More praise for Patricia Highsmith and *Small g*

"[Highsmith's] characters astonish themselves, and us, by discovering love in the very last places they ever expected to find it."
—Francine Prose, *O Magazine*

"Its superabundance of characters is only one of the elements that give 'Small g' its air of Shakespearean complexity."
—David Leavitt, *New York Times Book Review*

"*Small g* is a welcome addition to Highsmith's published novels, offering readers an insight into a fascinating aspect of Swiss society and an opportunity to explore Highsmith's final concerns and obsessions."
—Louise Welsh, author of *The Cutting Room*, in the *Washington Post Book World*

"For eliciting the menace that lurks in familiar surroundings, there's no one like Patricia Highsmith."
—*Time*

"[Highsmith] has an uncanny feeling for the rhythms of terror."
—*Times Literary Supplement* (London)

"An atmosphere of nameless dread, of unspeakable foreboding, permeates every page of Patricia Highsmith, and there's nothing quite like it."
—*Boston Globe*

"Patricia Highsmith's novels are peerlessly disturbing . . . bad dreams that keep us thrashing for the rest of the night."
—*The New Yorker*

"Patricia Highsmith is often called a mystery or crime writer, which is a bit like calling Picasso a draftsman."
—*Cleveland Plain Dealer*

"One of our greatest modernist writers."   —Gore Vidal

"[Highsmith is] a writer who has created a world of her own—a world claustrophobic and irrational which we enter each time with a sense of personal danger. . . . Patricia Highsmith is the poet of apprehension."   —Graham Greene, from his foreword to
The Selected Stories of Patricia Highsmith

"As in many of her other works, Ms. Highsmith here seems to relish the abnormal."   —Judy Alter, *Dallas Morning News*

"A powerful and mesmerizing read; highly recommended for public and academic libraries."   —Lisa Nussbaum, *Library Journal*

"Highsmith's last book . . . offer[s] an intriguing exploration of gay culture and the complexities of love, jealousy, possessiveness and friendship."   —Misha Stone, *Booklist*

"The best thing about *Small g* is the affectionate homage it pays to relationships that are not exclusive or possessive, that may or may not be sexual, but which have the power to create happiness or break a stranglehold that is choking off a full, delicious life."
                —*Lambda Book Report*

"All those qualities that have made Highsmith such an important figure—her carefully crafted prose, her understanding of human frailties and the randomness of life—are present in this final work."
                —Aaron Stander, *I Love a Mystery*

Small g: A Summer Idyll

Small g:
A Summer Idyll

Patricia Highsmith

W. W. Norton & Company

New York London

For information about permission to reproduce selections from
this book, write to Permissions, W. W. Norton & Company, Inc.,
500 Fifth Avenue, New York, NY 10110

Manufacturing by The Courier Companies, Inc.
Production manager: Amanda Morrison

Library of Congress Cataloging-in-Publication Data

Highsmith, Patricia, 1921–
Small g : a summer idyll / by Patricia Highsmith.—1st American ed.
p. cm.
ISBN 0-393-05923-5
1. Triangles (Interpersonal relations)—Fiction. 2. Bars (Drinking
establishments)—Fiction. 3. Gay men—Crimes against—Fiction.
4. Zurich (Switzerland)—Fiction. 5. Sexual orientation—Fiction.
6. Conspiracies—Fiction. I. Title.
PS3558.I366S63 2004
813'.54—dc22   2004044837

ISBN 0-393-32703-5 pbk.

W. W. Norton & Company, Inc.
500 Fifth Avenue, New York, N.Y. 10110
www.wwnorton.com

W. W. Norton & Company Ltd.
Castle House, 75/76 Wells Street, London W1T 3QT

1 2 3 4 5 6 7 8 9 0

To my friend Frieda Sommer

Small g: A Summer Idyll

1

A young man named Peter Ritter came out of a cinema in Zurich one Wednesday evening around midnight. It was January, cold, and he hurried to fasten his thigh-length leather jacket as he walked. Peter was heading for home, where he lived with his parents, and he had decided to ring Rickie from there rather than from a bar-café. Peter took an alley that was a short-cut. He was buckling the jacket belt, when a figure leapt out of the darkness on his left and said, "Hey! Give us your money!"

Peter saw a knife in the fellow's raised right hand, a longish hunting knife.

"OK, I've got about thirty francs!" Peter said, standing tense, fists at the ready. Sometimes drug addicts could be scared off, easily. "You want that?"

A second fellow had sprung up on Peter's right.

"Thirty with *that* jacket!" mumbled the man with the knife, and struck—a hard stab under Peter's ribs on his left side.

Peter knew the knife had gone through the leather. He was reaching under the jacket for the wallet in the back pocket of his jeans. "OK, I'm *getting*—"

The second man gave a funny shrill laugh and stabbed Peter in his right side. Peter staggered, but he had the wallet out.

The man on the left snatched it. More laughter, and a blow to Peter's throat now—not a fist, but another stab.

"Hey!" Peter yelled, twisting, in pain and thoroughly scared. "Help! Help me!" Peter hit the man on his left with his fist, fast as a reflexive gesture.

The second man bumped Peter, sending him toward the blackness of the house walls, where Peter hit his head. Trotting footsteps faded.

Peter was aware of lying on the worn stones of the alley, of gasping. Blood was choking him. He drank blood in order to breathe. Got to ring Rickie, as he'd promised. Rickie was working late tonight, as he often did, but Rickie would be expecting . . .

"Here! Look, here he is!"

Other people.

"Hey! Where're you hurt?"

"No, don't move him! Shine the *light* here!"

"That's *blood*!"

". . . *ambulance*?"

"Beni went to phone."

". . . young guy . . ."

"Is he bleeding! Wow!"

Peter felt as if he were going under an anesthetic, unable to speak, getting sleepier, though his neck was beginning to hurt. He tried to cough and failed, inhaled, gasped, choking and unable to cough.

Less than an hour later, someone had found Peter's discarded wallet in the same alley, and turned it in to the police. Peter Ritter of such-and-such address. The police notified his mother that Peter had been dead on arrival at the hospital. An intern had heard him say "Rickie." Did that name mean anything to her? Yes, she said. A friend of her son's. He had just telephoned her. She gave Rickie's address, on their insistence. Then the police came to escort Frau Ritter to the morgue.

That same night the police visited Rickie Markwalder, who was working in his studio. He was aghast at the news, or so he seemed to the police. He had been expecting a telephone call from Petey around midnight. Rickie wanted to speak with Petey's mother, but the police suggested tomorrow, because Frau Ritter had been given sedative pills tonight to take before trying to sleep. Her husband was away on business just now, the police said, a fact which Rickie knew.

Rickie telephoned Frau Ritter the next day, having waited

until nearly noon. "I am absolutely *shattered*," Rickie said in his simple, almost clumsy way. "If you would like to see me, I am here. Or I can come to you."

"I don't know. Thank you. My brother is here."

"Good. The funeral—shall I phone you tomorrow?"

"It's—a cremation. Our family way," replied Frau Ritter. "I will let you know, Rickie."

"Thank you, Frau Ritter."

As it turned out, she didn't let him know, but that could have been an oversight, Rickie thought. Or she might not have wanted him present with the relatives, the cousins, at the service which Rickie read about in the *Tages-Anzeiger*. He sent flowers to Petey's parents, anyway, with a card stating his "deepest sympathy," words that had become trite, Rickie knew, but were in his breast sincere.

Luisa would be shocked. Did she know already? The item in the *Tages-Anzeiger* had been short, and Rickie had found it only because he had looked for it. He preferred to keep out of the way in regard to Luisa and Peter, and he had the feeling Luisa didn't much like him, Rickie. Why should she? Luisa had been in love with Petey, maybe an adolescent crush, lasting a couple of months, but still—Rickie decided not to say anything to Luisa. He realized he was assuming she was over her attraction to Petey, because he wanted to assume that. It was easier than telling her in Jakob's, where Luisa was always in the presence of Renate something, her boss, and boss of a few other young apprentice seamstresses, who worked in Renate's atelier.

2

Rickie Markwalder, led by Lulu on her lead, clumped along his street en route to Jakob's Bierstube-Restaurant. This was

known as the Small g at weekends, but that name wasn't appro-
priate around 9:30 A.M. on any day. One of the guidebooks on
Zurich's attractions so categorized Jakob's—with a "small g"—
meaning a partially gay clientele but not entirely.

"Come on, Lulu! Oh, all right," Rickie murmured tolerantly
as the slender white dog circled purposefully and crouched. Rickie
urged her gently into the gutter with the lead, then pushed his
hands into the sagging and slightly soiled pockets of his white
cardigan. Lovely day, he was thinking, summer getting into its full
glory, the pale-green leaves on the trees brighter and bigger every
day. *And no Petey.* Rickie blinked, feeling again that shock and sudden emptiness. Lulu jumped onto pavement level, scratched with
her hind feet, and strained toward Jakob's with renewed zeal.

Aged twenty, Petey had been, Rickie thought bitterly, and for
no reason swung his leg and kicked an empty milk container off
the pavement into the gutter. Here he was, forty-six—*forty-six*—
still going strong (except for his own abdominal stab wound, ugly,
and which he had allowed to bulge a little), while Petey, such a
beautiful image of—

"Hey! Kicking refuse into the street? Why don't you pick it
up—like a decent Swiss?" A dumpy woman in her fifties glared at
Rickie.

Rickie made a turn to go back for the container—a little half-
liter one, anyway—but the woman had darted and picked it up.
"Maybe I'm *not* a decent Swiss!"

The woman's face twitched in contempt, and she went off
with the milk container in the opposite direction from Rickie's.
His wide mouth lifted at one corner. Well, he wasn't going to let
that ruin his day. Most unusual, he had to admit, to see an empty
container of any kind in a Swiss street. Maybe that was why he'd
felt inspired to kick it.

Lulu made a sharp right and drew Rickie through the front
gate of Jakob's, past the terrace tables and chairs which now were
unoccupied, because it was a bit chilly for outdoors breakfasting.

"'Allo, Rickie. And Lulu!" This from Ursie in the doorway, wiping her hands on her apron, bending to touch Lulu who raised herself a little and flicked her tongue at Ursie's hand, missing it.

"Good morning, Ursie, and how are you this fine morning?" asked Rickie in Schwyzerdütsch.

"Well as ever, thank you! The usual?"

"Indeed, yes," replied Rickie, slowly making for his left corner table. "Hello, Stefan! How goes it?" This to a one-eyed man, a retired postman, about to dunk a roll into his cappuccino.

"I see the world with a unique optimism," Stefan replied, as he replied half the time. "Hello, Lulu!"

Rickie took a *Tages-Anzeiger* from the circular rack and seated himself. Dull news, rather the same as last week and the weeks before, little formerly Russian states he had barely heard of, all near Turkey, it seemed, were squabbling and killing their inhabitants, people were starving, their houses blown up. Of course some lives—like these—were sadder than his own. Rickie had always known that and admitted it. It was just that, when tragedy struck, why not say it hurt? Why not say it was important, at least for the individual?

"*Danke*, Andreas," said Rickie with a glance up at the dark-haired young man who was setting down his cappuccino and croissant.

"'Morning, Rickie. 'Morning, Lulu." Andreas, sometimes called Andy, bent and gave a mock kiss to Lulu, who had seated herself on a straight chair opposite Rickie. "Would Madame Lulu like something?"

"Woof!" Lulu replied, every bit of her signifying a "Yes!"

Andreas straightened up and laughed, swung the empty tray between his fingertips.

"She'll have a taste of croissant from me," Rickie said.

Rickie returned to his paper. With croissant sticking out of his mouth, Rickie used both hands to turn the pages to "Recent Events." This was a short column with usually four or five items: a woman had had her handbag snatched; a youth not yet identified found dead from an overdose under a park bench in Zurich. Today an item was about a man aged seventy-two who had been hit over the head and robbed in a village Rickie had never heard of near Einsiedeln.

Ah well, seventy-two, Rickie thought, was getting on, and such a man couldn't be expected to put up much of a fight. But he'd come out of it alive, it seemed. Taken to hospital for shock, said the newspaper. Now Petey, in Zurich, had put up a fight (according to a witness), as many a young man would, and Petey had been in top form. Rickie made himself loosen his tight grip on the newspaper.

"Here, my angel." Rickie reached across the table and extended a crunchy morsel.

Lulu's pink tongue took care of the morsel, losing not a crumb, and she gave a tiny whine of pleasure.

At that moment, a smallish female figure in gray came in, cast a swift glance around, and made for a table against a wall opposite and to the left. Opposite meant quite far away, because Jakob's was a large establishment.

Jakob's Biergarten was three or four stories high, but nobody thought about the upper stories. The ground floor, walls and ceiling were of old dark wood, like the benches and tables and one later-made semipartition which was already old enough to blend with the rest. No formica, no chrome. The mirror behind the bar looked in need of a washing, but so many cards and sentimentalia were stuck all round its frame, it would have taken a courageous person to tackle it. The rather low ceilings had thick square rafters that looked even darker than the benches and booths, as if centuries of smoke and dust had become part of the wood. If Rickie was lonely, he came here for a beer, and if he tired of his own cooking, Ursie always had sausage and potato salad or sauerkraut till midnight.

The woman in gray was Renate something-or-other, and he

disliked her. She was at least fifty, always neatly attired and in curiously old-fashioned style. Though she was polite and left a tip sometimes (Rickie had seen it), few people liked Renate. She was somehow a spy, hostile, spying on all of them at Jakob's, contemptuous of all of them despite her smile, yet so often *here*, nearly always at this time, for her mid-morning coffee. Rickie was sure Renate got up early and wanted her girls at work before eight. From where he sat, Rickie could just make out little gray-tasseled scallops on the sleeves (somewhat puffed) of Renate's flower-patterned dress, tassels midway down the skirt, too, and of course at the hem. Practically Alice in Wonderland! A long dress it was, to hide as much as possible Renate's club foot, or whatever they called it these days. She wore high shoes with one sole thicker than the other. No doubt this had tended her toward the Edwardian gear. Rickie imagined her a tyrant with her young female employees. Now Renate inserted a cigarette into a long black holder, lit it, and focused a small automatic smile at Andy as she gave her order.

Rickie glanced at his watch—nine fifty-one. His helper Mathilde was never at his studio before ten-ten, even though when he had hired her, Rickie had asked her please to come by ten. Rickie knew he was not good at being forceful with people. Curiously, he was tougher in business deals, he thought, and this gave him consolation.

"Appenzeller now, Herr Rickie? *Oder*—" Or another cappuccino, Andreas meant.

"Appenzeller, *ja*, *danke*, Andy."

Rickie lifted his eyes from his newspaper as another voice said, "'Morning, *Rickie!*"

This was Claus Bruder, who had appeared from round the partition behind Rickie.

"Well, Claus! Still ogling your female clients?" Rickie smiled. Claus was a bank clerk.

Claus wriggled and replied, "*Ya-aes*. Hello, Lulu—*gut'n Mor-*

gen! I was wondering, can I borrow Lulu for this evening? Quiet
evening. Bring her back here tomorrow round this time?"

Rickie sighed. "All night? Lulu was out late last night. Someone had her out till two. She needs her sleep. Is it so important?"

"Here in Aussersihl. I have a new date tonight."

Lulu was a plus, that was all, even though any honest borrower
would have to admit to anyone that he didn't own Lulu. "No,"
Rickie said with difficulty. "The guy will like you just the same
with or without Lulu. You know? *C'est la vie.*"

Claus, younger by nearly twenty years than Rickie, had no
reply or decided to hold his tongue, and looked wistfully at Lulu.
"But, sweetie, you bring me *luck*!"

Lulu responded with an "Ooof!" and extended a paw toward
Claus's outstretched hand. They shook.

"See you, Rickie! Have a nice day," he added in English, a semi-
insulting thing to say.

"And up yours!" Rickie replied genially. He picked up his
Appenzeller. The first sip tasted as if it were something he needed,
its sweetness blended with the bitter cappuccino on his tongue. He
might have put Renate out of his mind with a cigarette and a
return to the newspaper, but Luisa had arrived to join Renate, and
Rickie's eyes were held. She was so young and fresh! Now Luisa
was smiling at Renate, taking a seat on the bench. Luisa had been
in love with Petey—yes, really in love, Rickie knew from what
Petey had told him. Petey had been a little troubled by it, polite,
not knowing how to handle it—handle Luisa's loving gazes. And
how jealous the old witch Renate had been, and had shown herself to be! Fairly audible lectures to Luisa right here in Jakob's!
There had also been "asides" to others, Renate on her feet, flounc-
ing her long skirt and turning like a flamenco dancer as she
announced, "It's *wahnsinnig* for a girl to get a crush on a homo!
These perverts are in love with their looking-glasses! With themselves!" Renate had got little support from the habitués of Jakob's,

quite a few of whom were gay and the rest at least rather *sympa*. But that hadn't stopped her. Oh no!

And it was horrid, had been, Rickie remembered, to see how Renate fairly gloated in triumph over Luisa's tears (alas, a few had been shed in public here) when it became apparent that Petey was not going to respond to Luisa's declaration of love. Poor Petey had been embarrassed, and Rickie had urged Petey to bring Luisa some flowers and he had, at least once, Rickie remembered, encouraged the boy to be understanding. What did that cost? Nothing. And you'll be a better *Mensch* for it, Rickie had said. True. Rickie drew gently on his cigarette and tried to cool his ire. The day was just beginning.

"Rickie—and Lulu!" said a female voice.

Rickie looked up. "Evelyn! So! How are you, my lovely? Want to sit down?"

An empty wooden chair stood beside the one Lulu occupied.

"No, thank you, Rickie, I'm already a little late for work. This drawing—"

Rickie watched her open a large manila envelope on the table, and pull out a pen-and-ink drawing on heavy paper, a castle with spires in the sky, a visible moat among the bushes and trees at the bottom. "Pretty!"

"The kids love it. Well, it is well done. It's by a boy about thirteen and I think good for that age. Could you—"

"Copies," Rickie filled in. "Yes."

"Copies." Evelyn's thin face changed with her smile. She looked younger than fifty-something. "Maybe ten? Eight? And I'll pay you for the paper, of course. Same kind of paper, if you can manage."

Rickie had a machine that copied, enlarged, reduced, and superimposed. More important, some people he liked and some he didn't. He liked Evelyn Huber, who worked in the library of the local school.

"You are sweet, Rickie! No hurry. Can I come by your studio in—maybe five days? Pick them up?"

"About, yes. See you then, Evelyn."

While Evelyn had been talking to him, Rickie had seen Willi Biber's tall form drift in like some sinister figure in a fairy tale, like a classic village idiot of yore, the vague handyman who would either overcharge you or work for nothing, people said. He was mentally retarded, according to Rickie's observation and also what he heard about Willi. He had been some kind of workman, brick-layer, Rickie thought, until either an industrial accident, like a load of bricks on his head, had cost him his job, or he had got the sack for stupidity.

Renate often deigned to speak to Willi, Rickie had noticed, maybe because both of them were damaged, he mentally and she physically. In a way, it was kind of Renate, Rickie supposed, which was something, because Renate showed nothing that could be called warmth toward other human beings, from what he could see. Rickie saw Renate nod a "Good morning," as Willi drifted past her and took a seat at the next table. Willi had a flat, blank face, large hands and feet, wore dark, shapeless trousers and a workman's dark-blue jacket, summer and winter. And Rickie had never seen him without a broad-brimmed hat of some kind, as if he were trying to protect himself from the sun.

Rickie paid his bill and did not leave a tip, as it was not the custom. Rather than go nearer to Renate and Luisa, Rickie chose a back door and went behind the brown wooden partition into another room of Jakob's, where a few workmen preferred to breakfast. The workmen had departed by a quarter to eight to get to their jobs, but there were a few in blue jeans now, come in for a second coffee.

Less than six minutes later, he was at the apartment building— four-story and light gray—where his studio was, unlocking one of the small metal boxes that contained his post. Rickie had what looked like a bill from an electrical equipment supplier, and two

letters with company logos that might mean work for him. Rickie
and Lulu descended eight or ten steps next to the building front,
past a couple of potted palms which belonged to Rickie, to
Rickie's semibasement door. Through the studio window as one
came down the last steps, one could see Frau Schneider and Frau
von Muellberg engaged in lively dialogue, each with a hand nervously raised. These were life-sized plaster-of-Paris figures seated on
a white settle of the same material, their twenties-style clothing
only delicately tinted to bring out the brown of a fur piece, the
black of a handbag. Newcomers to the studio nearly always stared
and laughed.

His studio was white, high-ceilinged, and had almost no
chairs, as three out of four big tables were meant to be stood at.
Lights with jointed supports craned over each table. There was a
sink with hot and cold water in a corner, next to this a stove with
two electric burners, and below the stove a square fridge.

Having removed his cardigan, Rickie put the kettle on for
more coffee for himself and Mathilde. He got a sack of coffee
beans from a cupboard and poured some into his grinder. The
reaching had given him a twinge in the midriff. He was in fact
ashamed of the bulge there, but had persuaded himself that the
bulge made him look casual, indifferent to keeping fit, such a fetish
among young and aging these days.

The twinge also reminded him, against his will, of goddamned
Renate who Rickie had vowed to keep out of his thoughts today,
in order to have a good day. This was because Petey had died from
being knifed, and Renate out of bitchiness and maybe inborn dis-
honesty had spread the story that Petey had been murdered in
his—Rickie's—own bed by a pickup that Petey had brought to
Rickie's apartment that night when Rickie had been working late
in his studio. Never mind that police records and newspaper
accounts gave the truth! People, strangers in Jakob's, for instance,
didn't bother to check stories like that. Rickie knew that *some*
people in the neighborhood believed the story. It was Ursie who

had told Rickie that Willi was murmuring a story about a stranger—or Petey and a stranger?—coming into Rickie's apartment via his outside steps to the balcony, and Petey meeting his death that way. Rickie had shrugged it off, though it had angered him. Willi had made that up? Well, maybe someone else had put the idea in his head, Ursie had replied. Rickie had said no more. Who else but Renate?

Rickie looked at his wristwatch—almost ten-thirty—just as his doorbell rang. Most likely Mathilde, to whom Rickie had not yet entrusted his key.

"*Good* morning, Mathilde!" Rickie said in his rich baritone, holding the door for the bulky female form that entered.

"G'morning, Rickie." Her eyes were pink-rimmed.

Rickie dreaded what might be coming, but at least coffee was on the way.

Mathilde let a large brown handbag slip from her shoulder to a bench at right angles to the two plaster-of-Paris ladies, but kept her white cardigan on. Unlike Rickie's, Mathilde's was rather clean, pocketless, and fitted her form snugly. Mathilde as a form was an assembly of curves. Her buttocks were broad and round, and the sweater cupped under them at the back. Rickie supposed that she thought this concealed her backside, but in fact the white sweater accentuated it. Her hip bones—they were somewhere under those lateral bulges—seemed to ride high, hardly preparing one for the really curvaceous and ample pair of breasts just above them in front. Rickie realized that Mathilde dressed to minimize all this mass—she tried—but the effect was just the opposite.

Rickie sighed. "Some coffee, yes? I'm going to have some. Only two letters to open today." In the kitchen, he poured coffee for both. Mathilde took hers with sugar. "Then if you can get the enlarger ready—for that perfume job, you know? Franck and Fischer. I'd love to get that done today."

"Thank you," said Mathilde tremulously, accepting the coffee.

A tear had found its way down her cheek and disappeared into two chins.

"Now come along, Mathilde. Take the coffee to the big table." Rickie had put the two letters on the big table, a central table for both of them, used for general work. "Now, what is the matter, dear?"

Mathilde looked at him, wet-eyed; her cup even rattled in its saucer. "I think I'm pregnant."

Rickie took a slow breath. Artificially, was his first thought. He couldn't ask, "What makes you think so?" Idiotic. The idea of Mathilde being pregnant stupefied him. The mere thought of kissing her shiny, red-lipsticked mouth was Rickie's idea of hell. The possibility that some man had gone further—

"I'm sorry," he said, since Mathilde seemed very sorry. He cleared his throat. "You're sure?" struck him as another inane question, so he checked that. "So what are you going to do about it?" he asked as gently as possible, and suddenly he didn't believe Mathilde. Wasn't she always full of drama? Maybe she should've been an actress. Still could be, maybe. She was hardly thirty.

"I don't know what to do about it," she said with a tremble, looking off into the distance.

"Well—" Rickie shifted. Frau Mueller who lived upstairs was always asking him, "Why do you keep Mathilde on? She's more of a drag than a help to you." Frau Mueller was right. But Mathilde needed the money. But then a lot of people in Aussersihl needed a salary and were prepared to work for one. "Well, for today—" Rickie moved toward his letters, but did not touch them. "Let's get moving, at least. Maybe—by this afternoon something will come to you."

"What?"

"An idea. What to do." If she had proposed then and there to go home for the day, Rickie wouldn't have tried to dissuade her. To set her an example, if possible, Rickie went to the enlarger and started getting it into position. This inspired Mathilde to go to the two letters at least.

One of the letters, which Mathilde brought to Rickie because she needed his answer, was from a firm called Logo Pogo, illustrated by a small black-and-tan design of a boy with feet on a slanting pogo stick. These people made sports equipment and wanted to illustrate a campaign, which was already on paper. Would Mr. Markwalder be interested?

"Tell them, yes," said Rickie. Mathilde could type, at least, and her German wasn't bad. Or maybe she would telephone.

"May I please have a beer, Rickie?"

"M–mm—of course." It was eleven; Mathilde had held out longer than usual on a painful morning too.

The telephone rang and Rickie answered. This was Philip Egli, asking if Rickie could come to "a small party" at his place that night, and please bring Lulu?

"Lulu needs an early night. She was out last night," Rickie replied. "But thank you, Philip."

Philip groaned. "*Think* about it. No need to phone me back. Just come if you can make it, OK? All fellows. Two new guys— young guys. Well—just to *talk* to, you know. Do you good. Eats too."

"Like the lasagne last time?" Rickie laughed genially, rocking back on his heels. Someone had managed to dump a huge platter of cooked lasagne on Philip's kitchen floor, and Philip and another guest had salvaged what they could from the top of the heap. "Thank you, Philip, I'll think about it," Rickie said as he hung up, but he wasn't going.

Mathilde did telephone the Logo people, and Rickie got on the line and made an appointment: they were to come to him.

"That way you can have a look at my workshop," Rickie said in the casual, friendly tone he unconsciously used with business people, at first. It broke the ice, certainly, but it also helped Rickie later to drive a hard bargain if he needed to, not that Rickie had worked this out, it had simply evolved.

With eyes still wet, Mathilde had set up his enlarger and had treated herself to a small Dubonnet, Rickie noticed. There were quite a lot of beverages in the fridge besides milk, Coca-Cola, soda, and tonic. There was tomato juice and a bottle of good vodka, Cinzano and the tail end of an old crock of Steinhäger, which had sentimental associations with a nice blond boy from Hamburg, so he neither drank from this bottle nor offered it to visitors.

Just after twelve noon, when Rickie had attended to the second letter and finished his enlarging job, the waters burst for Mathilde.

"Boo-hoo-*hoo!*" loud in the big room, a classic.

Rickie had been then glancing at an orange-backgrounded lipstick ad with a lightning zigzag of bright red through it—Rickie disliked it but the lipstick company loved it—and he stared at the design, tormenting himself for a few seconds before he forced himself to start administering comfort.

He began with the usual, after all. "Now, are you sure? Have you told your mother?" She had not. Was she going to? No answer. "Who—who is your man friend?" asked Rickie, treading on unknown, even incredible ground. What man could be roused by Mathilde sufficiently to impregnate her? Suddenly to Rickie his thought seemed a guarantee that she wasn't pregnant.

Mathilde lifted her dismal eyes to Rickie. "A man I've been seeing. Karl—"

"Does he know?"

"No—" Here came a great sob.

Rickie inwardly gave up. Was it his business? Mathilde had been with him only three months. She had answered his advertisement in the *Tages-Anzeiger* for a secretary-receptionist, salary and hours to be arranged. Out of three, Rickie had chosen Mathilde, because she had looked cheerful, healthy, and strong. Well, he had not been totally correct, he admitted.

"Now look, you go and have a good lunch at Jakob's. All right, Mathilde? Promise me."

Mathilde did like to eat, and at Jakob's she could have another beer.

"Telephone me, if you're not coming back this afternoon. I'd advise you to tell your mother—and decide what you want to do. I assume it's been only a month or so." Rickie was doing his level best.

Lulu had raised her pointed nose at the big "*Boo-hoo-hoo*," and had been concentrating ever since. She lay curled on her blue pillow, following each word, glancing at Rickie and back to Mathilde.

"You are so nice to me, Rickie." Mathilde seemed to be trying to conjure up more tears.

Rickie knew what was coming next, and he hated it. Gay men were so nice, so understanding. Why couldn't other men be as nice as gay men? It came, and Rickie switched off and barely heard it.

"Hm-hm," he said noncommittally. "Now I've got to go off to lunch soon, or I can't get back for this afternoon's work."

That got Mathilde on the move. Rickie gazed for some seconds critically at the big sheet of white paper under his enlarger: motorcycles—maybe twenty of them—zooming from upper left to lower right, all blurred. Speed. That was sure. Not bad, Rickie thought. He waited till Mathilde had exited before he moved. He fastened the lead to Lulu's collar, and she led him to the door.

Rickie's apartment was several meters away in the same street. The building had a garden at the front and one side, with bushes, three or four handsome trees, and a hedge along the pavement. Rickie's flat, on the first floor, boasted an iron balcony with steps down to the garden. French windows in his apartment gave onto this little balcony—alas, hardly big enough for a table, though sometimes Rickie ate out here with a friend.

Inside, a teal blue dominated. There was teal-blue wall-to-wall carpeting, darker blue wallpaper in nearly all the rooms, conservative furniture, all of wood and unpretentious. Here on the walls hung at least six of Rickie's cruising-white-bird paintings of vary-

ing sizes—all oils—the bird's slender outspread wings long in pro-
portion to the body, of which little was visible. The bird's head was
slightly turned in a direction that varied in each painting. The
subject was a seagull, though one painting was of a white stork
gliding over houseroofs.

And here too Petey Ritter was apparent in photographs
framed and unframed, in color and black and white. Rickie had in
six months progressed to the point of not looking at them, certainly not staring any longer at any of them, but not to the point
of taking any down. Yes, one he had taken down a month ago, the
least good, he remembered. When one entered the flat, Petey
loomed from the left on his motorcycle, blond, smiling, the wind
blowing his hair back, the motorcycle slanted as if on a curve,
though he had been still, posing for Rickie. Another that Rickie
loved showed him and Petey at a pavement table, black and white
and in dappled shadow and sun because of the vine-covered terrace. A good photo. Rickie had had that one blown up.

Rickie opened a small beer, and pulled out his leftovers of
spaghetti and cheese and tomato from last night, which had been
delicious. More butter, a dash of milk, and Rickie eased it into
a pan.

How long had it been since Petey? Rickie found he wasn't
sure any longer of the number of weeks, only of the date. His
absence was the point. What they might have had together! Helping each other, being happy. Murder was the point. Murder and
drugs. Rickie glanced at his pan, whose contents had not yet
begun to bubble, and walked with his beer to the french windows,
which were in his dining area, as some called it. Here was a well-
polished table that seated six comfortably.

He opened the french windows, which in fact didn't lock. The
doors were so loose—though they looked closed from outside—a
mere push could cause the horizontal bar to give, the doors to part
a little, and a hand could do the rest. Ought to get that fixed,
Rickie told himself.

Rickie began his lunch at the coffee table before his sofa. After less than a minute, he went to his cassette shelf and chose a female singer, American, singing some of his favorites. Several minutes later, there came a song that recollected Petey so strongly that he jumped up and turned the machine off, pushed it again to rewind.

"Lulu! One more little biscuit?"

Lulu, silent, stood up and wagged her tail, and looked at the biscuit box by the sink.

Rickie gave her one. Then he went into his bathroom where he had a full-length mirror on the wall, not a meter wide and some two meters high. Rickie pulled his shirttails out of his trousers and jerked his shirt up to his nipples.

He went forward and took a good look at his scar. Now there was a nasty job, from just under the sternum nearly to the umbilicus, and worst of all *broad*—as if the surgeon had messed around a bit or had been drunk. The scar was a mottled pink and white, pointed at top and bottom, as if the surgeon had begun and ended properly but got lost in the middle. It *was* a bad job, another doctor or two had said that, and Rickie hadn't worn his Velcro girdle as he'd been told to do during the critical days after the stitching, hadn't worn it day and night, Rickie had to admit.

That gash had happened about three weeks after Petey's death. Rickie had gone to a section of Zurich dense with bars, without his car, intending to enjoy his drinks, but he'd had one too many, that was certain. Suddenly it had happened, in those seconds of blackout as he stepped out of the bar into the street, intending to try to find a taxi, and tripped. The blackout lasted until he woke up in hospital, hours later, when the dawn was breaking, and a nurse was asking him his name.

The point was, his midriff was a horror to look at, and Rickie winced at the very idea of anyone seeing it, even a doctor or nurse, much less a lover. But compared to what Petey's body had suffered, this incompetent suture was nothing! Suddenly it seemed to Rickie that all his self-pity left him, drained out of him. He found himself standing straighter and felt better for it. "*Nothing*," Rickie said aloud.

He decided to go to Philip Egli's party tonight. And take Lulu.

But there was the afternoon ahead, with weepy Mathilde. Could he send her home, offer her a free afternoon, or would she be somehow offended, take it as a forerunner of getting the sack? Should he buy some posies from the news kiosk on Jakob's Bierstube corner? Sometimes there were flowers there, sometimes not. Funny that people thought gay men knew how to handle women better than straights, whereas Rickie (if he spoke for himself) simply didn't. Surely a married man would learn a lot more about women than a gay. Rickie reminded himself that he had a sister, whom he had always got on with and still did.

A tie for this afternoon? Why not? Rickie donned a pale-blue shirt and chose a blue tie with a red stripe. He thought he had a business date this afternoon, but wouldn't be sure till he checked it in the studio. That sort of thing, of course, was exactly what Mathilde should remind him of. Lots o' luck.

3

Mathilde was waiting on the steps in front of his studio door when Rickie got there.

"Oh Mathilde, you are early and I am late!" Rickie tried to assess her state by a glance at her eyes as he fished out his keys. Wettish, new eyeliner, he observed. "Come in. No, you first."

Rickie carried on as if it were a day like any other. He did have an appointment at 4 P.M., with Perma-Sheen, a nail-polish firm. Claws, Rickie thought, with a mild twinge of dislike. Cleanliness, a care for appearance and grooming—he supposed manicured nails implied all this. But to live with? And in bed? Clawing a man's back? Or anything else. No! Of course, nail polish earned money for him, for the manufacturer, the manicurists in beauty parlors. For perhaps the third time that day, Rickie tried to sweep his daydreams away.

"You look nice," said Mathilde, as Rickie was putting on the kettle.

"A business date at four. Mathilde, there are two errands this afternoon. One to pick up those color slides from the Foto Flash people. You know? Can you ring and see if they're ready? If so— you fetch them. Then the hundred-watts. Six more. Make a note, will you?"

"*Jawohl*, Rickie." Mathilde went first to the fridge and extracted the Dubonnet, what was left of it.

Rickie got his Perma-Sheen correspondence out. He had a cat idea for the ad campaign, and wanted to make some pencil sketches.

Mathilde wrote her shopping list and pulled on her cardigan. Rickie felt relieved when she had gone.

Perma-Sheen. His cat idea. Various colors of polish, a different one for each ad, but the same motif: close-up of a woman's fingertips stroking or gently massaging a cat's head. The cat would change in each too: Siamese, Burmese, tabby, marmalade, black, white, Persian. Rickie added color with his pencil crayons. Finally he had four to show.

Another idea? Of course. Accidents, mishaps, when a woman had to show her fingers. Her handbag drops, everything spills— either on the street or at a dinner party. *You can still look your best.* Or something like that. Lipstick, comb, purse on a carpeted floor, maybe a man's hand with jacket and a shirtcuff showing, coming to the lady's assistance, as her hand, nails done in Perma-Sheen, retrieves her own lipstick (which might match nail polish) from among the objects spilled.

By the time Mathilde got back, Rickie was in cheerful mood. Lulu remained sound asleep, even when Mathilde entered. "Success?" Rickie saw that she had two items, a big plastic sack and a smaller one.

"Ye-es," quavering. Mathilde stuck a couple of slips of paper on the expenses nail on the telephone table.

Rickie opened the hundred-watt bag and checked that Mathilde had bought the right screw size (she had), then glanced at the color slides, which looked good. During Mathilde's absence, a comforting thought had come to Rickie: he would not say another word to Mathilde about her "condition." Rickie judged this attitude to be even tactful, a further relief to him.

And Mathilde said nothing on that subject during the afternoon, and typed a few letters for Rickie, including a reminder for an outstanding invoice.

Perma-Sheen, by 4:25 P.M., did not much like his cat idea, but liked the humor of his "You can still look your best" idea.

Half an hour after the Perma-Sheen man had departed, the telephone rang, and the same man said that his colleague did like the cat idea, and could Rickie come up with two samples, layouts with room for a hundred words in two sizes of type, as he had described?

The day was shaping up well. But Rickie mentally tiptoed around Mathilde, as if she were someone in hospital, or someone in the delicate condition she had described. And if she were not at all pregnant, not even a little bit? Rickie smiled inwardly. Wasn't fantasy what made the world go round? All that kept up the morale? Like love, ambition, hope, and trying. All abstract, all fantasy, yet as vital as bread. So Rickie felt.

He even fancied that Mathilde's faint smile was one of gratitude for his tact, as she said good-bye that afternoon. They wished each other a good weekend.

Rickie stayed on at the studio another good hour, working, tidying, drifting, dreaming, as he could do only when alone.

Back at his apartment before seven, Rickie telephoned his sister Dorothea, who was married to a radiologist and lived in

Zurich. Did they, he and his sister, really have to go to their mother's for her birthday in a week? Was Dorothea going? She was not. She was going to telephone and send a present.

"Good," Rickie said, relieved. "I could drive, of course, but I don't drool down my chin at the thought." The childhood phrase made his sister chuckle.

"Rickie, sweetie, you driving—after Mummy's party!"

"Oh, I'd stay the night."

"Even so! You're doing all right, dear? Everything fine?"

Rickie assured her that it was. "And Elise?" he asked. This was Dorothea's daughter.

"Still hasn't finished her thesis—and she's met a new young man, so we can only hope." Here Dorothea gave a laugh. "That she buckles down and does it, I mean."

Elise was Dorothea's only child, who was taking her master's in business administration. "Keep well, dear sister. I'll sign off. Love to my niece—and to Robbie." The latter was Dorothea's husband. As he hung up, Rickie imagined his sister's orderly and somewhat heavily furnished apartment, leather chairs, dark-wood furniture, much of it gifts from their mother's and Robbie's family. Ah, well, pillars of society.

By nine-thirty that evening, showered and in the same pale-blue shirt and wearing a raincoat, Rickie rang Philip Egli's bell from a bank of twenty in the building entrance.

"Rickie!" he shouted into the speaker.

Someone buzzed him in. Lulu, sensing a party, danced on her feet as she walked, expending energy like a jet plane. Such was her nature. The show! She was a circus dog, from circus stock, and had been stolen from her mother when two or three months old. Out of the lift, and apartment 4G. Rickie rang.

Philip Egli opened the door, tall but not as tall as Rickie, with wavy, light-brown hair, an earnest, alert face. "Welcome, Rickie! And Lulu! Our honored female guest! Ha-ha!"

The living room was completely occupied, including part of the floor, and a few fellows were standing. The hum did not entirely subside with Rickie's and Lulu's appearance.

"This is Rickie Markwalder," Philip began. "Joey, Kurt—"

"Who needs no introduction," Kurt said.

"Heinrich," Philip continued.

"Weber," Heinrich put in from the floor, where he lay propped on an elbow.

"Peter, Maxi, Fr—"

"Peter here too!" cried a voice from a corner.

"OK!" Rickie said, embarrassed as ever by introductions. He knew half the group vaguely, and had been to bed with a few in years past.

"And that's enough!" someone said. "Give Rickie something to drink!"

Rickie had been to Philip's apartment a few times. Where books did not line the walls, photographs—many enlarged—filled the space, teenaged boys, many naked, gazing forward, some smiling invitingly. Another photo showed two sleeping heads, the rest of the subject under a sheet. The books, apart from a small paperback section, were heavy textbooks with dense titles pertaining to physics and engineering, of which Rickie knew nothing, a deadly contrast to the merry boys. Philip's family was not wealthy, Rickie knew, so Philip worked hard, not wanting to prolong his education, therefore the expense for his family. Rickie admired that, because Switzerland was full of students who spent years at their theses, decades even, living nicely on parents' charity and government loans that were essentially interest-free.

Rickie accepted a Chivas Regal. There were also wine bottles on a table by the window, and beer bottles in a couple of buckets of water. "Thanks," Rickie said. "Just a splash of water—good. And what's the occasion for this party, Philip?"

"Nothing. It's Friday," Philip said, pushing up his shirtsleeves, ready to dash off again to attend to his guests. "Well, to tell you the truth, Harry and I exploded—disintegrated. So I'm throwing a party to forget it."

"I see," said Rickie, in his serious baritone, searching for a comforting phrase, but before he found any, Philip was gone. Harry? Maybe Rickie had met him, but he couldn't attach a face to that name.

"Lulu!" said a young man Rickie knew as Stefan. "You're going to do some tricks tonight?"

"If you don't press her too hard," Rickie said with deliberate fussiness. "She's had a busy week."

"Meaning you too?"

Rickie savored his drink. "Busy enough. Who's that dealing out the favors tonight?" He nodded toward a corner of the living room, where a young man in a white shirt and black waistcoat was chopping out a few lines of cocaine. Two fellows watched him intently.

"His name's Alex. More I don't know!" Stefan laughed as if he had made a bon mot. "And don't want to."

It was unheard of—drugs at Philip's. Rickie watched the thin tubes of rolled paper being passed by Alex to a couple of rapt observers. Go ahead, through the nose, Alex's gesture said. Then he lifted the dinner plate so that his neatly radiating rows could be more easily inhaled. Alex knelt with the lifted plate, like a figure in a religious painting of the Middle Ages. The cocaine accepters had merely to bend a little at the waist.

Rickie looked over the restless, talkative crowd, meeting the glances of men whose eyes had been attracted by Rickie's passing survey. One was rather handsome, with short brown hair, but absorbed in the man he was talking with, it seemed to Rickie. And how would Rickie look to this group, he wondered, whose average age was under thirty? He would look like a saggy-jowled, out-of-condition old fellow of at least forty, on the prowl for young flesh. Disgraceful, embarrassing! Dirty old man! Stay home with your dreams of the past!

In the kitchen, Rickie made himself another drink, not too strong. When he returned to the living room, one fellow, maybe two, gave a sharp whistle, and suddenly "Gaieté Parisienne" was taken up by one after another of the guests, whistling, clapping.

And Lulu barked and pranced.

"Let 'er go . . . ! Take it off!"

Lulu was free.

"Here! Look, Lulu!" A young man held out an umbrella horizontally.

Lulu cleared it, circled round and cleared it again, noiselessly, with ease and pleasure.

Laughter! And some applause apart from the palm-smacking to the music's beat. Two men stood and made a circle with their hands and arms.

"*Lower!*" Rickie yelled. "She'll hit the glasses back there!"

Lulu leapt and barked once, circled again to repeat her act.

Rickie always felt a thrill at this, because he had acquired Lulu when she was such a pup, he was sure she'd never been taught these tricks, they were just in her blood.

"*Wheet! Wheet!*" The whole room seemed to be whistling, those who weren't laughing.

"That's enough! Enough!" Rickie broke in, clapping once, standing tall with his arms upstretched. "Lulu needs a break! Come, Lulu, we'll go on an ocean cruise to relax. All right?"

Here Rickie pulled some dark glasses from a jacket pocket, and went in quest of his red muffler in his raincoat sleeve. He draped the scarf around Lulu's head and secured it at her throat. Then he stuck the dark glasses on the bridge of her nose, and fixed the curves of the glasses under the red scarf.

"Whoo-oops! Ha-ha!"

More applause.

"Beautiful, Lulu!"

She had coiled herself in an armchair with head lifted, and her eyes might have been gazing at a distant horizon. Even Rickie grinned, though he'd seen Lulu so attired before. She did suggest a distinguished actress in a deck chair who might want to be incognito. Now the undisciplined musical background staggered into the waltz from the same Offenbach work.

Rickie caught a glimpse of himself in a looking glass, a fleeting picture which cheered him: he looked happy, his shirt and tie and straight dark hair contributed to the picture of a rather handsome man, after all. And he had yet to find a gray hair.

Someone was talking about food. Spaghetti, wieners, were coming up. Bowls of pretzels and Ritz crackers stood everywhere, nearly empty.

"Alex, what's this?" Philip asked. "Money?"

Rickie, rather near, overheard this.

"Hey, now, no selling in my house, eh? OK if you want to *give* it." Philip was on his feet now.

"Nobody gives it," said Alex, rising to his feet a little unsteadily. "Not even me. I'm a convenience store." He said the last sentence in English, and laughed.

"Sorry, Philip. He just said twenty francs and I had it, so—" This from a fellow on his knees on the floor. The paper tube was still in his hand.

"OK, I'll give it back," said Alex, fishing in a pocket.

Now Philip was embarrassed. "It's just the idea of *selling*— here."

Rickie moved closer. "Sure, Philip's right. It's a party, and Philip's not selling drinks, is he? It's not that Philip is *against*—that, I'm sure," he added soothingly, with a glance at Alex's remaining rows, two.

"Sure," someone echoed. "Just don't sell it, Alex."

"OK, I'll put it away!" Alex's eyes flashed with anger, because at least six people were looking at him.

"And no hard feelings, eh?" This drawling voice from the background sounded slightly drunk.

Rickie moved off to the kitchen in search of a beer. The fridge

was full of beer, plus a big bowl of potato salad. But Rickie chose
a beer from a bucket on the floor, wiped the bottle with a tea
towel, and opened it. Then looking for the bathroom, he opened
a bedroom door, and espied two of the younger guests standing
before the mirrored armoire, not looking at themselves but kissing
in such a delicate, new way, that he thought it must be their first
kiss, and he stepped backward and closed the door. The next door
was the correct one.

When he emerged from the bathroom, carrying his beer bottle, the apartment was quiet, except for one angry voice saying, or
yelling, "Well, somebody must've invited him!"

"*Ja-a*—who told him about a party?"

"Doesn't even take his hat off in somebody's house!"

"What's he, stoned? Mute?"

"Who the hell is he?" asked a young voice.

A frowning young man stood in the doorway to the living
room.

"What happened?" Rickie asked him.

The young man shrugged. "Doorbell rang—and this guy—"
He gestured.

Willi Biber, Rickie now saw to his astonishment, stood smack
in the middle of the living room in his usual garb, dark trousers,
old work jacket, and broad-brimmed gray hat.

Rickie called out, "Willi!"

Willi in his doltish way replied with a "Hee-aay!" and raised a
finger, pointing at Rickie, but whether the gesture was an accusation or a greeting was dubious.

"You know him, Rick?" a voice asked.

"I have *seen* him—in my neighborhood," Rickie said in the
careful manner that often came over him when he was feeling his
drink.

"But did you invite him?"

"Certainly *not!*" Rickie replied, loud and positive. "Word of
honor."

"Come on, fellows, let's cool it." This was from Philip. "Carry on and have fun."

"He's a troublemaker, this guy!" a new voice said. "I've seen him at Jakob's. He's a basher!" The voice meant gay-basher.

Philip approached the unwanted figure. "Look, Willi—we'd all be just as happy if you left. OK? Would you like a taxi?"

"*Ja-a!*" yelled someone. "A taxi!"

"I just answered the bell, opened the door," said another voice on a defensive note. "Am I supposed to vet everyone who—"

Willi Biber turned slowly, as if trying to make all the faces sink into his memory, or he could have been looking for a face he knew among the dozen men in the room. His gray eyes were dull, and he wore a dazed expression. Suddenly he opened his arms, raised them stiffly sideways, and said, "*Faggots!*"

Raucous laughter, mild applause. "We love you too!"

"OK, I know this guy and it's *out* with him!" said a short, dark-haired man, getting to his feet. He came forward like a wrestler, took Willi by the elbows and thrust him toward the door.

A cheer went up! "Good for you, Ernst!"

Ernst had helpers. Willi was lifted off his feet. Someone held the door open.

"Yee-hoo!"

Wine bottles circulated, people sat down and relaxed and smiled. Philip started the water for wieners and spaghetti.

When Ernst and his helpers came back, they got a roar of congratulation.

"A taxi?"

"No, we let him walk!"

"If that bell rings again—don't answer!"

RICKIE STOOD IN AN APRON, helping Philip in the narrow kitchen. It was as if Rickie had suddenly come awake, after perhaps twenty minutes of blackout, though he had been on his feet all the time. By now there was no one in the apartment but him-

self and Philip and a man whose name Rickie didn't know. Philip
was carefully putting back knives, forks, spoons in their compart-
ments in a kitchen drawer.

"So—I'll be taking off!" said the tall blond young man, swing-
ing a long scarf round his neck.

"OK, Paul, and thanks again for all your help," Philip said.

"*Bitte!*" Paul and Philip kissed each other quickly on the
cheeks. "See you soon."

He was gone.

Philip smiled at Rickie, looking different, younger.

"C'mon on, we're finished here."

"True," said Rickie, undoing his apron. They had even collected the ashtrays and washed them.

Philip gave a shy squirm. "I—would you like to stay the night,
Rick?"

Rickie's lips parted in surprise. "Me?" He smiled. "Do I look
that pissed?"

"You don't look pissed at all."

Neither did Philip, looking straight at Rickie. Somewhere,
deep in the core of him, Rickie was flattered. Philip—twenty-
three at most, maybe not handsome but not bad-looking
either, and above all young. Youth was the valuable thing, lasting such a short time! "Very kind of you," said Rickie. "You
know, I—"

Philip spoke on Rickie's hesitation. "I know. I know you're
thinking of Petey still. Everybody knows that. Perfectly normal. An
unusually nice boy, he was."

"Yes," replied Rickie, beginning to consider Philip's invitation. But no: Rickie thought of his age again, and of his unattractive abdomen, bulging not just because of the surgical job, but
because of a little embonpoint, softness, self-indulgence too. Then
there was the other thing.

"We're both—you know—trying to forget someone, as Cole
Porter says in—in—"

"'It's All Right with Me,'" Rickie supplied in English and at once laughed, chuckled. "Funny. I mean the song."

"Rickie—" Philip shook his head. "You don't realize that people like you. A lot, you know? Well—I can see you don't know." Philip looked at the floor.

Sure, people liked him because he was a nice old uncle to them, ready to lend a hundred francs and forget about it. To listen to someone's troubles, pour another drink, offer a bed in a crisis, and Rickie had a bed even in the studio where he worked. That didn't mean he was an Adonis! Rickie stood taller, tightened his tie. "Um, well," he said vaguely, not looking at Philip. "I must go. Maybe you can phone for a taxi, dear Philip."

"Nonsense, I'll drive you!"

Philip insisted, there was no dissuading him, his car was just downstairs in the garage, and so Rickie and Lulu went down with Philip in the lift. Philip opened the garage and backed the car up the steep slope to pavement level. The garage door closed automatically.

Rickie had to direct Philip, who had been to his apartment before, but couldn't quite recall how to get there. Philip parked at the curb, and turned off his lights.

"Can I invite myself for a nightcap?"

Rickie knew what that meant, but he could hardly say no, since tomorrow was Saturday. "Of course!"

A walk up the front steps. Keys.

Rickie poured two whiskeys, small and neat, which was what Philip had asked for—Chivas Regal. "*Prost*," Rickie said.

"*Prost*," Philip echoed. He and Rickie sat on a large white sofa, elegantly sagging and comfortable, its cotton covers clean.

"Yes, very handsome—your friend," Philip remarked, looking at the photographs on the walls. "What—what work did he do? Or was he still in school?"

Rickie sighed. "Petey was studying photography—but not as an apprentice. And other subjects too—literature, English, Euro-

pean history. Oh, Petey was interested in so many things!" Rickie
had suddenly spoken loudly, so he reined himself in. "I feel sure he
would've—decided about his life within a year. Maybe photography. He was only twenty."

"How long ago was it—that he died?"

"That he was stabbed. Six or seven months now." Rickie
drank. "January the twelfth."

"Not so long."

"No."

Philip glanced toward Rickie's fireplace, and back at him.
"Rickie, do you remember about four years ago—when we all got
so drunk at a party here and took off our clothes and danced
and—somebody dared us to run up and down the *street!*" Philip's
voice cracked as he laughed. "And some of us—were dropping our
clothes in the street. Remember?"

Rickie did remember, as if it were an old fuzzy photograph,
that he himself had gone out and collected all the garments he
could see in the street and brought them back here, and left them
in a heap, shoes, trousers, shirts. He must have gone out at least
twice to collect it all, while some fellows slept or wandered about
singing, he recalled. "Such lovely days—and not so long ago."

"*No!*" Philip agreed. "May I?" He meant the whiskey.

"Of course, Philip! No, not for me. Well—just the least bit."
Rickie held his glass.

Philip poured himself a small one. "I wish I—could make you
realize that you're popular. Everyone likes you. It's always been
so—ever since I've known you."

Rickie laughed. "All of six years, maybe?"

"Longer. Oh, I've seen—oh, never mind."

Seen old photos of him, maybe, Rickie thought. Yes, sure, he
had been tall, slim, and handsome at thirty, thirty-five. He had
known some of the fellows at the party tonight when they had
been hardly seventeen.

"What is it? Afraid of AIDS? I haven't—"

"I thought—" Rickie stopped in confusion. "In case you haven't heard—via the grapevine—I'm HIV positive. I heard—"

"*What?* Oh Rickie!"

"Yes. My doctor— Well, I had the bad news from him a few weeks ago." Rickie sipped, swallowed with difficulty. "Not something I like to tell everybody, only somebody I might go to bed with, and anyway since Petey—there's been no one."

"No, I hadn't heard." Philip was still frowning his sympathy. "But you know—well, you can live *years*—decades."

With a sword over your head, an ax at your throat. "Sure, I take B-12 and my doctor says I've a good supply of—the white corpuscles to—to fight infections."

"These days everyone's doing safe sex, anyway, HIV or not," Philip said more cheerfully. "You know, Rickie, you're the first fellow I ever went to bed with?"

"Re-eally?" Rickie, half incredulous, sought rather drunkenly for something to say. He couldn't recall the first time he'd gone to bed with Philip. There had been, Rickie knew, several times, but he was vague about those too. "Well-l," Rickie said, thoughtful.

"I brought some—condoms," Philip said, showing reluctance to utter the word.

"No. It's for your own good." Now Rickie was the elderly schoolmaster. He meant it, deep down. Philip was healthy, and he should not take chances. Rickie got up unsteadily. "Now I have to go to bed, Philip. God knows what time it is."

Philip stood up, polite. "Twenty past two," he said after a glance at his wristwatch. "G'night, Rickie. Something I can do, though—to help you now?"

"No—thank you, Philip. And good night, m'boy." Rickie moved toward the door, but by the time he got there, Philip was gone.

Then Rickie set about undressing, washing, turning the bed down in his bedroom, as he had done scores of times before when so drunk he knew everything was taking twice the time to do that it should have taken. At some point in this ritual, he gave up and fell face down on his bed and fast asleep.

4

The following Wednesday would have been Peter Ritter's twenty-first birthday. Rickie had thought of a long weekend in Paris, or Venice, and he remembered he had been going to ask Petey his preference, when the night of the stabbing came. Rickie thought of telephoning Petey's parents to say a friendly word. After all, he had met them, and they had been quite cordial to him. They had long before become reconciled to the fact that their son preferred his own sex. But on second thoughts, Rickie gave up the idea of telephoning Herr and Frau Christian Ritter, because it might make them sadder.

Then he thought of Luisa—Zimmermann, wasn't it? He might think of something to give *her* on Petey's birthday. Not that she knew when Petey's birthday was, probably, but she looked so wistful often, when Rickie saw her, which was always when she was with Renate at Jakob's. But what to give her? A nice card would be easy, and he could make it. But a gift? Petey had left two scarves here, a couple of sweaters. A pity there wasn't a ring, though Rickie admitted he would have kept a ring for himself. A scarf. One was dark maroon, the other narrowly striped in red and blue, and made of finely pleated cotton. Rickie had given Petey that. OK, that was it. He washed the scarf in tepid water, then twisted it to make the pleats return.

By Tuesday morning at his late breakfast at Jakob's, Rickie had still not seen Luisa, and Renate only once, on Monday. He wasn't going to give a message for Luisa via Renate!

Then Rickie saw Luisa crossing the street toward Jakob's, as he was nearing its back terrace gate. He hailed her.

She stopped on the pavement, looking surprised.

"Hello—Luisa," he repeated, looking for Renate whom he did not see. "Rickie, remember?"

Her young face smiled, and she brushed a long straight tress of dark hair back. "Of course I remember."

Rickie recalled that when she had come to work for Renate, her hair had been short and unruly. "I have something for you— something I'd like to give you. Nothing important. But it's back at my studio."

"Give me? Why?" She shifted, as if ready to fly off.

"My idea. Petey's birthday is tomorrow. Would have been. I can make a coffee for you at my studio, but maybe you have a date." He was thinking of Renate, probably due any minute at Jakob's, maybe already there.

"No, I'll manage." She glanced behind her, in the direction of Renate's house.

They walked quickly, Rickie making an effort to keep up.

"I've forgotten your dog's name."

"Lulu," said Rickie. "You still work for Renate, don't you?"

"Yes, along with three other girls." Her brown eyes glanced up at him, shining and alert.

She was so pretty, Rickie thought, with her glossy brown hair, clear complexion, and rather narrow lips, ready to smile. She carried her straight nose high. Today she wore brown slacks, a white shirt, a short black jacket full of pockets and metal snap buttons.

"Here we are," said Rickie, though Lulu was leading the way down the cement steps.

"Oh! I remember this!" Luisa had espied the two plaster-of-Paris females on the bench. "I was here once, you know?"

Rickie had forgotten. "I hope so," he said affably. "Now would you like some coffee?"

She wouldn't, thanks, and she glanced at her watch. Rickie

supposed she was expected by the old witch Renate at Jakob's, and right away.

"Just this. A small thing," Rickie said, presenting a flat, gold-paper-wrapped package. "Something Petey once owned. N-not exactly valuable," he added with a smile.

Her mouth opened a little with surprise. "Thank you, Rickie. . . . I think I'll open it at home, if you don't mind."

Rickie laughed. "Of course I don't mind! And where is home?"

"I have a room at Frau Hagnauer's place. It's a big—"

"Really? You sleep there?" Rickie had recognized the name.

"Yes," said Luisa, looking straight at him. "It's much cheaper, of course, than an apartment—which I couldn't afford anyway." She gave a laugh.

"I've heard she's so strict when it comes to working hours." Here Rickie laughed. "Doesn't she try to tell you when to be home at night, not to mention when to get up?"

"Oh yes. Home by ten—unless it's a special film I'm going to with friends. Then up—" The corners of her mouth rose on the word, and she looked at the floor. "Well, before seven, I'll say that, but then I sometimes have to go and buy the rolls and the sweet stuff for morning break for the girls, and make the coffee for Frau Hagnauer and me. We sign on for three years, you know. But the others don't sleep there."

To Rickie it sounded like a voluntary prison sentence, or a three-year voyage on a whaler, in the old days. "A big apartment," he mused.

"Yes. If I counted the rooms—at least five. And the main workroom with all the sewing machines and the tables, that's made from two rooms with the wall knocked out. Fluorescent lighting—"

Rickie could imagine. He knew the old apartment house without a lift, and even with fluorescent lighting, the picture of four diligent girls bent over machines or needles, doing buttonholes, cutting material, while Renate cracked the whip in her high-pitched monotone—Rickie had heard it—all this made him shiver. Better sloppy Mathilde, a bit tiddly by noon, at least she was human. "The girls—" Rickie couldn't go on. "Luisa, one more thing. You know that tall fellow, always in an old hat—at Jakob's. Willi—"

Her eyes showed recognition. "Willi, sure."

"I'm wondering how he knew about a party last Friday night given by a friend of mine in town. Did Renate say anything to you about it?"

"No. Why?"

"No reason. Just that Renate sometimes talks to Willi. And Renate's very observant."

"True. She picks up everything—about everybody. I don't know how she does it." Luisa looked desperate to fly off. "You know—I'd better leave this. She'll ask me where I got it. I do have a date with her."

"Really," said Rickie, not at all surprised. He took the gold-wrapped package back into his hands. "But you will pick it up some time? I can't deliver it to your house!" Rickie grinned; his eyes grew moist with mirth at the idea.

"Oh, she wouldn't have it in the house!" said Luisa, smiling. "'Bye, Rickie!" At his studio door she looked back. "I won't be able to say hello or nod to you, you know—in Jakob's."

"I know." He watched the girl race up his stone steps, glimpsed her running sneakers as she dashed off to his right.

Rickie realized that he wanted to see her again. She was somehow a link to Petey. Why hadn't he tried to make a date with her in regard to her picking up the scarf? Well, his two numbers and addresses were in the telephone book, and he felt sure Luisa would telephone or turn up soon unannounced. That was nice to expect.

He went out with Lulu. Today he would make a quick ritual

of breakfast, and not keep Mathilde waiting on the doorstep. One
of these days soon, he'd give her the key.

Today Tobi, nicknamed Baconhead, was on duty instead of
Andreas. Tobi was tall and blond, just over twenty, and as
acquainted with Rickie's menu as was Andreas.

"Good morning, Rickie and Lulu!" said Tobi with a slight
bow. "The usual, sir?"

"Yes, and the Appenzeller soon," said Rickie, opening the
Tages-Anzeiger.

A few meters distant and opposite Rickie, Luisa sat in her dark
jacket, and Renate in something blue today, at least on top. He did
not glance directly at them, and was sure Luisa was acting her part
too, not even absently letting her eyes rest on him for two seconds,
as she might have done any other morning. He felt that he shared
a secret with Luisa, and he liked the feeling.

Rickie had to devote much of that morning to improving a
design—a running female figure in short Grecian gown. He had
done a better design for this company, but it was unpleasant to
argue, and a couple of times he had lost clients because he did
argue. By just after twelve, Rickie was tired of drawing in pencil,
erasing a bit, taking another piece of paper to do nearly the same
thing. The client was coming at 4 P.M., one Beat Scherz, an amusing name to Rickie, as *Scherz* meant joke. Having bollocksed one
sketch beyond repair, Rickie amused himself by adding an
enlarged penis to the long-haired, long-limbed figure.

This made him laugh with a single "Hah!" which caused
Mathilde in the corner to look round at him.

"Spoilt something. Excuse me," he said, ripping up the small
page.

"I'm glad when you laugh!" replied Mathilde.

Rickie smiled back at her. The pregnancy scare had eased two
days ago, when something had happened: had Mathilde said she'd
actually *had* a urine test? Because Rickie disliked thinking about

personal, feminine things, he had forgotten exactly what she said. No matter, the great news was that she was *not* pregnant.

In mid-afternoon, Mathilde informed him that a woman was on the telephone, and had said her name was Luisa.

"Hello," Rickie said.

"Hello. I am out to buy a newspaper with a certain blouse advertisement," Luisa said, laughing a little. "*True*. But—"

"Would you like to come to my studio now?"

"No, I can't. I was thinking—quarter to six at your apartment?"

"But of course! I'll be there, Luisa." Rickie noticed that Mathilde went on pecking at the keys. She wasn't interested in his female acquaintances.

Mr. Scherz by nearly five had chosen three sketches to take back to his office, with a preference for the one Rickie thought was best, which was a bit unusual. And Mathilde did a good job of her letter-writing, and invoices, and Rickie told her so.

"Thank you, Rickie. You're a nice man to work for."

"Am I now? Not a dirty old man?"

"Oh no-o!" She gave a long, lazy shriek. "You? Never! Ha-ha-ha-ha!"

Maybe that was a compliment. For an instant, though, it had made Rickie feel as if he were a castrato.

HOW MUCH TIME would Luisa have? Rickie fussed with a bottle of Dubonnet and glasses on his shining table. Of course, he had Coca-Cola too. Or orange juice. He stepped out on his little balcony to get some air and to see, maybe, Luisa walking toward his building.

At last she came, from his right, under the tree leaves that overhung the pavement, head up and with quick steps. She looked for his house number, then noticed him on the balcony and raised an arm. He did the same. She came in the iron gate, looked up again, and at the steps up to the balcony.

"This way?" she asked.

"Well—you could," said Rickie, smiling.

She climbed the cement steps that were partially covered with ivy. "Funny way to enter an apartment!"

"Welcome!" Rickie opened his french windows, and let her precede him. She had not been here, Rickie was sure. "Yes, and this doesn't even close. Well, it closes but it doesn't lock." He pushed the two sections together, without the bar across, and they parted slightly.

Luisa was staring at a nearly life-size photo of Petey from waist up, suntanned, in a white shirt, blue-sky background, his eyes nearly closed as he gazed at the photographer—Rickie.

"Of course I have quite a lot of Petey," Rickie said on an apologetic note. "It's only natural."

"Yes—of course."

"And your famous little present! But first, can I offer you something? A Dubonnet, Coca-Cola, fruit juice—tea?"

"I can't stay long."

Dismal words. "Now, who says so? Half an hour? Have you a date?"

"Oh no." She had opened her jacket. "I said to Renate I was going out just to walk for a few minutes. I've been sitting."

"But—sit again, and I'll bring you—well—" Rickie fetched the yellow package. "Only if you sit."

Smiling, she sat on a straight chair near the table.

"Open it. It's so simple—for all this fuss."

Luisa opened the package, took out the long scarf and held it up. "Petey's."

"Yes, he left it here. I thought you might like it."

"Of course I like it." She pressed it to her nose, then looked at Rickie. "Thank you. Thanks for thinking of me."

Rickie looked at the floor. "Now I'm going to have a cool beer—and if you change your mind—" He got a small Pilsner Urquell from his fridge. A beer, anything in his hand, would make him appear more relaxed, he thought. "Why is it," he began, addressing the girl who was in a corner of the room, looking at a smaller photo of Petey and him in Ascona.

"Why is what?"

Were the girl's eyes moist? Rickie hoped not. "Why is it this Renate keeps such a tight rein on you? Is she jealous of your boyfriends?"

"Ha! I haven't any boyfriends—just now."

"But she makes you come home at a certain hour? Eat with her too?"

"Supper? Yes—usually." Luisa looked embarrassed by his questions. "She's a good cook—and by then it's just the two of us."

Rickie sipped his beer. "But for instance, if I asked you to have dinner with me this evening. Out somewhere. You'd telephone her—"

"Oh sure, telephone her. But I wouldn't tell her I was with you." Luisa smiled, amused.

"No." Rickie understood that, of course. "She bosses all the girls around like that?" He was sure Renate didn't.

"No. But the others don't sleep there, you know. They live with their family."

Rickie hesitated. "I remembered Petey told me you'd run away from home."

"Yes, my family, well. I don't want to talk about that."

Rickie watched her brown eyes move from one object to the next, not evasively, but as if she sought something to help her collect her thoughts. "My parents quarreled. My real parents. Then there was a divorce. Then my stepfather—I was about twelve. Then—I suppose not so many quarrels but my stepfather would hit my mother and sometimes me." Here came an attempt at a shrug and a smile. "So finally I ran off. Took a train to Zurich—last October. I even washed dishes for a while. Don't ask me where I slept!"

"I won't!" Rickie managed a smile.

"*Not* the railway station." Now she smiled. "I met a girl where I was washing dishes. She was a waitress living with her mother. They let me sleep in the living room. Maybe I will have a Coke."

Rickie went to his fridge and returned with bottle and glass.

"Thank you," Again she seemed to struggle to organize what she wanted to say. "Then I got *very* depressed. I went to the railway station, not knowing where I should go with just a few francs. That was worse, the sight of young people sleeping—you know, some of them drugged. So I started walking—through the Langstrasse tunnel, you know?"

Rickie knew, under the railway line of the main station, the Langstrasse was for cars and pedestrians and led to the district of Aussersihl.

"I was having a coffee somewhere—with not enough money to eat, really, and I got to talking with a girl on the stool next to me. I asked her if she knew of any jobs—anything, like a salesgirl, I thought. She asked if I had any *skills*. Some people make it sound like a *Doktorat*. So I said I'd done nearly two years as an apprentice seamstress, and this girl said she knew of a woman in the neighborhood who employed seamstresses. And she gave me Renate's name but not the exact address." Luisa gave a big sigh and drank some Coke. "Anyway, I finally got to Frau Hagnauer's house—and I thought it was the luckiest thing that ever happened to me—a job and a place to sleep."

Rickie could understand. "But why is she so strict—with you? Just because you're alone?" And because on an apprentice's salary, Luisa couldn't afford a Zurich apartment, Rickie was thinking. It was sadism, of a sort.

"Y-yes," Luisa said thoughtfully, "and also she's teaching me all the time. She wants to make me a designer and—she thinks I have talent." She spoke with a pride and amusement combined.

"And you? You like that idea?"

"Yes. I like inventing clothes. It's fun. I sketch a lot. New ideas. Renate has stacks of cheap paper everywhere in the workroom. I do as much of that as sewing!" Luisa laughed, and finished her drink with a gulp. "Now I must go." She stood up and her smile went away, as if she imagined facing Renate.

"Are the other girls jealous of you?"

"No. Because I can help them in little ways. They know I'm not conceited about special attention from Renate!"

"She's not married, is she—Renate?"

"She was—for about seven years. She's divorced." Luisa shifted. "Rickie—I have a question."

"Yes?"

She curled the red-and-blue muffler gently around both hands. "It was here—wasn't it—that Petey—in the bedroom, I mean."

Anger and frustration surged in Rickie, hot and confusing. "He was stabbed to death when he came out of a cinema. He took a shortcut toward home—a dark street." With effort, Rickie kept his voice steady and low. "I can't understand why people think— he died here, when the stabbing was reported in the newspapers, the *Tages-Anzeiger*, *Neue Zürcher*, even the street name." Rickie felt warm in the face. "Maybe Renate said he was murdered here."

"Yes. She did. She said by someone Petey had brought here one night when you were working in your studio."

"She hates homosexuals. I don't think I have to tell you." Rickie was inwardly boiling. "Funny, she goes nearly every day to Jakob's, when she could go to that little tearoom nearer her— espresso machine, brioches—such a nice clientele."

Luisa's lips gave a twitch of a smile. "I know. She loves to make remarks about people."

"Whole stories, it would seem!"

Luisa looked embarrassed, unsure of herself. She went to the french windows, which were partly open, and looked cautiously out, stooped to see past the tree branches.

"What's the matter?"

"I don't want to bump into Willi. I'll go out the front door, Rickie. Thank you!"

"A pleasure! Come again, Luisa." He opened the apartment door for her.

"G'bye!" She opened the front door herself and fled down the front steps.

5

Some three streets away from Rickie's flat, Renate Hagnauer waited nervously for Luisa. Had she started talking with someone, given in to an offer of another coffee? Renate clumped into the kitchen—clump, scrape, clump, scrape, dragging her right foot—to check the potatoes—still in their water with the gas ring off, all right. Clump, scrape. Renate didn't care how she clumped when she was alone, and if the couple below didn't like it, they could lump it. The nerve of them once, complaining about a handicapped person! Renate had given them a piece of her mind, made them feel wretched, she hoped.

Luisa deserved a strong word. Not even the courtesy to telephone to say she'd be late!

At last Renate heard the key in the lock.

Frowning, Renate entered the high-ceilinged hall. Coat hooks sprouted all along one wall, as if a regiment had dwelt here, though the hooks were useful for the girls during the workweek.

"What happened to you?" Renate asked sharply.

"Nothing. I'm sorry if I'm a little late."

"A little? You could have telephoned."

Luisa calmly hung her jacket on a book.

"What is this, you're getting fat? What's under your shirt?"

"It's nothing. I lowered my vest because it was hot. Let me go and wash, all right?" Luisa turned right in the workroom, then entered a small room which had a toilet and washbasin, washed her hands quickly, and with the water still running pulled her shirttails out and extricated the muffler. She folded it small, and hearing nothing outside, exited, intending to make a dash for her room.

But Renate stood in the hall. "What's that in your hand? You bought something?"

"Yes. Not important."

Renate followed her to the doorway of her room. "Well, what is it?" She was always curious about clothes.

Luisa shrugged. "Just a scarf." She tossed it on to her bed, and walked toward the door.

But Renate advanced. "A long muffler? This time of year?"

"In a sale. I liked it. Can I do something to help with dinner?"

"Was this what you had under your shirt? What is this, you are shoplifting now?" Her accent, German-Romanian-Jewish, a pot-pourri of Mitteleuropa, had come to the fore. "Come on, or we ruin the dinner."

The meal interval was cool. Renate suspected something, but wasn't sure what. Had Luisa met a boy? Had a beer or a Coca-Cola with him just now at Jakob's? Or at some other place, because too many people knew Luisa at Jakob's, and might report it to her, Renate?

"Another little scaloppini Good for you." Renate had got up and was bringing the iron pan in her mitted hand, lifting a tasty length of veal with a wooden spatula onto Luisa's plate.

"It does taste good," replied Luisa pleasantly.

"It's good meat. It pays to buy the best—in everything, material, thread, machines. Don't forget that."

Several minutes later, when Luisa had removed the dinner plates and set the table for dessert—Renate's own lemon mousse—Renate said, "Your hair looks lovely. That shampoo I bought you is good, no? Makes a gloss."

Renate ate, savoring her mousse, her eyes fixed on Luisa. Renate fancied that Luisa had a slight crush on her, that Luisa would appreciate, enjoy, a quick embrace before bedtime, a kiss on the cheek, the pressure of her hand in both Renate's, for instance. Renate was aware that she took the place of Luisa's mother, to some extent, that selfish mother who was plainly wrapped up in her second husband (a good-looking bully, Renate gathered) and in her son by him, a child who would be nearly six by now. Poor Luisa had been shoved out in the cold, emotionally speaking. Just as well for her, Renate thought, and indeed had said more than once. Luisa had not replied to Renate's compliment on her hair. She was unusually pensive this evening.

"You didn't meet a new boy," Renate began on a light, teasing note, as she served them both a little more mousse. "Had a Coke with him maybe?"

"No," Luisa said firmly, looking Renate in the eye.

"I don't mind if you do, you know. Why should I mind? A nice boy. It's these *homos* everywhere that are the problem! So many— you'd think AIDS didn't exist!" She forced a titter. "They are the silly ones. Always changing partners. They have no partners, just sex en masse, you know. At the same time they flirt. They think they are handsome." Renate glanced at Luisa who was still looking straight at her, and fitted a cigarette into her long holder, reached for her silver lighter.

"They certainly don't flirt with me," Luisa said, and drank the last of her red wine. "They don't bother me. What're you worried about?"

"I'm not worried!" Renate retorted at once. "Worried about homos? Hah!" Her right hand played with her silver napkin ring, turning it over and over, and realizing this, she banged the ring down on the tablecloth. She went on, aware that she had made the same speech before, but unable to stop herself: "You see, don't you, what happened with this Petey you were infatuated with. He teased you. Oh, they love to be the center—"

"He did not tease me," Luisa interrupted. "Ever. Petey was very serious. And honest."

"You see what happened, though. Stabbed to death in the bedroom of this overaged man friend. It's the company they keep! What else can you—"

"He was stabbed in a *street*." Luisa's voice shook on the last word. "It was in the newspapers. It's only a few people like you, maybe, who say—"

"Who told you that?"

"Told me? Now I remember Ursie and Andreas saying it. Petey went to a film that night. He took a shortcut home, a dark street." Luisa went on, determined, sure of herself. Her words tore at the picture Renate and a few others had created, even Willi Biber, maybe, that Petey had been stabbed by a pickup of Petey's, "I didn't read it in the newspapers. I was so shocked to hear about him—from you. I thought you had real information—the *truth*, I thought. Maybe from Rickie even. But it wasn't true. He was killed in a street."

"Luisa, who are you to say that I and my neighbors are wrong?" Renate rapped out the question.

"I'm sure I could find it in the newspapers. Mid-January."

"Luisa, you are recently arrived here. What do you know about the neighborhood, the people who live here? Stop scowling and stop mooning over this worthless—homo boy!" Renate stirred, about to get up to signify her disgust at all the emotion. "A kept and worthless homo!"

"Petey was not kept. He was living with his parents and going to school. He wasn't poor."

"You've been talking to this Rickie Mark—something—or one of his entourage. I don't want to hear about Petey again, do you understand? Not in this house!" Renate stood up.

Luisa stood up too.

"Let's have coffee, Luisa. It's silly to—"

"No coffee. I'll come back in a minute, help you with—"

"Never mind the dishes. Where're you going?"

"Just to my room!"

Renate stomped after her, clump, scrape, not caring. "The last episode of *Hit Squad* is on—in twenty minutes!"

"I don't care! Thank you!"

Then Luisa appeared, carrying a summer jacket.

"What's all this?"

"All what? It's eight-forty, not even dark. I'm going out for a walk."

Renate had an impulse to seize her arm as the girl swept past her. Luisa was stronger, taller, and never had they come to a struggle. "Where're you going?"

Luisa took a breath and it sounded like a gasp. "For a walk! Do I have to say where? Nowhere!"

The apartment door slammed.

Renate went and opened it. "You may find it bolted when you come back!"

Luisa's quick steps kept on, downward.

Renate ducked back into the flat, and locked and bolted the door. How she would have loved to follow Luisa, see where she went, what kind of stranger she decided to talk with, even if—after a walk to cool her temper, she only stopped for a glass of wine somewhere. Renate's bad foot prevented that: she was both conspicuous and slow. But as she often reminded herself, there were compensations, too—she got special privileges from strangers.

Willi Biber. See if he was at Jakob's, Renate thought, give him a small task: to see if Luisa was there this evening and remember whom she was talking to. Renate hesitated, however. Sometimes she disguised her voice when ringing Jakob's, and she considered herself good at that. But too often was too often. She suspected that Andy might know that it was she on the phone, though sometimes Ursie answered, and Ursie was always in such a hurry, all she wanted to know was what or whom the caller wanted. Willi? If he was there, Ursie went and got him.

But who in the name of God wanted to talk with the dunce except Renate? They had to meet and talk on the sly, almost, like star-crossed lovers. Her small, rather ugly face wrinkled, her eyes nearly closed, as she yielded to a few seconds of nervous amusement.

She could have convinced Willi Biber that he'd stabbed this Petey to death in Rickie's apartment. That balcony door was broken, Willi had so informed Renate months ago at the height of the Luisa-Petey infatuation—last December. That information hadn't interested Renate then, but after Petey's death, she had indulged in a little fantasy. Willi had a stout Swiss army knife. By now he looked on homos with almost as much revulsion as did Renate herself. She had convinced him that he'd served in the Foreign Legion; why not that he was the murderer of Petey too? But she had confined herself to telling Willi that she had inside information that a third man had come into the apartment, one night when Rickie had been working in his studio—invited or not by Petey, no one would ever know—and had likely made his exit via the balcony. Willi had passed this story on to a few in Jakob's, Renate knew, maybe to his employers the Wengers at L'Eclair, where he washed baking pans and took out dustbins. That satisfied Renate, or had satisfied her. It did annoy her that Luisa had, apparently, spoken with Rickie or someone who was sure of the newspaper account.

While she was putting soiled dishes into the dishwasher, humming tunelessly as she often did when nervous, Renate decided not to telephone Jakob's tonight.

"Hmm-mm-hmm-mm-hmm-mm," she hummed as she looked about, making sure that she had collected every object that the machine could handle. "Hmm-mm-hmm . . ." She would give Luisa an unpleasant time tonight, make her wait a while.

6

At about the same time, Luisa was walking back the way she had come a couple of hours before, toward Rickie's apartment, hoping she'd see a light behind the balcony. Then—she was sure she would find the courage—she would ring his doorbell.

But there was no light, just blackness at the tall french windows.

Well, there was Jakob's, not far away. Hadn't she been there a few times on her own after supper, to take a coffee? Certainly.

Since Willi the Dunce always sat at the long table in the front part of Jakob's, Luisa entered via a side gate that opened onto the back garden. A path led to the back terrace, where lights hung from grapevine-covered beams. Voices and laughter. Luisa's shoulders relaxed, and she felt her frown go away. All the tables but a small one seemed occupied. She would sit at the little table and not care when Andreas or Ursie appeared to take her order. It was wonderful to be among people who were having a nice evening, people who weren't Renate Hagnauer and didn't know she existed.

She was about to sit down, when a male voice called, "Luisa!" Rickie had half risen from a full table at the other end of the terrace, tall and very visible in a white cardigan. "Come over to us!"

Luisa made her way.

"Welcome!" said Rickie, indicating a chair that someone had secured for her.

There were five or six people at the table, one of them a woman. A single candle burned low between ashtrays.

Rickie introduced the woman as Evelyn Huber. "And Claus—Bruder," he went on. "Philip Egli—"

"Enough!" said a dark-haired young man, smiling and a bit drunk. "I'm Ernst."

Lulu barked from her own chair.

"And Lulu," said Rickie.

"I know Lulu!" said Luisa, smiling.

"This is Luisa—Zimmermann." Rickie was happy that he had managed to recall her last name. "And what would you like to drink—or eat?"

"There's wine! Where're the glasses? Give me the—" This from Ernst who was extending an arm in Rickie's direction.

Andreas arrived.

"A Coke?" asked Rickie, who had sat down. "Wine? The peach tart is lovely tonight." He was aware that he had drunk enough, but he had not made any mistakes as yet. "Another espresso for me, please, Andy. And for the young lady," Rickie continued, "our guest of honor tonight—"

"A Coke, please," said Luisa.

"Rickie," the man called Philip said, "the glasses—the funny ones!"

"In due time," replied Rickie, raising a finger, looking round for Renate and happy not to see her.

". . . no, I'm an apprentice seamstress," Luisa was saying to Ernst.

"Really? You mean—fancy—sewing work?"

Luisa looked at Rickie. "Ernst thought I was a model!"

"That is because you are pretty," Rickie replied.

"I have seen you here—with the couturiere." This was from the woman called Evelyn, who looked the soberest of all present.

"Yes. Frau Hagnauer often comes here for a coffee in the mornings."

"And to snoop," Rickie put in genially.

A giggle rose in Luisa, irrepressible.

"Ha!" This from Philip. "What else has the old witch got to do? Goggle-goggle!" He put his hands up to his eyes, as if he looked through binoculars. "Rickie, show Luisa the glasses! Put 'em on Lulu!"

Lulu barked once on hearing her name, and put a white foot

gently on the table edge. She looked around for orders, making an "Ooo-ooo" sound as if she were dying to talk.

"Sit till I finish my coffee, Lulu," Rickie said and the dog took her paw from the table.

"Evelyn, show Luisa your castle," said the young man called Claus.

Evelyn carefully unrolled a cylinder of paper that she had been holding across her lap. "This is for children, you understand, Luisa. I'm a librarian—in a school." She stood up, and with the aid of Claus held the corners of the black-and-white drawing of the spired castle.

It looked dreamy to Luisa, reminding her of stories half remembered, when she had been small. The castle made her feel for a few seconds like a four-year-old looking into picture books when she could believe in them.

"Rickie copied a boy's drawing for me—on his machine," Evelyn shouted over the table conversation.

"You're going to pin them on the wall? Or give them as prizes?" There seemed to be at least six.

Luisa never heard an answer, because of a clap of laughter: Rickie had put on a pair of joke glasses, and was clowning with his espresso cup in hand. Luisa's Coke had arrived, and a few more beers. Rickie's glasses had eyes painted on them, rather sleepy, stupid dark eyes with blue eyeshadow above them, set farther apart than Rickie's own.

"Put 'em on Lulu!"

Lulu pranced in her chair.

"Anyone got a scarf?" Rickie asked.

Philip Egli pulled a blue muffler from a jacket pocket.

Lulu's winter-cruise tableau again. Rickie obliged, and settled the glasses on Lulu's nose.

"Ha-ha! Look! Look!"

Applause for Lulu! Rickie glowed with satisfaction.

"Take her on a tour!" Ernst yelled.

Rickie went with Lulu on the lead into the larger, more lighted part of Jakob's, now bordered with tables and chairs. One by one people spotted Lulu and pointed.

"Look at the *dog*!"

"Hello, Lulu."

"*Very* becoming!"

Patters of applause.

"Hi, Rickie!"

A few were Rickie's neighbors, lived in his building. Steadied by Lulu's confident lead, Rickie walked past the table where Renate and Luisa usually sat, and returned at a leisurely pace to the back terrace.

Luisa had watched from the open doorway between terrace and the big section, trembling inside with laughter, while her eyes filled with tears, tears that even ran down her cheeks. Was she laughing or crying? It had turned into a wonderful evening!

"Friend of Petey's," Luisa heard Rickie say to someone at the table. "And you know, Petey's birthday is tomorrow. He'd have been twenty-one." He went on, "It's my party tonight. Nobody pays anything."

The librarian Evelyn groaned, smiling. "Come on, Rickie."

"Thanks, Rickie, some other time. I left some money under my glass. No argument!"

Luisa found another Coca-Cola in front of her. She glanced at her watch and saw that more than an hour had gone by since she had left the house! "Rickie—"

He was on her left, and at that moment he looked down at the table and grimaced. Then she saw that his eyes were wet. He wiped them quickly with the back of one hand. His other hand held Lulu's lead.

"G'night, Rickie. Many, many thanks," said Evelyn, departing with the white cylinder under her arm. "Don't get up."

But Rickie, somewhat wobbly, was on his feet.

In the next minutes, Rickie settled the bill with Andreas, who gave Rickie change, no doubt exact, as Andreas was honest. Just as Andreas walked away toward the inside room, Luisa saw Willi standing in the doorway, looking straight at her with the gray-eyed, fixed but neutral gaze with which he looked at everything. He was going to report her presence here to Renate, Luisa supposed.

Ernst was the only one left at the table besides Luisa and Rickie. "Thank you, Rickie," he said. "Want me to walk you home?"

"I am seeing this young lady to *her* home," said Rickie.

Luisa took an uneasy gulp of her Coke. "But I live so near. You don't have to see me home, Rickie." Glancing, Luisa saw that Willi had disappeared as if he had been a bad dream. She stood up.

So did Rickie and Ernst. The three went through the garden to the gate, the way Luisa had come. The two men took her gently by an elbow, one on either side.

"Now this is an escort!" said Luisa, amused and anxious too.

"And an honor. An honor guard!" said Ernst.

Three or four streets away, St. Jakob's Church tolled once for half past ten.

"Isn't she a darling?" asked Rickie.

Ernst said, "What a shame we're not the marrying type. We're what the English call 'confirmed bachelors.' Ha-ha! It means something like the Small g, only bigger!"

Somehow it was funny, and harmless. Luisa laughed, not knowing why. They were approaching the whitish house where she lived. Formerly this had been a capacious private dwelling, big enough for a growing family and a couple of live-in servants who would have had to climb to the little rooms at the top, with their small peaked windows in the roof, to sleep. The window below the servants'-rooms level was lighted. This was the sitting room, where the TV set was.

"Thank you—both. Thank you, Rickie—for the wonderful evening." Luisa almost whispered.

"Soon again, I hope," said Rickie. "Phone me, any time."

"G'night, Luisa."

Luisa opened the front door with her key, and waved to the two watching her. Then she climbed the stairs, second key at the ready.

As she had expected, Renate had slid the inside bolt. Luisa knocked gently.

But nothing came, no sound. Luisa's thoughts jumped: Renate was going to make her wait half an hour, longer, maybe. Keep calm, Luisa told herself. She had found calmness a good defense against Renate, who preferred to see her hurt.

She knocked again. Luisa was sure Renate was not far away, probably standing in the hall, listening to her difficulties. She rang the bell briefly, and hearing no response, tried her key again, hoping. The bolt still held.

Luisa turned to the banistered stairs with a crazy thought of dashing after Rickie and Ernst. Nothing more certain than that Rickie would let her sleep on his sofa tonight. Angry now, Luisa tried a trick: she went somewhat noisily down the stairs, halfway down the next flight, and waited.

And waited. After two minutes, she decided to creep back up. Again she tried the key, and then knocked. And waited.

At last, the bump and scrape, a bit slower than usual, which heralded Renate's approach. Luisa straightened, taut; why should she say she was "sorry," when Renate hadn't needed to double-lock?

"So," said Renate, in nightdress and dressing gown. "A little late tonight."

"Thank you," said Luisa, coming in. "I don't know why you bolted it. I wasn't going to be out long."

"Long enough! Woke me up!" Renate sniffed. "Where were you?"

They were standing in the hall. Renate had turned off the sitting room light, where she had probably been watching TV.

"At Jakob's, having a Coca-Cola," replied Luisa, hoping to take some steam out of Willi's report tomorrow. "When I wasn't walking, that is."

"Walking. If you have so much energy, you might start working as our *putzfrau*, no?" Here Renate gave a twitch of a smile.

The storm was over. Luisa was able to walk on to her room.

To Luisa's relief, Renate did not follow her to her room with a last thought. Luisa had near the end of the hall what she could call her own bathroom, albeit a small one: toilet, basin and shower, and hot water. In five minutes, she was showered and in bed, with the light out, eager to think about the evening.

What had Rickie meant when he said, "Come to the Small g Saturday night?" Luisa knew there was dancing Saturday nights, sometimes Friday nights too, if the crowd was big enough. Jakob's boasted an old jukebox, and there were amplifiers in the corners.

What a really nice evening it had been! Such friendly people! Petey's birthday tomorrow—meaning an hour from now. Luisa remembered the tears in Rickie's eyes, and she was sure he had loved Petey quite as much as she had. *A dream!* She knew Petey had been "a dream," because he didn't like girls, not in a romantic way. Now she remembered distinctly Petey's smooth, handsome face with the worried look, saying, "You mustn't fall in love with *me*." Now she felt she understood, at least understood a lot better.

Pleasantly drowsy, Luisa drew her knees up nearly to her chin, stretched her legs and turned face down, to sleep. She would see Rickie again, she was sure, and the white dog Lulu with the soft ears and alert eyes—sitting on a chair at the table listening to everything, like another person. Luisa shook with silent laughter. She had the feeling that something important had happened this evening, something happy and lucky.

7

Luisa's Wednesday began between six-thirty and seven with coffee and roll in the kitchen. By seven-thirty Renate's "girls"
began to arrive, usually Vera first, the oldest and a coworker (higher
than an apprentice), then Elsie (serious and conscientious), then
Stephanie, of cheerful disposition and usually the last. Stephanie
came on a tram from the center of Zurich. The others lived in
Aussersihl, at least, and Vera often walked.

By seven-thirty the fluorescent lights had flickered on down
the long ceiling of the workroom. The six big windows might
have given adequate light, certainly in summer, but Renate had
grown accustomed to bright light and insisted on it.

"Hi, Luisa!" Stephanie had called on entering the "factory,"
the workroom, where Renate and Luisa were checking things for
the day's work, scissors handy, thread for work-in-progress. A private client was having a suit made, requiring a certain pink thread:
Vera's project, that suit, with help from Renate. There were six
sewing machines, a steam-ironing board and two normal ones.

Yesterday afternoon, Renate had fairly given a eulogy about
Luisa's latest creation, a two-piece suit for autumn, drawings of
which were now pinned to the long bulletin board on the wall
opposite the windows. This was without lapels and had a generous
stand-up collar, large flaps on two side pockets, a skirt with pleats,
two front and back. Today Luisa was to cut the pattern in two sizes
to sell first as "exclusives." Three of the sewing machines had tables
on their own, the others lived on the table which was some six
meters long, made of three well-worn flush doors supported on
six trestles. Luisa supposed that at forty-two or -three, Renate liked
the old-fashioned, the near antiques that could be chic if one
announced that they were chic. Such was the old table with its
scratches and scars from Stanley knives, slight burns from irons,

even some splotches from the days of ink, though this was draw-ing ink, black.

Luisa sensed tension in Renate this morning as she drifted among the girls, as usual looking over their shoulders, though not so close as to annoy them. Renate usually made a comment, some-times a moderately contented, "Hmm-m," sometimes, "That looks nice," peering at a girl's work through her hand lens. Renate demanded especial care with buttonholes.

Stephanie went to the telephone-radio and pressed the num-ber three button for classical music. Classical was permitted, not too loud, but not the pop music of the German, French, or Italian channels.

Luisa was well into her pattern of the suit jacket, when Renate rapped out, "All right, girls. A nice cup of coffee?"

It was after nine-thirty. Luisa wished she did not have to go to Jakob's this morning with Renate (still cool), but she might see Rickie, might see the librarian Evelyn—friendly faces. The girls drifted toward the kitchen. Vera took care of the kettle. They made drip coffee in a large pot. Renate as usual put out a cake and a knife on a plate. If the girls got sticky fingers, the sink was right there. Crumbs on the floor much annoyed Renate, and it was a rit-ual that Elsie swept in midmorning and Luisa after lunch, which the girls took in the kitchen, while Renate and Luisa usually ate in the front sitting room.

That morning Renate walked in ominous silence with Luisa toward Jakob's, and Luisa's remark about the beauty of the chest-nut trees met with a preoccupied, "Um-m."

Renate's favored table was not free, but big enough for them to share with a smallish man sunk in a newspaper at one end of it.

And nearly opposite were Rickie and Lulu, Rickie with newspaper, but he saw her and waved discreetly.

"*Morgen, meine Damen*," said Andreas in *Hochdeutsch*, to be funny. "And what might the ladies like?"

"*Guten Morgen,*" replied Renate, then gave her usual order in Swiss German, and for Luisa too. Espresso with cream.

Luisa saw Willi, entering this morning from the back rooms behind Rickie. He beckoned to Renate in a sly way as if his gesture would not have been noticed even by a child, and Renate did not bother to acknowledge it. Willi seated himself at a table with a couple of men in work clothes.

"Did you see Willi last night?" asked Renate.

"I don't think so. I wasn't looking."

From Willi Biber's gesture—unusual—Renate thought Luisa was lying. Luisa would've noticed Willi, and known that he would report her presence to Renate. Renate enjoyed her near total control of Luisa, though at the same time realized that it had a sadistic element. Whenever these self-critical thoughts crossed her mind, she absolved herself utterly from blame or overcaution by remembering Luisa when she first presented herself—unkempt, even in need of a bath, broken fingernails, hair cut short and abominably by herself, Luisa had admitted. She had run away from home and also her apprenticeship in Brig (so Renate had had to straighten that out for her), run away also from a stepfather who had sexually abused her, Renate felt sure, but she disliked querying Luisa on the subject. More important, Renate was tutoring Luisa to become a first-rate dressmaker and designer, if Luisa heeded her.

"A French paper?" Luisa asked, ready to go to the paper rack.

"I'll go," Renate said.

Luisa watched her, knowing that Renate did not like walking in a public place like this more than was necessary. Renate lifted *Le Matin* and carried it on its stick toward Willi, with whom she began talking.

Here Rickie made comic gestures with his hands as of two people talking, and mimed silent laughter that bounced him up and down the bench.

Luisa was seized with nervous hilarity, looked down at her

empty coffee cup and nearly exploded. What could Willi be narrating? That she drank a Coke? Renate would try to stop her from
seeing Rickie, Luisa warned herself, but even this did not make
her sober up completely. It was as if Rickie were a knight in
armor—in that castle in the picture—and the armor protected her
from Renate somehow.

Renate was returning, head high, taking small steps. She had
left enough coins for their coffees. "What're you smiling at?"

"Nothing. I didn't know I was smiling."

Renate was not going to sit down. "So—you were at quite a
party last night, it seems."

Luisa had stood up. "I sat at a table with my Coke."

Renate went off to hang her newspaper. Luisa followed,
avoiding looking at Rickie.

"You seem to know some of the people—this Rickie—and
others."

They were going out the door. Luisa nodded a good-bye to
Ursie, who was sweeping the path across the front terrace.

"I saw Rickie, yes. The others—just a few friends of his."

"All these homos. All homos." Renate continued as they
walked, "What's the matter with you?"

"With *me*? Last night there was a woman called Evelyn—a
librarian. Other people—with jobs. Just talking. I don't know
what's the matter with having a Coke with them."

"These people get murdered. Robbed! You ask *me* what is the
matter?" She seemed all at once in a teeth-shaking fury.

Luisa decided to stay quiet, not sure at all that it would help.

So the day began.

THAT EVENING AFTER DINNER, Renate proposed a game of chess.
This they always played in the front sitting room, where a bridge
table stood folded against the wall. There was a sofa covered in
pale-green cotton. A full-page photograph of a model wearing a
winter-coat creation hung above the sofa; a famous Zurich store's

name was prominent at the bottom. The slender blonde model looked out with amused arrogance, and Luisa found her face, not to mention the coat, truly *démodé*. But of course the coat and the page in a sleek magazine had been a triumph for Renate then.

By a fluke, Luisa did not do badly at chess that evening. She did not really like chess, and felt that the game had helped her to realize that—it seemed—she was not aggressive by nature. "Attack!" Renate sometimes said during a game. "Always attack!" Luisa lost the game finally, but she did not feel the usual inferiority that Renate, even wordless, could make her feel, because tonight she had given Renate a bit of a struggle to win.

More coffee. Luisa declined. Renate could drink coffee till midnight and still get to sleep at once.

"You must work, work, work—to get anywhere. No silliness, do you understand?" She looked Luisa in the eyes, as if Luisa had done something wrong in the last hour.

"Yes, of course. I understand," replied Luisa, in a tone that asked, why shouldn't she understand such a simple statement?

"Then be sure that you act on it. Practice—draw—get new ideas, try them on paper, watch what the younger generation likes—though that may be temporary, still . . ."

Luisa listened with solemn face, sometimes looking down at the chessboard (which often remained on the table a few days), aware of the aging photographs, two or three in the room, of Renate's skinny brown-haired husband, rather handsome with long dark sideburns and heavy brows and pleasant smile: married in Casablanca, Renate looking like a dwarf compared to him, in white with white veil over her head. *White!* Then Renate's mysterious family in the photos, numerous cousins and aunts on a long bench outside a country house with two chimneys, somewhere in Romania. A couple of the women had babies wrapped in white in their arms, the men were all in dark suits and white shirts.

"We must pay a visit to the newspaper archives soon," Renate went on, "see all this on computer screen. The history of fashion.

Fashion is not oversized metal buttons or these vulgar short skirts that look like a towel wrapped around and tucked somewhere at the waist!"

Luisa was thinking of the one date she'd had with Petey Ritter. They'd gone to a film, then had hamburgers and Cokes afterward. She had been proud to be with him. That same week he had given her, at her request, a photo of himself, bigger than passport size, which Luisa still carried in her wallet.

8

Rickie Markwalder cruised in his Mercedes. He had bought the Merc, as he called it, secondhand, but still it was a Mercedes-Benz, and when clean and shining, as it was now, it made an impression. The car even inspired Rickie to don a jacket and tie on excursions like this, at 11 P.M. on a Friday night.

As slowly as traffic conditions permitted, Rickie crawled along the Limmatquai, his eyes out for solitary young men whose eyes might be also looking around. This was where the strollers strolled, and Rickie was not the only cruiser, of course. In his mirror, he saw the car behind him stop, had a glimpse of the driver grinning, talking, looking out the window. Music, loud pop, came from somebody's car radio, and the mangled words sounded like something out of Africa. But who wanted a street pickup? Or was that sour grapes? Pickups could be nice, he'd known at least two nice ones, if he thought about it. And any street around here was a pickup area, Niederdorfstrasse for pedestrians only, Zähringerstrasse where the Bagpiper and the Carousel were. Or there was the Barfuesser, if he felt up to it, in Spitalgasse. Rickie cruised with open windows.

"Hi, Papa!" yelled a blond boy, whom Rickie had indeed been ogling.

His two companions laughed, a bit tipsily.

Rickie managed a smile too, waved a hand as if to dismiss them as they had dismissed him. Still, it hurt. And what if they saw his abdomen, if he walked into a bar like the Barfuesser, for instance? Rickie hadn't been there for six or eight months, he supposed. Really hip, that bar was, all the latest and the youngest. He'd taken Petey there a couple of times—and with such pride! A lot better than Mercedes-Benz pride!

By a little past midnight, Rickie decided to head for home. What a waste of an evening, or part of it. So now, at slightly more speed, he rolled past the lighted façades, the BAR CÉSAR, CAFÉ DREAMS, beer-brand names in neon, the CLUB HOTEL, the drifting beer-can-sipping males—homeward.

Rickie pressed a bit hard on the accelerator, but he felt quite in command, more sober than drunk certainly, and his car behaved well. In a dark street somewhere—everything looked dark compared to what he had just left—Rickie put on more speed. Watch it, he told himself, and so he did at the next quiet and residential intersection where there was no traffic but a STOP written on the asphalt. Rickie stopped, then on again.

A minute or so later, he heard a siren behind him, saw a car flashing its lights, and Rickie thought: Certainly not for *me*. He slowed a little, not enough to look guilty, and kept going. He was nearly home. One big curve and he would be back in his nest, in his own garage under the building in which his studio was.

The police car followed him round the big curve.

The flashing lights signaled to Rickie that he had better stop, which he did, at the curb. Had he been going *that* fast? Rickie composed himself, and tried to forget the couple of Scotches he had had more than one hour ago.

The short cop touched his cap and asked to see Rickie's license, which Rickie produced. "You were speeding. You know?"

"I didn't realize. I'm sorry," Rickie said with polite contrition.

The little cop was writing a ticket, pad in one hand, ballpoint pen in the other. Carbon copy of course.

This would be a couple of hundred francs, Rickie supposed. "Didn't realize I was going so fast," he repeated, accepting the paper.

"Over sixty in a residential area," said the cop, going off to his car. "See yuh."

Rickie put his car in his garage, and walked off to his apartment down the street. He felt depressed, defeated. Only Lulu welcomed him when he opened the door, and he took her out for a short walk.

When he had finished his shower and put on pajamas, the doorbell rang. Rickie was instantly wary. He went to his still unrepaired balcony window and peeked, but could not have seen a figure on the doorstep, because a high bush concealed anything there. Rickie's old building had no speaker, so he put on a dressing gown and went into the hall.

"Who is it?" he asked at the locked door.

Seconds of silence, then, "Police. Open up."

Rickie curled up inside. More queries, and he'd just had a nip, and he felt vulnerable in pajamas and dressing gown. Rickie opened.

A short, blondish man smiled at him. He was the cop who had just given Rickie a ticket, but now he wore ordinary clothes. "Hi. Can I come in?"

What was this? But Rickie had begun to suspect. He was still cautious, polite. "This way," Rickie said softly, leading the way to his flat door, which was ajar.

"Nice big place," the cop remarked on entering. "My name is Freddie." He was still smiling. He looked about thirty-five, certainly not handsome, just ordinary.

"Freddie," Rickie repeated.

Lulu gazed, silent, from her pillow bed on the floor.

"I think you like boys. What else were you doing in that area, eh?" The cop was certainly getting down to business. He pulled a folded paper from the back pocket of his blue trousers and tore it up, smiling. "Your ticket. Hee-hee! Hah!" He seemed genuinely amused. "Well—do you feel like it?" He walked toward Rickie, arms open.

Rickie thought, tried to. It wasn't a frame-up, because he could report the cop, thanks to the ticket in his own jacket pocket. What else was he doing tonight? The cop was *here*, the man. "One thing—I'm HIV positive—so I—"

"Me too."

"I use condoms, though."

"So do I."

Less than ten minutes later, they were horizontal, with unfinished vodka and sodas on the floor beside Rickie's large bed. Rickie considered a low bed sexier. Freddie left around half-past two, after a second shower. He had written his name and two telephone numbers on a piece of paper, in case Rickie was ever in a bit of trouble.

"Small trouble," Freddie had qualified with a smile.

His name was Freddie Schimmelmann and he lived in the Oerlikon direction, in Zurich.

ON SATURDAY, Rickie pottered in his studio, putting stacks of paper in order, throwing things out. Finally he had a meter-high stack of cardboard, newspapers and outsized publicity material on the floor inside his door. He took a length of sturdy twine and tied it up. This was for recycling, to be stored in his garage till paper-collection day in about a week. Ah, the tidy, thrifty, law-abiding Swiss! Uptight. Why else did the Swiss have the highest drug-abuse rate per capita in the drug-abusing world—meaning the world? Too uptight. Rickie finally swept even the corners of his studio.

Three P.M. now. He had been to the supermarket with the

Merc that morning, laying in the usual, tonic water, beer, milk, dog food, orange juice, coffee, heads of lettuce, a couple of fillets of beef, fresh spinach, and from a good bakery an apple tart.

Rickie thought hardly at all of Freddie. He had had such encounters before, he reminded himself, more than he could reckon up. But none since Petey. Therefore Freddie was different, and in a way memorable. But by no means a marker, in his experience. Freddie had a wife, he had told Rickie, volunteering this information as if to discourage Rickie from getting too deeply involved with him—not Rickie's intention. Was he worried about what his wife might think? Maybe he'd ring Freddie some day, but probably he wouldn't.

Rickie was about to leave, when his telephone rang.

"Hello?"

"Hello, Rickie," said his sister Dorothea's voice. "Working this afternoon?"

"No-o, I am dreaming, sweeping—tidying here. Ha-ha!"

"Tried to get you at home. You didn't phone after Mum's— you know."

Mum's birthday. "I did send flowers. And I phoned her. Maybe I phoned the day afterward."

Such was the case. Dorothea told him that she and Robbie had driven up to Lausanne, but daughter Elise had not come with them, which did not surprise Rickie. Their mother had given a dinner party for six or seven people, and seemed in fine health.

"You sound sad, Rickie."

"Sad? Not at all, Dorothea! Why? I wasn't even saying anything."

"Maybe that's why you seemed sad."

Rickie laughed. It was a conversation like others they had had, comforting to Rickie. Dorothea knew about Petey, of course; she had said the proper sympathetic words, and in her way she had meant them. After all, Petey had been in Rickie's life for nearly a year. The months might be intense, hopeful, Rickie supposed, but it still wasn't a marriage in his sister's eyes or in anybody's eyes, Rickie knew.

"Now cheer up. Come and see us soon. Come for dinner—bring a friend, if you want. You know. Elise would like to see you too." Dorothea laughed. "And you can meet her new heartthrob, maybe."

"Looking forward."

"Don't joke, Rickie. Phone us. Promise? Room to stay the night, you know."

"I promise. Thank you, dear sister." They hung up.

Rickie looked around at his visibly tidier tables, chrome this and that, unframed blowups on the walls, metal wastebaskets, his little sink and two-burner that looked like something in a hospital. There were times when Rickie was proud of his workplace, times when he was ashamed. Just now, he felt somehow ashamed.

Silly inferiority complex, Rickie told himself. He didn't live here, he worked here.

And tonight—he'd go to the Small g, where dear Philip Egli might be, despite his exams, where Ernst surely would be, and maybe the darling Luisa. Maybe. And shitty Willi.

Rickie chuckled at the thought of Willi on a Saturday night, when everyone was merry but Willi! Rickie went out and strolled to his apartment house, greeting a neighbor on the way, old Frau Riester, a widow who lived in his studio building. She was carrying two shopping bags, one of woven rope that sagged with age. She wore a wide-brimmed hat, a mauve cardigan.

"And how are you faring, Frau Riester?"

Her wrinkled, smiling face looked up at him. "Pretty well, Rickie. And I'm *Ruth* to you, remember?"

"Of course I remember—"

"You taking care of your laundry well enough?"

Out of the past, more than a year ago, Rickie recalled: he'd been down with flu for several days, and Ruth Riester had called for his laundry and washed it in her machine, and brought it back with his shirts and even his socks ironed. "Yes, Ruth—I swear. I wield a fine iron." Rickie pantomimed ironing. "You should come to our local pub more often. Jakob's." Ruth hardly ever came. "It'll cheer you up." Rickie was drifting away.

"Oh, I'm cheery enough. So people say." Smiling, she trudged on.

Rickie went to Jakob's just before 10 P.M. that evening, wearing a new white cotton jacket, dark blue summer trousers, well-polished black loafers. He preferred sneakers, but at his age he thought sneakers suggested that he was trying to look younger than he was. *I'm just looking around tonight,* he told himself as he walked in with Lulu in her pale blue leather collar, which happened to match Rickie's shirt.

"Lulu!"

"Hi, *Lulu!* Good evening!"

"Hello, Rickie! Sit with us?" This was from a sextet at the table where Renate and Luisa usually sat in the morning.

Rickie vaguely knew two of the fellows, the blonde girl with them not at all. "Not just yet, thanks, maybe later."

A young boy and girl were dancing to music that came from a radio behind the bar. There was an amplifier on the other side of the dance floor, which Rickie now circled, drifting toward the back terrace, which he wanted to look at, see who was there.

"*Rickie!*"

Rickie saw Ernst Koelliker in the far right corner, half standing up as he hailed Rickie. There were four or five people at this table. "*Evening!* Maybe in a minute!"

"Hey, you on luxury cruise tonight?" a voice on his right asked, just as he was about to enter the back terrace.

The man who had asked that was about thirty-five, blue jeans and denim shirt, blank-eyed yet aggressive, the drug type. Rickie kept a neutral expression and walked on.

"Hey, what's your dog's name?"

If he didn't know by now, Rickie thought, too bad.

The back terrace was noisy and somewhat drunk. But there was Luisa in the far corner! With her was a brown-haired fellow, in short-sleeved shirt, focusing on Luisa as she talked, but she had seen Rickie and smiled.

"My dear Luisa!" said Rickie, bowing to her. "I'm Rickie," he said to the young man.

"Uwe," replied the young man, looking not happy to see Rickie, but if Rickie was a friend of Luisa's—

"Want to sit down?" Luisa asked Rickie.

"No-o—I shall walk a little with Lulu, thank you, and come back." Rickie looked round at the doorway where a few days ago he'd seen Willi standing, observing the scene. "Have you seen our mutual friend this evening?" He saw Luisa hesitate, as if wondering if he meant Renate. "Willi," said Rickie with a smile.

Luisa nodded toward the dark garden beyond the terrace. "He was here a minute ago—heading out there."

"I am going to join Ernst inside. See you later, Luisa." Rickie looked over the terrace once more, then took the garden path which ended at a gate on the pavement. He strolled along the pavement where more cars than usual were parked tonight, then turned, intending to enter again by Jakob's main door. Before he and Lulu got there, a car door slammed behind them and two young men in white trousers and shirts walked past Rickie and entered Jakob's front terrace.

"... both ... *white*!" one of the young men was saying in an annoyed tone, and gave a quick laugh.

Nice-looking boys, Rickie thought, especially one of them. By the time Rickie entered the main door, the two in white were standing at the far end of the bar, every stool of which was occupied.

The music was now a tango; several couples were trying it, some clowning, and laughter broke out in the main room. Rickie much wanted a beer, but Ursie and Andreas looked frantic behind the bar, and Tobi was nowhere to be seen, though Rickie had seen him a minute ago.

"You want to dance?" This was from a slightly tipsy but not bad-looking fellow in his mid-twenties, arms already extended.

"I am trying to get my first *beer!*" Rickie replied with a smile. "Maybe later—if my *carnet de bal* is not entirely filled."

The younger man laughed. "I shall *hope*—"

"Andreas!" Rickie had his attention. He was after all tall, visible. "*Ein Bier, bitte! Danke!*"

"*Jawohl*, Rickie!"

Rickie drifted toward the bar and found a niche which he barely secured with an elbow. He was constantly mindful of Lulu's safety. She danced out of the way of people's feet quite well, but when Jakob's got impossible, he took her home and returned.

Rickie vaguely knew half the clientele tonight, which was to say he had seen them before. Amazing how word of mouth advertised Jakob's, and crammed it on Saturday nights. His beer arrived with a nice head, set before him by Ursie, who had a second to nod a greeting before whirling to fulfill more orders. He studied the two boys in white to the right of him. One looked about twenty-five, with crinkly blond hair, strong of build, a dark blue sweater's arms tied round his neck. He drank beer, and kept talking to his friend whose back was to Rickie. His friend was more slender, with straight black hair. The blond one glanced often at the door, as if they were expecting someone.

Lulu could stay with Luisa, Rickie thought, for half an hour anyway. Relief for Lulu. Then maybe take her home?

Rickie had just lifted his beer, when the black-haired boy looked round at the door, past Rickie, with anxiety in his face. But what a handsome face!

Ernst Koelliker appeared at Rickie's other elbow. "Can I borrow Lulu for five minutes or would you come—"

"What're you going to do with Lulu?"

"Did you bring her dark glasses?"

Rickie shook his head. "No glasses tonight, no. Take her but—

carry her across this." He indicated the throbbing dance floor.
"Lulu? You go with Ernst. Up!"

Lulu was up, caught by Ernst at his waist-level, and instantly
cool, surveying the crowd from her better position.

"I'm going to get Luisa," said Rickie, gesturing with the beer
glass. "You'll be in that corner?"

Ernst nodded, and carried Lulu off.

As he wove his way through people toward the back terrace,
he saw Luisa moving in his direction, and she saw him. "This way,"
Rickie gestured.

But Luisa wanted something from the bar, and Rickie waited.
He saw Luisa trying to get the attention of Ursie, saw the young
man Luisa had been with on the terrace pursuing her with a
dampened but determined air, and saw the pair of boys in white
look at Luisa. Rickie had a second glimpse of the handsomer one.
This boy's lips moved as he said something to his blond companion. Then their eyes once more turned toward the door. Luisa
appeared with a glass of Coke.

"Would you come and join Ernst and me in the corner? And
your friend?"

Luisa gave a shrug and a glance that implied she would like to
lose her new friend. "I just met him!"

At that moment, Rickie's eyes looked into the eyes of the
handsomer boy, who had glanced over his shoulder. In the next
second, his blond companion turned and walked quickly toward
the dance floor, and vanished. Then two policemen entered from
the front terrace, conspicuous in caps and blue uniforms. They sur-
veyed the crowd.

Then one said, "Anyone with Zurich registration number
four six one—one nine one?" This in a loud, clear voice.

A few patrons at the bar looked around for reaction, but there
was none.

"Can't remember!" called a tipsy male voice.

Chuckles among the assembled.

"Dark-blue Opel," the officer said, looked around again and repeated the number.

No reaction, and the officers walked to the edge of the dance floor, where the music kept on but nearly everyone had stopped dancing.

"What happened?" a woman asked the officers.

One of the officers waved a hand to indicate that he was not going to reply.

Rickie saw the dark-haired boy in white moving toward the dance floor and onward, not hurrying, toward the back terrace.

"I'll see you in a minute!" Rickie said to Luisa. "Go where Ernst is."

Rickie entered the back terrace, where he supposed the boy had gone, if he hadn't stepped into the toilet which was between dance floor and back terrace.

But neither the boy nor his blond friend was on the terrace, where every table was full. Rickie looked at the dark garden, which had only one light near the pavement gate. Was that a white-clad figure near the gate, or a trick of the streetlight? Try it, Rickie told himself, and set his beer down on the corner of a nearby table. He heard someone say as he stepped into the garden's dark that he must be in a terrible hurry to pee.

Now Rickie could see the boy's figure. Maybe at the sight of him, the boy went hurriedly through the gate and turned left. Rickie followed. Were both boys running from the police?

The white figure wasn't running, just walking purposefully onward. Rickie walked faster.

"Hey, *I'm* not the police!" Rickie said, not too loudly.

The boy stood where he was, frowning.

Rickie glanced behind him: no one. "Hello. Good evening."

The boy's eyes were fixed on Jakob's lighted corner, far away. "*Abend*," the boy said automatically. "I'm getting out of here. Don't bother me, OK?" He walked on.

Rickie hurried after him. "I'm not bothering you, I—" Rickie had to laugh, because he was bothering him. "My name's Rickie and—and I'm sorry we can't have a beer together."

Now the boy stopped short, looked at Rickie as if he were amused. "Yes, sure—I understand." Again he glanced back at Jakob's lights. "I've got to move away from that place, so—" The boy walked.

So did Rickie. "What happened with the police?"

"*Nothing.* And I don't *want* anything to happen."

"And your friend? Do the police want him?"

"The hell with them all," the boy said nervously. He was still walking at a brisk pace.

They were almost at Rickie's apartment house. Give it a last try, Rickie thought. Plainly he hadn't smitten the boy with his advances. Now Rickie spoke softly in the residential area. "I live here— couple of meters on." He jingled his key ring. "No one home but me, if you want to come in—to be safe for a few minutes."

By then they were at his front gate, and Rickie unlatched it, watched the boy hesitate, then follow Rickie on to the path, and relax visibly as the tall black hedge hid him from the street.

"I'm going back to the Small g in a few minutes. My dog's there with a friend." Rickie paused, hesitated, because the boy was hesitating, shifting from foot to foot. "I have an idea," he whispered. "I'll call my friend Ernst from my house—he's at Jakob's— and we'll find out if the police are still there." He moved toward his door. "OK?"

The boy came with him.

There was a ceiling light in the front hall, usually on till about midnight, and it was on now. Rickie heard his front door click shut and thought: A dream is ended, the wonderland he had just left, beginning with Jakob's Small g, with following the handsome boy, with *persuading* him into his apartment building. In a minute, Rickie's apartment lights would go on, the boy would glance at his watch, Rickie would have a better look at him (and vice versa), reality's curtain would fall. End of fun, end of hope. End of story.

Rickie opened his apartment door. He had left a small light on. "Come in!"

The boy came in. He was not quite as tall as Rickie. A wallet bulged his back pocket. He wore a black belt with his loose white trousers.

"Now—well—" Rickie saw that the boy was every bit as good-looking as he had thought at Jakob's, shining dark eyes and an intelligent mouth. "Sit down, if you like, and—as I said—I'll speak with Ernst. Sooner the better, don't you think?" Rickie hated saying that, it sounded as if he wanted the boy out in a hurry. "What's your name, by the way? If you don't mind telling me."

"Georg," said the boy carelessly, and looked behind him at the darker dining area. "You live here by yourself?"

"Oh yes. No one else here." Rickie headed for the telephone; Jakob's number was written at the very top of his current direc- tory. "Would you like to sit down with a beer?"

"N-no. Thank you."

Rickie again turned back from the telephone. "The police were looking for your friend?"

The boy shifted a little, took a breath. "In a way, yes. He stole somebody's car tonight."

"He had the keys?"

"Jump-start."

"And you?"

"I got in with him. I don't know why."

"You're good friends," Rickie said casually, curious but not wanting to push too much.

"No. He works in a men's gym in my neighborhood. I just happen to know him."

"Before Ernst—I'm going to open a beer. Not to mention a Chivas Regal, first of the evening." Rickie proffered the bottle, but Georg shook his head. Rickie poured a small one, then went to his fridge for a Pilsner Urquell. He offered Georg a glass of it.

"All right. Thank you," said the boy with a polite smile.

Rickie dialed Jakob's, and hectic Ursie answered. "Hello, Ursula, Rickie speaking. *Ernst*, please?" He had to shout and talk clearly.

Ernst came on, surprised at Rickie's voice. "You running from the cops?"

"*Ja, natürlich!* And I am calling to ask if they are still *there*."

"No-o. They left five minutes ago!"

"What was it all about?"

"Somebody stole a car, parked it near here, so they were looking the place over. Didn't find anybody. Where *are* you?"

Lulu was fine and they all wanted Rickie to come back.

Rickie hung up and conveyed the good news to Georg. "I'm going back. You're coming or—? If you're still afraid, you can stay here. I'll be gone just an hour or so."

Georg looked the least surprised at this; his brows went up. "No, well—if the police are gone—"

"*You* didn't steal the car."

"No."

"Was the car damaged?"

"No. Hermie didn't wipe his fingerprints off, I'm pretty sure. I did—tried. Hermie thought we were being followed. So we just parked the car somewhere and ran—went into the Biergarten." The boy finished his beer and glanced at Rickie. "OK, I'll go—to this place for a while. Then I'll catch a taxi home—if it's very late."

He meant if it was after midnight and the trams had stopped, Rickie supposed. Rickie much wanted to—suddenly he blurted, "You are most welcome to stay the night, if you're worried." About what, Rickie wondered. He simply wanted to be with the boy and realized that he had zero reason to think the boy was gay, or that he himself had the slightest chance—except for the fact that Hermie worked in a men's gym!

"No. I don't think I will. But—thank you."

Rickie went and got his best cardigan, a black cashmere, from his bedroom. "You're going to get cold—in just a shirt tonight."

"Thanks. I'll borrow it. Nice one. I'll be sure to return it. I promise you."

9

Rickie entered the Small g so proud of having Georg with him that he hardly breathed. Head high, really looking at no one, Rickie walked into the lighted bar area, acknowledged a couple of "Hi, Rickie!" greetings, and managed to gesture and say to Georg, "The back corner!"

The place was busier; people shouted more loudly to make themselves heard. And there was old Renate, barely visible to Rickie through the crowd, drawing coolly on her long cigarette holder, wearing a shocking-pink blouse tonight, and at her usual table! She'd probably asked somebody to move, in her arrogant way. Rickie thought he had seen her little sketchpad on the table, ready to record what the weirdos were wearing.

"Georg!" Rickie said by way of introduction, when they had made it to the back-corner table, trying to appear cool at having such a handsome boy with him, merely another capture, like a rare butterfly.

"Georg," a few at the table echoed, staring.

"Hello. G'd evening," Georg replied.

"Luisa," Rickie said, gesturing with upturned palm. "This is Georg."

Luisa smiled and replied something inaudible.

There were no chairs, but if Rickie could keep out of people's way, he preferred standing. Someone had ordered several beers, and here they came. Ernst was giving Georg a thorough visual examination, Rickie saw.

"Dance?" Georg said to Luisa, and when she got up, he set his beer down in a big ashtray.

Philip Egli, closer than Rickie, righted the beer glass at once. "Where'd you pick up Golden Boy?" he shouted at Rickie.

Rickie took a deep breath, looked at the ceiling and smiled, as if to say it was due simply to his usual luck. He watched Luisa and the boy dancing, Georg graceful and easy, Luisa looking happy. It was a French tune, rather fast. Georg had the arms of Rickie's black cardigan tied round his neck now. Rickie was aware of his own heaviness, of the fact that he was too shy to make a trio with them, as people often did here. Rickie wasn't a bad dancer.

Lulu, in the corner with Ernst, wriggled with expectation when Rickie looked at her.

"Let 'er *go!*" Rickie said to Ernst.

"Off the leash?"

"*Ja!* Up, Lulu!"

Lulu rose like a rocket from the bench seat over the table into Rickie's arms. A fine catch!

"Bravo, Lulu!"

Rickie swung her round his neck, held her feet, and Lulu relaxed as if she were a limp scarf. "*Dum-dum-dum*—dum—*dum-dum-dum*—dum," he sang, dancing, turning in a circle.

On his far left, he saw Renate staring at him and Lulu as if frozen. Hadn't she as yet noticed that her darling was with a boy? Rickie was in the center of the dance floor, humming, swaying to the samba. He could feel that Lulu was in her element, with the crowd pointing her out, laughing.

"What the well-dressed homo is wearing this year!" Rickie said to a smiling couple. "His dog!"

Luisa surely knew that Renate had arrived. Rickie imagined an osmosis between them, an unhealthy symbiosis, if that was the word.

Seconds later, it was all over, that song, that dance. Rickie saw Georg shake his head at an offer from a gay man to dance. He was back at the table with a seat now, as was Georg, because a couple of people had left.

"Don't you have to go sit with Renate?" Rickie asked Luisa. "But how nice if you *don't*!"

"Oh, she'll *say* something," Luisa replied. "But I don't know why after all *day* . . ." Some words were drowned out by noise. ". . . all evening too!"

"Who is this Renate?" Georg asked, frowning.

"She is—a couturiere," Rickie said, "and Luisa is employed by her. Renate comes here to observe—and snoop and criticize people like you and me. Everybody!"

"Employs Luisa?"

"She employs four girls. They sew clothes—" Rickie suddenly burst out laughing. Renate seemed funny just then, though he couldn't have explained why if his life depended on it.

At least Georg was smiling at him now.

The boy had stopped glancing behind him, perhaps stopped worrying. It was past midnight, and would Georg really take a taxi or— And here came Willi in his drab clothes and brimmed hat, like a dark cloud, edging his way round the dancers. He came from Renate's direction. The messenger! Bringer of bad tidings!

"Willi!" Rickie still stood with the draped Lulu. "Some unpleasant news? You want Luisa? Right there! Ha-ha! *We* are feeling very merry tonight!"

Willi's long face under the old hat did not change. He bent and said something to Luisa, then slunk away. The rest of the table might not have existed for Willi.

"What's all that?" Rickie asked.

"Renate's leaving. Wants me to come with her," Luisa said to Rickie.

"You've got your own key, haven't you?"

"Oh, she'll double-lock it. Anything to—" Luisa looked

embarrassed at having said this much. "It can be unpleasant," she
finished with a forced smile.

"You are welcome at *my* house," Rickie said.

Then Luisa gave a lovely, amused smile that showed her pretty
teeth, clear brow, and calm brown eyes. Georg was watching her.
Luisa got up, holding her little bills, looking at them. "Nine forty."
She had a small handbag, but reached in a trouser pocket.

"Oh no!" said Rickie. "Leave that!"

"Don't worry, don't worry." Georg pulled out a ten-franc note
which he dropped on the table. "Can I walk you home?"

"Best not," said Luisa. "But thank you, Teddie. And thanks,
Rickie."

"Old witch would bite your head off!" said Rickie to Georg,
now Teddie. "I'll see you to Renate."

Rickie did, led the way for Luisa between tables and dancers
toward the old witch's table. Lulu kept her calm on his shoulders,
her eyes on a level higher than his.

"Look at *Lulu!*" someone yelled.

"Good evening," Rickie said politely, bowing as much as Lulu
permitted.

Renate, elegant in probably real gold earrings, slender necklace, the shocking-pink blouse and a satin skirt—long, of course—
did not remove the cigarette holder from her mouth. She stood
up, ignoring Rickie neatly, he realized, and shuffled her way round
the corner of the table. Willi Biber stood at the table end nearer
the bar and the door, without the wit to pull the table a little way
toward him to assist Renate in getting out.

"*Bonne nuit,*" said Rickie sweetly to Renate. "*Und schönen Sonntag!*"

Pretending he was invisible, Rickie supposed, was Renate's
highest order of contempt. But Luisa was able to throw him a quick
smile, at least, before she had to give ear to Renate. They were
walking toward the door and home, the short, tense Renate and the
lithe young Luisa, so politely listening to Renate's mumbling.

And there was Dorrie Wyss! With a girl Rickie didn't know. They were dancing, the short-haired blonde Dorrie moving with a beautiful energy, jumping as if on springs. People chanted, "One—two—three—*four!*"

"Dorrie!" Rickie cried, but she couldn't hear him. The brunette with her was quite pretty, about twenty, with large silver circles in her earlobes. A new romance, Rickie supposed. Dorrie didn't come every week to the Small g.

The music ended before Rickie got back to his table, and he sought Dorrie's attention again, raised a hand.

And with a look of surprise, she raised a finger, index first, then a different finger, laughing.

Rickie pointed to the corner to tell her where he would be, and he saw her nod agreement. People shifted to make room for Rickie and Lulu on the bench. Georg was standing at the other end of the table, looking over the scene.

"Is your handsome friend tied up tonight—completely?" Ernst whispered in Rickie's ear.

"Don't you know by now?" Rickie replied. "What were you doing while I was gone?"

"Anything's possible. My motto. Philip's interested, too. He just went to the gents."

"Philip is gadding about too much," said Rickie with deliberate primness. "Exams coming up—" He saw Ernst's gaze move again to Georg, or Teddie, dreamily.

Dorrie arrived, by herself. "Rickie! I'm back! Haven't seen you in . . ."

Philip returned, Rickie introduced him, and from a distance Georg. Dorrie did know Ernst. Dorrie wasn't in a sitting mood.

"Who was the pretty girl with you?" Dorrie asked, gesturing toward Renate's table.

"You see? You don't come here often enough!" Rickie said. "We have lovely girls here—"

"Answer my question!" Dorrie tugged her red waistcoat down

gently. She wore attractive garb tonight, dark blue corduroys, white shirt, red waistcoat with brass buttons.

"*Luisa*," Rickie said finally, and saw Georg glance at him.

"One of us?" asked Dorrie.

"Not sure," Rickie said. "But you never know." He felt mellow now, and loved the din around him.

"Kim," Dorrie said, as her dark-haired friend with the earrings came up. Unlike Dorrie, whose straight blonde hair and blue eyes hardly needed adornment, Kim wore lipstick, and her short hair had been lacquered *en brosse* on top, while the short sides looked like a prison job. "She works with me just now. My assistant!" Dorrie said.

"How convenient," Rickie replied, thinking that Kim's hair reminded him of certain shoe brushes.

Dorrie Wyss was a windowdresser, and worked freelance for some of the finest stores and shops in Zurich. A crazy occupation, persuading window-shoppers to buy at the highest prices what they didn't need. But wasn't his work exactly the same—except that he made drawings?

"May I offer you beautiful girls something to drink?" Rickie asked.

"Thanks, Rickie, we want to dance." Dorrie smiled, tense with nervous energy. "See you!"

"Come back—here!" Rickie shouted, pointing, not knowing what he himself meant—tonight or next week or both.

"If you bring Luisa!" Dorrie yelled over her shoulder.

10

A little after 1 A.M., Rickie and Teddie stood talking outside Jakob's. His name was Teddie Stevenson, his mother was

Swiss, his father American, Teddie had explained. He had told Rickie a different name, because—well, why?—because he liked to feel like another person, somebody else now and then.

"I've never done anyone any harm by it," Teddie said. "I'm not trying to cover up anything."

"Oh, I understand," Rickie said, only half understanding.

Rickie had by now learned that Teddie had finished his military service, had acquired his *Matura*, and had told his mother that he wanted to relax for a few months, maybe several months, and decide what he wanted to do in life, and would she put up with that, let him live at home? And even be a little patient, Teddie had said. His mother had agreed. Rickie gathered that she was ambitious for her son. Teddie's father was a "business consultant," a term of vague meaning to Rickie.

"He had a company in New York, but he travels—to Paris, Milan, even Miami. Even Zurich, but when he's here, he doesn't usually see my mother. They may speak on the phone. After all, they're divorced."

From Jakob's now came a drunken whoop.

"Big family?" asked Rickie, stalling for time, thinking that Teddie was going to aim for a taxi, phone for one in the next seconds.

Teddie looked as if he were tired of talking about family and self. "One sister. Married, lives in Boston."

"Look—" Rickie took a breath. "As I said—Teddie—you're welcome at my house tonight. Plenty of room."

Teddie hesitated a couple of seconds only. "OK. All right. I will. Thank you, Rickie."

They began to walk.

"*Rickie!*" A last tipsy hail from Jakob's. "'Bye, Rickie—Lulu!"

Rickie lifted an arm in reply, half turning, and Lulu for an instant had pointed her nose at the shouter. "You phone your mother from my place, if you like."

Teddie nodded. "I will."

Rickie, once home, became the gracious host. "The tele-phone," he said with a gesture.

The boy grimaced at the prospect but went and phoned at once.

Rickie barely heard him saying, ". . . I *am* sorry it's late, but—perfectly OK . . . Yes . . . definitely . . ."

"All right, is it?" Rickie asked when the boy had hung up.

Teddie nodded. "Fine. No problem. Saturday night—my mother always reads late, so it wasn't so bad."

Rickie had been finding a clean towel and face cloth. "This will be in the bathroom," Rickie said, going in that direction, and on returning, asked, "Are you hungry?"

"No, thank you."

But twenty-year-olds were always hungry. Somewhat tipsy, Rickie had decided that Teddie should have his bed, the double one, while he would take the oversized sofa in the living room. He so informed Teddie, and turned his own double bed down and changed the sheets doggedly over Teddie's polite protests. Teddie went to take a shower, Rickie seized the interval to put on paja-mas, got a blue pair out for the boy, and laid them at the foot of the double bed.

Teddie came out of the bathroom wearing only his under-pants. An unbelievably handsome figure, a moving statue, barefoot, lithe, indifferent to Rickie's gaze.

Rickie then took his shower, and emerged in pajamas and slippers.

The boy had donned the blue pajamas and was reading some-thing, sitting on the edge of Rickie's double bed, with the lamp on. He got to his feet. "I wanted to say good night, Rickie. And thanks. You're sure it's all right—like this?" He meant taking Rickie's bed.

"But of *course*," said Rickie, the affable host. He went to the kitchen, took a waxed paper with sliced prosciutto from the fridge, plopped it all on a plate and brought it into the bedroom.

"Let us have *one*," Rickie said. "A housewarming—a bite before bedtime, a—"

Teddie smiled and took a slice with his fingers, shook it, and tilted his head back as if he were eating asparagus.

Rickie set the plate on his dresser and did the same. "Good, is it not?"

"Delicious!"

"More."

"No, thanks," said Teddie.

"Some wine?" asked Rickie. "Coke!"

"No, I'm pooped. Glass o' water."

"Mineral? Cold?"

"*Vom Fass!*" Teddie said, grinning, looking tired.

Rickie presented a glass of tap water. "Milk? There is plenty."

"Really, no. And thank you for the pajamas."

Rickie looked at his slightly blurred vision of the Golden Boy, as Ernst or someone had called Teddie tonight. "I wish I had a color photo of you—like you are now," Rickie blurted. "Good night, Teddie." Rickie turned, just a little unsteadily, and feeling very noble.

"'Night." The boy reached for the lamp switch.

Rickie crept between the folded sheet on the big sofa in the next room, pulled a thin blanket over him, intending to savor the evening, feel to his core the fact that Teddie Stevenson, the handsome one with his dark, level eyes, his dark hair still short from the military (so Rickie supposed), his body beyond Rickie's power of description, more like an aesthetic impact than something solid—this creature of dream was sleeping in the next room and in his own bed! Rickie fell asleep while preparing himself for luxurious cogitation.

Around dawn Rickie awakened, and realized that he had to urinate, before he recalled that—*Teddie* was in the next room! Quietly Rickie got up, though with carpet everywhere, it would have been difficult to be noisy. He went via the hall, not glancing

at the pale rectangle of his bed past the open door. And what if he
were dreaming that Teddie were there, that he'd put a fantasy to
bed there? And maybe Teddie had got up in the last couple of
hours and departed—via the balcony window? Was he real or not?
Teddie might as well be a fantasy for all the luck he would have in
becoming Teddie's lover!

Once more, Rickie slept, more lightly and with dreams. In
one of the dreams, he and Teddie were in Venice. Teddie wore a
blue-and-white-striped seersucker suit and a straw hat, and presented such an attractive figure that everyone, and all things, like
pigeons, turned to look. Teddie rode in a gondola, standing up, lifting his straw hat.

Rickie awakened. He had drawn the curtains, and had to peer
at his watch: eight twenty-five. Teddie. Really Teddie? He was
afraid to look and see. Breakfast. Good coffee. He had bread, eggs,
the prosciutto. He went down a short hall to the kitchen. With the
drip coffee started, he entered the bedroom to get some clothes.

Now he looked at the bed. Yes, there was Teddie, sound asleep,
and it seemed with an erection. He could see it peaking the sheet.
Normal, Rickie thought, especially at that age. How nice it would
be to creep into that big bed, to begin without waking Teddie, to
have him in his possession, as it were, before Teddie came fully
awake! Rickie almost tried it, almost let his clothes drop (those in
his hands), and didn't. It might ruin everything, if there was anything to ruin.

Rickie dressed, shaved in the bathroom, tidied the sofa back to
normal, and set the shiny table in the dining area with plates, napkins, orange juice.

Teddie woke up after nine, and sat up, visible through a doorway.

"Good morning!" Rickie called. "Coffee?"

Yes.

The dream continued. Coffee, and Teddie disappeared for a
few minutes in the bathroom and came back. A boiled egg for

each. Toast and Rickie's best strawberry preserves, English brand. There he sat, in Rickie's blue pajamas! He had a small mole on his right cheek, heavier black eyebrows than Rickie had thought. But the overall effect dazzled Rickie.

"Have you plans for today?" Rickie dared to ask.

"My mother and I— It's a friend of hers. We have to go to lunch there." Teddie smiled, licked coffee from his upper lip. "I promised."

Rickie was focusing on the faint fuzz of a beard, some darker hair along Teddie's jawline. It could not be said that Teddie needed a shave, not in Rickie's opinion, anyway. He cleared his throat. "I'm glad you—do things to please your mum." Then Rickie burst out in a short laugh, sounding and feeling like himself.

So did the boy laugh. "Sometimes," with a shrug. "She was nice to me when I was at school—when my father was calling me lazy—"Teddie squirmed and glanced at his wristwatch. "Sorry. I'm OK for time. When my father more or less gave me up because I had to take a couple of subjects twice—my mother was always patient about it."

"Good." Feeling stupid, Rickie looked down at his empty eggshell. "I hope to see you again, Teddie! At our local, the Small g. It's so marked in gay bar and restaurant guides; not totally gay, just partly, that means. Otherwise known as Jakob's for an owner who died—ages ago. Best on Saturday nights, but not bad on Fridays. And—you must see my studio—where I work. Just two steps from here. Same street. If you have a couple of minutes."

"Studio? You're a painter?"

Rickie waved a hand deprecatingly. "Mediocre one. Some of these." He gestured toward his gliding white birds. "The birds."

"You did these?"

Rickie could see that Teddie was impressed. The boy got up for a closer look. Impressed, Rickie thought, because the paintings were neat, on canvas, brought off, successful. But great, no.

Then it seemed, in no time, he and Teddie were out on the

pavement, the boy in the white clothes of last evening, and not
needing to borrow a sweater, unfortunately, because the day was
already warm. Teddie was going to take the tram home.

Click!

Rickie unlocked his studio door, and the yacking pair of
white plaster ladies caught Teddie's attention first.

"Oh, I like that!" Teddie smiled broadly.

Rickie showed him his work-in-progress—acrylic lipstick yet
again—his enlarging machine, the kitchenette and the little room
off it with a couch that was a single bed, and the bath with shower.
Rickie got one of his business cards from a box, and added his
home number. "Keep this. And if you ever want a change of
scene—a meal—an evening at Jakob's—"

"Thanks." Teddie stuck the card in a back pocket.

"You've got your wallet?"

"Oh yes," said Teddie, slapping a front pocket now.

"Enough money? If you need to take a taxi—"

"No, I don't. I saw a tram stop . . ." He was ready to fly.

Lulu, sitting near the two plaster ladies, observed and listened.

"Phone me some time," Rickie said.

"Oh sure. It's an interesting place, Jakob's," shifting on his feet.

"May I kiss you on the cheek—good-bye?" Rickie saw the
boy give a quick, shy smile, before the boy's arms enveloped him,
squeezed hard, and Rickie had no time to respond before Teddie
laughed and released him.

"*Thank* you, Rickie. And I'll phone you."

And Teddie was out, climbing the cement steps two at a time.

Rickie closed the door, looked at the attentive Lulu, then let
his eyes wander around the emptiness of his studio. Had it all happened? Yes. Teddie had just been here, Teddie Stevenson. Rickie
wandered slowly the route that Teddie had taken, past the sink and
the short hall that led to the WC behind a white door, past a couple of tables and the tall bamboo in its white pot, past the window
that revealed part of the cement steps.

A few minutes later, he was back in his flat, dreamily tidying, leaving his tousled bed to the last. It would be a long time before he changed those sheets.

And he hadn't asked Teddie for *his* number! On the other hand, Rickie didn't fancy Teddie's mother answering. His voice didn't sound like a teenager's. He suddenly recollected Teddie's hard embrace on his departure, like the embrace of a comrade before setting off—for the North Pole, maybe, or the Matterhorn. Nothing sexy about it. And Rickie remembered his interest in Luisa. Well and good. Luisa in the neighborhood—she was a nice attraction, a reason for Teddie to visit again.

Rickie opened a small beer, and forced himself to give thought to a decision he had to make about an all-purpose liquid detergent called Star-Brite.

The telephone rang so shockingly loud in the silence that the little bottle nearly slipped from his fingers. He was suddenly back with Teddie, thought it might be Teddie ringing—hadn't he had time to get home?—and Rickie picked up the telephone with slightly trembling hand. "Hello?"

"Hello, Rickie," said a female voice, his sister's. "What're you doing?"

"Oh—" hesitantly.

"I'd like to invite you for lunch . . . Come on. The Kronen-halle. Something *nice*. Robbie's off for a motorboat ride with his friend Rudi on the lake . . ."

Rickie wavered. After all it was Sunday, and Dorothea sounded so warm and friendly. "The Kronenhalle—" One of the fanciest, heaviest places in town. "All right, Dorothea. With pleasure. And what time?"

"One? I'll book a table. I'm pleased, Rickie! I need cheering up!"

Rickie didn't ask what had happened. Dorothea was never very depressed about anything, never had been.

For this occasion and because it was Sunday, Rickie put on his next to best suit, a dark blue summer worsted, kept his clean shirt on, and added a striped red-and-cream tie, conservative and proper. He could not take Lulu, so he gave her a light lunch for consolation, and said good-bye.

Rickie walked. He felt full of energy, happy, optimistic, and he was walking directly away from snooping Willi Biber's terrain, from Renate Hagnauer's too. Rickie opened his jacket and strode on. He greeted two of the neighborhood denizens, Adolf, a retired baker, and Beata (he had forgotten her last name), a widow exercising her elderly St. Charles. Finally Rickie paused at a curb, and let the breeze erase the moisture that had gathered on his forehead, under his shirt. Ahead of him, beyond some tall pavement trees, a woman sat on her windowsill, polishing the panes. Rickie decided to take a taxi the rest of the way, if he could find one or find a stand, but he came to a tram stop first, pulled his bus-tram carnet from his wallet, and got on the next to Bellevue.

Familiar streets drifted by, residential with prim window boxes, red geraniums dotting the gray cement façades, then more and more shops at pavement level: household pots and pans, appliances, dummies modeling wedding clothes, shops that offered handbags, suitcases, then a haberdashery. Rickie got off at the stop before Bellevue. He still had time to spare, and he felt like walking. It was such a splendid day!

An eye-catching male figure approached and Rickie assessed it: about thirty, looking like a male model in a cream-colored raincoat with cuffs partly unbuttoned as if to prove that the buttonholes were real, porkpie hat, Tattersall shirt with yellow silk tie, and Gucci shoes. Rickie glanced behind him for a photographer and saw none. A few meters on, a couple of stoned hippies—or simply moneyless teenagers in worn-out jeans and scruffy, waist-length denim jackets—leaned against a building, attempting to share something with trembling fingers. A cigarette? A line of cocaine? No one paid them any mind, and no one had paid the swank menswear advertisement any mind either. That was Zurich.

Not far ahead, Rickie saw a man on a ladder, working with a screwdriver on a flagpole socket. Rickie hesitated only briefly—a ladder to walk under was always a temptation—and walked calmly on under the ladder, careful not to touch it.

A passerby noticed, and smiled. When Rickie turned to look back, the ladder was slowly sliding down the building front, as the man descended.

Whack! The ladder fell flat on the pavement.

The impact jolted the man off his balance, and he rolled onto his back, looking stunned. Another man offered him a hand up, and still another righted the ladder.

Rickie hadn't touched the ladder, he was sure. Suppose he had walked under at the time to get hit on the head, or his neck pinned between rungs?

Then the heavy door of the Kronenhalle, with its brass handle, a few steps up to restaurant level, then the full display of dark and heavy wood panels, partitions, tables covered in white linen, raftered ceilings of the same—not dark from old tobacco smoke or fireplace soot like Jakob's, but deliberately stained dark. There was the glint of silverware, the sparkle of stemmed glasses, and a discreet hum of Sunday noon voices, a far cry from Saturday night at the Small g.

"Frau Keller," Rickie said to a headwaiter in black who had approached him. "She has a table."

"Ah, Frau Keller!" The restaurant knew Dorothea Keller, but not him. "This way, sir."

Back and back, past the well-dressed patrons toward a cozy corner table. Dorothea had seen him first.

"'Ello, *Rickie!*"

"Dorothea! How goes it?" Rickie took the chair the headwaiter had pulled out for him. "Thank you."

"I am well and you look *very* well," Dorothea replied. She wore a pale blue cotton dress with white piqué trim—classic, fresh and pretty—and a heavy necklace of what looked like many twisted gold strings.

Costume jewelry, Rickie knew, but the effect was excellent. "And you," Rickie said, "look not a bit depressed."

His sister sighed. "It's only Elise, and she always pulls through. Doesn't she?" Dorothea went on, getting it off her chest before their lunch began. "She went off to Zermatt where a man friend of hers has a flat. Just for a change of scene, she says, and she took her work with her, that I know . . ."

No, it wasn't a new affair, Elise was still in love with her steady boyfriend Jean-Paul, but young people always manufactured such drama. "And I can't even call them young, if Elise's twenty-five and Jean-Paul's thirty and gets his *Doktorat* this year."

"I don't like his name, Jean-Paul, sounds like a pope."

Dorothea laughed.

That's why she liked to see him, Rickie supposed, he could make her laugh. Her family troubles were not so much: Elise delaying completion of her thesis by another few months? What was new about that?

"I have news," Rickie said. "Last night—"

A waiter stuck a huge menu on stiff white paper in front of him, practically into his hands, and Dorothea got the same treatment.

"A drink first, Rickie," she said.

"Very good. A Bloody Mary. Cheerful to look at—along with you."

"*Zwei* Bloody Mary, *bitte*," Dorothea said with a sweet smile to the waiter. "Then we shall order. You were saying, last night—"

She looked at Rickie with level dark eyes. Her hair was puffed out softly round her head. Dorothea looked younger than fifty.

Rickie took a breath, expecting criticism, something negative, but unable to suppress it. "I met the most handsome—boy. Well, I'm sure he's twenty."

"Oh Rickie—" deploringly, eager for more. "Just a little on the young side!"

"Lives with mum in town—and may not even be *schwul*."

"Oh. Then—" Dorothea looked as if she had been expecting an orgy, and was therefore disappointed.

"He is so handsome, I'm sure comes from a rather good family, has his *Matura*," Rickie continued, at the same time thinking that Teddie's arriving in the company of a car thief didn't sound too respectable.

"And what does he do?"

The old story, or problem; the boys were stumbling around, finding themselves. Rickie said it bluntly, "Stumbling around—finding himself."

Dorothea shook her head. "Aren't they all?"

"His mother apparently doesn't mind. Teddie phoned her last night to say he was all right and would be home this morning. And—I should add, he has rather nice manners." Rickie could see that this was a plus in Dorothea's mind. He sipped more of the excellent Bloody Mary. "He stayed the night—*chez moi*."

"Really. And you don't know—" Dorothea's mouth turned up at the corners in a provocative smile.

Rickie said that Teddie had slept in his bed, and he on the living room sofa. This did amaze his sister.

"You are watching out about—you know," she said.

She meant the HIV-positive business. Before Rickie could answer, the waiter returned, and this time they made up their minds and ordered.

"Yes," said Rickie, when the waiter had gone. For the past month and a bit more, Rickie reckoned.

"Taking your vitamin pills."

"Oh yes," He shrugged. "Vitamins. Safe sex. Oooh, la! Can't do any more." He was immensely grateful that his sister had stood by him, when he learned that he was HIV positive. It was like a death sentence, the only question mark being *when*? Neither of them had to say this.

"What kind of wine?" Dorothea was examining the list with the aid of a monocle on a black cord.

Rickie was unpleasantly reminded of Renate in Jakob's, peering at the little bills before she paid them. After they had chosen the wine, Rickie told his sister about walking under the ladder that morning and the ladder falling immediately afterward—*wham*!

Dorothea was alarmed, until Rickie assured her that the man had not been hurt at all. "I saw him standing up—smiling!"

"Rickie—you're always taking chances, and one day—"

When their lamb chops and tournedos arrived, they talked of family things, events in Dorothea's country house on the lake of Zurich. Robbie had acquired more tropical fish, meaning another aquarium had been added to the living room. Rickie rather liked gazing at the tiny royal blue or quite transparent milky little fish in their bubbly, illuminated water.

"Because Robbie's a radiologist," Rickie said, "maybe he likes looking at their spinal cords without having to X-ray them."

"You might be right! He talks about retiring—but that's as far as it gets. Fifty-nine! He could afford to retire. But no, up at the crack of dawn, into the car and driving to the hospital. All he reads is medical journals. But—"

"But?"

"He's an indulgent husband. Never says no to anything I want. That's something." She smiled.

It was during these minutes with his sister that Rickie felt convinced that he had fallen in love with Teddie. Yes. That important phrase. That feeling that didn't come every year, that some people said they'd never had. That madness based not on how pretty or handsome someone was, that mysterious power—Rickie realized that he was under that influence, which was both pleasant and dangerous.

And to be practical, he hadn't Teddie's telephone number. Of course, it might be in the book, and Stevenson being not such a common name in Switzerland, he might find it.

AT ABOUT THAT TIME, Luisa Zimmermann and Renate Hagnauer were looking at a "German paintings and drawings" exhibition at the Kunsthaus, half a kilometer away from Rickie and his sister. Renate—besides enjoying the vast display of talent in the form of painting, sculpture, and photography that the Kunsthaus offered—felt it her duty to introduce Luisa to the cream of the art world, to educate her. Incredible, the gaps in Luisa's knowledge, and not merely in regard to the visual arts. A person would think that she had come from one of the pocket villages of Switzerland, in the notch of some valley where people never read a book, seldom went anywhere, and in the past perhaps had intermarried with appalling results. Luisa's childhood had not been that benighted, but neither of her parents had cared about art, good music, or books, that was plain. Luisa was even reluctant to talk about her family. Fortunately, the girl had a liking for good classical music, which was a blessing. The rest needed prodding.

"You see—this Kandinsky—this spiral so delicate and perfectly balanced. Probably not the first he made to achieve this. The kind of perfection a *machine* could not achieve! He achieved it, freehand, no pencil first, I feel sure."

Luisa looked closely, appreciative, taking pleasure from the drawing, Renate could see. Renate had spoken softly, not wanting to annoy other people with what to them might sound like a lecture.

Renate made a quick and almost furtive sketch of a woman's beige dress. Handmade Italian, Renate could see from across the room. She pointed out her find to Luisa, and waited patiently until the woman turned and she could see the front. Interesting collar, one button, two pockets. Renate sketched.

Several minutes later, they were having cappuccino and apple torte at one of the little tables in the café section on the ground floor. Renate's treat for the young Luisa. The girl did seem in cheerful and relaxed mood today, interested in the show, and not in the least impatient when Renate had wanted to see the very last room of it. Not daydreaming either. Or was she really daydreaming about the boy she had met last night? The good-looking boy with the dark hair?

Renate fitted a cigarette into her holder, lit it. How would she bring it up again? Plunge ahead and repeat it, she decided. "You know, Luisa, if you are dreaming about that boy you danced with last night—"

"I wasn't!" said Luisa, waking up. "I was thinking about something quite different."

"I told you already—Willi saw him leaving Jakob's with Rickie about one in the morning. Willi said they went into Rickie's apartment house. No doubt for the night." Renate sighed with an air of futility. "It would be the same story over again, if you—if you got to know this boy any better. Or if you were stupid enough to fall in *love* with him!" Renate became excited as she spoke, and forced a laugh. "A homo is a homo—forever."

Luisa looked at Renate and said, "I was thinking—about—something else."

Renate stirred in the plastic chair. "Why do you speak to me in *that* tone? I don't care for it."

11

Monday morning. One of the first things Rickie did was telephone a locksmith in regard to his balcony door. Dorothea had asked him yesterday about it, and Rickie had had to admit that he hadn't got round to the repair. Dorothea was appalled, she'd visited him six or eight *months* ago, she reminded him, and been surprised by its state, and he still had done nothing? Then a lecture on the dangers the drug addicts presented now, after the government and the police had cleared them out of the Platzspitz, where they had been able to obtain clean needles at least, and meet their dealers. Oh, Rickie knew. The park had become such a slum really, a dealer's paradise, a public toilet too, that the police had been ordered to clear them all out, take the addicts by busloads back to their homes, often in small towns. But a great many of them had made their way back to Zurich for their drugs, and they were still hanging around, nearly three hundred of them daily drifting in Zurich's streets, according to a recent news bulletin that Rickie remembered. Street holdups, mugging at knifepoint, had come back, Rickie knew. Not to mention that he could see a few almost any time of the day or night in the St. Jakob's church area, sleeping in a nook somewhere, or sitting on the pavement propped against the building, too far gone to stand up to beg.

Anyway, by eight-thirty Rickie had telephoned the locksmith company and made an appointment for ten-thirty that morning. He had said it was urgent, because Rickie knew Dorothea would ring him this evening to ask if he'd done it. Then Rickie had his breakfast at Jakob's, with newspaper and Appenzeller, and as happened most mornings, Renate and Luisa arrived before ten, got their usual table, and before Rickie departed, he was able to give Luisa the most discreet wave of his fingers, and she a big smile to him, as he exited by the main door with Lulu on her lead.

Star-Brite. His ideas. Rickie put his three sketches on the table. They were little more than doodles, but sometimes these won the day. These had action.

Mathilde was opening the post.

"If the Star-Brite man telephones, Mathilde, make a date with him—anytime this afternoon."

"Really? I thought Friday."

Rickie was pleased she remembered. "Things got changed. If I'm not back by noon—I'll phone you, OK? C'mon, Lulu."

The locksmith was only five minutes late, a fortyish man in beige work clothes with a tool kit. Rickie let him in the front door and into the apartment, and explained the problem—

instantly apparent, of course—something broken inside the lock; the key kept turning without moving the bolt. A new lock. So be it.

Rickie had absently looked the man over on first sight, as he usually did—was he gay? This time definitely not, he thought. Not a handsome type, at any rate. So many were gay, and when Rickie forgot to size a man up, something odd could happen, like the gay policeman coming back to his house that night and knocking. Rickie realized that if this one had been gay, even given him a positive sign, he would have declined, because he was dreaming about Teddie.

It would take at least half an hour, the workman said. Rickie stayed, made hot water for instant espresso. The workman didn't want a coffee. Rickie stood sipping, looking out his bedroom window, and was shocked and annoyed to glimpse through the leaves Willi the Snoop directly across the street, staring up at the workman on the balcony. What else had he to do, of course, but patrol the neighborhood—for gossipy purposes, and at public expense, considering that national health insurance was certainly contributing to the dolt's upkeep?

Rickie tried to repress his anger. Good, at least, that Renate would learn in a matter of hours the earthshaking news that Rickie Markwalder's balcony door lock had been repaired—provided Willi wasn't too dim to realize what the workman was doing! There was the workman's little van below, saying "Schlosserei Kobler" in red letters on white, to give Willi a hint.

He yielded to an aggressive impulse, and raised the window, put his hands on the sill. "Hi, Willi!"

Willi heard and saw him, Rickie could sense. But no word, no movement from Willi. His heavy brown shoes hadn't moved on the pavement.

Rickie kept staring at him, remembering that Willi had said a murderer had come in that broken door. Rather Renate had invented that story, and Willi had probably helped to spread it. He

watched as Willi drifted off, giving one backward glance after a
few steps, as if nothing but Rickie's repair job interested him at the
moment. Except reporting it now, of course. Rickie hoped Willi
would spread it all over the neighborhood.

The workman did accept a small beer when the work was
nearly finished. Finally, collection of tools, sweeping up of metal
fragments with Rickie's broom, and the man was gone. Great! Perfect. He *did* feel more secure, and he could make a good report to
his sister.

"Let's go, Lulu!"

Lulu leapt to her feet, ready for her lead.

Back to the studio, and Mathilde informed him that the Star-
Brite man had telephoned, and she had made an appointment for
3 P.M. That was fine.

"Anything else?"

"This bill—needs a check. And someone called Georg phoned
around eleven-thirty. Said he would call back."

"Just Georg?" Rickie asked casually, though his heart had
jumped.

The telephone rang, and Rickie laid the invoice down.

"I'll take this one," said Rickie, not hurrying. "Hello?"

"Hello, Rickie. Teddie. I'm—um— How are you?"

"*Gu-t, danke,*" replied Rickie. "And where are you? Home?"

"I'm at Jakob's."

Rickie instantly saw the semi-sheltered stand-up booth—if a
hood with shoulder-length sides could be called a booth—against
a wall near the toilets. "So-o—well—um—I am still working, you
know. For a few minutes. Could you—" He saw that Mathilde was
doing something at her desk, paying him no heed. "You know my
home address."

"Just the telephone there."

Rickie gave him the house number. "Say, one o'clock?"

"Sure, Rickie. Thank you."

Rickie smiled, hanging up, feeling happy. A polite boy to say

"Thank you." He hoped Teddie hadn't got into some kind of trouble, and at once thought it was possible that Teddie liked him a
little.

He took a spare key from a drawer. "A key for you, Mathilde.
I'll be back by three for Star-Brite, but maybe not before. You have
work for this afternoon. I think."

She sipped her Dubonnet before she answered. "Yes, indeed,
Rickie. *Guten Appetit!*" she added more cheerfully.

Rickie waved and departed.

He saw the boy from a distance, standing under a tree, in blue
jeans and a tan jacket, sneakers. Then Teddie saw him, and raised
an arm.

"Hi, Rickie!" A manly handshake from the boy.

Rickie almost trembled. "Want to come up? Have you had
lunch?"

"No. Be nice to talk for a minute." Teddie looked in a cheerful mood.

They went up the steps, into Rickie's flat.

"Welcome—again!" Rickie said with a big smile.

Teddie nodded. "Thanks. I talked with my mum today. I feel
better."

Rickie felt a start of alarm. "Talked—about what?"

"About what I might do with my life. I'm thinking of journalism. I wrote a column this morning—just two pages but it's
something."

"Very good," said Rickie. "Would you like to sit down? Something to drink? A Coke?"

The boy might not have heard the questions. His alert eyes
gazed into Rickie's. "I just wanted to talk to you. I'm going to try
to start a column—twice a week, maybe. 'Georg's Hiccup,' something like that—sort of for young people, though I hate the term
'young people.' Just—things I've been doing."

Rickie knew. Hiccup—well. "How about 'Georg's View' or—
'Georg's Adventures'?"

"'Adventures'—that's possible. I'll think about it."

"Did you bring your piece?"

"I sent it off just now." Teddie smiled. "To the *Tages-Anzeiger*. Aiming high, eh?"

"Aha! My newspaper. But you have a copy of your piece."

"It's at home. It's—about Saturday night, the joy ride, ha-ha— and ending up in a strange neighborhood and dropping into a friendly bar and restaurant like Jakob's and meeting—"

"Did you write 'Jakob's'?" Somehow Jakob's was private, like a club.

Teddie laughed. "I called it 'Artur's.' And meeting—friendly people like you, and others—and a pretty girl and dancing with her. It's a whole new world."

It was only a whole new neighborhood, Rickie thought.

"And even if it doesn't last," Teddie went on. "A night's adventure, as you said. Like an episode, you know?"

"Yes," Rickie replied, puzzled. "Look, can I invite you to Jakob's for a snack? Because I haven't anything interesting here."

Rickie felt more at ease going into Jakob's at lunchtime, because the hostile eye of Renate Hagnauer was never here at midday, and seldom was the dunce Willi Biber, who had vague jobs at a tearoom a few streets away, Rickie had heard, and very likely he ate there. He and Teddie entered by the main street door, and walked on to the back terrace, he and Lulu being greeted by a few of the patrons as usual.

Bratwurst and sauerkraut for Teddie, sliced ham and potato salad for Rickie, and a Coke and a beer. Again a lovely day, with sunlight through the grapevines over their heads.

"Does Luisa come here for lunch sometimes?" Teddie asked.

Rickie chuckled, enjoying his meal and the beautiful image— the fact—of Teddie opposite. "I'm pretty sure Luisa has lunch with Renate at home there."

"And the evening?"

Rickie quaffed some beer. "Never saw them for dinner here.

Later, maybe—when the crowd gets interesting. Especially week-ends."

Teddie's brows looked troubled. "They're always together?"

"No. But Renate's possessive. You'd think Luisa was her daughter." He added, "I've heard she's very jealous, Renate. So watch out—if you want to see Luisa again." Nothing more obvi-ous to Rickie than that Teddie did want to see Luisa again, and that that was why he was here.

"Well—um—why has this Renate got such a hold?"

Rickie didn't answer at once. "Luisa—her family's in Brig, I think. Renate gave her a job—continuing her apprenticeship, a place to sleep, about a year ago—less. Renate takes advantage, bosses Luisa around." He added, as if it would explain the situa-tion, "Everyone knows that."

"Because—I wouldn't mind seeing Luisa again," Teddie said with a smile, laying his knife and fork diagonally across his empty plate. "That was good, Rickie. Great place!"

Rickie smiled a little, for some reason recalling the night he had barely made it home in his Merc, drunk and tailed by a police car. He had parked his car outside Jakob's and staggered in, and Ursie had hidden him in the kitchen. Yes, *hidden* him, while the police had taken a look round the bar and the restaurant rooms, and had given up. Oddly, Rickie had not received a ticket in the post for that, because certainly the police had had his license num-ber, if they'd cared to use it.

"This Renate—is she in the telephone book?"

Rickie reached for his nearly empty beer glass. "I think so. And if you try to telephone Luisa, she'll likely pick up the telephone first." He laughed.

Teddie wagged his head to indicate indifference. "I can try it. What's there to lose?"

Rickie looked at his watch. "I'm checking because of an appointment at three," he murmured, as if thinking of something else, which he was. He was trying to see into the future.

"My mother says I can have the car more or less when I want," Teddie said, "since I have a good record. Haven't got it today, though."

And it would be nice to invite Luisa for a drive, Rickie was thinking, and to dinner at a restaurant in the countryside. Teddie's handsome young face looked as restless as his left hand, whose fingers drummed on the old wood of the table. "I'm serious about the newspaper column idea. I'll try it for a couple of months. Might improve with practice."

Rickie lit a cigarette. "But of course—with practice. A column for—people your age. If the *Tages-Anzeiger* turns you down, try somewhere else."

"I was writing articles and a couple of short stories in *Gymnasium*. I think I'm better at nonfiction. I don't mean I'm very good yet—but I had some praise at school."

Rickie felt that Teddie gazed at him hopefully for approval, as if he, Rickie, had become a father figure. He frowned down at the ashtray. "You know, it might be better if you wrote to Luisa instead of telephoning, because if Renate answers"—he had lowered his voice, as if the old witch was at the next table—"she's not going to pass you on to Luisa. She'll ask your name, your business."

"Oh. That bad."

"Yes, Teddie."

Teddie stood up. "Excuse me. I'll take a look. The telephone book—Hagnauer."

"Yes," Rickie said reluctantly, as softly as the boy had spoken. Then he picked up the four little bills, and reached for his wallet.

Teddie was soon back. "I took the address and so on."

"So you'll write a note."

"OK. But it's so much slower."

Rickie had to smile. "Coffee?"

"Not for me, thanks. I had a lot this morning, working."

Teddie reached for the bills, firmly. "I'll pay. I think it'll bring me luck."

Ursula was in sight, and came at Rickie's beck. She wore a limp, slightly soiled white apron over a dark blue dress, and carried her pad and pencil at the ready.

"So-o, my dear," Rickie said in jocular tone. "We pay. Rather my friend does."

"Ah-h—our friend from Saturday night!" said Ursula pleasantly, on recognizing Teddie. "Welcome!"

"Thank you," said Teddie.

Ursie's pale blue eyes focused on her reckoning, and she announced the sum.

"Thank you very much, Teddie," said Rickie.

They went out via the garden path with the gate at the pavement edge.

"By the way, Teddie, are *you* in the telephone book? Your mother?"

"Yes. Under K. J. Stevenson. Here." He pulled his wallet again from the inside pocket of his jacket, and took a small business card from it. "One of my dad's old cards, but it's correct."

Rickie recognized a street name and postal code of a residential section of Zurich. "Not that I mean to phone you. But it's somehow nice to know where you are."

"You could telephone me," Teddie said in a frank tone. "Why not?"

Just then, past Teddie's shoulder, Rickie saw Willi Biber crossing the street, apparently heading for Jakob's main entrance, Willi in his broad-brimmed gray hat, and looking downward, as if afraid of stepping into dog excrement. When Willi reached the pavement, he glanced in their direction. Impossible to know what the dimwit's brain had registered, and depressing to realize that if Willi reported sighting him with Teddie, if would be in Rickie's favor: Renate would warn Luisa, maybe with redoubled strength, that she'd be consorting with a homosexual, if she made a date with Teddie.

Teddie turned to see what interested Rickie. Willi fixed his gaze on Teddie for a couple of seconds, then disappeared into the greenery that enveloped Jakob's entrance.

"That guy again," said Teddie. "Wasn't he here Saturday night? Sure. At Renate's table—funny-looking guy."

Rickie strolled toward his office, and Teddie came with him. "Every village has its idiot, I suppose."

When Rickie was almost at his apartment house, he made a decision. "Teddie, come in for a minute. There's something I want to tell you and I can't tell you out here."

"What?" asked Teddie, unwilling.

"It'll take two minutes and it's important." Rickie pulled his keys out as if he meant business.

The boy followed him. Rickie entered his flat and closed the door. He had fourteen minutes before Star-Brite.

"Look—this—it's Renate," Rickie began. "I told you she was possessive about Luisa. I had a young boyfriend—Peter Ritter. His pictures are all around here. He was killed in January this year. He—"

"Killed?"

"Stabbed one night as he left a cinema. In Zurich. Stabbed and robbed, you know? Bled to death before he got to a hospital. I wasn't with him, he was by himself."

"That's terrible, Rickie. I'm sorry." Teddie's eyes flickered toward the big picture of Petey with his motorcycle, then away.

"The *reason* I tell you this is that Luisa was very fond of Petey, in love with him even. For several weeks. Renate was most upset. Petey was gay. Oh, I know it's a different situation. But Renate told Luisa that Petey was stabbed by a pickup of Petey who came in through the balcony window or some such when I was out—that he was stabbed right here in my apartment."

Teddie began to frown. "But wasn't there anything in the papers about the stabbing?"

Rickie nodded. "The time and place and the hospital he was taken to. Not a big item. Not everybody read it, of course. And people believe what they want to believe. *Some* people. Like Willi who's practically a moron. Renate has a lot of control over him."

"And the people around here? In Jakob's?"

"Oh, Ursie and the help at Jakob's, they know the truth. But— people who just come in for a beer—any stranger, they're going to believe a story like the stabbing in my apartment, because it's interesting—dramatic. I feel sure Renate can tell it as if she believes it. She convinced Luisa. I had to set Luisa right."

Teddie said with utmost seriousness, "It's hard to imagine Renate's that cracked."

Rickie hesitated a moment. "She's not cracked, she's shrewd. Greedy, maybe. Now she's concentrating on Luisa. Renate wants to make her a very good dress designer."

"She's gay, Renate? A lesbian?"

"Ha! Maybe a repressed one. I don't know what she is, because it's all sort of distorted—I heard she was married once, for years. No children, I think."

Teddie nodded. "I've heard of a hundred percent repressed gay people. Men *and* women."

"I warn you about Willi Biber too. A real snoop—and full of lies. It seems Renate convinced him he was once in the French Foreign Legion—years ago. Ursie told me that one!" Rickie could not repress a smile. "I hadn't heard it but it seems Willi tells it to a lot of people."

Teddie stepped back and gave a laugh. "The Foreign Legion. That scarecrow!"

Rickie moved toward the door, keys still in hand. They went out and descended the front stone steps.

"I don't know how this Renate can look you in the face."

"She doesn't look at me—usually. You haven't noticed yet. I don't exist for her. Here I am at the factory. Phone me some time—if you feel like it." Rickie felt noble with his casualness, his easy smile.

"Right. I'm sure I'll feel like it."

They were standing beside Rickie's studio railing, where the steps went down to work, discipline, the telephone, and Mathilde.

"And I'd love to see one of your efforts with 'Georg's Adventures.' If you send me a carbon copy, I'll return it if you want me to."

A vague gesture, a murmured word and a smile, and Rickie's vision of perfection—health, good looks, and sex appeal—turned and hurried off toward Jakob's again.

12

Two days later, Luisa Zimmermann prepared cautiously for her first date with Teddie—sometimes Georg—Stevenson. She was to meet him one street away and around the corner of the street in which she lived. His car was an Audi four-door, brown, and if she didn't see it parked, she would see him strolling along, wearing a light-colored jacket.

> Can you invent a reason to stay out long enough for dinner, etc? A sick friend? A film you want to see? Whether you can make it or not, I'll be there by seven-fifteen and I'll wait—how long? A long time anyway!
>
> Till then XX
>
> G.

It was hard for Luisa to invent something to tell Renate, because Luisa's circle of friends was small, and because Renate suspected anything that was out of the ordinary. *Why* did she feel like taking a walk just now? Because she hadn't stretched her legs all day, Luisa might reply, which was the truth, but Renate's eyes would stare like knives cutting her brain open.

For this occasion Luisa had said, taking a big chance, that it was too hot to eat anything, at least at 7 P.M., and she wanted to stroll along the Sihl for a while. She would probably be back by ten, she said. *Daring*, that had been, but here she was out, *out*, at one minute to seven, freshly showered, wearing a full blue cotton skirt she had made, and a white, long-sleeved cotton blouse, carrying a small handbag that held her keys, a little money, paper tissues, a comb, and over her arm a black sweater for later when it became chilly. Luisa wondered, was Renate baiting her, letting her line run out quite a lot, so she could haul it in with a big catch? Renate had attacked every boy or young man Luisa had made acquaintance with in the last—well, all the time she had lived in Renate's house, nearly a year. Renate would make a devastating remark: "Shabby clothes," or "Looks like a farm worker," or "Common as mud! Just because he smiles and invites you to a Coke, you intend to make a *date* with him?"

Luisa strolled away from home and Jakob's, and past the place where she was to meet Georg-Teddie. She was thinking of her "circle of friends": Elsie, one of the apprentices who lived in the neighborhood, would certainly help her out. Luisa could still ring her up (she lived with her parents) and say, "I was with you this evening for dinner, in case Renate questions me. All right, Elsie?" Vera would be cooperative too. Impossible that Luisa could have arranged such an alibi during working hours, when Renate was present in the big apartment. Luisa wouldn't have dared try. It was as if the walls had ears, as the saying went, or that, despite her audible gait, Renate could sneak up and hear every word before Luisa was aware of her presence. Luisa had captured Teddie's letter safely, only because she'd fetched the post herself from the box.

Seven past seven. Maybe Georg was already at the meeting place? At the next corner, she turned right, into the appointed block, and still slowly walked along the pavement overhung with birch and plane trees. There were a couple of dark figures ahead, but she saw a pale blur which became a jacket, she thought.

"Hello, Luisa!" Georg-Teddie said softly. "You made it!"

"Yes!"

"Car's this way." He still spoke softly. "Round the corner. No, at the corner. I'm so glad you're here!"

He smiled, and opened the door of a large and shining car that had appeared black to Luisa. "Please."

Luisa stepped in and sat on a broad beige passenger seat, and Teddie came round and got behind the wheel. Luisa had a glimpse of a complex-looking dashboard, red arcs, dials, then Teddie closed the door and the engine purred.

"What a big car!"

"You think so? No-o. Well, I'm used to it, I suppose. What kind has your—well—your friend got?"

"Renate?" Luisa didn't like saying her name. A VW Golf. With special brake and patrol pedals. She has a handicap—a *Klumpfuss*." Luisa used the common term for it instead of talipes, which Renate preferred. Were people supposed to puzzle over what talipes meant, Luisa wondered, since Renate's foot was hidden beneath a long skirt? "Maybe you noticed that she limps," Luisa added, hoping that finished the subject.

"If I did, I forgot," Teddie said, as if he couldn't care less. "Do you like shish kebab?"

"Oh yes."

"Because I know a good place. That's where we're going. Ten—no, eight kilometers away. You don't mind?"

The summer air blew against her face, her arms, and the car rolled as smoothly as if they were flying. "No. I don't mind. An Arab place?"

"I think it's French but they do a good shish kebab. Chez Henri, it's called. Has a terrace, so it's cool. Also a little orchestra." Teddie laughed. "You like to dance, I know."

The breeze was louder in her ears than Teddie's voice. He wore a red vest under his white jacket, which he had now unbuttoned, and Luisa thought of the girl named Dorrie with her red

vest last Saturday night. This coming Saturday was the first of
August, Switzerland's National Holiday, which meant a big event
at Jakob's. Would Renate invite all her girls for an evening at
Jakob's? Bratwurst, cervelat, and bread, wine and beer. Luisa rather
hoped not, but Vera had said Renate had made a party of it last
year.

"You're very quiet. What did you do today?"

"You want the truth?" Luisa asked.

"Of course I do!"

"I phoned Rickie—while I was out buying something for *la
fabrique*. Renate calls it *la fabrique*, the workplace. I wanted to tell
him I was seeing you tonight."

"Good. I'm glad." Teddie flicked his lights and overtook a car
on an upward stretch. "And the rest of the time?"

"I worked. But I spent some time wondering how to make it
this evening, what to say. To escape."

"To escape! Can't you see someone for dinner? Why do you
take it?"

Luisa foresaw two awkward statements, like confessions,
ahead—if she made them. She began, "Maybe I didn't tell you. It's
not all that important, but—Renate thinks you're *schwul* because
she's seen you with Rickie—or Willi has. He reports to her."

"Ha! Ho-ho. You can tell her I find her stuffy. Add *creepy*. I like
Rickie, queer or not. Or don't tell her anything!"

Luisa was silent. She also liked Rickie. He would be a friend
in case she needed one—she sensed that. Now she tensed herself
for the next confession. "The other reason"—Luisa closed the
window to make herself more audible—"I'm not so independent
is that Renate gave me a job and a place to live last year when I
ran away from Brig. I wasn't twenty but I had to say I was—to
some people, so I wouldn't be sent back home. And Renate had to
speak for me to the *Schneiderin* I'd been apprenticed to in Brig. My
parents—mother and stepfather—well, they don't know my
address and I'm glad. I wrote to them that I'm in Zurich and OK,

and I don't think they want to ask questions. Anyway they've got my younger half-brother to bring up. So that's the end of it, Teddie. Or are you Georg tonight?"

"I'm Teddie tonight. Did you sign a contract with Renate?"

"Not yet. She assumed I'll sign. We have to get a legal release from the woman I was apprenticed to in Brig, you see. Renate wrote to her. Renate's not satisfied. It's not straightened out yet."

"Don't sign it, don't sign anything with her. She's an oddball, you know? Liar too. Rickie told me a few things, and I believe Rickie."

So did Luisa believe Rickie. "Do you mean about Rickie's friend Petey?"

"I do. Well—I went to the newspaper archives in town yesterday. Looked it up. Peter Ritter—stabbed in a Zurich street in January, dead on arrival in hospital. The idea of a presumably sane person like Renate telling a lie about a death! Now I have to be careful so I don't overshoot. This place is on the other side of the road." Teddie concentrated.

Teddie was right, Rickie was right, Luisa knew.

He swung across the road to a small white sign that there was no time to read, and they climbed a narrow road with a couple of bends in it, and came on to a level. The lights of a long, one-story restaurant showed a terrace with tables and a parking area. Teddie parked in a row of fifteen cars or so.

Luisa wished she was in her new pink dress, but how would she have escaped for the evening in it?

A headwaiter came onto the terrace to greet them.

Teddie had made a reservation for two under Stevenson, and the maître d' seemed to know Teddie. "Is the terrace all right?" Teddie asked Luisa.

Of course.

"To drink?" Teddie asked when they were seated. "Please have something—to celebrate!" He said it as if one or the other of them had a birthday. "I had such a good day today. And now you're— I'm with you!"

"What I would like is a gin and tonic," Luisa said, feeling daring.

"Good. And I'll join you in the tonic." Teddie gave the order.

"No drinking when you drive, I suppose." Luisa meant it as a compliment.

"Sure, I could, you know. One, anyway. But I promised my mother." Teddie set his jaw and scowled at the menu. "Well, I know the kebab's good, but we'll wait. Maybe you'll have two gin and tonics. I wrote another column," Teddie said. "My third or fourth. 'Georg's Adventures,' I call my efforts—for now. I admit the *Tages-Anzeiger* turned the first two down. Well, three."

"What kind of column?"

"About—someone like me. Just an incident. What happens— what we're thinking about. Even just a date like tonight. Who knows?"

Just a date. Luisa was thinking that Teddie Stevenson looked elegant, like a young millionaire, in his fine off-white jacket and black bow tie. And she was dressed as if she had stepped out to buy a liter of milk! Her nails clean now, but devoid of polish. Yet Teddie was looking at her as if he liked her, and liked being with her.

"As I said to Rickie Monday, I'll give it a good try for a couple of months, this journalism. My mother thinks what I wrote— might have a chance somewhere, anyway. Or so she said. Here we go."

The drinks had come.

"To you. To us," Teddie said, lifting his glass of tonic with lemon slice.

"To us," Luisa said, and drank some. She imagined that she felt the gin at once. "Have you—"

"You make—" Teddie interrupted, and smiled. "You make me think of a chestnut," he said with determination. "All shining— somehow."

"A chestnut?" Luisa ducked her head, embarrassed, not knowing why. "Have you been to America? I suppose so."

"Tw—no, three times. New York. And once to California. I said chestnut, because your hair shines like a—"

The waiter was back, politely inquiring about their order. Teddie thought it a good idea to order, as the shish kebab took a time. With rice. No garlic? All right, a little. A green salad. A half-bottle of good red wine for Mademoiselle. Teddie looked at the list.

"A glass," Luisa said.

"No-no! A half-bottle." Teddie was firm. "And caviar maybe?"

Caviar. Yes. Renate—Luisa could not stop herself now from thinking of Renate indulging Luisa and herself in caviar at near Christmas time last year, and making it clear that caviar was a rare luxury.

"Now we could dance," Teddie said, "*if* you'd like."

Luisa wore pumps: she had had to tell Renate she meant to walk. Again, she felt the embarrassing contrast between Teddie's garb and her own, but once he touched her waist, held her right hand, her confidence returned.

"With a waltz," Teddie began, "what can you do but waltz?"

It was old-fashioned, elegant, beautiful. Teddie danced very straight, his head high. Luisa was aware that some of the people at the tables watched them. It was a dream, she felt, and just as in a dream, she had worn the wrong clothes and was ugly in contrast to Teddie. Yet people smiled at both of them.

Then they were back at their table, Teddie holding her chair until she was seated.

The waiter arrived with the caviar.

"One more gin and tonic, please," Teddie said, "and one plain tonic. Thank you."

"No, Teddie, I can't! This one is enough." She was not even finished with the first.

Teddie yielded, and dropped the order.

Caviar. Symbol of luxury.

Teddie was now talking of scuba diving when he'd been fifteen. Luisa suddenly saw herself at fifteen and sixteen, as clearly as

if she gazed at a film in black and white, wearing an ugly gray cov-
erall suit like a mechanic's, hair short and jagged, yanking her
motorbike into upright position, throwing her head back as she
guffawed with the local boys. They were assembling in the square,
waiting for a last pal—maybe Franz, always late—before they tore
off, making as much noise as possible in the small streets, rushing
past private houses, scaring cats, causing drivers to blink their lights
in silent fury. Luisa recalled her sense of "success" when strangers
looked at her twice, as if asking themselves, "Is that a boy or a
girl?" She had affected a tough gait, a rough toss of her head, an
aggressive way of mounting her motorbike. Her nails—uneven
and dirty! Of course! But she'd got free of her stepfather by these
maneuvers—or at least they had helped. He had tried to laugh at
her toughness at first, but he hadn't been able to shake her from
her intent. Freedom! Out of the house!

Now she was dancing with Teddie to a really good song, Teddie with jacket unbuttoned and its whiteness flying, like his patent
leather slippers.

A raspberry ice each for dessert, Teddie insisted.

Then Luisa was saying, "I must be going soon. I *must.*"

Ten to eleven. The tension had returned. Not another dance
tonight, she knew. She didn't dare. The last dance had been a dare.

"I know, I know." Teddie said it with patience, but with annoyance too.

There's just so much I can get away with, Luisa thought of
saying, but checked herself.

In no time, it seemed, because the atmosphere had hardened
into reality, they were back in the car, racing toward town and
Aussersihl. Luisa tried to rehearse her answers, in case Renate
quizzed her. She'd grown tired and had to wait an extra long time
for a tram? No. Renate knew when she was trying to lie.

"I'll walk you to the house," said Teddy boldly, turning off his
engine, his lights. He had parked near where Luisa had met him
tonight.

"But—no, Teddie. What if she looks out the window and sees you?" Luisa's gaze took in the length of the dark pavement under the trees—no one, and she was ready to open the car door.

"Kiss me good night?"

He kissed her first quickly, then gave her a longer kiss, still gentle, with a lick of his tongue between her lips. He pressed her hand against the car cushion between them. Luisa opened the door. Then Teddie was beside her, holding the door open for her.

"Go back!" She was thinking of his very visible white jacket. "I'll say good-bye here. Thank you, Teddie."

"I thank you. Go—if you must!" he whispered, clowning with arm upraised.

Luisa walked. For a few seconds, she expected Teddie's long brown car to glide by—he had to drive in this direction, unless he attempted a U-turn. She turned right at the next corner, not having seen him, braced in fact for the sight of Renate who just might be taking a late walk, returning from an espresso at Jakob's, hoping to spy on her, on anyone with her. Luisa stole a glance at her wristwatch under a streetlight. Twenty-two past eleven. Not horrible, but bad enough. A mere walk along the Sihl? Yes, that was possible, if she'd stopped somewhere like a buffet-restaurant for a Coke and a frankfurter. Caviar and shish kebab! Luisa imagined that she still felt the effects of the gin and tonic and the wine.

Luisa was suddenly at her house steps. She looked nervously at a dark figure coming from the Jakob direction, male, but it was no one she knew. Looking up, Luisa saw a light in the TV room. And she had her keys, good. She opened the front door.

"Hello. Luisa!" This from Francesca, a plump, fiftyish woman with whom Renate sometimes chatted in Jakob's. Francesca was walking her Pomeranian.

"'Evening, Francesca," Luisa replied with a smile.

Luisa climbed the stairs. The old paneled white door opened easily. The TV was audible, a male voice.

And Renate appeared in the TV room doorway, wearing her

pink-and-white floor-length negligee and an anxious expression, hair tied back and hanging down her nape now. "Well—so—a long walk. And how was the Sihl?" The tone was not particularly hostile.

Luisa had heard that middling tone before. It was unpredictable. She threw her shoulders back, feeling strong. "Very pleasant. A little breeze. I had a wiener and a Coke."

"Did you? Where?"

"Oh—somewhere. You know. A kiosk with a couple of tables and chairs." She could see the place. Luisa felt ever more certain as she spoke.

"Where were you really?" Renate's tense, slender figure, not so tall as Luisa's, had come between Luisa and the back part of the hall, where Luisa wanted to go.

Luisa did not hesitate. She laughed and said, "Really—taking a walk! And I enjoyed it! Excuse me, Renate."

Luisa moved past her, down the hall to the bathroom. She realized that she had seen something new in Renate's face just now, heard it in her voice. It was different from uncertainty, or simple questioning, it was something like fear. Bizarre thought! Renate was fearless. She'd said so many times, not boasting but as if she stated the truth.

Yes, she'd had a date with Teddie Stevenson, and so what? And she would see him Saturday evening too at Jakob's! They hadn't made a date, but he'd be there. Jakob's was a public place, after all, and Renate couldn't dictate who'd be admitted and who wouldn't. She might dance with Teddie, and he might dance with another girl. And why not?

Luisa took a delicious lukewarm shower. Renate had returned to her TV.

She fell into bed, washed and combed, with her head full of Teddie—taking her hand gently before they stepped onto the dance floor, saying that she would have to meet his mother (why?), saying so many things that had made her smile and made her smile now. What was Teddie doing now? Would she always remind him of a chestnut? What was always? Two months?

13

Saturday night. Rickie had worked alone in his studio most of the day, worked well in the silence. A gentle rain around 4 P.M. had cooled the air wonderfully. Rickie worked on until after eight on the Star-Brite jobs. Finally he collapsed for several minutes on the single bed in the back room, hands behind his head.

Would Teddie be at the Small g tonight? Should he wait and eat a bit there, instead of making something at home? If Teddie came, he'd be looking for Luisa, of course, maybe already had a date with her. Perfectly normal, Rickie told himself. He'd watch them dancing together. He couldn't dance with Teddie, oh no. Teddie wouldn't like that, and of course Rickie wouldn't propose it. In a mixture of reality and fantasy about Teddie Stevenson, Teddie dancing naked and by himself, and inaudibly singing—Rickie fell asleep.

When he lifted his head and peered at his wristwatch, it was only five past nine. He closed up shop, summoned Lulu to her lead, and walked to his apartment house. Here he gave Lulu her supper, put on a cassette of Dietrich—he loved "Johnny, wenn du Geburtstag hast"—showered and got dressed. A yellow linen jacket for tonight, a nice white shirt, no tie but a good foulard at his neck, blue stay-pressed cotton trousers. Not elegant, Rickie thought, just maybe *neat*. He thought of the English word, which to him had many facets: adroit, clean, chic, and a bit dismissive—somehow. He felt his garb meant he was not going to try to make a conquest tonight, yet if something came along—

The telephone rang when Rickie had his hand almost on his own doorknob. He turned back.

"Hello?"

"Hello, Rickie! Tried to reach you twice before. This is Freddie—Freddie Schimmelmann. Remember?" A hearty laugh. "The *cop!*"

Rickie's brain spun a couple of times. Of course, Freddie the cop who'd let him off. My God, he'd been to bed with this man! "Freddie, sure—how are you?" Rickie saw again the smallish figure, the affably pleasant face curiously wrinkled at the corners of the eyes.

"I'm fine. I'm free tonight—wondered what you're doing. What *are* you doing?" Freddie's smiling voice was suggestive of wild fun.

Rickie thought fast, tried to. "Well, I'm—" Rickie thought of Teddie, of seeing him very likely tonight, even of possibly seeing him. He didn't want to be tied up with Freddie, didn't want to suggest Freddie come to the Small g tonight, because it would look as if—"I've got a date, to tell you the truth."

"Oh—not the kind I could join maybe? Are you tied up later too?"

Rickie had to answer no to the first question, yes to the second. At the same time, he wanted to be nice to Freddie, because Freddie had been nice to him, and because Freddie might well be of help in some predicament in the future. "Another time—I'm sure. But just now I'm pretty busy, Freddie. I was working all day, that's why I wasn't at home."

Rickie had got out of that fairly easily. Freddie made sure that Rickie had his card, still, with work and home numbers. Rickie had.

Then Rickie went out and strolled toward the Small g. Certainly Freddie wasn't a knockout, Rickie was thinking. Was that why he was so hard up, that he phoned him, Rickie? Or was he again belittling himself, seeing himself old and ugly, when the truth was not nearly so grim? Rickie put on an optimistic air, head a little higher, as he walked through the main entrance of Jakob's. The outside terrace's six tables were nearly full. Jakob's had put out little Swiss flags along the trees, the flags on strings, white crosses on red. A couple of firecrackers went off but from a great distance, as if from some dark mountain. More red-and-white altered the dark-brown-and-tan interior of the Small g. Bigger flags here, but not many of them.

"Hello, *Rickie!*" from someone standing at the bar.

"Rickie and Lulu! Hoopla!"

The usual. Rickie casually greeted a few faces he knew and moved toward the now-empty dance floor where the tables and booths that ringed the room gave off murmurs and shouts and some spontaneous singing. Rickie, looking for Philip or Ernst, stole a glance at "Renate's table," and there they were—Renate in white tonight and Luisa.

She saw him and flashed a smile, lifted her right hand quickly. Renate, apparently lecturing Luisa as usual, had been too occupied to notice him, or so he hoped. A woman whom Rickie didn't know was on the other side of Renate.

"Hey, Rickie! This way!" This was Ernst, conspicuous in French sailor's striped sweater, half standing up from a smaller table. Here were Philip Egli and also Claus Bruder with what seemed to be a new catch, a blondish boy.

There was room for Rickie on a bench against the wall, and for Lulu beside him. A beer. Exchanges. How was everybody? Claus's new boy was called René, and sported the short-side haircut with bushy top now such a favorite of the young. He looked stupid, Rickie thought, but maybe honest. Of course Rickie could have turned up with a new face from the Bahnhof this evening, but who wanted such? The kind of boy who'd do it for money, who'd pick your pocket besides at the first opportunity. And what a comedown from Petey. No, the Bahnhof Rickie would not cruise. Better the Bahnhofquai, even if he got a brush-off from the young! Better Freddie Schimmelmann!

"To eat, Rickie! Anything?" Ernst was apparently ordering, Andreas standing near with his tablet.

Rickie soon had grilled cervelat, dark bread, and a mustard pot plus a green salad before him. It was getting on for eleven.

Renate had begun to sketch, Rickie saw, the object of her attention being a young woman in a long black tunic over orange slacks, Rickie thought, who had taken to the dance floor. Renate's white dress was set off by two broad red bands from shoulder to waist, effective and unusually bold for the Edwardian Renate. And here came Willi Biber, hat in hand tonight, and Rickie watched Renate shoo Luisa and the third woman farther down the bench with a flick of her hand, so Willi could sit beside Renate and face the crowd.

"Hey, Rickie! Did you bring her *glasses*?" This from two tables over to Rickie's right. A man pointed to Lulu.

"Her glasses? No!" Rickie replied, smiling a little. "Sorry!" He didn't know the people at that table, not even by sight.

The crowd was bigger and noisier, because of the holiday. Rickie looked out for Dorrie Wyss, not at all sure she'd come, if she had a good party to go to in town. Rickie had finished his meal, lit a cigarette and ordered another beer, when he caught sight of Teddie and his heart gave a jump. Teddie in a pale blue jacket, bow tie, so handsome that he was anyone's Golden Boy— Rickie's, girls', boys', his mum's Golden Boy, of course. Rickie lowered his eyes, flicked his ashes into an ashtray, looked up again just as Teddie and Luisa saw each other—it seemed. There were a few dancers between them. Rickie saw Teddie stop, lift his head and smile, as if he were going to head for Luisa's table, but he turned in Rickie's direction. Luisa continued to watch Teddie.

"Teddie?" Rickie called, lifting an arm.

The boy hadn't seen him until then.

Rickie made room, asked one fellow to get himself a chair, in fact, and put Lulu on his other side, so Teddie could sit beside him. "Well, Teddie! You know nearly everyone, I think."

Nods and hellos.

"You are looking very smart tonight," Rickie said.

Teddie shrugged. "Dinner out with my mum. And another— well, my godmother," Teddie said, laughing. "Had to look nice. Godmother's birthday. Did you get my—my article, Rickie?"

Now Rickie had a slight sinking feeling, the opposite of a few moments ago. He had got Teddie's page and a half and hadn't liked them. About motorcycle riding, racing with a friend. "Ye-es."

"Like it?" asked Teddie, as directly as a child might. Then, "OK—you can be frank."

"Then frankly—I'm not sure it's going to appeal to many people. Motorcycle people—sure. But the way you wrote about speed, noise. Risk also—"

"Yes, sure."

"Interesting," Rickie said, making an effort, "but I'm thinking about a majority who wouldn't like it."

Teddie smiled. "Well, you're right. I got it back this morning. I send self-addressed stamped envelopes; otherwise I wouldn't get anything back." He forced a laugh.

"Did the editor have any comment?"

"Oh—'limited appeal.' 'Not worked out' or something. I admit I wrote it fast—to keep in the spirit, you know."

Rickie felt easier. "What would you like to drink? A Coke?"

"Got to be a Coke, I've got the car tonight."

That was that. Fine, Rickie thought, raised an arm for Andy or Ursie, or maybe Tobi was on duty tonight too. None of them in sight. Claus Bruder was concentrating on his new friend, who was sitting in the far left corner, back against the wall, one foot on the bench.

"I'd love to ask Luisa to dance, but the old witch is right there!" Teddie gave a short laugh.

"Ask her anyway!" said Rickie aggressively, feeling his drink a little now. "Who is she to say Luisa can't dance—at Jakob's!"

"Did Luisa tell you we had a nice date—this week?" Teddie asked with visible pride.

"No-o. I don't see her every day, you know. A date where?"

Bang! Then a few seconds of silence. A gun?

That had come from the room behind Rickie and the partition, and he half stood up. So did others.

"Who's got the gun?" a woman's shrill voice cried.

Someone laughed, then came an explosion of anger. Curses. It was a fist fight.

"*Hugo!*" That was Ursie from the bar direction.

The tall blond Tobi appeared first, shouting and waving his arms, then Hugo, a bulky man with a long apron over his shirt and trousers—the cook—crashed his way through what was left of the dance floor, and seized one of the men under the arms. Rickie was now standing on his bench, and he could see over the partition. Two men got dragged out, thrown out.

"Fireworks tonight!" Someone yelled. Others laughed.

"Outsiders," Rickie said, settling down again. He hadn't recognized them. Drunken outsiders. Lulu had kept her calm, and Rickie passed a hand over her white head and back.

"I'm going over to ask Luisa," said Teddie, optimistic.

Across the room, Luisa watched Teddie appear through the crowd, and bow slightly.

"Good evening," he said, including the whole table. "Would you like to dance, Luisa?"

Luisa was aware, as she slid out from the bench, that Willi Biber's eyes—little pale blue eyes—bored like nail points into Teddie. Renate stared, stony-faced.

It was a fast song. Teddie took both her hands in his.

I can't believe you're *here*, Luisa wanted to say, but felt it was exactly what a stupid and unsophisticated person would say.

"National colors." Teddie nodded at her garb. "On purpose?"

Luisa was wearing a scarlet shirt and white cotton slacks.

"Did you catch it Wednesday night?" he asked.

"No!" Luisa fairly gasped. "Incredible. I was lucky."

"I wrote about us—yesterday and this morning," Teddie said.

"What do you mean 'about us'?"

"Wednesday. The nice evening. Well, for *me* it was nice. A page and a half. Sent it to the *Tages-Anzeiger*."

Luisa was alarmed. "You don't mean it's going to be *printed*?"

"Who knows?" said Teddie dreamily. "I called you J. Just the letter *J*. And what'd we do wrong?" His voice cracked and he laughed.

Nothing wrong. Just that she'd been with him at all. She was conscious of both Renate and Willi Biber staring at her and Teddie as if they were creatures from outer space, deformed humans, somehow.

"Let's go—" she began.

"Anywhere." Teddie still held one of her hands.

"Just to the bar."

Teddie forged a way for them toward the bar near the front door. Because of the crush, he didn't quite make it to the bar, but now standing people made a wall between herself and Teddie and Renate's table.

Just then Renate, out of hearing of Francesca, who was not at all interested anyway, was saying to Willi, "You see how he looks at her? Tch-h!" A shake of the head. "That pretty boy is a homo—a friend of Rickie's. You know that."

Willi nodded, and continued staring dully at the bar crowd into whose thicket the young man and Luisa had vanished.

Renate went on, "It's going to be the same story again—as with Petey, you know? Why do they do it, these boys?" Renate's usually throaty voice grew thin and shrill on that question, wailing even.

Willi Biber looked at her, surprised by the tone. His thin lips worked, then he lifted his glass of beer and drank.

"Vanity! Worse than girls!" Renate concluded with a cynical smile. "He needs a good scare, this one." She nodded toward the bar, not knowing whether Luisa and the boy were there or had gone on to the front terrace. She glanced at the apparently deaf Francesca—the place was loud—and said, "Give him a scare tonight, Willi. Follow him. Does he have a car usually?"

Willi was slow with an answer. "I think—usually."

Renate didn't one hundred percent believe Willi. She never did. That was the drawback in dealing with him, of course. "Give him a good big scare, Willi. You know how. You're bigger than this boy."

At that moment, Luisa and Teddie had secured Cokes, though not an elbow's room at the bar, so they stood each with a bottle in hand.

"Alone at last!" said Teddie, pretending to swoon. He looked at his wristwatch. "Got to be home by one. I've got the car."

"I wish it were last Wednesday night."

"Y'know," Teddie yelled over a loudmouth near him, "it's a good column, this last that I wrote."

"Maybe they'll buy it." Luisa felt on a crest of optimism, for no reason, as if everything was going to turn out well. What was everything? She didn't want to try to answer that. Teddie looked confident, and his confidence spread through her.

"I've got nearly an hour. We could take a spin—very short. I'd bring you back."

"Where is your car?" A drive would be nice, but even short, impossible. Renate would somehow know, and scream about it.

"Same place. Like Wednesday night. Want to?" He was ready to set his Coke somewhere.

Luisa shook her head.

Teddie collected himself. "Can't you just tell her you want to have a date with me now and then? You're not her prisoner."

Luisa squirmed, hating herself for squirming. "She'd somehow know. If I took a ride with you. And she saw you go to Rickie's table tonight."

"I couldn't go straight to you with *her* sitting there! Don't you think I'd have preferred to sit down by *you*?"

At that moment, Luisa, facing the main door of Jakob's, saw Willi sidling, making his way out, pushing his old hat down with one big hand on the crown, as he reached the terrace path.

Over at Rickie's table, a couple of fellows were arguing about foreign immigration into Germany, arguing not intelligently, Rickie thought, because one kept asking, "All right, but why should Germany ever have agreed to such a law? To let everybody in?" And the other: "Germany lost the war. They were in no position to . . ."

These were newcomers, Rickie didn't know their names. Claus Bruder had René on the dance floor, a willowy pair, the boy tall and thin, all arms and legs. Rickie realized he was feeling his beer a little. How inelegant, *beers*, Rickie was thinking, as the din or roar in Jakob's hit a new height.

Midnight! Firecrackers from afar! A vague roar from the assembled!

Rickie noticed that Teddie and Luisa seemed to have disappeared. Here came Andreas, and also Dorrie and Kim. They didn't care to sit, didn't want a drink.

"Your little friend's got a good-looking boyfriend," said Dorrie.

"Luisa?"

"Who else?"

Was Dorrie trying to pique him? The last time, Teddie had been his boyfriend. "No comment," said Rickie.

"Rickie, you're becoming timid!" Dorrie joked. "Won't do!" She wagged a finger. "Won't catch any fish that way!"

Rickie finished the last of his beer.

IN THE TREE-BORDERED STREET where his car stood, Teddie walked in near darkness, and reached for his keys in a trouser pocket. A couple of streets away, someone sang an unrecognizable song, gave up and laughed.

Teddie hadn't the keys quite out of his pocket when something hit him in the back, something like a big hammer, low, just above his waist. Teddie was aware of the breath knocked out of him, that he buckled, and fell forward. His arms scarcely broke his fall. His chest, then his face, struck the pavement and a tree trunk, all in a split second. Teddie gasped, getting breath back painfully. His back hurt worse; the pain spread like a fire. What had happened? He struggled against fainting, gasping through his mouth now. He could hardly lift his cheek from the tree trunk. The pain is not going to stop, he was thinking, and what if he were bleeding, inside or outside, both? He tried to call out for help, and managed something like a groan.

He heard voices. A couple of fellows. Questions.

"Hey, what's happened?"

"He's drunk, you think?"

They lifted him up clumsily, tried to set him on his feet, and Teddie let out another groan, eyes shut in pain. He was aware that he couldn't stand up by himself.

"Got hit," Teddie said. Couldn't they see that?

"Where?"

"In the back."

"Where d'you live?"

Teddie didn't think of home, he thought of Jakob's, which was nearer. He said he had friends at Jakob's, and could they help him get there?

Sure, they knew Jakob's. Then began a dragging walk, Teddie trying, till one fellow said, "Just relax." They had him under the elbows, which hurt, but not like his back. And they were going what seemed to Teddie the long way, round the block, so as they neared the lighted, noisy place, Teddie said, "Back terrace. Quicker— Thank you very much."

One young man chuckled at this. "Where're your friends? What're their names?"

"Rickie—"

"Rickie? With the dog?"

"Rickie!" said the other. "I'll get him." Seconds later he was saying to Rickie, "Hey! Got a friend of yours on the terrace! He's been hurt—somehow."

"Who?" said Rickie, getting up. "Hurt?"

"Come this way."

Rickie saw Teddie sitting limp in a chair, and three or more people around him. Teddie's cheek was dirty and scratched, oozing red. "What's *this*? Teddie! What happened? A mugger?"

Teddie managed to focus on Rickie. "No—something hit me in the back. Like a brick, I dunno." He sipped from a glass of water that someone held to his lips.

"You're bleeding—" a male voice began.

"—was just by the car," Teddie said. "It happened right by the car."

"Bleeding here," the man behind Teddie continued. "Look, can you take off that jacket?"

"I'll help him." This from a female voice.

Rickie thought: Was there perhaps a doctor at the Small g tonight? He watched as a man and a woman eased Teddie's arm out of his jacket. There was blood on Teddie's white shirt above the belt, a little blood also on the white trousers at the waist.

Teddie made a vague movement with his head. "Right, take the shirt off."

Rickie helped now. Teddie was a little more alert, and moved his arms to ease the shirt off.

The wound was three or four centimeters wide to the left of Teddie's spine, not apparently deep, made by something blunt.

"Wow! Looks like a rock did that!" one young man said.

Rickie went through the wide doorway to the dance floor. "Is there a doctor here?" he yelled. Then more loudly, "Is there a doctor here tonight?"

The dancers slowly stopped.

"Somebody's passed out!" yelled a would-be wit.

A small voice came from the left. "I am. I am a doctor," said a man of about fifty, coming toward Rickie, a bespectacled man in shirtsleeves. "What's the matter?"

"Come!" said Rickie.

The doctor peered. Teddie leaned forward, giving a yelp of pain at the bending.

"That's quite a swat," said the doctor. "Should be cleaned and bandaged. I haven't my kit here."

"I can telephone my doctor," said Rickie promptly. "I live near here. I think my doctor would come—or we go to a hospital."

"One or the other," said the doctor. "My kit's in Regensdorf. Want me to help you?"

Rickie said he knew his doctor's number by heart.

Now Ernst Koelliker had joined the group on the back terrace.

Dr. Oberdorfer's telephone gave Rickie his answering service, and Rickie cursed aloud, then a female voice interrupted: the doctor's wife? Rickie didn't care who it was, the sober voice was willing to take a message and to reach the doctor. Rickie identified himself and explained the situation.

"Please! I think it's urgent. Dr. Oberdorfer knows my address. My *home* address." Rickie gave it anyway.

It sounded as if the doctor might be able to arrive in minutes: he was at a party in Zurich, and of course he would have to pass by home to get his kit.

Back on the terrace, Rickie saw Ursie setting a cup of tea before Teddie. "*Thank* you, Ursie!"

"What happened to the boy?" she asked.

Willi, Rickie thought suddenly. Having suspected it minutes before, Willi Biber as the culprit suddenly was a fact. "Attacked," Rickie replied, frowning. "Couple of streets from here." The direction in which Willi lived too. Rickie had seen Willi leaving, seen his old hat above the throng. The time fitted.

Ursie went off, busy elsewhere. Teddie had his shirt back on, unbuttoned. He wore a thin gold chain round his neck.

"To my place!" said Rickie, giving orders now. "Let's go!"

"How far . . . a taxi! Shall I—"

"My car's *there!*" said another, pointing to the street.

Plenty of willing hands. They got Teddie upright. The boy threw his head back and shut his eyes. Two fellows, one the sturdy Ernst Koelliker, had Teddie by the elbows, lifting his feet off the ground. Philip Egli was now with them. Another man was going to walk.

Rickie hovered, seeing that Teddie was as comfortable as possible in the front seat. Rickie got in the back with Lulu on his lap. Whose car?

At Rickie's apartment house, Teddie was lifted up the front steps by a couple of fellows who kept telling him, to Rickie's annoyance, that he was going to be all right in no time.

"My bed! Here!" Rickie said, turning his own bed down.

Teddie of course had to lie prone. Someone had taken his shirt off, another wanted his trousers off, and still another said the doctor could perfectly well see the wound, couldn't he? The blood colored the white pocket under the belt, but the bleeding had all but stopped.

Rickie had barely gulped a small Chivas Regal from a glass and brought the bottle in for any who wanted it, when his doorbell rang. It was the good Dr. Oberdorfer, smiling, looking puzzled as he walked into the apartment with Rickie.

"Evening! What's happened, Herr Markwalder?"

"Come—please. Friend of mine . . ."

All made way for the doctor, who had his brown leather kit, Rickie saw. The doctor called for a clean towel and some water. Philip Egli obliged, after Rickie indicated the towel cupboard. Rickie brought water in a saucepan.

"What happened?" asked the doctor. "It's going to be a bad

bruise." His gray eyes peered up at Rickie over the top of his glasses.

"A mugger on the street!" It hadn't occurred to Rickie till now to see if Teddie still had his wallet. "Teddie didn't see the person."

Dr. Oberdorfer had washed his hands at the kitchen sink, and now he swabbed gently, cleaning the area around the injury, and Teddie winced.

". . . metal or a piece of wood," Rickie heard the doctor say in answer to someone's question.

Here came a square bandage, affixed with stripes of white adhesive. The doctor murmured an apology to Teddie for the jolt of an anti-tetanus needle in his arm. They got the boy's belt undone; the stained trousers were pulled off, then the stained slip. The doctor pulled the sheet over Teddie, added a blanket too, and proffered two pills.

"One against pain, the other to make you sleep," said the doctor, and took the glass of water that Rickie had hurried to fetch.

Teddie dropped the second pill on the sheet, picked it up and swallowed it with water, then sank the right side of his face into the pillow again. The doctor had washed the left side of his face, which bore some scratches.

Then Dr. Oberdorfer took from Rickie Teddie's name and age, twenty or twenty-one. The address?

"Just put mine for now. He lives in Zurich but I don't know his address by heart."

"If there is blood in the urine—telephone me, Mr. Markwalder."

"Got to telephone my mum," Teddie said suddenly and clearly, as if the pills had woken him up. "What time is it?"

"Thirteen minutes to two," Ernst replied.

Rickie got the telephone. "Can you say the number, Teddie? It won't reach."

"No!" cried the doctor. "You're not to sit up just now, you'll start the bleeding again!"

Rickie suddenly remembered the telephone lead near his bed, unplugged the cord in the living room and brought it in. He had removed the cord months ago from his bedroom, because the phone near his bed reminded him too much of talking with Petey. Rickie dialed carefully from Teddie's dictation.

"May I talk first?" asked Rickie, firmly.

Teddie's mother sounded shrill and anxious.

"Frau Stevenson—Rickie Markwalder. Your son is late, but he is quite all right and—"

"And the car too," said Teddie into the sheet. "Give it to me."

Rickie did.

"Hello, Mum . . . Well, a—somebody swatted me in the back. You know, August the first . . . I am *not*—not much hurt . . . No, Mum, it's not serious, but it's better if I stay where I am tonight . . . Yes, we got a doctor, Rickie's doctor."

Dr. Oberdorfer was making signs that Teddie should conclude his conversation. *Peace, calm!* his spread hands said.

"He just put a little bandage on . . . Mum, I wasn't even in the car."

The doctor took the telephone, to Rickie's relief. He said the boy had an abrasion on his back, but it was not deep, more a bruise. Exchange of names and addresses. The doctor wrote, and assured Frau Stevenson that he would see her son tomorrow and report.

Meanwhile, Rickie had started heating water for coffee. The doctor declined coffee.

Teddie, with eyes shut now, might have been asleep.

"I'm off, Herr Markwalder," the doctor said. "Two pills by the lamp there. Anti-pain. He may wake up with pain in a couple of hours. Four-hour interval between each of those pills."

Then the doctor was gone.

14

They had all drifted into the living room with the doctor. There was silence for a few seconds, then Ernst looked at Rickie, smiling, and said, "Wasn't it lucky that—"

"Rickie! Jesus, man! What a crazy *night*!"

"The doctor gave him *two* needles, didn't he?"

Laughter. "A rough neighborhood . . ."

Rickie said authoritatively, "Sh-h! Everybody! Who can sleep with all this? Sh-h!"

One man took his leave. No one wanted coffee except Rickie and Philip.

Rickie said to Ernst, "The night is young! What do you say two or three of us call on Willi Biber? Wish him a happy August the first?" Rickie gave a deep chuckle. Just what *was* Willi doing now?

"Where does he live? I'm game." This from Ernst.

"Behind that teashop. What's it called?"

"Milady's Piss!" cried someone in falsetto, maybe Philip Egli, because he was grinning, lifting his coffee cup.

"*Someone* hit—Teddie. We can just ask Willi about it. No?" asked Rickie.

"Yes," replied Ernst, as if Rickie's proposal showed absolute logic. "I'm with you, Rick!"

"So—" This left Philip. "Philip, you stay, will you? Because of Teddie. Snooze here on the sofa if—"

"Oh sure, Rickie," said Philip. "I can stay. How long you going to be—about?"

"Oh-h, an hour. Less maybe. And if—maybe you heard the doctor—any blood in Teddie's urine, I'm to tell the doctor. So tell Teddie if he wakes up."

"Right," said Philip.

Philip might snooze, read something, but he could be trusted. So thought Rickie as he found himself out on the pavement walking rather briskly with Ernst toward Jakob's, which still had a lot of lights on, but was slowly closing, Rickie could feel in the atmosphere. The front terrace's tables were all empty, though a few people stood at the bar. Rickie thought of looking in for Willi, and decided not to: Willi was never out this late.

"You know how to find this place, Rickie?"

"I know where the tearoom is. Willi works there. Not with teapots."

Ernst grinned. "So we wake the tearoom people up?"

"We've got to ask them—exactly where he lives. Maybe right there."

L'Eclair—this was the tearoom's name—was dark, and its glass door far from any visible dwelling. Rickie knocked with increasing loudness, and ended his efforts with a kick.

Ernst laughed nervously. "They'll love us!"

Rickie repeated the knocking and with a "Hello-o?" instead of a kick.

At last a woman's voice asked from a dark first-floor window, "Who is there?"

"Markwalder," said Rickie soberly, as if he were a police officer. "I have a question to ask, Madame, and I am sorry to disturb you. Can you tell me where Willi lives? Willi Biber?"

"He—has he done something wrong?"

"No, Madame! Just a question or two—to ask him."

"I am not responsible for Willi, you know. It's the little passage to your left, then second door on your right—in the wall there."

There were two steps down into the dark alley, and both nearly fell.

"Shoulda brought a torch," Ernst murmured.

Rickie had a cigarette lighter. The alley was narrow, and the next obstacle would have been two dustbins which took half its width. Rickie saw the second door, and lit his lighter once more. To the left of the door was a single dark window, closed and dusty-looking.

"Willi–i? Happy first of August! Open up!" said Rickie, trying the friendly tone first, sure that Willi wouldn't recognize his voice.

"Willi–i?" Ernst called.

Silence.

Rickie tried knocking with his fist. He could see better now and was not using his lighter.

"Who's there?" Willi's voice asked, somewhat shrill.

"Open *up!*" Rickie now gave the lower door panel a hard kick and he heard it crack.

"Hey!" Willi yelled.

Rickie grabbed the knob and put his shoulder to it. The door only creaked.

Ernst took a dustbin lid and charged the door.

The door made a snapping sound and opened. They were again in darkness, and the lighter came into service. There was a door to the left, which moved and shut even as they watched. This door had no lock, it seemed, and Rickie simply shoved it open.

"Put the light on, Willi!" Rickie said. Again he used the lighter, had a glimpse of Willi hunched and wide-eyed like a mad figure in a Munch painting, a lamp by an untidy bed. "The light, put it on!"

Willi did.

The room had a look of being a hundred years old, Rickie thought. The lamp had a crumbling beige shade, the carpet had been worn to something like burlap, and the armchair oozed its upholstery. The place stank of sweat and dust. Skinny Willi stood trembling in short underpants and an indescribable shirt.

"You hit a boy tonight, didn't you, Willi?" asked Rickie, holding his right fist at the ready. "The boy in the blue jacket? You waited by his car, Willi?"

"You can't come in like this—break my door in, you homos! Faggots! I'll tell my landlady!"

Rickie gave a laugh. "What did you hit him with, Willi? Big piece of wood? Piece of metal?"

"He's not dead! Why're you—get *out*! Out of m-m-my house!"

Ernst, fists clenched, watched both of them. "Rickie, the land-lady—she just might phone the police, y'know?" He spoke quickly, softly.

"Is Renate giving you orders, Willi? You take orders from her? And money—a little money?"

"A little," Willi echoed, as if to beg off with this.

"Rickie," said Ernst, "let's take off—while we can."

Rickie moved his fist, not intending to hit, and Willi flinched, stumbled backward onto the sagging single bed.

"You admit you *hit* him," Rickie said.

"*Ja.*" Then seconds later, "*Nein!—nein!*"

Ernst moved to the door, and Rickie reluctantly followed.

"See you again soon, Willi," Rickie said.

The alley was silent. Rickie remembered the two steps and so did Ernst. They headed for home, Rickie's place. Again the cozy glow of the Small g, a smaller glow but still there. Now Rickie didn't want a nip of anything, though he knew Ursie or Andy would've obliged. Rickie felt odd, quite strong, though just then he staggered, and Ernst caught him.

"You heard him, eh, Ernst? He's our man! *Willi!*"

They both heard a police car's siren then. It sounded far away. Then it was behind them in the direction of the tearoom.

They were home.

Philip awoke from a sleep on the sofa.

"How's Teddie?" asked Rickie.

"Still asleep." Philip spoke softly, looking half asleep himself. "His mother phoned—said she wanted to make sure she had the phone number and address right. What did you find out—just now?"

"Shitty Willi—he confessed! Didn't he, Ernst?" Rickie looked at Ernst in triumph. "Says he takes 'a little bit' of money from Renate Hagnauer."

"Gotta wash, Rickie. Look!" Ernst held out his palms which were as black as if he had been handling coal.

So were his own, Rickie saw. He peeked into his bedroom, and saw the boy lying as before, face to the wall. A dim bedlight stood on a nearby table. "Did he pee?" Rickie whispered.

Philip shook his head.

Ernst washed at the sink, and so did Rickie. Someone had turned the electric burner on under the kettle.

"Got any cheese, Rickie? Or cake?" Ernst asked.

"Both!" said Rickie proudly.

Ernst helped with coffee mugs, Philip with the rest. All went on the coffee table.

"So Rickie, what're you going to do about this Willi nut? He is a nut, isn't he? The one who came to my place the night of the party, isn't he?"

"Yes. I'll tell the *police*," said Rickie, sure of himself. "Let the police handle it. And tomorrow when it's light—"

"Hear that?" Ernst nodded toward the window.

They all heard a faint police siren.

"Maybe I should skip while I can," Ernst said, setting his coffee mug down.

Rickie knew: the police knew his name, not Ernst's, from Willi's landlady.

Ernst turned at the door. "No. I'll stay, Rickie—if they're coming."

"What happened at Willi's?" Philip asked.

"We broke his door in," Rickie replied.

The police car had audibly stopped at the curb. Rickie glanced nervously at his watch. It was just after four now.

His bell rang. Rickie smoothed his hair, pulled in his bulging waist, glanced at the living room.

"*We* look respectable!" Philip said solemnly, meaning all of them, imbibing coffee.

At the front door, the police identified themselves; Rickie confirmed his identity.

The outcome of all this went through Rickie's mind as he led the two officers to his apartment door. He'd get a fine for breaking a door down, and he'd pay it. Had he even touched the bastard who'd hit Teddie? No!

Rickie entered his flat, followed by the officers, who barely nodded at Ernst and Philip.

". . . at Leckler tearoom about an hour ago . . ."

Rickie calmly admitted everything: he had been noisy, knocking, he had broken a door in.

"Two doors."

"All right—I wanted to speak with Willi Biber. I don't think he was going to let me in."

"You were with another man, Frau Wenger says."

"I was with my friend," Ernst said, and gave his name and address to the police.

"But I'll take responsibility," Rickie said to the two cops, one writing, one staring.

"You may be responsible for the damage, Herr Markwalder, and for—menacing this Willi—Biber. You'll probably have to appear before a magistrate for that."

Rickie frowned. "Menacing?"

"He said you knocked him backward—hit him. He fell on his bed, he said."

"I was *there*," Ernst put in. "My friend didn't touch him. He fell backward all by himself. Why don't you ask why we wanted to see him? Because he attacked—"

"Ernst—" Rickie felt suddenly protective of Teddie, and had no confidence that the police here could grasp Willi's motivation.

"Attacked?" asked the officer.

"Well, show them, Rickie!" Ernst gestured toward the bedroom, whose door was partly open. "If you don't explain—"

"All right. Have a look. There is a young man here—we had a doctor." Rickie hated it.

Ernst beckoned, and the officers followed him into the bedroom where Teddie slept. Ernst pulled the sheet down to Teddie's waist.

The officers looked impressed.

"I shall mention this assault"—Rickie indicated the bedroom—"when I speak to the magistrate."

"You say this Willi hit the boy?" asked the officer.

"No. But we have reasons to think he did. Thank you, gentlemen," in a tone of dismissal.

The cops smiled vaguely, shifted. They looked warm in the face, warm all over. With caps off for coolness, they still sweated. The night had brought little improvement in the temperature.

"Keep this." One officer tore a page from his notebook, a carbon of something. "Are you going to be here in the next days? At home?"

"Oh yes. And I work just down the street. I have a studio. I'm in the telephone book, of course."

Gone they were.

"I'm bushed," said Ernst. "I think I'll phone for a taxi, Rickie."

A low groan came from the bedroom, then, "Ow!"

Rickie went in, followed by Philip.

"You're not to sit up, Teddie. Remember? There's a pill here, if it hurts."

"Hurts! Ch-rist!" Teddie gently lay down again. "Gotta—pee."

Rickie had thought of that. "One second!" He went to a kitchen cabinet and returned with a liter Italian wine bottle. "Can you manage with this, Teddie?"

Painfully, eyes shut, Teddie managed. "Thanks, Rickie."

Rickie took the bottle. Clear, he thought, but in the bathroom, he held it to the light, before he poured it out and flushed it. Clear.

Teddie was awake, and Rickie persuaded him without much trouble to take one of the anti-pain pills.

Ernst was just hanging up the telephone. He said he would wait for the taxi outside. "Good luck, Rickie, and I'll be in touch."

Philip said he would stay a while. "I'll grab a nap in the chair. You take the sofa." He turned out the one lamp, because there was light enough. "Don't argue. I had some sleep on that sofa, you know?"

Rickie didn't argue. He took off his trousers, with a mumbled, "'Scuse me," to Philip, folded them over a chair back, and lay down on the sofa. He was aware that Philip brought a mug and set it on the coffee table announcing, "Water."

15

Rickie opened his front door the next morning to a trim, dark-haired woman of about forty, in raspberry-colored linen slacks, sandals, and a woman of about the same age with fluffed-out pale reddish hair, who Frau Stevenson said was Jessica somebody.

"A pleasure," Rickie replied.

"I'm sorry to be early," Frau Stevenson said to Rickie, "but Jessica arrived so soon, ready to bring me."

"Perfectly all right. My apartment is this way, please."

More introductions to Philip, but brief indeed, as Rickie said at once, "Teddie's expecting you."

"Teddie!" cried his mother, who bore a startling resemblance to Teddie, Rickie thought, or vice versa. "Well, you're eating! Now what hit you?"

Both women were in the room, staring at Teddie and at the

bandage which was nearly fifteen centimeters square on Teddie's back. Propped on his right elbow, Teddie had been eating with fork in left hand.

"Since it was behind me, Mum, I couldn't see." Naked now, Teddie was careful to keep the sheet pulled up to his waist.

"Any stitches?" asked Jessica.

"No stitches, eh, Rickie?"

"No. It's a bad bruise—that broke the skin. My doctor put that bandage on last night. I know he intends to see Teddie today."

"And you were right by the car at the time, Teddie," said his mother.

"Walking, Mum, ready to open the door. It was dark. Then a wallop and I fell forward. I think I was knocked out for a minute."

Frau Stevenson shook her head and looked at Rickie, then at her friend Jessica. "As I said, I don't care for this neighborhood. Is the doctor coming at a certain time, Herr M—"

"Markwalder. No-o, Madame, I am supposed to telephone him—about now, in fact. Maybe you would—"

The doorbell again.

Rickie repressed a curse, said, "Excuse me," and went. He overheard Frau Stevenson asking Teddie or Philip, "Do the police know anything about this?"

Luisa stood at the front door. "Hello, Rickie. How is Teddie?"

"Better." Rickie held the door open for her. "He's eating breakfast."

"Ursie told us this morning. I was just there with Renate, you know." Luisa had come into the front hall. "Is it a stab?" she asked softly.

She was thinking of Petey, Rickie supposed. They moved toward his apartment. "No. Something blunt. But it broke the skin."

"And Willi," she whispered. "What happened? I'd rather hear it from you."

"I went over to see him—with Ernst." Rickie had his apartment doorknob in his hand, the door closed.

"You broke his door in, Ursie said."

"Well, yes. I don't think he was going to open it."

"And beat him up," she whispered, looking pleased at the idea.

"We didn't touch him, I swear, Luisa! Teddie's mother's here now. She wants to take him home."

"Oh!" Luisa was suddenly tense. "But maybe I could say hello to him?"

"I would think so," said Rickie, opening the door. They went into the living room. "Philip, Luisa's here."

"Hello, Philip," Luisa said.

"Philip, can you be a darling and take Lulu out? Her lead is on the chair there."

"Sure thing, Rickie."

"Lulu—go with Philip. Be a good girl." Rickie went to the bedroom door which was ajar. He knocked.

Teddie's mother had laid clean white trousers over a chair. Now she was looking at Teddie's pale blue jacket which she held in both hands.

"Look at this. This should—" Frau Stevenson stopped on seeing Luisa with Rickie.

"Frau Stevenson—Luisa Zimmermann," said Rickie.

"Hi, Luisa!" This from Teddie, who had turned himself in order to see her. "Can hardly move, sorry!"

"How do you do, Frau Stevenson," said Luisa.

"The girl I was telling you about, Mum," said Teddie.

"Yes, Teddie. How do you do, Luisa? Herr Markwalder, I suppose you saw this?" She indicated the L-shaped tear in the pale blue cloth.

Around the rent was a grayish smudge from some dirty object, that was plain. The sight of it pained Rickie. "Last night we were so busy taking care of Teddie—" He felt that Frau Stevenson was playing the detective, discovering things he hadn't.

Rickie went to the telephone, now atop a chest of drawers, and dialed his doctor's home number. His wife answered, not the machine, for which Rickie was grateful. He identified himself. "I was expecting the doctor this morning. Can he—"

"He's not here, but he did say he was calling at your house this morning."

Rickie put the phone down, reassured, and announced to the room that the doctor would be looking in before noon.

"Rickie," said Teddie.

Rickie came closer. Teddie wanted to whisper. Rickie guessed what it was about before Teddie had the words out, and Rickie made his second announcement, "Since Teddie cannot walk to the toilet, I must bring—something—"

The room smoothly cleared of the three ladies, like a ballet, it seemed to Rickie. Having handed Teddie the liter bottle, which had been on the floor near the night table, Rickie strolled toward the door, and closed it.

Seconds later, Teddie said, "OK, Rickie. Many thanks. Sorry."

By a door on to the hall, Rickie was able to reach the bathroom unseen. Still no blood, he saw. He returned with the clean bottle.

"I swear, Rickie, the idea of walking—" Teddie eased himself flat again, cheek against the pillow.

Rickie could tell from the voices in the living room that the good doctor had arrived. "I can get some more pills for you now, Teddie. Doctor's here." Rickie went out.

The doctor greeted Rickie, on his way to the bedroom. "How is the urine?"

"No blood. Otherwise I'd have telephoned."

A painkiller first, Rickie saw to that. Dr. Oberdorfer had a cheerful air: yes, it was painful, but it was going to get better every day now. Today would be the worst day. Frau Stevenson and Jessica had come into the bedroom, while the others remained in the living room.

The bandage was gently peeled back, and Teddie winced a couple of times.

His mother gasped.

Both the pink border and the red center had darkened, so the whole looked like a surrealist flower, maybe a kind of poppy. Dr. Oberdorfer put white powder on the wound and a new bandage which he taped in place.

Frau Stevenson talked with the doctor. Of course her son could go home today, but the trip in the car would be painful, the doctor said, and the boy was comfortable here.

"I'm free all day today," Rickie put in. He saw Frau Stevenson eyeing a blown-up photograph of Petey Ritter smiling, near a palm tree, and Rickie knew what she was thinking.

A compromise was arrived at: Frau Stevenson would go home soon, with the car, and return around 7 P.M. for Teddie. That would give Teddie all day to rest.

Frau Stevenson carried Teddie's trousers of last night, plus his shirt. "Get some rest, dear, and as for food—"

"Oh, there's a restaurant nearby," Rickie put in. "I can fetch something—*anything*. Teddie can just give me his order."

"Teddie—the street where the car is—" said his mother.

"Yes, Mum." Teddie explained, and Rickie listened.

Wasn't that Feldenstrasse? Luisa confirmed that it was, and she was quite sure, when Teddie said the car was in the same place as where she had once met him. Rickie said he would like to accompany Frau Stevenson, if he might, as he wanted to see what might be lying around by way of a weapon.

"Herr Markwalder—I'm off!" said Dr. Oberdorfer. "Four more pills there in a little container, four-hour intervals, don't forget. That ought to see him over the worst. Good day, everyone!" He turned back and said to Rickie, "I'll phone you. Maybe tomorrow or the next day. Something to say to you." Neutral yet foreboding. He was gone.

A pang had gone through Rickie. *What* kind of news? He could have told him any good news now, out in the front hall.

Frau Stevenson calmly and seriously asked, "Do you know

what the police are going to do—for instance? Anything? I can
speak with them."

Rickie took a breath, hesitated as he looked at the woman's
dark eyes that were disconcertingly like Teddie's. He went ahead.
"The first thing, they're going to come at me again for breaking
in somebody's door last night. With a friend. In fact the police
were here last night."

"Whose door?"

Luisa was listening.

"Someone I suspect. You see—" Rickie glanced at the ceiling,
feeling for words. "Since I didn't see what happened—it's wisest if
I don't say any more just now." He glanced at Luisa, who kept
silent.

Rickie appreciated that. That was neighborly solidarity.

Jessica was to drive Frau Stevenson to her car, and offered to
take Rickie. Luisa asked if she might come, but modestly said she
could walk, if she made a crowd. Smiling, Jessica told her the car
was quite large enough.

Philip was to stay with Teddie.

16

They got into a comfortable dark red BMW belonging to Jessica, and rolled toward Jakob's. Rickie hesitated, then said,
"This corner place—Jakob's—is our local Biergarten and restaurant, where Teddie was last night."

"I see," said Frau Stevenson noncommittally, glancing.

"Now make a left, please," said Rickie, "and it's three streets
farther."

And after another left, they saw the Audi. They found a parking place half a street away, and walked back. Now Luisa showed a

curiosity that made her the lead figure in the walk back to the Stevenson car.

All of them were looking, in the gutter, at the ground round the big trees.

"Must've been here," Rickie said, pointing at the base of a tree trunk near the car door. "Teddie said his face hit a tree trunk." Rickie looked also for drops of blood, but saw none. The weapon is the most important, he told himself.

Luisa was a little distance away, looking into the gutter as she walked. Rickie did the same on the other side of the car, walking in the direction of Willi's home. Nothing, merely a few leaves and pebbles. When he looked back, Luisa was walking toward him with her eyes on the low garden walls, the front paths. She picked up a loose brick from a wall top, and put it down again.

Now Luisa was past the car, beside which the two women were standing, talking. Suddenly, in a front path she saw a metal piece not a meter long, yellow, and somewhat rusted. At one end of it was a broken fixture, dangling. Luisa picked it up, instantly thought of fingerprints, and it was too late.

"Rickie?" Luisa held the thing in her hands. It weighed at least a kilo.

Frau Stevenson was watching also. "Where'd you find that?"

"Just—a couple of meters back. On a front path."

Rickie recognized a piece of tripod. It could certainly be used as a ramming object. He took it from Luisa. A handy weight. "It's a possibility—isn't it?"

All agreed. Yes.

Luisa went on looking at front paths, behind pavement walls, oblivious of a woman at a lower window who watched her, curious.

Frau Stevenson looked at the tripod piece with a slight frown. "I can keep it safely, you can be sure."

Rickie put it into her extended hands. Still she was able to hold it in one hand and unlock the car, declining Rickie's assistance. Luisa said she lived near by, and would walk home.

"And where's the house where you broke the door in?"

"That way," said Rickie, pointing in the direction her car was facing. "You can't see it from here." He recalled Frau Stevenson taking Teddie's wallet from his inside jacket pocket this morning, pulling notes halfway out, pushing them back. Willi wouldn't have bothered trying to rob, Rickie thought, he'd have been more concerned to quit the scene at once.

"I'm glad to have met you, Luisa," Frau Stevenson said.

Polite good-byes, then Rickie walked with Luisa toward her house.

"Was Willi Biber in Jakob's this morning?"

"No," Luisa said. "At least I didn't see him."

"And Renate—how's she acting?"

"What do you mean?"

"As if it's all news to her?"

Luisa understood. It was a horrible thought, but Luisa had thought it this morning—before she had heard about Willi's door—that Renate could have persuaded Willi to hit Teddie. "Well, yes."

They were approaching the front path of the house where Renate and Luisa lived. They both glanced up at the same time.

Rickie knew the girl had to go back, climb the stairs to Renate's establishment. He felt angered, felt like cursing. "I would bet you that if Renate didn't get Willi to do this—she'll convince him he did it." Rickie had lowered his voice to almost a whisper. "Keep in touch with me. You understand?"

Luisa knew. Rickie wanted to know how Renate behaved, and what she was saying. "I know. At the moment, she's just saying what a tough crowd you associate with. Of course she's saying you were drunk last night. Got to leave, Rickie. Can I phone you later? Maybe I can even come by."

"But of course."

They parted. Rickie walked on to Jakob's.

Almost one o'clock now. The lunch crowd would be in full

swing. Ursie's cook Hugo made a fine goulash on Sundays. Rickie entered by the main door.

Ursie was behind the bar, looking a little tired around the eyes. "Hello, Rickie! And how is your friend?"

Rickie edged closer to the bar, set both shirtsleeved elbows on it, briefly, as if to claim territory. "Improving," he replied. "Can I have a nice beer, Ursie please, with a head on it? Now—how is the goulash today?"

"Oh, excellent, but not so much of it because it is hot today. We have cold lobster salad—"

"Can you give me three portions of goulash to take out?" Rickie felt ravenous. "And with the little noodles, I hope?"

Rickie was thinking that he ought to telephone Freddie Schimmelmann, who might be of help, though Aussersihl was not Freddie's territory. What would they soak him for shitty Willi's door plus the "misdemeanor" itself? Screw them! Rickie didn't care what it cost. And the idea of comparing a damaged door to what had happened to Teddie! A kidney blow could have put the boy in hospital. By the time he had finished the beer, a big opaque plastic sack had arrived: lunch. Rickie left thirty francs in notes on the wooden bar.

"Thank you, Ursie dear! Greetings to Andreas!"

"His day off!" Ursie grinned. "'Bye, Rickie!"

Rickie exited by the back terrace, which was quicker to his house, and acknowledged a couple of greetings, friendly as ever.

At his house, Rickie used the front door key, and enjoyed knocking at his apartment door, knowing people were there.

"Stuff!" Rickie said, handing Philip the plastic sack. "Good goulash. Can you heat it up, Philip, while I take a fast shower? And how is the patient?"

Philip's face brightened. He wore the same shirt and trousers, but looked as if he'd just showered and washed his hair. "Got his underpants on. And I gave him a wet towel to swab down with—you'll see."

Teddie was up on one elbow in bed, looking happier, and said he'd made it to the bathroom and back.

"Good." Philip had laid one of his cotton dressing gowns on the bed, Rickie saw. "Hope you're hungry, because I have brought lunch."

Under the shower, Rickie let cool water run on his head, then washed his hair and himself in warmer, then cool water again. He chose different trousers and a shirt from a cupboard in the hall.

"Philip—you are a gem! Marry me," said Rickie, gazing at the table Philip had set with glasses and yellow napkins in the dining area. A mouthwatering smell of goulash came faintly from the kitchen. "Three places?"

Teddie made a try, and had to admit that he wouldn't be able to sit up for long as yet.

Rickie put up a bridge table in the bedroom, so they would eat in company. Teddie was served a tray, and could stay in bed. Beer, even for Teddie. The meat was so tender, it did not require a knife.

"I have made the acquaintance of a cop," Rickie said to Philip.

Philip chuckled. "Just tell me something new, Rickie. Where? How?"

"Hm-m—rather not say. He may be just traffic department, but—well, I intend to give him a call this afternoon. Tell him about this. He's friendly."

Philip's blue eyes showed interest. "Won't do any harm, I suppose. If he's a friend."

A friend. Could the affably smiling Freddie be a real friend? Rickie decided to sound him out, but to be cautious. "How are you doing with your left hand, Teddie?"

"OK. Getting used to it. But maybe that's about enough," he said, laying his fork on the plate, sinking slowly on to the sheet.

Rickie got up. "I'll relieve you of the plate. Ursie gave us some coleslaw—a free extra, I'm sure. Would you like some?"

"Maybe later, thanks."

Philip accepted coleslaw. "Rickie, I'll be shoving off soon. You can manage alone till seven, no?" Philip's smile had just a hint of mischief.

"I'm pretty sure. I intend to sleep—like a stone—on the sofa."

The telephone rang.

"I forgot to say Ernst phoned to ask how things were," Philip said. "Maybe that's him again."

It was Frau Stevenson. Rickie informed her that Teddie was looking better, and would she like to talk to him?

Rickie and Philip went into the living room to give the boy some privacy.

"Did you learn anything at Jakob's?" Philip asked. "I mean about Willi?"

"No—several people seem to know I kicked his door in. Oh, and Luisa found"—he moved toward the window, farther from the bedroom—"what might have hit Teddie. It's a piece of metal." Rickie indicated its length. "Looks like from a camera tripod. Luisa found it in the front path of a house. Teddie's mum took it with her."

"So any fingerprints are gone."

"True, but if you saw this thing, partly rusted. Not the shape to keep any fingerprints." Or was he right, since there was always something new in detection technique? "It could have been the weapon, anyway."

"Interesting," Philip said. Then with a smile, "Show it to Willi." He collected his sweater and a serious-looking, thin school notebook which he had hung on to last night. "I wonder how you'll ever prove anything. It's almost an advantage if Willi's a nut, you know. Advantage for Willi."

"I know."

Philip took off. Rickie, in pajamas, had arranged the TV so Teddie could watch it in the bedroom, and was about to set his alarm clock for a quarter to seven, when the telephone rang. It was Luisa.

"Can't talk long," she said. "Is it possible to talk with Teddie?"

Of course. Teddie was already aware that the caller was Luisa. Rickie continued his tidying up from lunch. In the kitchen, he heard Teddie say, "Well! Hey, Rickie!"

Rickie went to the bedroom door. Luisa had suddenly had to hang up, Teddie said, because Renate had come from somewhere.

"Imagine! She won't let Luisa out of the house, because she knows I'm here."

"Nothing new. Another pill, Teddie? Against the pain?"

17

The alarm awakened Rickie from a heavy sleep. Frau Stevenson, he recalled. And he hadn't rung Freddie Schimmelmann yet. He peeked into the bedroom and saw Teddie lying face down, chin on folded arms, watching TV.

"Got to dress, Teddie."

"I know. Could you maybe hand me my trousers, please, Rickie?"

Rickie did. The day was still warm, breezeless, though the windows were open top and bottom. He took a fresh hand towel and brought it, damp with cold water, to Teddie. "Can you use this?"

Teddie groaned appreciation. "Thanks. Just what I need." Grimacing, Teddie rubbed the back of his neck, started to drag a foot up and dropped the idea. He washed his chest and a thigh.

"I'll do it," said Rickie, took the towel and rubbed the boy's feet quickly.

"Do you know where my sneakers are, Rickie?"

Not sneakers but black leather shoes. Rickie got them from his cupboard. "Never mind socks. I'll get your shoes on after you—"

The doorbell rang.

Florence Stevenson. She said her name. There was a man with her whom she introduced as David somebody, about her own age.

"I think the patient is feeling better," Rickie said.

She carried a blue shirt over one arm. "We'll manage," she said over her shoulder, with a slight smile, as if to dismiss him.

So the David somebody helped Teddie get dressed.

"OK, but slowly, please. *Ow!*" from Teddie. "OK, *I'll* make it."

A chiding murmur from his mum, and something unintelligible from David. Was David Frau Stevenson's boyfriend, lover? And who gave a damn? He watched Frau Stevenson and David—a slender type with blondish hair and rimless glasses—partly supporting Teddie by the elbows, one on each side. Rickie was ready to help, but it appeared he was not necessary. Teddie seemed to know David well.

"Rickie's been very good to me, Mum. So was his friend—Philip."

Frau Stevenson seemed to force a smile. "I do thank you, Herr Mark—"

"Markwalder."

Her smiled warmed. "I have a little trouble with that name, I don't know why. I realize you've been very kind to my son. I do thank you."

Rickie made a gesture. "Only natural! It happened in my neighborhood—I'm sorry to say."

Teddie, supported, shifted gently from one foot to the other.

"May I ask—have you learned anything from the police today?" David said.

"No." The household had been rather busy with Teddie, Rickie felt like saying. "Two officers were here around four in the morning, as I told Frau Stevenson, but that was because I broke in a door near here."

"Ah yes. The door of someone you suspect, you said this morning," Frau Stevenson put in.

"What's his name?" asked David.

"Willi Biber. But I have little to go on." Rickie spoke reluctantly. "It's more of a guess on my part."

"You should see this Willi, Mum," Teddie said. "He's *weird* to look at."

"When you mentioned a suspect—I thought you would talk to the police," said Frau Stevenson. "Would you like us to do it?"

Rickie tried to think. Would the police act if Frau Stevenson told them someone suspected Willi Biber of assault and battery? "I think Willi should be questioned, shown that piece of tripod that you have."

"Can you give us his address?" asked David.

"We can get that by telephone," said Frau Stevenson. "I'd like to get home soon."

"The fact is," Rickie pushed on, "I didn't *see* Willi doing anything wrong."

Frau Stevenson looked at her friend. "I think we should talk to the police, David. Don't you?"

David murmured something. They were moving.

"I'll come out with you." With housekeys in pocket, Rickie came with them out to the brown Audi. Teddie was taking ever longer steps. Frau Stevenson unlocked the car and opened a back door. Teddie's forehead glistened, and he was biting his underlip.

"Other side's easier, Mum. I have to lie on my right side—sort of."

Rickie held open the door on the other side, finally had to grip Teddie's left hand for his painful slide onto the back seat.

"Ow! Oh boy!" Teddie said miserably.

It was Frau Stevenson who wanted the boy moved home, Rickie was thinking. Finally, after more smiles and thanks, the car rolled off.

Rickie went back to his flat, closed the door, and felt a huge emptiness, an aloneness that was familiar. He put his hands over his face, his eyes for a moment, but the darkness did not change the emptiness, the rude shock of the rumpled white sheets on the bed.

Try Freddie, Rickie told himself. What was he getting into? Always dangerous, police. Might seem to be friendly, and then— He moved to get Freddie's card, now in a little box with at least ten others on Rickie's writing table. *Your work*, an inner voice said. Next assignment—that dry-skin job. Could yet another dry-skin softener be hitting the market? Well, yes. Rickie stared at the telephone, and the image of David's slender waist came to him, encircled by a brown alligator belt. Fitness. Money. Skiing and swimming in season, and a fat-free diet. Of course. He could keep up with that lifestyle, Rickie told himself, food and dress department, he just didn't want to.

Lulu stood up and licked his hand quickly, whimpering.

"I know, my angel, you are right! Just one quick phone call first."

Rickie dialed.

A woman answered, to Rickie's shock, then he remembered: Freddie was married. "Freddie's out just now, but he ought to be back in less than half an hour. Can I—"

"I'll phone again then. Thank you."

Rickie took Lulu out.

When he rang again, Freddie was home, and sounded surprised and happy that the caller was Rickie.

"Got a problem," Rickie said. "Are you alone—sort of?"

Freddie said he would close a door.

Rickie told about Teddie being brought back wounded, supported by two strangers last night at Jakob's. And Willi's smashed door. "Willi needs a goddamn scare—the right cops. Or cop," Rickie finished.

"You *sure* about Willi? He did it?"

"N-not a hundred percent sure—just almost. There are other things too. Facts, I mean. That I *know*. I was wondering, can I see you this evening?"

Freddie was going to have a snack with his wife now, then he could come to Ricki's place by about nine.

That suited Rickie. He asked Freddie to bring his workpad or notepad. "What you give tickets with. Looks authentic. We might visit somebody tonight."

As soon as he had hung up, Rickie thought of his next duty: ring Dr. Oberdorfer. What was it the doctor wanted to tell him? Something worse in regard to the unmentionable? Something new? Tomorrow.

Rickie's doorbell rang at a quarter past nine. The smiling Freddie Schimmelmann in civvies stood at his door with his curiously crinkly eyes, his shy yet confident manner. Freddie's pad was a big lump that partly projected from a back pocket of his black cotton trousers.

"Heineken's or Hopfenperle?" asked Rickie.

Hopfenperle. Over their beer at the dining table, Rickie enlightened Freddie about Renate's attitude toward Teddie, and her control of Willi Biber.

I think if Willi didn't hit Teddie, Renate could persuade him he did—and if he did, she could convince him he didn't."

"What's the matter with the guy?"

"You've heard of morons. Mentally challenged, maybe that's nicer."

"And you're hung up on Teddie."

Rickie squirmed, happy. "Not really hung up. He's a nice boy. Likes me quite well, I think."

"And he's in love with Luisa. Rickie, you're asking for trouble!"

"And not getting any!" Rickie laughed.

Finished with his beer, Freddie strolled around the big living room, hands in trouser pockets. "Who's this again? The pretty blond?"

Rickie took a breath. "That's Petey Ritter. I—" Rickie had told Freddie how Petey died, because Freddie had asked about the

photos the first evening he had come to the house. "There's something else I might tell you," he said, then he told Freddie Renate's
story—that a pickup of Petey had stabbed Petey here in Rickie's
bedroom.

Freddie took this in solemnly. It was the first time Rickie had
seen Freddie frown, as if he had a problem he couldn't deal with.

"Well, let's take off."

"Where're we going?"

"Up to Jakob's, I thought. The Small g. By the way, got your
identification card with you? Police?"

Freddie nodded. "Yup. Why?"

"Because I thought I'd introduce you—as a friend. Unless you
have any objection. My friend in the police force."

Freddie pondered. "No. I suppose that's OK. OK, Rickie!"

As they neared Jakob's, Rickie heard an organ-grinder's music.
Yes, there he was, visible now through some trees and bushes, near
Jakob's back terrace.

"Organ-grinder! Most exceptional, Freddie!" It was an exceptional day all round, however, Rickie thought as he reached for some
change. "The Blue Danube." How corny could you get? Rickie
chose a five-franc piece, a heavy coin. "No monkey?" Rickie said,
dropping it into a tin pie plate.

Freddie contributed too.

"Thank y', sir! *Schö'n Sonntag!*"

They went in, Rickie with the intention of standing at the
bar. Did Freddie look like a cop? Not today, with a brown cotton
jacket, no cap.

"Rickie! Back again? How was the goulash?" asked Ursie
behind the bar.

"Ursie—superb! And you're going to drop dead one of these
days if you don't get more sleep."

Ursie gave a laugh, as if he'd said something funny. "What will
the gentlemen have?"

"I—a small beer, please. Freddie?"

"Same."

Before Ursie moved away to the taps, Rickie said, "I'd like to introduce my police officer friend—Freddie Schimmelmann. Ursie—queen and guiding spirit of Jakob's restaurant and Biergarten."

Ursie's face betrayed that she was impressed, or surprised. "How d'you do? A police officer."

"Show her, Freddie."

Freddie reached for his wallet, and opened it to a plastic window.

Rickie glimpsed a picture of Freddie in cap above a lot of printed lines and signatures, and he saw Ursie's pale blue eyes bulge almost to normal size. "It's true," said Rickie.

"Ruth told me your young friend went home," Ursie said, working at the draught tap.

"He was taken back home. Practically carried. But he's on the mend." Rickie looked over his left shoulder toward Renate's table: no Renate, no Luisa. No Willi Biber in sight either.

Their beers arrived. Rickie laid out the coins for them, over Freddie's protest.

When Ursie was back in the area, Rickie said, "We're going over to see *Willi*—if he's home. Has he been in this afternoon?"

He hadn't, that Ursie had seen. "Going to *see* him?" she asked, curious, Rickie knew, because he was with a policeman.

"Social call. Freddie would like to meet him," Rickie said calmly. "What's the name of the tearoom people—Waengler?"

Ursie thought for moment, stayed her hand on the draught handle and closed her pinkish eyes, then opened them. "Wenger." She was on the move again.

A quarter of an hour later, Rickie and Freddie approached the tearoom L'Eclair, now dark and shadowy.

Rickie said, "Willi lives behind here." Then he noticed a feeble glow at a front window, first floor. The tearoom owners were home. "Down this alley," Rickie motioned.

A somewhat brighter first-floor window showed in the alley,

but no light from Willi Biber's quarters. Freddie produced a flash-light the size of a fountain pen. "Bless you!" said Rickie. He knocked on the alley door, which had a lower panel missing. There was no answer; Rickie tried the knob and the door opened at once. The dark hall again. Rickie gestured toward the door on the left. "Maybe asleep." Rickie knocked. "Willi? You have visitors! Somebody wants to see you!"

Still no answer, and Rickie was about to try this door, when a female voice cried, "Who's there?" from the lighted window direc-tion.

Rickie tried the door anyway. The lock held. He and Freddie went into the alley. "'Evening, Frau Wenger. We would like to speak with Willi, please."

"Who would?" Frau Wenger had her hands on the sill.

"Markwalder—I'm with a police officer. Is Willi at home?"

A pause. "Are you saying he's done something this afternoon? We're not responsible—my husband and I."

"No, Madame. The police would like to *see* him. Is he with you?"

"Police, Madame," said Freddie, showing his wallet's identifi-cation, which Rickie illuminated, illegible at this distance for Frau Wenger, but impressive enough.

"So—come up," she said.

She buzzed them into a well-appointed little hall with table, looking glass, and carpeted stairs up. They climbed, Freddie with identification at the ready.

Frau Wenger, a plump blonde of about fifty, plainly recognized Rickie and disliked him. Rickie not even vaguely found her face familiar.

"Officer Schimmelmann," said Rickie. "Frau Wenger."

And there was Willi Biber, the scarecrow scared, standing now at the end of the living room sofa, and visibly shaky, his droopy blue eyes sunken with fatigue. "Willi Biber—" Rickie said for Freddie's benefit.

Herr Wenger stood to one side of Willi. Rickie exchanged a "Good evening" with him. Rickie said to Freddie, "It's about last night at midnight and just after that I'd like to ask a question."

"Herr Markwalder," said Frau Wenger, finding her tongue, "last night around two or three in the morning—this morning— you broke in two of my doors. You—"

"For which I shall pay," Rickie said in a pacific tone.

"You hit Willi—frightened him—"

Rickie had told Freddie that he might have to face such an accusation. "I have a witness—last night—that I didn't touch Willi," Rickie replied.

"The man who helped you break the door in? Is he a reliable witness?" asked Frau Wenger.

The woman had a point, Rickie supposed. "I would like to ask Willi—if he knows anything about a piece of metal—" Rickie turned to Willi and continued. "About this long, Willi? A little rusted, painted yellow? Did you use it to hit Teddie?"

Willi visibly tried to collect himself, shifted, smiled a little, looked at Frau Wenger and back to Rickie. "Di'n' even see him."

"By his big car, Willi. Under the trees? Young man in a light blue jacket—remember? Feldenstrasse." Rickie gestured. That street wasn't far from here.

"I was—was in Jakob's last night." Willi stuck his thumbs in the top of his cotton trousers, hitched them up on his flat waist.

"So was I. I saw you leave a few minutes after midnight. Out the main door, Willi. Front door."

"Herr Markwalder, you are putting ideas in his head," Frau Wenger murmured, as if to keep her words out of the hearing of a child. "You can see, officer—Willi is not the most—able type, but he has his rights. He shouldn't have it suggested to him that he did something he didn't do, if you understand me." She looked sharply at Freddie.

"I do, Madame," said Officer Schimmelmann. "We'll be asking a few other people the very same questions, though. Jogging their memories. It's the usual procedure." Freddie had pulled out his pad, and he continued to take notes.

The doorbell rang, and Frau Wenger lifted her hands and let them drop at her sides, as if the evening were already too much for her. "I suppose——" She looked at her husband with a doubtful expression.

"I'll get it, Therese," said the mild-mannered Herr Wenger, and went to the buzzer in the front hall.

Murmurs at the apartment door, then to Rickie's surprise Renate entered, a nervous cloud of rose, pink, and blue in a long, full-skirted dress. "Therese, I——" She saw Rickie, glanced at Herr Wenger, and again at Willi Biber, who stood as if frozen. "I see you have visitors tonight!"

"Ah yes, and last night too," said Therese Wenger. "As I told you, Willi's doors are broken."

"This is fortunate, Officer Schimmelmann," Rickie said. "You can meet one of my neighbors, Frau Hagnauer. Madame—Officer Schimmelmann of the police force. We came to see Willi."

Freddie nodded to Renate, and displayed his open wallet once more.

Renate looked at it, long enough to compare the photograph with the man before her. "So—came to see Willi. And I hope Frau Wenger's doors too. Herr Markwalder and a friend were doing some celebrating last night, it seems." She addressed Freddie. "Kicking people's doors in. Drunken vandalism!"

"Oh well, Renate," said Herr Wenger, "I told you Herr Markwalder will pay for the repairs."

"Gladly," Rickie put in. "We came to ask Willi a question—Madame," he said to Renate. "Does he know anything about a young man being injured last night—or this morning about half-past midnight. Feldenstrasse. Teddie Stevenson. Hit in the back." Rickie watched Renate turn her lavender-mascaraed eyes to Willi.

"And what did you say, Willi?" Renate asked him.

Willi shook his head slowly. "Never seen him—this boy. What boy? No." The head kept shaking, no.

Renate began a slow nod of approval, and checked herself. "You should look elsewhere—among your own rather odd acquaintances, Herr Markwalder—and let other people *and* their property alone. Otherwise you'll simply get yourself into trouble." Renate felt better now, on the attack. Not too much, just enough, she told herself: keep the enemy off balance. "Officer—Herr Markwalder—one would think he is a law unto himself. Couldn't wait for Willi to open his door, it seems, so he broke in!"

Rickie glanced behind him at the two open windows, where thin curtains stirred not at all, and dragged his palm across his wet forehead. "Maybe you have heard of Peter Ritter, Willi—or you remember him? A young man—stabbed? He died seven—eight months ago."

Willi continued to look blank, no blanker than before, but no less. He shifted slightly.

"Why do you try to put ideas into his head?" Renate asked with impatience. "These names?"

"Just what I said a few minutes ago." Frau Wenger drew herself up and went on. "People can give Willi the idea he's done something wrong—or accuse him when he *hasn't*."

Rickie sensed an opportunity. "Yes. Maybe you know, Frau Wenger, that some people believe my friend Peter Ritter was stabbed in my apartment? That's the story Willi tells, in spite of the newspapers stating that he was found stabbed in a street in Zurich." Rickie glanced at the Wengers and at Willi.

Renate, head high, turned her attention to the Wengers, whose male half listened with a frowning attention. "You see? Some kind of fantasy here, Karl. Willi talking about a *stabbing*?" She put on an amused smile. Rickie's balcony door had been unrepaired then, for months on end (Willi himself had noticed that the french windows didn't close). Renate knew she had taken a small risk, telling Willi such a story, but he had so swallowed it! That had given her satisfaction, plus the pleasure of taking Rickie down a few pegs—hoodlums in his apartment! The story would get around, Renate had thought, and it had—just enough. Renate laughed with feigned gaiety, and her thin cheeks creased for an instant. "Can you imagine?"

"No," said Herr Wenger, still frowning.

"That," said Rickie, "is my point too. Talk about putting ideas into Willi's head! The French Foreign Legion—deeds of— Did *you* tell him that, Frau Hag—"

"I was there!" Willi interrupted, waking up. "France! The Foreign Legion." Willi Biber nodded, sure of himself. *"Jawohl, mein Herr!"* Willi might have been addressing a Legion superior.

"Frau Wenger, does Willi talk to you about the Foreign Legion?" Rickie asked.

"Once, yes—I think he did."

"And did you believe him—about being in it?"

Therese Wenger looked at her carpet and smiled. "No, to be honest. But then I know how Willi is."

"What's this got to do with Herr Markwalder attacking Willi in his home?" Renate asked.

"Don't you want to sit down, Renate?" asked Frau Wenger. "It's ridiculous, all of us standing."

Renate Hagnauer might not have heard. She glanced at Willi, who was staring most of the time at her, and maintaining his nearly catatonic position at the foot of the sofa. "Thank you, Therese. What Herr Markwalder is saying is fantasy—even libelous, I'd think. I'm pleased that an officer of the law is here tonight." Renate turned and clumped toward the door; her skirt swirled, and a laced boot was briefly revealed to Rickie's gaze. But she stayed.

"Herr Markwalder," said Karl Wenger, stepping forward, "I think tonight, the main thing is that a police officer has seen our damaged doors—I believe?"

"Yes, indeed, sir," said Officer Schimmelmann.

"And Herr Markwalder agrees to pay for their repair. I don't see that anything else much matters tonight—at least not to us." His tone was polite.

Rickie frowned. "*I'm* here, sir, to ask a question about Teddie Stevenson—early this morning." He addressed Karl Wenger. "A nasty wound in his back. It happened two streets from here."

"But why do you think Willi did it?" asked Frau Wenger.

Because he's been told by Renate Hagnauer to hate Teddie, Rickie wanted to say, but would these people believe it? Rickie had the feeling that he had a wonderful argument in hand, all on his side, and that he was not presenting it properly. "May I say, Willi is influenced by what Frau Hagnauer tells him, and I know that Frau Hagnauer disliked Petey Ritter and now dislikes Teddie Ste—"

"Nonsense!" Renate interrupted. "Teenaged boyfriends of Luisa! Why should I waste *time* disliking them?"

"You can make Willi dislike them," Rickie asserted.

Here Karl Wenger shook his head, as if to say Rickie's argument was personal and hopelessly thin.

"Officer, why do you bother writing things that aren't facts?" asked Renate.

"My work, Madame. May I have your address, please, Madame?"

"Yes, why not? Since it's easily found in the phone book too." Renate gave him her address, and cast a smiling supportive glance at Therese Wenger.

"Herr Markwalder," said Therese Wenger, "my husband and I believe in tolerance. Live and let live. If you look closely—"

"I wasn't talking about you, Madame," Rickie interrupted. "I was talking about Frau Hagnauer. Her attitude."

"Attitude? You're giving me *attitudes* now!" A toss of the head, a clump closer to the door, followed by Herr Wenger who may have intended to open the door for her, but again she turned. "I would like to say, Officer—"

"Schimmelmann."

"Schimmelmann, that you can't entirely trust what Willi may say. He is somewhat handicapped—as you see." Her last words were soft and gentle, as if to spare the weak.

"Yes, Madame, I realize."

Now Renate departed. In the silence that followed the door closing, Rickie took a deep breath.

"Frau Wenger—Thank you for giving us so much of your time tonight."

Rickie and Freddie were at the hall door, when Frau Wenger said, "May I ask, Herr Markwalder, just where you heard this story—that your friend was stabbed in your apartment? Your friend called Peter?"

Rickie was aware that her voice was loud enough for Willi to have heard. "In Jakob's. I think from a stranger—who asked me had the killer been caught. Willi, *you* know that story, someone came into my apartment when the balcony door lock was broken."

"Yes," said Willi, calm as ever.

"And the story is," Rickie went on, "a friend or ex-friend of mine killed Petey with a knife." He felt breathless on the last word.

"Yes," Willi repeated.

Rickie made a gesture to Frau Wenger, as if to say, "You see?" He cleared his throat. "Who told you that, Willi? Do you remember?"

Here came the slow head-shaking.

It was as if Renate had rehearsed him, Rickie thought, to shake his head whenever she was in danger of being mentioned. "A stranger, maybe, Willi?"

After a pause, Willi nodded.

Rickie gave a smile, rather to himself. "A stranger to me too, you see, Frau Wenger. It gets retold until—it's like something in the air, a gas you can't see, this balcony story. But Luisa had heard it—from Renate." Rickie reached for the doorknob. "Good night."

"Good night," said Freddie.

Out in the slightly cooler air, they walked in the direction of Rickie's apartment.

Rickie glanced up on his right, and saw a light in what he thought was the Hagnauer floor. "That's where she lives."

"Who?"

"The old witch. Renate. Luisa too. I told you. It's the seamstress factory."

Freddie made no comment. At Jakob's corner, he said, "Look in?"

"No, I'm dead."

"I'll walk you home."

Freddie came in with Rickie, and asked to use the toilet. When he came out, he said, "Can I stay the night, Rickie?"

Rickie had to muster the kind of strength he hated. "No. I'm sorry, Freddie. I'm whacked and—talking about Petey tonight—"

"Just to go to sleep, I swear. My wife's not going to phone here."

Rickie was not worried about Freddie's wife. "I really want to be by myself."

Somehow they embraced. In the next seconds, they were holding each other tight, and Rickie felt a wave of gratitude, of strength, wash over him as if from Freddie's hard, smaller body. Freddie had been a friend tonight. Rickie recalled with shame that he had brushed Freddie off as to a date on Saturday night last, because Teddie was going to be at Jakob's, because Rickie might have met a more handsome stranger.

"G'night, Rickie. Call me anytime." Freddie went out.

18

The telephone woke Rickie just before eight the next morning.

Luisa's voice said, "Rickie, sorry to phone so early. I'm in the booth at L'Eclair—out buying groceries. I spoke with Teddie last night when Renate was out."

"Yes?"

"His mother doesn't want him to come to Aussersihl anymore, for one thing."

"I could have predicted that. Frau Stevenson talked with the police?"

"Yes! She got the police to come to the house and look at that piece of metal. She gave them the address of the house where I found it. It seems nobody's living there now, or they're away. The police wanted to ask about people hanging around."

Rickie frowned. "Do you know what the police intend to do now?"

"No, I don't. Teddie said he'd tell you any news. Rickie, I'd better go now." The line went dead.

So Teddie couldn't come to the neighborhood anymore; at least not with his mother's car, Rickie was sure, maybe even without. Yet love would find a way, it always did.

Rickie went back to bed, intending to sleep for an hour. Lulu leapt up and joined him with a lick of her pink tongue at the empty air, then she lay down on the top sheet and closed her eyes. On the bottom sheet was a dark red circle of Teddie's blood, the size of a five-franc piece.

The telephone awakened him.

"Dorrie Wyss," the voice said, and Rickie at once saw the jester in red vest, with her short blonde hair. "Tried to get you last night. Now how is our dear boy?"

Rickie was sure she didn't mean him. "Doing well. He's

home now, in Mum's care." Dorrie had been at Jakob's late
enough to see Teddie on the back terrace after he'd been hurt,
Rickie recalled.

"And Luisa?"

"She reports this morning that Teddie's mother doesn't want
him coming to this neighborhood again."

"I can understand. Rickie, I had an idea. Can't we visit Teddie? You and I, Luisa, bring him some flowers? What's his number?
I'll phone. I'd imagine you can't—or maybe shouldn't." She gave a
laugh. "I've got a BMW hatchback, you know. I could swoop by
anytime after five today—take us all in my car."

They planned. Rickie would reach Luisa somehow. Dorrie
could park at or near the Small g. Dorrie would ask Frau Stevenson if they could pay Teddie a visit around six. Rickie took Dorrie's work number, and made sure she had his studio number.

Rickie closed shop before five that afternoon, in order to go
home and change. He showered and put on black cotton trousers,
and chose his yellow jacket, which was still clean. A white shirt—
no tie but a good silk scarf at his neck.

"Farewell, Lulu, I'll be back before eight anyway." On second
thoughts, why not take her? She could stay in Dorrie's car while
they visited Teddie. Lulu didn't mind that.

Dorrie Wyss's shiny black van was parked near Jakob's when
Rickie approached, which was five twenty-five. And here came
Luisa, crossing the street, smiling on sight of him.

"What's up?" asked Luisa.

"We're going to see Teddie! All three of us," said Rickie. "Didn't
Dorrie tell you?"

Luisa looked startled. "My fault. I had to hang up so fast."

"We're going to Teddie's house. Dorrie's idea," said Rickie.
"Hello, Dorrie, angel! Now let's escape while we can!" Renate
might appear at any instant, he was thinking.

They were off, Lulu beside Rickie in the seat behind Dorrie,
Luisa in front with Dorrie, heading toward the town's center.

"The address, Rickie!" said Dorrie. "Do you know how to get there?"

Rickie had consulted a city map in his studio, and was able to instruct Dorrie.

It was a large beige apartment house some ten stories high, with a few trees in front. They had to park a street away, and Rickie made sure the car was locked, that Lulu had enough air. The car was out of the sun, anyway. They had stopped at a florist's shop, and Rickie had bought two bouquets, one for him, one for Luisa to give.

"Swank," said Dorrie, on entering the glass-doored lobby. Up they went to the ninth floor, exactly on time.

The door of apartment 9B opened as they stepped out of the lift. Teddie stood there, in blue jeans and a white T-shirt and sandals.

"Welcome, honored guests, come in! Hey, I'm not dead yet!" Teddie said, on Rickie's thrusting flowers toward him.

Frau Stevenson stood in the living room, smiling a greeting. The apartment was air-conditioned with wide windows, a baby grand piano in one corner, and one wall of books.

"Dorrie Wyss," Rickie said, "Frau Stevenson."

"A pleasure," both said.

Dorrie was looking quite chic, Rickie thought, with small green earrings, a good shirt, and narrow black slacks.

"May I, Frau Stevenson," said Luisa, presenting her bouquet to Teddie's mother.

"Oh, thank you, Luisa! Excuse me, I'll get a vase or two."

"I'll get 'em, Mum," said Teddie, looking eager to debarrass himself of the flowers.

"Teddie, don't leap about like that! You promised." This from a frowning mother.

"I wasn't leaping, Mum. Please sit—all of you—anywhere," Teddie said with an effort at calm. "I'll give my mother a hand. Excuse me."

Rickie saw a bulge of bandage under the T-shirt, as Teddie left the room. "If the ladies don't sit—"

The ladies smiled. They were looking the room over.

"Then I'll sit."

"I'll beat you!" said Dorrie, darting for an easy chair, landing before Rickie touched the brown leather sofa.

The flowers returned in vases, followed by iced tea and lemon cake.

Frau Stevenson asked what kind of work Dorrie Wyss did. She called her Dorrie.

"I put the clothes on mannequins," Dorrie said. Then with a laugh, "Pose them. Mainly female—but not always. Then I do backdrops too—with the help of a man called Bert."

Rickie shuffled his feet. Bert! Rickie could see him: either long-haired or skinheaded, and very likely plucked eyebrows.

"Stores in Zurich . . . ? Such as which?"

Dorrie mentioned a couple, in the Bahnhofstrasse. "I work freelance."

Rickie began, "Frau Stevenson—that piece of metal—what did the police say?"

"Oh!" She was suddenly all alertness. "Well, they took it with them. They're not optimistic, to put it mildly. Not enthusiastic about fingerprints, either. But they think it could be the weapon. It could have made a tear—as in Teddie's jacket. And a wound like that." She paused, then went on, "But this to happen by the car as early as just after midnight. Maybe the neighborhood doesn't like Teddie—somebody doesn't—because he's *not* from that neighborhood."

Luisa exchanged a glance with Rickie. "The neighborhood's not considered dangerous, Frau Stevenson," she said earnestly. "Really. We all more or less know one another there. I realize it was the evening of the National Holiday. There were a lot of strangers at Jakob's that night."

Rickie had a vision of Willi's lank figure slipping through the crowd at Jakob's, exiting at the right time to have struck Teddie. Had he possibly put that weapon beforehand in the front path near Teddie's car? Willi might carry a small torch, considering the darkness of that alley in which he lived. "Madame, did you . . ."

"We could talk about something else," Teddie began at the same time. He leaned forward in his chair, with tea glass in both hands. "Sorry, Rickie."

"Yes, um-m—I was about to ask, Frau Stevenson, if you have the name of the police officer who came to see you here?"

"Ye-es," said Frau Stevenson, seemingly reluctant to share her facts. She frowned as easily as did her son.

"Because I have a friend in the police force," said Rickie, with a sense of pride. "It might help, you know—a word to keep them on the job. My friend could ask about their investigations." Rickie's hands opened for an instant between his knees. His tea glass was on the coffee table, and he had abstained from cake. He wanted a cigarette and was afraid to light up.

"Excuse me a moment." Frau Stevenson went into a hall where Rickie had glimpsed a telephone table moments ago. She returned with a card.

Rickie wrote: Thomas A. Senn, 73rd Station, Zurich Eggstr. (01) 275-4556. Ext. 5. "Thank you." He stood up to hand the card back to her.

"And what's your friend's name?" she asked.

Rickie replied carefully, "Friedrich Schimmelmann. I think he's with the traffic department now, but he's based in Zurich. Easy to reach."

Frau Stevenson chose this moment to pass the cake plate round again, to Dorrie then Luisa. "Not even just a little?" she said to Luisa, who accepted. "And you, Teddie? No need to ask."

Teddie took a piece with his fingers and put it on his plate. "I should've offered it, Mum, sorry."

"You—*sit*," said his mother softly but firmly, as if she had said it many times in the last couple of days. She returned to the sofa where Rickie sat, her dark eyes again puzzled. "I haven't much confidence in what the police are doing or can do. Oh, they did telephone this afternoon, to say they'd inquired at four or five houses near where Teddie parked that night—also on the opposite side of the street—asked if people had seen or heard anything. No news there, I'm afraid. It's not punishment that I want, but I think people who do such things ought to be identified and warned. A meaningless act. Not even for robbery! What does one do with such a person?" She was ready to smile at herself, at her impotence.

Silence for a few seconds.

Rickie heard Luisa asking Teddie if he played the piano.

"Yes, but I'm not great. My mother plays."

"Luisa, you must tell me when we should take off," Dorrie said. To Frau Stevenson, she added with her quick smile, "I'm the driver today."

"Talking about going?" Teddie said, annoyed. "I want you to see my room at least, Luisa—all of you." He was on his feet, insisting.

Dorrie stood up and extended crossed hands to Luisa, who was deep in a leather chair. Luisa took her hands and Dorrie pulled her up.

Frau Stevenson held back. "I'm sure the room's neater than usual."

The four went down a hall to an open door.

To Luisa, the room suggested the British Navy, blue and white, perhaps an officer's room, full of severe lines. The bed, a three-quarter against the wall, bore a neat dark blue fitted cover.

Rickie, blinking once, took in the CD player, the World Receiver near the bed on a shelf, books that seemed of a technical nature, a new-looking, dark red Olivetti typewriter, a beer mug full of pencils and ballpoint pens.

"Cool," Dorrie said, impressed.

"See, Luisa, if you ring me—that's where I can take it," Teddie said, indicating his telephone.

"Any news from the *Tages-Anzeiger,* Teddie?" Rickie asked.

Teddie ducked his head. "Not good news, if that's what you mean."

They went out, back to the living room, and said their thanks and good-byes in the foyer.

"I think your apartment is lovely," Luisa said to Frau Stevenson. "Thank you for having us."

"Thank you, Frau Stevenson. I appreciate very much your air-conditioning," Dorrie Wyss said with a smile. "Take care of yourself, Teddie."

Rickie merely bowed and said, "Thank you." He realized he was too intimidated—if that was the word—to ask Teddie to telephone him tomorrow, because Teddie's mother was present.

They were silent in the lift down, then on the pavement they broke into laughter.

"How the other half lives," said Dorrie Wyss.

"*So* swank? No-o," said Rickie. "Medium swank."

At the black BMW, Rickie called Lulu out and let her walk for a little. Then back into the warm car. Dorrie announced that she was putting her cooling system on, a fan, the best she could do.

"Wasn't that a great room, though?" Dorrie said. "Teddie's. The size! My whole apartment could fit in Teddie's room, I bet."

Luisa was thinking of the time, seven twenty-seven, and of what she was going to say to Renate about being late for dinner, or late in helping to prepare it, anyway. If she said she'd been in Jakob's, Renate might say she'd looked in there (whether she had or not), and Luisa hadn't been there.

"By the way, Luisa, any time you want a ride to Teddie's neighborhood, I'll take you. No trouble, you know, to pick you up in Aussersihl and bring you here," Dorrie said. "I'll give you my card, once we're up by Jakob's."

Rickie thought, a card now! Dorrie was coming up in the world, even if her apartment was small.

"And," Dorrie went on, "I'd imagine Teddie could take you home in a taxi, providing he didn't get out of the taxi!"

Rickie hesitated over the question he wanted to ask, and decided to go ahead, "Luisa, did Renate say anything about last night? Willi and so on?"

Luisa gave a start, and turned to look at Rickie. "No. But I heard something from the Wengers, you know, where I phoned you from. They know I talk with you sometimes. They said you came by with a police officer."

"We think—I think Willi might've hit Teddie with that piece of metal that Luisa found. But since we're not sure—"

Luisa described the piece of tripod to Dorrie.

"You talked with Willi?" asked Dorrie.

"Yes, and he says he never saw the boy," Rickie replied. "Doesn't know Teddie, didn't see him Saturday night or any other night."

"Of course the Wengers think we're trying to blame Willi because there's no one else to blame," Luisa said.

"It's next to impossible with someone so dim-witted as Willi, you know?" This from Rickie.

"Impossible?" asked Dorrie.

"You can't go after a retarded person—the way you would a normal person. Even if I had more facts, or the police had," Rickie said in a discouraged tone, "you'd probably never get Willi to admit anything. He acts sort of guilty now, but he's like a machine pro-grammed to say he never saw the boy in his life."

Silence again.

"Renate was extra nervous today. Very cross with me. It's going to be a mess tonight, because I'm late." Luisa gave Rickie a tense glance. "My usual problem."

"How much longer is your apprenticeship?" Dorrie asked.

"About six months."

"Can't you switch to another atelier? Isn't that allowed?"

"Maybe *allowed*," Luisa answered, "but Renate would give me the worst references possible. I know her." She didn't want to add the dramatic statement that Renate simply wouldn't turn her loose. With a jolt, Luisa recognized her own neighborhood, and stopped her daydreaming. They were nearing Rickie's studio and Jakob's. "I can walk a couple of streets, you know. Best if I do, Dorrie."

"If you say so. I'll go up to Jakob's and make a turn there." A few seconds later, Dorrie said, "Can't you tell this Renate that you had a lift to go to Teddie's and you wanted to visit? Has she got something against boyfriends too, this gay-basher?"

"Well—y-yes," said Luisa.

The car stopped, and Luisa got out.

"Oh, my card!" Dorrie groped in a briefcase, then leaned over to hand a card to Luisa. "Good luck, my sweet. Call me anytime!"

Rickie was reminded of Freddie Schimmelmann saying that. "Me too! Good luck with the old witch." He watched Luisa walking briskly toward Renate's, as Dorrie turned her car.

"You're aiming for home, Rickie?"

He was, and Dorrie said she had an eight-thirty date. They parted in front of Rickie's apartment building.

Rickie telephoned Freddie at once, and was surprised to get him. He told Freddie about the police agreeing that the tripod piece could have been the weapon. And he gave Freddie the name and particulars of Thomas Senn.

At about that moment, Luisa was taking questions from Renate. What had kept her so long? Renate had eaten dinner. Tomorrow was a working day, and routine had to be kept.

"You could have telephoned, no?" asked Renate. Her tone was mild—dulcet—compared to her voice when really in anger. She wore a Chinese red-and-gold kimono with wide sleeves, which she adroitly kept immaculate, regardless of kitchen activities.

"I was at Teddie's house. I went to see him, because I got a lift," Luisa said calmly.

"Oh! And they have no telephone, I suppose! Who drove you, this Mark—walder, whatever it is?"

"No—a woman."

"Who?"

"I don't even know her name—Beatrix, I think."

"Friend of his? Was he with you?" Renate scowled.

"Yes," Luisa said, feeling bold. "I don't want dinner, it's so warm. I may have a glass of milk."

"You will *eat!*" said Renate, glad to focus on something definite. "You worked today, you'll work tomorrow, and you need to eat. There's a pork chop. And potato salad. You help yourself!"

Luisa hated it, but it wasn't worth fighting about.

19

It was a few days later, as Rickie was taking his first bite of croissant at Jakob's, that his eye fell on a name that made him pause. Georg Stefan. Why was that familiar? Rickie was gazing at a page of the *Tages-Anzeiger*. Georg Stefan had written an article called "An Old-Fashioned Date in a Brand-New World" and Rickie started to read it. With a shock, a twist of his thoughts, as if someone had turned his head full circle, Rickie realized that Teddie had written the piece about his date with Luisa at a mountain restaurant, dancing under the stars, a first date with a pretty girl who, like Cinderella, worse, had to be brought back home *before* eleven, or just a little after. The big car belonging to his mother, his promise to drink not even one glass of wine, his pleasure in the girl's company *now*—but would she, could she make a second date with him? Teddie wrote that "her father" was the stern disciplinarian, which made Rickie smile. Caviar, a daring gin and tonic for her, the girl with eyes and hair like shining chestnuts.

Alone, alone, the piece ended, after the drive back to the city to deliver the girl (she had no name) safely to her home. Funny,

Rickie thought, that the paper would print it, and yet its naivety, its intensity, was much in its favor. Rickie supposed Teddie would be exploding with pride this morning. He thought Teddie really had not known about its acceptance last Monday.

Rickie, having stuck a crisp bit of his croissant into Lulu's pointed muzzle under the table, lifted his eyes just as Luisa and Renate arrived, and Andreas also with his Appenzeller. "Thank you, my good man," said Rickie, putting on an English gentleman accent.

"Do mansion it," replied Andreas, "sir."

Catching Luisa's eye, Rickie gave a smile and a nod, that from this distance might have included Renate too, but she was not looking, or pretending not to, as she fixed a cigarette in her long holder. Rickie wanted to point to his newspaper to pique Luisa's curiosity, but she wasn't looking his way now. He had lifted his drink for a second sip, when Fred Schimmelmann walked in, wearing uniform. The day was indeed shaping up!

"Freddie—good morning!" Rickie relished every second, watching Renate stare with surprise at the police uniform. "Sit down, my friend. Off duty?"

"Couple of hours ago, yes." Freddie sat down on a chair. "Traffic again, twenty-two hours till six, how about that?" He took his cap off, laid it on the big table. "I went by your apartment, no answer, so I thought you might be here."

"Breakfast. Nearly every morning."

"I talked with Thomas Senn this morning, went to his home station," Freddie said. "He's a serious guy, had the house number, photographs—of the scene."

"He's a detective?"

"Same as. He's with a squad. He's not too hopeful about finding who did it. But"—Freddie lowered his voice— "I told him about Willi, and I asked, how do you go about questioning a mentally handicapped person? Maybe with a doctor present?" His blue-gray eyes looked sharply at Rickie. "So this Senn says it's perfectly legal to question him, and thinks a doctor present is a good idea—quietly present, y'know? A doctor could confirm that we're not trying to give poor Willi the third degree."

"No," Rickie murmured, agreeing, but he saw another hitch. Ursie was heading toward them to take Freddie's order.

"Ah, our police officer! Good morning, sir."

"Morning," said Freddie. "And I'd like a cappuccino, please."

"Our *friend*," said Rickie, pleased that Ursie was well disposed toward Officer Schimmelmann. He continued when Ursie left, "It'll be a neat job if we can make a date with Willi without Renate Hagnauer finding out and butting in." Rickie had lowered his voice.

"I know she's sitting behind me," Freddie said, gazing at the old scarred and sleek wooden table top. "They're that close?"

"Oh—she pretends to protect him. If Willi has an hour's warning about a date with the cops, he'll tell her—or tell the Wengers."

"We'll have to surprise him—somewhere. With Senn plus a doctor from the police station."

Just the idea made Rickie happier. "Fred—to change the subject. What do you think, my friend Teddie sold an article to the *Tages-Anzeiger*." Rickie folded the paper on its stick, so the piece in question was visible.

"He's a journalist?" asked Freddie, taking the paper.

"Wants to be—just now. This is about his first date with Luisa. Sort of naive—but it's charming."

Freddie was taking a look at it. "Rickie, you'd say it was charming if it stank."

"Maybe. But if it stank, it wouldn't be in the *Tages-Anzeiger*."

RICKIE GOT TO HIS STUDIO just as Mathilde did.

"You're looking happy today," she remarked.

"Oh—a small bit of good news," Rickie replied as he unlocked the door. Mathilde was curious, he saw, so he didn't wait for her to ask what. "My friend Teddie—the boy who was hurt. An article by him is printed in the *Tages-Anzeiger* today. I just read it in Jakob's."

"That he wrote? And he's just a kid! An article about what?"

"A first date. He signs it Georg Stefan."

"I'll read it. We take it at home."

Coffee. Always more coffee. Mathilde opened envelopes.

Rickie was cheerful for another reason: he had a "dry-skin" idea that he thought might work. It was true, some things are better dry, like champagne, some white wines, Dry Sack, and a dry martini cocktail, but not your skin. Rickie's layout would have no person in it, only attractive wine and cocktail glasses. With his coffee and a cigarette, Rickie began to sketch.

"Ah, Rickie, here's something not so nice." Mathilde came over to hand a piece of paper to him.

This was a bill, with a small handwritten note from the Wengers, saying they were sure he would like to settle this as soon as possible. It was an estimate of two thousand, six hundred and forty-five francs for the two doors of Willi Biber, which had to be custom-made, because of the house's antiquity.

"*Two* doors. Why can't these crooks stuff themselves," Rickie muttered, and broke out in a grin, when he saw that Mathilde had heard him. "For a couple of flimsy doors that anyone could kick in. And I did!"

They both laughed.

"One pays for one's fun, no? Make a check out to those people, please, Mathilde, and I'll sign it." He went back to his work.

A little later, he was consulting a much used address book for a number for Dorrie. He found three, and tried one in the Bahnhofstrasse. This place knew Dorrie and thought she might be at another store, whose name they gave. At least he was able to leave a message: please telephone.

Dorrie did, just before noon.

Rickie told her about Teddie's article. "I'd love to let Luisa know, but I'm afraid to phone there." That was the absurd truth, afraid.

"I'll call her! Of course I want to read it first," Dorrie said with a laugh. "What's the old witch's last name again?"

When Dorrie's call rang in the Hagnauer house, Renate and Luisa were having their lunch in the sitting room. Renate answered the telephone, though one of the girls, Vera, happened to be in the hall and had been nearer.

"Dorrie?" said Renate.

Luisa was instantly on her feet.

"This is the lunch period," Renate said, cold as a recorded message.

". . . will take just a minute . . . *message*," Dorrie's voice said.

"I think you are a friend of Herr Markwalder? Then I'd be grateful if you would *not* call here again." Renate put the telephone down. "Rude people—*en plus!*" she snorted to Luisa, and started to clump back.

"She said a short message," Luisa began.

Renate resumed her place and her meal. "If that telephone rings again—"

It did, just then.

"*You* answer it!" Renate said, standing up, ready to come with Luisa. "You tell that person she's not to telephone here again! Tell her!"

Luisa walked past the eerily silent kitchen, where Stefanie, Vera, and Elsie were having their lunch. She picked up the telephone. "Hello?"

"Hello, *sweetie*! Teddie has an article in the *Tages-Anzeiger* today! Under the name—"

"*Tell* her!" cried Renate.

"Dorrie—"

"Georg Stefan. Got that? About you and—"

"Dorrie, I have to say—not to phone here again. That's from—"

"Don't tell *me*! Tell her to get stuffed!" Dorrie said loudly. "I'll write to you—or something. You know where to reach me."

"Hang up!" Renate commanded.

Luisa hung up. She hoped Renate had heard Dorrie's words. Luisa returned to the sitting room, not wanting any more to eat, but if she had excused herself, Renate would have complained.

"I hope that sank in?" said Renate. "The nerve! The gall!"

Why, Luisa wondered. To telephone someone during the lunch hour? She was curious about Teddie's article, though in a way she dreaded facing it: about their date at the mountain restaurant; Teddie had mentioned working on the piece.

"Finish your lunch."

Luisa made an effort, washed it down with tea whose ice had melted, swallowing hard. Teddie's article, strangely, had become one more obstacle in the day. Renate watched her now. Luisa longed to talk with Rickie—or did she? What good could he do? He was a friend, and sympathetic, but what could he *do*?

A quarter of an hour later, Luisa was at her sewing machine, working on the skirt of a suit she had designed, on Renate's orders. Renate had had a word of praise for the waist of the jacket, the small and unusual lapels. Every now and then, Renate asked Luisa to "create something," even a nightdress, which Luisa had once done. Luisa rechecked her basting of the zip panel. She had glanced over the bench where the girls put their handbags and other items, and had spotted a *Tages-Anzeiger*. Luisa chose a moment when Renate was out of the room, and went to the newspaper.

"Can I borrow this for a couple of minutes? Whose is it?"

It belonged to Stefanie, who said of course she could borrow it.

With careful haste, Luisa carried it down a short hall with windows, to the toilet used by the girls. She found the page and stood reading, so rapidly that she had to go back after a couple of paragraphs and read it again to make sense of it. Here was the nervous excitement of the evening when she had met Teddie in the dark near the big car that belonged to his mother, and which Teddie couldn't borrow unless he kept his promise not to drink any alcohol. Dancing under the summer sky, and Teddie feeling unreal and elegant in a light jacket, sharply pressed trousers, and patent leather shoes. And the girl! Luisa forced herself to read it. She had to smile. One would have thought she was a fairy-tale queen, all beauty and shining eyes. She even had a lovely voice and could dance well! (Surely Rickie had laughed, reading this, Luisa thought.) And the food which sounded ethereal, the wine for her, and all too soon the drive back to the city, to deliver her at the hour she had to be back. The brief kiss good night. The Audi which seemed to take flight with Georg, when he drove it alone back to its berth.

Would Renate guess the truth if she read it? Luisa thought not. And what if she did? What had been wrong?

Now, hardly thinking, Luisa pulled the toilet chain with its old black knob, for proper sound effect. Tucking the paper under her arm, she rinsed her hands at the undersized basin which had only cold water, icy in winter, but pleasant now. Luisa went out.

"Thanks," she said to Stefanie, replacing the paper on the bench.

Renate was just coming into the big room.

"Looking for another job?" Vera said softly, leaning toward Luisa. Vera's shoulders hunched with laughter.

Luisa smiled. Another job. Yes, that was starting to sound nice. She bent again to her work.

Renate was making her rounds, checking, commenting, giving a suggestion here, a criticism there, and rarely a word of praise. That morning, when Luisa had awakened in her room, she had lain for a few minutes, letting herself swirl down into what she felt were the depths of—discouragement.

There was Renate's hostility toward Teddie, though she didn't even know him. Then Luisa's own sharp memory of Teddie's fine apartment, of his mother who, though pleasant enough now, would probably never countenance Teddie's taking seriously a girl like herself. Teddie had his *Matura,* he had been to America at least twice, he dined at fine houses—not that he had said this, but he would know just how to behave, while Renate was still, often, correcting Luisa about something she did at the table, especially when they went to a good restaurant, as they had on Renate's birthday. One could *not* make up for all that just by trying, Luisa felt. Anyway, for how long would Teddie have any interest in her? Maybe not as long as the six months to come of her apprenticeship, maybe not half that.

"This is quite good," Renate said, bending over Luisa's zip panel which she was just finishing. "*Very* nice." She moved on.

The other girls were working on beige or blue trouser suits, all the same model. Production number: four, in three sizes.

Teddie would be walking on air, and maybe he would dare to telephone her today. Luisa hoped not.

She had Dorrie's telephone number, two of them. That was comforting. Someone to talk to! Like Rickie. In a way better, because Dorrie was a girl. And so cheerful! Luisa liked that. When could she try to reach Dorrie? And from where? L'Eclair was the closest public telephone.

Maybe this afternoon around three, when Renate sometimes sent her out to buy bread for dinner or a cake from L'Eclair as a treat for the girls. Luisa realized that it was possible she could see Dorrie this evening. Wonderful! In the next instant, the old question raised itself: *how,* meaning what excuse would she give Renate?

Might it be easier to meet Dorrie at Rickie's place? Then she and Dorrie could go off to a café somewhere, drink something cold, talk for half an hour, anyway.

"Luisa—you're dreaming today!" Stefanie was bending toward Luisa, offering a tray of variously colored thread.

"Oh! OK, I'll take a black. Thanks, Stefanie."

Luisa started at every phone call. Since Renate was more often on her feet than the others, she usually answered. The fourth call brought Renate back into the workroom after she had answered it.

"Luisa—someone for you," Renate said.

Luisa went into the hall. Renate's eyes were on her, and Renate followed until she was hardly two meters from the telephone.

"Luisa!" said Teddie. Then more softly, "Did you see my article?"

"Yes. You know—it's hard to talk now, so—"

"Can we have dinner tonight? Something in town? If I come in a taxi around seven? Please!"

"It just isn't so *easy*."

"Tell him good-bye!" Renate said with a wave of a hand, turning her back. But she turned again, listening.

"It's just—impossible," Luisa finished with a gasp. "Try Rickie!" That was the best she could do now, as far as communication went. She hung up, and faced Renate with an eye as steady as Renate's. Then Luisa looked straight ahead as she made her way past Renate to the workroom.

"Try Rickie indeed! He should *live* with him!" Renate said grimly but quietly, not wanting the workroom to hear.

Luisa ignored the comment. Rickie, yes. Luisa thought of Rickie as a fortress she could run to. Indeed, Luisa supposed, Renate probably wouldn't enter Rickie's apartment or studio under any circumstances, because Renate would consider his dwellings contaminated.

Renate had an appointment that afternoon. Frau Huttmann, a buyer for an expensive Zurich shop, was coming to look at the trouser suits. This would be at four. So Luisa was sent out to choose the best in the way of a torte—a whole cake, Renate said—that L'Eclair had to offer. During this time, Luisa rang Rickie at his atelier, whose number she knew by heart.

"You didn't make a date with Teddie," Rickie said.

"I couldn't with Renate listening to every word! Rickie, can I see you later? Maybe—before dinner? I'll try it."

"But of course, dear Luisa. You mean at my studio?"

Luisa hesitated. "I want to see you alone." It sounded so
romantic, it was funny. And she'd said it in a passionate tone.

"Can you come to my apartment if it's at six? It's even closer
to you."

Luisa made the tea, and got the cups ready, enough for the
girls too, plus plates and forks, and the large blue paper napkins.

The clock did not creep, it leapt to a quarter to six. Stefanie
and Elsie had taken their leave, only Vera remained. Frau
Huttmann was gathering herself. Luisa removed the empty teapot.
Good-byes and it was a pleasure, and until soon—with the deliv-
eries, that meant.

"I'm going out for a few minutes," Luisa said, almost as soon
as the door had closed on Frau Huttmann.

"Where?" asked Renate.

"Just to get some air," said Luisa as if she meant it, and she
went out, empty-handed, with no money.

"Luisa!"

She was racing down the stairs in her sneakers. Had Renate
called her name? Was she dreaming, having a nightmare? Anyway,
Renate couldn't possibly catch up with her, and she wouldn't try.

20

Rickie was home, Luisa saw from the slightly open french
windows. She rang the bell.

Seconds later Rickie opened the door into the front hall. Luisa
restrained herself: she felt like embracing him. Instead, she held his
left hand, squeezed it as they walked toward his door.

"Luisa—what's the *matter*?"

"Nothing!" She smiled at Lulu. "Hello, Lulu!"

"Arf!" Lulu wriggled a greeting, recognizing her.

"You're all out of breath," Rickie said.

"I was just running. We had a showing—sort of. Renate had an important buyer—tea. You know. I had to make the tea and serve the cake."

Rickie looked at her. "And what else?"

"Nothing! I just felt like seeing you. So I ran out!"

"I—see. I am honored. Sit down—somewhere. A Coke?"

"No, thanks. Well—yes. Thank you."

Luisa leaned back against the sofa pillows, and took a deep breath.

Rickie came with her Coke and what looked like a Scotch on the rocks for himself. "Your health!" He lifted his glass. "Did you talk with Teddie today?"

"He phoned. Wanted me to have dinner with him. I couldn't just *arrange* that with Renate standing there, trying her best to hear! I had to say no, of course. He'd have picked me up in a taxi, he said. Maybe he'd have to lie to his mother, since she doesn't want him in Aussersihl. Why is life so complicated?"

Rickie shrugged. "Other people," he said calmly. "Six more months, you said—with Renate?"

Luisa nodded. "Yes. Sounds like years to me sometimes."

Rickie lit a cigarette, and spoke with deliberate objectivity, as much as he could muster. "But you're almost nineteen. You need to live somewhere else, Luisa."

"And keep on working for Renate?" Luisa gave a laugh. "Not to mention that I can't afford an apartment on my stipend from Renate."

Rickie knew. Luisa was welcome to sleep on his sofa, he was thinking, but hell would break loose, Renate would call the police and invent weird stories! "Did you know I have a bedroom, a shower, a kitchen in my *studio*? Where I *never* sleep at night, and seldom take a nap in the day? You are most welcome, Luisa! Free of charge."

"Thanks, Rickie." Her voice sounded weak to her, although she meant the thanks. "That would be heaven—just not having to eat with her. But—it still belongs to you. It—" Luisa allowed herself a few seconds of dreaming: living in Rickie's atelier, borrowing some of his novels and big art books which she saw here, *not* having to play chess with Renate in the evenings, being able to call the atelier her own in the evenings, Luisa was sure. Independence! And Rickie's studio was so attractive with its white walls, its good lights, and his sketches and cartoons tacked up.

"But *think* about it," Rickie said.

"She'd absolutely have a fit! She might throw me out, you know, because—she'd say I was associating with—maybe not criminals but homosexuals."

"True. Renate would have a hard time catching me in bed with a girl."

They both laughed. It was suddenly funny for Luisa to imagine.

Rickie was glad to see her laugh, but sorry his atelier idea had been rejected. Luisa would have been out of his studio at precisely the hours when he needed to work there.

Luisa had wanted to talk about Teddie, why trying to make dates with him seemed not worth it as long as she was apprenticed to Renate. But this, Luisa knew, would have led her to talk about Petey, and she didn't want to remind Rickie of Petey now. It was not that she was still in love with Petey, but that Teddie came nowhere near inspiring in her what she had felt for Petey, that feeling that the world had totally changed, that the air she breathed, the space she walked in, had been different and special, and that everything small and large that she set her mind to she would succeed in, and with ease. That was being in love, and only with Petey had she felt this.

The doorbell rang.

Luisa thought at once: Renate has followed me here and there's going to be a war! Then she remembered that Renate would consider the premises dirty, out of bounds.

192   PATRICIA HIGHSMITH

"Forgot to tell you, Dorrie's coming for a drink," Rickie said, getting up. "So smile," he added with a wink, and went to open the doors.

"Hey! Luisa!" Dorrie said on coming in. "What a nice surprise!"

"Surprise, yes," Rickie said. "Luisa had a rough day, so I am the lucky one, she pays me a visit. What'll you have, dear Dorrie?"

"First a glass of water, please, Rickie." Dorrie said to Luisa, "Isn't that nice news about Teddie's article?"

"Nice—yes," Luisa said.

Rickie was inspired to say, "It's Renate cracking the *whip* today. Unburden yourself, dear Luisa."

"My troubles, nothing but my troubles," Luisa said, embarrassed. "I've said enough."

"Luisa feels she must decline the offer of my studio as a cost-free dwelling place," Rickie said in a precise manner, "because Renate doesn't like queers. Luisa escaped this afternoon and came running to me. I am most flattered. But I hope you have your housekey, Luisa."

Luisa knew her keys weren't with her. "They're in my handbag at home."

"Good. You have a bed here and in my studio too," said Rickie. "You have a choice."

"And I've got a spare! Sort of a camp-bed, but still. That makes three beds. You mean the old bitch might not let you in? Why?" asked Dorrie.

Luisa took a breath. "Because I'm supposed to be there right now—helping to get dinner for us."

"Call her. Tell her you've got a date for dinner tonight, eh, Rickie?"

The two of them exerted a force. Luisa went to the telephone at the end of the sofa. She dialed, said, "Hello, Renate," and started to speak.

"Where're you calling from?" Short and angry.

"I'd like to have dinner out tonight. I have a—"

"Who're you with?"

"I'll be home—before eleven." Luisa felt a light sweat breaking out again.

"And just what brought *this* on?"

"Good-bye," Luisa said in the middle of Renate's question, and hung up.

"Wow! Good for you!" said Dorrie. "I could hear her! And she doesn't know where you are?"

"No. Maybe suspects."

"What do you say we phone Teddie and we all roll out to dinner somewhere air-conditioned? I've got my car with me. What's Teddie's number?"

Rickie knew the number, but protested that Dorrie and Luisa should go out together, as he had to do some accounting. They could phone Teddie from here, of course.

"I really don't want to see Teddie—tonight," Luisa said.

Rickie stopped himself from asking why. Luisa had her moods, she would have her reason.

Dorrie looked surprised. "OK, the three of us. Come on, Rickie."

"Can't. Won't."

Then Luisa was in the BMW with Dorrie, heading toward Zurich's center. Dorrie said she knew a restaurant called Der Fang.

"Cold lobster salad—a speciality," Dorrie said.

They lifted stemmed glasses of white wine. The restaurant was air-conditioned and had some space between tables, a luxury. Dorrie was asking her questions about her family, how she had encountered Renate, but the questions were light, not like an inquisition.

"And your stepfather?"

"Oh—a child-molester," Luisa replied bluntly. "This went on till—I suppose I threatened something when I was fourteen or fifteen. It's funny how I forget, maybe because I don't want to remember."

"Really a molester?" asked Dorrie, wide-eyed. "Fooling around in bed and all that?"

Oh yes. And it was a miracle she hadn't become pregnant, though she had made an effort to wash herself. Luisa spoke flatly. If her biology was uncertain, so was that of a lot of girls and women who became pregnant when they thought they couldn't have been impregnated (Luisa had read about such), and after all she was talking facts.

"My God," Dorrie said, impressed. "I think you look remarkably normal—considering."

This made Luisa laugh. She told Dorrie about the years from fifteen to seventeen when she had done her best to look and act like someone who slept in the streets, riding motorcycles with boys, smoking and drinking wine in bar-cafés, making her mother and stepfather furious, for different reasons.

"I wanted to be a tough and I was. I can still see myself talking with the fellows and the town whore in the neighborhood square—and people staring at me, wondering if I was a girl or boy."

"Trying to make yourself as unattractive as possible to girls *and* boys, it sounds like."

That was true, for that period. Unattractive to her stepfather, for sure.

"I wanted to say something about Petey tonight."

"Petey? Rickie's friend?"

"Yes. I liked him very much, you know."

"I know. I heard—something."

"Sometimes I think I'm not over it yet. I suppose I *am* over it, it's just that I haven't felt like that since."

Luisa tried to describe those weeks, maybe only six or seven, when she'd been so happy and sure of herself. It hadn't mattered that Petey hadn't been in love with her. She had felt outside herself, like a person everyone on the street might look at twice—though people hadn't. She had been *happy*, and she wondered if that feeling would ever come again. Luisa told Dorrie about Petey saying so earnestly and gently, "Don't be in love with me . . . I don't want you to be sad." That hadn't mattered. She had assured Petey she wasn't sad, wasn't going to be disappointed, no matter what. And that was true, until Petey had been killed. Then she had thought: Petey is no more, but her love was still alive, which she supposed was a natural feeling for a while, maybe a long while. Now she wondered if she would ever again exist in such a special way, because of another person.

"Does that come just once in a lifetime, do you think?"

Dorrie looked into a corner of the room for a few seconds. "I dunno. Maybe only once. And maybe three times. You're not even twenty, after all."

Dorrie was perhaps twenty-four. Luisa didn't want to ask. "I wanted to say—tonight, it's not like that with Teddie. Never could be. I couldn't have said all this in front of Rickie, you know. And I didn't want to say Petey's name. And yet—he knows, I'm sure, the way I cared for Petey."

"Does he? I knew Petey. A nice, serious boy, but what you're talking about is all one-sided, your own idea of Petey—isn't it? Because you were never very close to Petey, let's face it. So it's like a dream."

"I know," said Luisa firmly, as if she meant to hang on to her dream, and why not?

"You see, here—I reach a point where I can't say one more thing. So I'm going to change the subject. The lemon meringue here is especially good."

They ordered, and espresso to follow.

"I have an idea. Come to my place. I'd like you to see it. Telephone Renate, if you want to, to make sure you can get in tonight." Dorrie had to laugh here. "If not, you stay on my camp-bed tonight, and I'll take you to Renate's around the time the girls arrive in the morning, and you go in with one of them."

Luisa had thought of that. She felt better suddenly. But Renate was not going to say on the telephone whether she could get in or not tonight.

When the bill arrived, Dorrie said, "I'm inviting you tonight, OK? Suppose when you phone Renate, she's all sweetness and wants you to come home?"

"I don't think I will phone her."

"Good! That's progress."

Independence. But the truth was, Luisa did not want to hear Renate's yelping voice on the telephone. Put it off till tomorrow, Luisa thought, and don't ruin tonight. They got into the car, and Dorrie drove first across a large avenue Luisa knew, then into darker residential streets, some tree-bordered.

"And here we are," Dorrie said, pulling in at an unlit curb, "with a parking place, extra lucky. I have a garage though."

Then Dorrie was unlocking a partly glass front door, turning on a light in the lobby. They took a lift to the third floor, and Luisa saw the lobby light go off as they rose. Dorrie unlocked another door and put on a light.

"My place is disorderly—but no more than usual. Welcome!"

A short hall with a doorless cupboard for coats was followed by the one room Dorrie had mentioned. A low double bed showed an expanse of rumpled white sheets.

"Bed still unmade. This morning was a rush." Dorrie gave a laugh. "I'd ask you to sit down, but my bed's the sofa once I fold it. However—there's a chair." She gestured toward a white-covered easy chair. "Excuse me."

A naked female mannequin, bald-headed, stood in a corner by the front windows, one foot raised as if to step up a curb. A blue-and-red dishcloth hung neatly over her forearm. There were two big bookcases, a record player, a small TV set.

Dorrie was back from somewhere, bearing what looked like firewood. It was the camp-bed. Luisa helped.

At last it was up, stretched taut, hard as the floor, Luisa

thought, amused. Here came a pale blue sheet, so large, Luisa suggested they just fold it over. Then a pillow.

"Now I'll check the facilities." Dorrie disappeared again, and
returned after a minute, waving a still-wrapped toothbrush.
"Yours. Standard equipment here, for the unexpected guest."

Luisa went and took a shower, cool and delicious. There were
cartoons on three walls of the bathroom, half of them by Rickie.
On the back of the door was a large photograph of Japanese
wrestlers in action, and by some retouching of breasts and rouging
of lips, these had become convincing females. Luisa got into the
pajamas.

Dorrie went into the bathroom.

Luisa stared at the TV that Dorrie had turned on, and thought
of tomorrow morning. An impulse to ring Renate vanished as
soon as it had come: the damage was done, and phoning so late
would make things worse.

"Now, set chronometers," said Dorrie, reappearing in blue
pajamas, strapping on her watch. "Ten to midnight, I've got. I'm
usually up by seven. What time do your girls go in?"

"Around eight. Not exactly on the dot, but—"

"I'll have you there by ten to eight. All right?"

"Perfect. Thanks."

"Glass of something? Anything—water?"

Luisa didn't want anything. "I like your place."

"Really? I hope so."

Lights out.

Luisa lay listening to the traffic noises, the closer, more fre-
quent *whoosh* of cars. She felt that Dorrie was not asleep either,
that they both lay thinking, wanting to sleep because they had to
get up. Luisa blinked, watching the car lights ripple and flow over
the ceiling. Independence, Luisa thought, was sweet. And tomorrow, of course, she must fight for it, defend it. She sensed a battle
just beginning.

21

Dorrie Wyss stopped her car almost in front of Renate's house at seven minutes to eight. "How's that for timing?" she asked, proud of herself.

Luisa was already opening her door. She realized that she didn't want any of the girls to see Dorrie, lest they report something to Renate. And here came Vera.

"'Bye, my sweet. And call me anytime you feel like it. OK?" Dorrie gave a kiss to the empty air between herself and Luisa.

Luisa nodded and slammed the door.

"We-ell, you're up early," Vera said, brushing her long dark hair back, smiling. "Or up late."

"'Morning, Vera. Up early," Luisa said in a casual tone. She hung back and let Vera ring the bell.

They were buzzed in, and began climbing the stairs.

A man passed them, coming down on his way to work. Murmured good mornings, as Luisa didn't know his name.

Renate was holding the door open. "Good morning, Vera. Another hot day ahead—or so it seems."

"Ye-es, tough luck," said Vera, cheerful as ever.

"'Morning," said Luisa without thinking, and realized that Renate was taking the I-don't-even-see-you tack. Fine, better than scolding. Scolding would come later; Renate wouldn't be able to resist that.

Luisa returned to her work of yesterday. She had had a cup of coffee and part of a bun at Dorrie's, and one of Dorrie's cigarettes. And they'd left the beds! What a happy atmosphere at Dorrie's compared to this! Today Renate would go out silently on her way to Jakob's after nine-thirty, Luisa supposed, but to Luisa's surprise, Renate said around that time, "Coming out for your second coffee?" It sounded awkward.

"Yes, sure," Luisa answered. Then she understood: Renate

probably wanted to watch Rickie this morning, to see if she could discover anything from his behavior.

"It is warm again today," Luisa said as they walked. "Worse than yesterday, I think." She had slowed her usual pace, as always, to match Renate's step-and-drag, step-and-drag, though in public Renate made more of an effort at a normal gait than at home.

"Hm-m," was the reply.

In Jakob's, Luisa went to reach the *Neue Zürcher Zeitung* down from the circular rack, as she often did. As she turned to go to Renate's table, Rickie came in with Lulu on the lead.

"Hello, Luisa!" Rickie called.

"Hi! Hello, Lulu!"

Lulu, happy at hearing her name called, stood on hind legs for a moment to greet Luisa.

"Had a nice time last night?" asked Rickie in a normal voice, as if unaware that Renate was within hearing.

"*Very* nice. Thanks," Luisa said. "Talk to you later, maybe."

"Do that!" A smile, and Rickie went on to his usual table.

Luisa saw that Renate's eyes had fixed on Rickie. Luisa felt curiously sure of herself this morning. What had she done wrong, after all? Spent the night in a girl's apartment, so what? And Dorrie Wyss had been a good hostess, considering how small her flat was.

Andreas bade them good morning and took their usual order, espresso with cream.

"You stayed at Rickie's house last night?" Renate asked.

Luisa answered slowly, "No-o."

"Then where?"

Renate didn't know Dorrie's name, but would know her by sight as one of the gay group, Luisa thought. "Does it matter? I was back in time for work—as usual."

"It matters because you are in my *employ*," Renate said with an effort at keeping her voice low, "and I can report you to the authorities."

"For what?" asked Luisa, in a polite tone.

"For disappearing—not telling me where you are in the evening—the night."

Andreas was serving, putting two little pieces of paper with the tally under Renate's saucer.

"That is not in order," Renate continued, when Andreas was out of hearing, "unless you tell me beforehand where you're going—that you'll be *out* all night!"

She said the last three words as if the phrase were a sin all by itself.

"I am not managing a hotel, Luisa. In a hotel you would have your freedom, of course."

Where was all this written, Luisa wondered. Nowhere that she knew of. Luisa was mustering a reply, when Willi Biber appeared on her left, staring at Renate, apparently wanting to speak with her.

"Frau Renate," he mumbled, hands shaking. He gestured toward the door. "Today—"

"What about today, Willi?"

Luisa stared at Willi's thin, pale face, fascinated by his struggle. What was he trying to say?

"—coming to my house," Willi said.

Renate showed impatience. "I think they are repairing your door. Didn't Frau Wenger say so?"

Willi shook his head in long, slow twists.

"Luisa, could you leave us just for a moment? I think Willi does better if there are just the two of us," Renate said with a pained expression. "Sit down, Willi." She gestured toward the end of the table, where the bench curved against a partition.

Luisa slipped out at the other end. She had been at pains not to glance at Rickie. Now she walked toward him.

"Luisa," he said softly, "I think you have been dismissed. Please sit."

Renate was listening to Willi with concentration, making a

downward movement with one hand, as if to ask him to keep his
voice low.

"And what did you do last night?" Rickie asked.

"Oh—a very nice dinner. Dorrie treated me, because I hadn't
a franc in my pocket. And then, I was sure Renate was going to
make it hard for me to get in the house. So I stayed the night at
Dorrie's place."

"Did you? Good! You mean you didn't phone Renate last
night?" he asked in a whisper.

"No." Luisa had to smile.

Now Rickie chuckled, and his eyes strayed to Renate and
Willi, still in conversation. Rickie reached for his cigarettes. He
was thinking that Willi was talking about something more important than his doors being repaired, and that could be that the
police wanted to see him today. But would the police ring up first
and make an appointment? Maybe, via the Wengers. Rickie
decided not to mention this possibility to Luisa. Best to try to
reach Freddie Schimmelmann. Renate seemed to be concluding
matters, trying to nudge Willi into departure.

"I think your jailer is requesting the pleasure of your company
again."

Frau Hagnauer was not beckoning, but the toss of her head as
she tried to catch Luisa's eye meant, "Come here, now."

"A happy day to you, dear Luisa, and let me have your news,
will you? Phone me today or this evening," Rickie said.

Luisa was on her feet. "I'll try."

Willi Biber, shuffling toward the main door, disappeared from
Rickie's view. Renate had been giving Willi orders about something, Rickie thought. Her bony forefinger had struck the table
again and again as she spoke. It was time he got to the studio, so
Rickie left some coins and went out with Lulu, deliberately not
glancing at Renate's and Luisa's table.

Renate was saying, "You never told me where you were last
night."

Luisa had drained the last cold drops of her espresso. Frowning slightly, ready to depart, she said, "At a friend's."

"A boy or a girl?"

"A *girl*," said Luisa, annoyed.

She'd done nothing wrong, but Renate had been deprived of the pleasure of locking her out last night, or at least of delaying her getting in! Luisa had a premonition of a lucky, happy day, despite Renate's sourness. And Luisa realized that a lot of her happiness—yes, happiness—was because she felt able to count on Dorrie Wyss now as a friend, just as Rickie was a friend, someone who would lend money, a key, a bed, in case of need. *I'm not an orphan anymore,* Luisa thought.

MATHILDE BROUGHT A COFFEE to Rickie's worktable. He was looking up Freddie's two numbers which he had noted in a business address book.

Freddie's home did not answer. His work number said that Officer Schimmelmann was on duty in a car, and was the message urgent?

"Yes," said Rickie. "If you can reach him, would you ask him to ring Rickie Markwalder—just Rickie—when convenient. But by noon, if possible."

Then Rickie forced himself to concentrate, pencil in hand.

The third telephone call that morning was from Freddie. "I was going to phone you," Freddie said. "Senn and a doctor are coming at three this afternoon—to talk with our friend, y'know?"

"I suspected that."

"At his place," Freddie continued. "The Wengers'. I'd like to be there but I wouldn't care to bet I can make it today."

"Try," Rickie said at once. "I can't, of course. Listen—I think you remember—the woman at the Wengers' in a long dress?"

"Um-m—yes."

"I have a hunch she'll be there—to help her protégé. You follow me?"

"Yep, Rickie."

"I've a hunch she was rehearsing him this morning in the Small g. Where can I reach you—say around six?"

"Um-m—you can't. I'll get back. At your house tonight?"

"Likely enough. Try anyway, Freddie—and my thanks!"

RENATE WENT VERY SOON to the telephone after she and Luisa returned from Jakob's. She wanted to speak to Therese Wenger, whose L'Eclair number she had to look up in the book. She used the telephone in the sitting room, which offered more privacy than the hall.

Therese answered.

Renate said, "I gather our Willi will have visitors this afternoon at three?"

"Ye-es, he had a notice—in the post—and he brought it to us to read to him. And they also telephoned. A man called Senn, *Detektiv*. And another who is a doctor." Therese Wenger spoke softly and clearly.

"Oh? What kind of doctor?"

"I didn't ask. But we'll be here to help Willi. Of course it makes him nervous," said Therese calmly.

"Of course! I don't know why they want to see him *again*. I shall come over, Therese—just before three, if that's all right with you."

It was of course all right with Therese.

Just after two-forty, Renate spoke to her girls, said she was going out, probably for less than an hour, and were there any questions now?

There were not.

When Luisa heard the blessed click of the apartment door, she stood up. Check with Rickie. Something was going on.

"Who wants another coffee?" Vera yelled.

"With cake? Yes! Who's serving?" asked Stefanie, grinning, her blonde hair dark with sweat above her forehead.

"I will," said Elsie, and got up.

Luisa knew Rickie's studio number by heart. She dialed it in the sitting room.

In a few seconds, Rickie was on the line.

"Excuse me, Rickie. Is there something happening today—now—"

"They're asking our simple friend a few questions today at three. Freddie told me. At L'Eclair, you know. The—authorities."

"I think Renate just went there," Luisa said.

"I am not surprised. Can you phone me around six today at my apartment?"

"I'll try. I'll have to get out, of course, to phone."

IN KARL AND THERESE WENGER'S TEAROOM, five ladies were having tea and pastry, two pairs and one single at the tables. And Willi Biber was at work in the generous kitchen behind this room, washing mixing bowls and baking pans in the big sink. On Frau Wenger's orders, he wore a loose yellow shirt over his sagging T-shirt, but he had already got the rolled-up sleeves wet, because they had sagged with his activities. Still, the arrival of the police and their entry into L'Eclair's kitchen came at a time when Willi was respectably employed, and not three meters from his modest dwelling.

"Willi?" said Frau Wenger, who preceded the men into the kitchen. "Your friend Frau Renate is here. And here is—"

"Thomas Senn," said the sturdy blond man in civvies, with a polite smile.

"Officer Schimmelmann," said Freddie. He carried a brown paper-wrapped package which he held in both hands.

"Dr. Faas," said a smallish, mustached man of about forty.

Willi looked but didn't even vaguely acknowledge these introductions.

"Willi, if you dry your hands—I thought we might go up to my apartment." Frau Wenger stood straight and attentive.

"No, Madame," said Thomas Senn, "we would like to go where the accident happened. That was in a street near here, I believe." Senn was ready to move.

Out they all went then, except Frau Wenger, into the warm sunlight. Feldenstrasse with its row of plane trees was two streets away. Hatless now, Willi towered over the others, even over Senn who was a tall man.

"So," said Senn, having glanced at a house number on his left. "Here by this tree—"

Renate could see an X in chalk, worn but still there, on the pavement near the tree. She caught Willi's eye, gave him a nod and a small smile of reassurance, almost a wink. He was sweating with nervousness, she could see.

"Officer—" Senn gestured.

Officer Schimmelmann at once pushed the cord off an end of the package, and pulled out the tripod section with its scratched yellow paint.

"Do you know this object, Herr Biber?" asked Detective Senn. "Seen it before? It was found in the walk there—just behind you."

Renate said, "I think you should not put ideas in his head, sir. You see that he is handicapped." She wished that Therese—so helpfully pro-Willi, so used to him—had come along, but she had casually stayed behind to tend the tearoom.

"That's why I'm here, Madame," said Dr. Faas amiably, "to make sure Herr Biber is treated fairly—no pressure. I understand the situation. We all do. But it is necessary to ask a few things."

"Yes," said Senn. "Just names to begin with. Teddie. You know a young man called Teddie?"

Willi shook his head slowly. "No."

"Or Petey," said Officer Schimmelmann. "You knew a young man named Petey, I think—several months ago?"

Renate stamped a foot. "What are we talking about—and who?" She shot a glare at Schimmelmann, the little chum of

Rickie Markwalder, an evasive type, no friend of hers or of Willi's, certainly, and why a friend of Markwalder's? Had Markwalder given him money? "I thought we were talking about a boy called Teddie—whom Willi does not *know*. Willi said to the officer here the other day that he didn't know Teddie. Remember, Officer?"

"Yes, Madame," replied Officer Schimmelmann.

Detective Senn said, "There are some coincidences. Peter Ritter was a friend of Herr Markwalder. So is Teddie Stevenson. Herr Markwalder has reason to know that Willi Biber—frankly, knew both by sight, anyway. Willi Biber was at Jakob's bar last Saturday night and departed at a time when he could—*could* have followed Teddie—"

"Stevenson," Officer Schimmelmann put in. He had set one end of the metal piece on the pavement and kept his hand on the other end.

"I'll show the way it could have happened." Senn reached for the metal piece, and the police officer presented it horizontally. Senn had stuck his notepad into a pocket. He took a couple of paces into the front path, turned, and held the metal in a position to use as a ram or to throw a short distance. He took a quick step toward the curb with it.

Renate flinched.

Willi's expression did not change.

Senn said, "Like that." His voice was calm and neutral, and he was watching Willi Biber without staring at him. "But of course we're not sure this was the weapon—" He went into the path again and stamped on a part of it. "Just because it was found here. Do you remember anything about this, Herr Biber?" Senn asked casually.

Renate looked at Willi, but he was not looking at her.

"No," said Willi.

"Have you ever seen this yellow—tripod piece before?"

"No," said Willi, shaking his head now.

Renate sighed, as if with impatience. "This neighborhood has its share of drifters—troublemakers—on a Saturday night." She addressed Senn.

A window rattled above them. A man on the second floor of the next house looked out, curious. Senn paid him no mind.

"What's the trouble?" the man asked.

After a few seconds, Senn said, "Nothing."

The man continued to watch.

"Willi, did you know Teddie's car was here?" Officer Schimmelmann asked, pointing toward the X on the pavement.

"Yes," said Willi.

"He—then you know Teddie, Herr Biber? By sight, I mean. You know Teddie when you *see* him?"

Willi looked to Renate, who was frowning and taking a deep breath.

"Again," said Renate, "you're trying to tell him what he knows or doesn't know! Dr. Faas—"

"No, it's a fair question," said Dr. Faas. "Herr Biber, do you know Teddie when you *see* him?"

Willi looked at a loss, as if he were thinking: Yes or no, and why? "Yes," he said finally, positively.

"Good," said Detective Senn, visibly relaxing. "At least it's something!" he added with a smile to Renate and to the police officer. "Herr Biber, do you remember seeing Teddie at Jakob's Biergarten—last Saturday night? The fireworks night?"

"Yes," said Willi, with a nod.

"Do you remember when he left? Went out of Jakob's?"

Willi thought. "No."

"When *you* left?"

"When?" asked Willi.

"What time was it—about—when you left Jakob's?"

"No," said Willi. His tone was flat.

"He's quite vague about time," Renate murmured. "That question is useless."

Senn wiped his forehead with a handkerchief and made a note.

"When you left Jakob's—Saturday night—what did you do?"

Renate gave a short, positive nod, which she doubted if Willi saw. She had rehearsed this one with Willi.

"I went home."

Renate felt relief. Willi was not going to be shaken here, she was sure.

On that note, the questioning seemed to be over. Senn looked at the doctor, who gave no sign, but merely closed his notebook.

They began to walk in the direction of L'Eclair and Renate's street. Willi, practical in his way, had lowered the sleeves of his yellow shirt to let them dry during the questioning, and now he rolled them up again in preparation for dishwashing.

Good-byes and thank-yous and forced smiles all round, except for Willi, who didn't bother with either.

The police car was parked near L'Eclair with a POLIZEI card behind its windscreen. Renate lingered, looked back long enough to see that Officer Schimmelmann got into the car along with the doctor and Senn, who was driving. The car was not going in Markwalder's direction.

FREDDIE SCHIMMELMANN TELEPHONED just after six, when Rickie had been home hardly ten minutes.

"Not great news," Freddie said. "I was there, so was Renate. I thought it was better if I didn't go over to see you afterward, Rickie, with the doctor and Senn there. I don't want them to think we're that chummy, y'know?"

"And what happened?"

"Not much. Willi denies he even saw that piece of metal, which we had with us today. He does admit knowing Teddie's car was parked in that spot—admits that he knows Teddie on sight. But the rest—Renate was there, trying to steer him. Rickie, my hunch is it may be best to forget it. After all, Teddie's not badly hurt. It's a . . ."

Rickie's attention drifted. Yes, Teddie would mend, with an ugly but not big scar there.

"Happens often that we can't find the person who struck the blow, or stole the car—or we can't prove anything if we do. So we have to let it go. But the incident is on record, of course."

"I know. I understand."

Rickie hung up, feeling that Renate had scored another little victory. Not so little with Willi unscathed, and maybe the police would not question him again. He should've asked Freddie about that. And Teddie scared off the premises, forbidden the neighborhood by his mother. Not bad, Frau Hagnauer.

Frowning, he stood taller, and drew in his abdomen as much as he could. He felt rotten.

Again his telephone rang.

"Hello, Rickie, Luisa. Have you got any news?"

"Willi says he never saw that piece of metal—that he went home from Jakob's that night. But you know, Renate is just too interested. Why is she so interested, if he's innocent?"

"*Yes.*"

"Want to come here for a nice cold Coke?"

"Yes, but I can't. I'm out buying buns at L'Eclair and I'm a little shy about phoning from here."

Rickie understood. "You know, my sweet, pop into my studio or apartment whenever you have a spare ten minutes. You don't have to telephone first."

22

"The news is good," said Dr. Oberdorfer in anything but a cheerful tone.

Rickie squeezed the telephone. The doctor had rung him.

He was standing in his atelier, looking at Mathilde, who was paying him no mind, pecking out something on her computer, a pink Dubonnet at hand. "Then—why do you want to see me? Can't you tell me now?"

"I'd like to tell you face to face," said the doctor. "Unless you have something very important to do just now, could you come to my office within the next hour?"

Rickie of course said he could, even though he had an appointment at four that he might not be able to get back for. A new client. Wristwatches. Rickie asked Mathilde please to ring that company's number, and beg off for him. "Something more important has turned up," Rickie said. He felt that he was pale in the face.

Before Mathilde telephoned, Rickie dialed for a radio taxi. "Soon as you can, please." He'd get there with minimum effort. Then Rickie told Mathilde he thought he would be back within an hour—if not, he'd telephone. He went up to stand on the pavement till the taxi came. Had Dr. Oberdorfer heard of some mitigating drug in regard to HIV? Something that definitely prolonged the "incubation" stage in the lymph cells, before hell broke out somewhere?

So what? Rickie asked himself, trying the philosophical tack. It was only a question of time, wasn't it? Death, for anybody, was only a matter of time, wasn't it? *When* was the very personal question, unfair to ask, except that with HIV it was sooner, or soon. That much was certain. Rickie had succeeded in squelching his anxiety about every little lump, real or imagined, on his neck, for instance. He had gone at least twice to Dr. Oberdorfer with pounding heart and unnecessarily. He no longer looked daily for a purple spot on his legs, Kaposi's syndrome, just maybe twice a week. Now Dr. Oberdorfer had brought the time factor back: he had "good news," meaning (what else?) some means, some new drug that was going to prolong his life, maybe by three years, maybe by a few months. Nice, of course, when you're at the end. Maybe not to be sneered at.

Rickie rang the bell at Dr. Oberdorfer's office door, and was admitted by the fiftyish female nurse whose face Rickie knew well. It was a lean, neutral face with an expression that Rickie felt was professionally acquired: though very slightly "pleasant," it gave away no hint of life or death in the news to come.

"Oh yes, I think he's ready now, Herr Markwalder."

Rickie went into Dr. Oberdorfer's private office, which had a desk and chair and two other chairs, and whose walls bore no pictures, only framed diplomas.

"Sit down," said the doctor, words Rickie had dreaded.

Rickie thought people were asked to sit when the news was going to floor them. He sat with head high, attentive.

Now the doctor smiled. "And what do you hear from your young friend—Stevenson?"

"Oh—better every day, I think. Doing well."

Dr. Oberdorfer cleared his throat. "Herr Markwalder, I have good news for you. You are clear of the HIV problem."

Rickie didn't understand. "What?"

"Yes. You've been using condoms? Lately?"

Rickie's mind spun back to Freddie, Rickie's latest, that night with him. "Yes. Yes, indeed."

"Not so difficult, is it?"

"N-no."

"I was testing you. I'll confess that. A two-month test, you might say. Do you understand?"

"Not entirely."

"I confess I wanted to give you a real shock." The doctor's voice had become soft and Rickie had to strain to hear. "For your own good. I wanted you to find out you can live with 'safe sex,' if you understand me."

Rickie was beginning to. He was beginning to relax, and he had a long way to go.

"It's—no doubt out of order, what I did. You could sue me. I mean what I say. Go ahead and sue me, if you want to."

At that moment, Rickie felt like embracing Dr. Oberdorfer, shaking his hand, pressing it till the doctor cried for mercy.

"I've never done such a thing before," said Dr. Oberdorfer, still speaking in a clear, low voice. "Maybe I won't ever again. It would've been quite awkward for me, if you'd committed suicide, and left a note."

Rickie gave a short, loud laugh, which sounded odd, like a dog's bark, not like his laughter. In fact, he didn't feel like himself. He felt simply odd.

"I like you, Herr Markwalder, but you lead a careless life. You take chances."

Now Rickie understood, completely. "I don't feel like suing you."

Dr. Oberdorfer gave a small, rare smile. "Good. Well, that's all. Except I shall say I hope you keep on—you know—taking life the safe way. All right?"

Rickie stood up. Their handshake was firm. Rickie had extended his hand first.

The inscrutable nurse again, then the second door closed.

Must tell his sister Dorothea. Rickie walked. What would she say about Dr. Oberdorfer's behavior? Rickie realized he was walking in the wrong direction for home or even a bus. He turned, and after a few brisk steps went back to his thoughtful pace. He was not going to die *soon*, that was the happy news. And he didn't hate his doctor. "They're very young kids," Rickie remembered himself saying to Dr. Oberdorfer, months ago, remembered with shame now: sixteen- or seventeen-year-olds he'd picked up, anywhere. The kind who would manage to clean out his wallet, if he took them home, which he did, often. "You think the young ones can't carry diseases just the same as the older ones?" Dr. Oberdorfer had asked. And he'd been looking for more of the same the night he had found Freddie Schimmelmann.

For the umpteenth time in his life, Rickie told himself he was lucky.

A quarter of an hour later, Rickie was pacing thoughtfully in the lobby of Dorothea's apartment building. Dorothea was out. Shopping, probably, but it was nearer five than four now, and he had a feeling he wouldn't have to wait long.

"Rickie!" Here was Dorothea with two big plastic shopping bags. "How nice to see you! Something the matter?"

"No. Got some news," Rickie said. "Tell you upstairs. May I?"

"But of course!"

The lift. Silence. Dorothea had a worried look.

"*Good* news," Rickie said.

"Oh." Her brows relaxed. She unlocked her door. "Now what is it?" she asked, and let the plastic bags slide to the floor. The worried look was back.

"Sit down," Rickie said pleasantly. "I'll sit too." The tables were turned! "Sit down" meant good news!

Dorothea took the sofa, Rickie a straight chair.

"I saw my doctor—Dr. Oberdorfer. I'm not HIV positive. I'm all right! He—"

"What? Was that an *error*?" The frown again, the outraged sister.

"My dear Dorothea—he told me he was trying to teach me a lesson. And he did. A very tough one, OK."

"Rickie, talk *sense*!"

Rickie took a breath. "In a word—he was determined that I should practice—safe sex. You know."

Dorothea did.

"So I did," Rickie went on, "since he told me that."

Dorothea seemed to struggle. "But Rickie, that's horrible—what he said."

Rickie shrugged. "He said I could sue him and to go ahead." Now he laughed. "I understand. I said, 'I don't want to sue you.'" Rickie looked down at the carpet. "It's tough—a tough lesson.

OK. I'm not angry." He said the last words feeling humble, like a child punished, knowing the punishment was justified.

"You're going to *live*, Rickie." Dorothea had a wide smile now.

"Live a little longer."

"You used to say it was a sword of Damocles."

"Well, that sword is gone—for me." He stood up. The correct thing was to go, he thought. No more emotion. "I'll take off, dear sister."

"A quick drink? A good brandy."

"No, thanks. Maybe I don't need it."

"Nor I—I couldn't be happier!"

"You can tell Mother." Mother was the respectful term, for rare occasions.

"Does she know? I never told her."

"No? I somehow thought you had. I never did," he said.

Dorothea gave a big laugh. "Just as well, isn't it?"

Then Rickie was descending in the lift, feeling odd and awkward, as if in another world. He wasn't going to go around announcing the news, he told himself, just if the subject came up. How many friends had he told, after all? Philip Egli. Freddie Schimmelmann, poor fellow. Take it easy, Rickie told himself. No celebrations.

THE NEXT DAY, Rickie found a lumpy envelope in his post with Dorrie Wyss's return address. The bulk was in a second envelope addressed to Luisa. A small sheet of paper bore a note to him:

Hello, Rickie,

I know Luisa's address but—

I trust you can get this envelope to her by hand, please. Important.

Love to you,

D.

A pity, Rickie thought; he'd just seen Luisa and Renate drinking coffee at Jakob's. The envelope had something rectangular and flexible in it, and it rattled when he shook it. A keycase. Dorrie's housekeys. What a good idea! And he could do the same.

"Oh Rickie," said Mathilde, swiveling. "You asked me to remind you, Unimat comes today."

"Yes. OK. Thank you, Mathilde." What was it? House paint? Make-up? No, *toothbrushes*. Rickie had finished his colored rough days ago, a neat drawing of brushes in bristling center and brush handles radiating, multicolored of course, like the petals of a flower, from white to dark purple. "What time?"

"Three," said Mathilde.

Rickie pushed his hands into his pockets and began to walk slowly round his studio, eyes on the floor, the walls, unseeing. His strolls didn't bother Mathilde. "I'm thinking. Pay no attention," he might say. He made himself stop pressing the envelope in his right-hand pocket.

His vision of Freddie Schimmelmann with police cap and thin-lipped, slightly twisted smile yielded to a stronger image of Teddie, the dark-haired boy with the quick, handsome eyes, saying, as he had on the phone two days ago, "Oh, I'm writing another article . . . Yes, aiming for the *Tages-Anzeiger*." Teddie wanted to keep trying with this paper, trying to get a toehold. He had been in to see the editor. And of course Teddie had asked Rickie about Luisa, how was she, how did she look, though the iced tea and cake party had been hardly a week ago. "I'd love her to come to my place . . . We could spend a whole day together, if she ever has a day." No comment from Rickie here. A day that Luisa didn't have to account for to Renate Hagnauer? Yet how could Renate deny Luisa a lunch date of an hour or so? Well, Renate could and did, that was the answer to that one. Just as drifting nobodies in Zurich could stab and rob someone—anyone—and slope off unpunished, victorious. The world wasn't dedicated to seeing justice done. Things were often the opposite of what seemed natural and right, which reminded Rickie of his early adolescence, childhood even, when without consulting a book or an adult, God forbid, he had known to keep his juvenile loves quiet, hidden, denied.

Rickie bumped into the corner of a drawing table, and paused. Teddie was wrapped up in his journalism and in Luisa. He lit a cigarette. Wrapped up in anything but him. Rickie was only a go-between. Teddie hadn't even expressed regret at not being able to come to the Small g any more: after all, Luisa could come to him.

And Luisa? He sensed a cooling toward Teddie, not that Luisa had ever been intense, Rickie thought, nothing like the way she'd been about Petey.

Mathilde, he noticed, was having a Dubonnet with ice. Rickie went to the fridge and took a Heineken. He decided to clean out a certain portfolio in what was left of the morning, chuck sketches that he would never need again. Rickie dragged over his largest metal wastebasket. The telephone rang.

"Markwalder Studio," Mathilde said. "Rickie—a girl. I think Luisa."

"Good!" Rickie said at once. "Hello?"

"Hello, Rickie. I'd like to see you—now. Unless you're tied up, of course."

Rickie said he was not busy till three, and to come over. She was at Jakob's. Rickie went on with his discarding, folding old sketches, sticking them in the basket already lined with plastic for paper conservation.

Luisa came on the trot, leapt down the stairs and knocked.

Rickie opened. "Unexpected pleasure!" He wondered if they could talk with Mathilde present. "Something happen?"

"Hello—Mathilde," said Luisa. She lingered near the door.

"Hel-lo," said Mathilde. "How're you?" She returned to her work on the computer.

Luisa whispered: Teddie had rung, and she had managed to answer, when Renate rushed up and snatched the phone from her hand. "'These are working hours.' Renate said and she hangs up. It was so shocking—I just ran out. I had to talk to someone—*you*. The girls heard it all, of course."

Rickie gave Luisa a slow wink. "It won't last forever. Now if you've got a minute—" He pulled the wrinkled envelope from his pocket. "From Dorrie this morning."

"Dorrie?" Luisa tore off a corner of the envelope. She saw a key case plus a note, an ostrich-leather case with two keys in it.

"I guessed it," said Rickie. "And I can do the same—with my keys. You have hideouts—safehouses, Luisa."

Luisa blinked, reading the note. "How nice! That's really friendly. I have to go now, Rickie. I feel so much better! I always do when I see you." But she was tense again. "'Bye, Mathilde!"

Rickie watched her vanish up the cement steps. The day was starting in a positive way.

LUISA HAD HER KEYS, and with the girls still at work, Renate had not played any trick with the inside bolt. Renate might suppose she had gone out to ring Teddie from a phone booth. Luisa felt she had done something bolder, made contact with both Rickie and Dorrie. In her room, Luisa pulled the key case from one pocket and Dorrie's note from another.

Dearest Luisa,
        You have a roof and a camp-bed any time in Zurich.
Not to mention shower, fridge, and TV.
        See you Saturday? I expect to come to the Small g.
                                            Love,
                                              D.

Saturday was two days off. Luisa rubbed her thumb across the light brown leather of the key case. Elegant! She dropped the case with deliberate casualness into a shallow tray on her dressing table, and left her room to go back to work.

Renate shot a look at her, but did not interrupt her lecture-in-progress to Vera about a piece of work now in Vera's machine.

That evening, Renate did not mention Luisa's dashing out that morning, and they watched a TV episode of *The Trackers*, of which Renate was especially fond.

Luisa would write a note of thanks to Dorrie, easier than phoning, even though she'd see Dorrie Saturday night. And what might she give Dorrie in return? She could make a black velvet vest for Dorrie, or design a jacket. No, a vest. But when could she make it, with Renate peering—everywhere?

SATURDAY MORNING, LUISA HAD A LETTER from Teddie. The envelope bore a typewritten address and had no sender's name. Having recognized the type as easily as if Teddie had written it by hand, she pushed the letter into her pocket and deposited the rest of the post on the kitchen table. Renate was in the workroom, where Luisa had emptied the five wastebaskets, and in a few minutes, they were going out to Jakob's, as on working days. Luisa opened her letter in her room!

Dearest Luisa,

I just sent off my finished article to the *Tages-A*. "A Bump in the Road" or alternative title, "Night Adventure 2," about being clobbered from behind, after dancing at a Biergarten. Be assured—no names! Didn't write Jakob's or the Small g. Or you, God forbid! About being knocked nearly out, and being helped to my nearest friends by total strangers! Human kindness!

How are you? Please write a note or phone me as I'm usually in by orders. This reminds me, I can't come to Jakob's this Sat. night, but shall be thinking of you—dancing, being happy. Doctor says I can go out by next Wed., if I am careful. I take showers now and never think about

it. No bandage. The scar will always remind me of you.
That may not sound nice, but I mean it in a happy way.

XX My love, my love, T.

Luisa and Renate were going to Jakob's Saturday night and Renate
was even creating a dress for herself. This was an electric blue satin,
embellished with flat gold braid depicting a serpent with a red eye,
and red open mouth. The frowning, spitting dragon might have
been a portrait of Renate, Luisa thought, so it was comical to Luisa
on Saturday night to see Renate's finely wrinkled face break out
from time to time in quick, polite smiles, almost grins.

By contrast, Luisa wore a white shirt whose tails hung out,
black cotton slacks, and a thin red tie tied in a loose knot, casual
gear, though Luisa felt tense and excited. She and Renate arrived
shortly before ten. The dance floor swayed to "The Tennessee
Waltz," and a few of the dancers clowned to the sentimental
melody. Luisa had a glimpse of Rickie at a table in the far corner
to the right, then she avoided looking at him, lest Renate make a
remark. Three strangers sat at the long table that Renate liked to
think of as hers.

"A coffee?" Luisa asked.

"A white wine," replied Renate.

Luisa took her time getting to the front bar to order. First
there was already a dense crowd, and second, Luisa loved feeling
lost for a few seconds, moving toward invisibility, among a lot of
people. It was the opposite of being stared at.

"'Evening, Luisa!" said Ursie, working two beer taps.

Luisa gave her order, wine and a small beer, and paid, then
made her way carefully back to the long table. She was glad to
render this service for Renate, because she knew Renate's shyness
about her crippled foot. It even pained Luisa a little that Renate
tonight hadn't bothered putting on one of her pretty slippers, of
which she had five or six singles. Some were of patent leather, one

of pale blue kid. One foot could show, the other must not, so most of the time Renate chose to hide them both.

"Who're you looking for?" asked Renate.

Luisa hesitated. "No one!" She had, in fact, glanced over the dance floor for Dorrie, and hadn't seen her. Still standing, Luisa saw Rickie in the far corner, talking with one of his friends. "I'll be back!" she said to Renate, and started toward Rickie, circling the dancers to her left.

Renate had a moment before pulled her sketchpad from her big handbag, and lit the cigarette in the long black holder. The present scene wasn't ideal for sketching: young people in cool and careless garb, older ones in square-tailed sportshirts and loose summer dresses. A loud young man occupied the half-open telephone booth, and another fellow yelled at him to wind it up.

"Rickie!" Luisa was smiling, making progress, but he hadn't heard her.

Then he shouted, "Ah, Luisa! Here she comes! Make room!"

But nobody did make room, though Philip waved cheerily and the dark-haired Ernst called a greeting. Beer and wine glasses and ashtrays covered the table.

Philip got up from a chair. "Dance?"

Luisa pushed her beer onto the table.

The lanky and limber Philip danced at a little distance from her. He wore white slacks, white shirt scarcely buttoned, and a T-shirt beneath. His hands were cool. How did he manage that? When Luisa touched his side, she felt his ribs.

"Weren't you taking *exams*?" she shouted.

"Yep! Passed 'em!" Philip waved a hand.

Luisa glanced toward the main door, the big bar, and saw Dorrie coming in, wearing a red vest, white shirt, and dark trousers. Was she alone? Luisa didn't look again.

They went back to the table. Above Rickie on the broad partition behind him sat an old-fashioned electric fan that turned slowly in a semicircle back and forth.

"Your friend—Rickie's friend," Philip began, "the one who was hurt—"

"Teddie. I heard from him today," Luisa said. "His doctor says he can go out next Wednesday. Leave the house, I suppose. I should tell Rickie. Or you can."

Philip did, leaning across the table. "Teddie's circulating again next Wednesday!"

Rickie gave Luisa a slow nod of thanks for this information.

Luisa realized with a start that Dorrie stood beside her, smiling, greeting Rickie, and giving a general "Good evening!" to the others.

"No chairs? Must we dance all ni-i-ight?" Dorrie yelled in English.

"Ye-es!" someone shouted.

"Are you by yourself tonight?" asked Dorrie.

"By myself—" Luisa, abashed, tried to laugh. Dorrie wore greenish eye shadow, spooky and effective. "Didn't you see my boss—over at the usual table?"

"No! I didn't and who wants to see her?"

"You alone?"

"Ye-es!" said Dorrie firmly. "I have a date with you. Want to dance?"

Luisa laughed, embarrassed. "Maybe later." It was a good song, and the dance floor was filling. "Dorrie—the key case—it's beautiful! Thank you."

"Most welcome—you are. You must make use of it." She turned to Rickie. "How're you, Rickie? And how's Lulu?"

"Umph!" said Lulu, which pleased Dorrie, but Rickie at once said, "That means she's bored and wants some action." Rickie sank out of sight, followed by Lulu, and reappeared on the other side of the table, wobbling to his feet. A man had got up to let him through. "Enough exercise to last me till next *year*! Come, dear Lulu!"

Rickie extended his palms, and suddenly Lulu was on Rickie's shoulders. "Bravo!" He steadied her with both hands on her sides, then off they glided to the music, Lulu's forepaws on one shoulder, her hind feet on the other.

"Look!"

"It's a statue!"

"A real *dog*! Sure!"

Lulu was as still as a white statue, however, her expression calm. She was doing her work. The crowd gave her a hand, not a big one, but a hand, because she was balancing herself now. Some shouted her name. Ernst Koelliker whistled his admiration. Rickie was taller than most of the crowd, the dog still higher.

"Yee-aye, Lulu!"

Rickie smiled. He had rehearsed Lulu once at home, but tonight she excelled herself, because the crowd put her on her mettle.

The music improved, which was to say it became a loud irresistible beat that got a lot of people up. Couples became groups. Luisa moved off with one hand held by Philip, the other by Dorrie. There seemed to be two circles of hand-holding people. Luisa had a glimpse of Rickie moving toward his corner table, with Lulu still on his shoulders.

People were chanting "Group-a" or was it "Grappa"? A teenaged boy in blue jeans fell, and stayed on the floor rotating on his backside, with arms and legs outspread. Laughter. A blur of faces.

Minutes later, when people at Rickie's table had ordered food and more drinks, it occurred to Luisa with a faint pang of guilt that she ought to go back to Renate for a moment and see if she wanted to order something or go home. It took Luisa a few minutes to get there. A stranger asked her about "the boy who was attacked . . ." and Luisa gave her cheerful "next Wednesday" news. Luisa got within sight of Renate's long table, and found it entirely occupied by people she didn't know. Luisa looked toward the crowded bar section. No Renate in sight. Five minutes past midnight, she saw on her watch. That did give her a shock, that so much time had passed. Was Renate going to be angry when she got home? But Renate could have sent Andy with a message, if the lateness were that important. Luisa went back to her friends.

23

"Can I *see* your room?" Dorrie whispered.

Luisa, surprised by the question, looked up at the house ahead: no light in the top window. See her room. And why not, Luisa thought? She and Dorrie had just been dancing together, not the only two girls or two fellows dancing together at the Small g tonight.

"Why not?" Luisa whispered back. "Renate's probably gone to bed, so we'd better be quiet."

"I can be quiet."

Luisa led the way. Keys. The feeble light of the *minuterie*. Alone, Luisa could have made it in the dark. She put a finger to her lips. They climbed two flights. Feeling for the keyhole with a thumb, then working the lock, Luisa got the door open. Again her hand found Dorrie's easily, and she led Dorrie down the hall to a door on the right. There had been no light under Renate's door on the left side of the hall.

"Come in," Luisa whispered.

Then she closed the door, and put the harsh main ceiling light on, because its switch was the nearest.

Dorrie stood in her dark trousers, red vest, looking round, smiling a little.

Luisa's bed was made, a single bed with head against the wall on the right, a night table near with a lamp. Her dressing table with its three drawers looked presentable, and so did two posters—

one a Toulouse-Lautrec from the Kunsthaus, the other a de Chirico from a smaller show. A bookcase. Two chairs, one straight, the other upholstered in a green-and-brown-patterned material which Luisa liked: this chair stood near the inner court window whence came some light for reading on good days.

"Really OK," Dorrie said. "Much higher ceiling than my place."

"Would you—"

Rap-rap-rap!

My God, Luisa thought, and turned to open the door, but the door was opening.

Renate stood in one of her Chinese kimonos, scowling, then advancing. "What's going on here? So much *noise!*"

"Noise? I'm sorry, Renate. We were whispering. This is—"

"Oh, I know, I know," said Renate, clapping a hand to her right eye as if the light hurt her. She jerked her hand away and stood up straight, balancing on the ball of her bad foot, which Luisa could just see, naked. "What're you doing here?" This in a throaty voice that Luisa had never heard before.

"I'm leaving, Madame," said Dorrie with a quick smile at Luisa. "Nice to've seen you."

Renate gazed at Dorrie as if at an object of horror, and stepped aside to let her pass.

"I'll come down with you," said Luisa, feeling her courage return. After all, she had said earlier to Dorrie that she'd walk her to her car.

"Oh, you will? To where?" said Renate, almost shouting.

"To her car," Luisa replied. "It's parked near where Teddie parked his." This to Luisa was a dangerous dark area now.

The hall light was on. Luisa slapped her left pocket: her keys were there. Luisa and Dorrie went to the apartment door and out.

"What a tyrant!" Dorrie said, laughing, when they were down on the pavement. "You mean you can't have any *visitors?*"

"She hates gays," Luisa said reluctantly. "Claims she does."
They were whispering in the silent street. "I thought I told you,
she thinks Teddie's gay because he stayed one night in Rickie's
apartment—not the night he was attacked but the first night,
when it got late or something."

"Here's my car, thank goodness," said Dorrie. "Apart from the
old battleax there—it's been a nice evening! Thank you. Can I call
you? In case something amusing turns up?"

Luisa hesitated. "Better if I call you. OK?"

"Sure, but do it."

Before Luisa realized, Dorrie had touched her shoulders, and
given her a quick kiss on the lips. Dorrie unlocked her car.

"Hope you don't get hell tonight," Dorrie whispered. A quick
wave, and she was gone.

Luisa walked back toward her home, hoping Renate had
decided to go to bed, knowing she probably hadn't. Tonight furnished such rich ammunition! A dim light showed in the window
of the sitting room. Once more the stairs, the unlocking. Luisa had
half expected the door to be bolted from the inside and for the rest
of the night.

Renate was standing in the hall, one hand over an eye. "Get
the doctor!"

"What? Which—"

"Call the doctor! I can't *see* to call!"

"Luethi?"

"*Yes*, you stupid girl!"

Luisa knew Luethi's number was among those on a list by the
sitting room telephone. She dialed the number, and got a recorded
message that was interrupted by a sleepy female voice.

Renate yanked the telephone from Luisa's hand.

The doctor had come on now.

"Hello, Dr. Luethi . . . Yes, Renate Hagnauer. It's the *retina*, I
think. You remember—I *am* keeping calm, as much as I *can* under
the circumstances!"

Luisa retreated a step. Yet Renate would want her to play nurse now. She heard Dr. Luethi saying, "If I were *there* even—" a couple of times, and being interrupted by Renate.

"Tomorrow—you *must*. Please!" Renate said. "All right. At nine o'clock."

At last, she hung up. Her right hand had stayed over her eye the whole time. "I've probably lost my *sight*!" she whimpered, almost in tears. "This shock—"

What shock, Luisa thought. Dorrie in her room? "Can I get you something? Tea?"

"Tea!" Renate scoffed. "A cold compress. Ice cubes. Oh, put them in a hand towel! Five or six cubes, not the whole tray!"

Luisa hastened to carry out this order, and found Renate in her bed, eyes shut, frowning. "Do you have pain?"

"Not so much, it's these *lights*. Darting red and white—the doctor warned me, you know."

Luisa vaguely remembered something about "a delicate retina" the last time Renate had been tested for glasses.

"If it's really torn, then I'll be blind in that eye. Or else have an operation that's probably not successful!"

Renate radiated energy and wrath. Luisa wanted to remind her to stay calm, and was afraid to. "Something else I can get for you, Renate?"

"No. I'm sure you'd like to be off. So—"

"No, I'm here. Just tell me—"

"Nothing," Renate interrupted. "So leave me."

Luisa walked toward the door, then stopped and turned. "Good night."

"Leave the door a little open."

Luisa did so, not liking to, because she felt Renate somehow pursuing her down the hall. She took a shower, brushed her teeth, then went to bed. She fully expected a summons from Renate for something else during the night. How much was Renate pretending? Blinking in the darkness, Luisa reviewed the evening, Rickie

with Lulu on his shoulders, waltzing and turning. And Dorrie—
what a good dancer! Luisa had a vision of her slim figure, black
trousers, white shirt, bobbing and spinning on Jakob's dance floor.

She awakened to the murmur of a voice: Renate was on the hall
telephone with the doctor, Luisa supposed. Eight-ten by her watch,
early enough for a Sunday morning, when Renate usually allowed
herself to sleep till nine. Luisa got dressed, instead of putting on a
dressing gown, as she usually did for her first cup of coffee.

The kettle was on, the drip pot prepared.

"'Morning," Luisa said. "How're you feeling?"

"Terrible."

"Can I get you anything, Renate?"

"Just bring me some coffee—when it's ready." Renate went
back to her room.

Luisa prepared a tray with bread, butter, and orange marmalade. Renate sat up in bed with a damp hand towel over her
right eye. At least she had dialed the doctor's number just now,
Luisa thought.

"Thank you," Renate said coldly.

Dr. Luethi arrived at half-past nine, carrying a brown leather
bag. He had a lean figure, a lean face, and a smile that pulled the
corners of his mouth, while his worried gray eyes stayed the same.
Luisa had let him in, and she lingered in Renate's room near the
door, ready to be of service or to be shooed out by Renate.

The doctor focused the reading light, plus his own head lamp.

"Happened last night," Renate said. "I had such a shock—"

"Look straight at me. Now up to your left—keep still—now
up to your right." After a moment he said, "There're no inflamed
blood vessels visible, and that's a good sign. Now these lights—"

"Red and white. You told me to take them seriously if they
came again."

"Your ophthalmologist told you that. Of course I'd like you to
see him."

"But of *course*. I started to telephone him this morning."

"He would tell you to lie still, not to try to lift anything. You mentioned a shock?"

"Yes! A stranger in Luisa's room. It was after midnight. I'd just—"

"An intruder, you mean?" asked Dr. Luethi in a surprised tone.

"No, but a *stranger*."

"A friend of mine wanted to see my room," Luisa put in. "She'd been there just a few seconds, not even sat down—"

"Dr. Luethi is talking to me, Luisa."

Luisa had expected that.

Renate focused on the doctor, recounting her surge of fear last night, a sense of something bursting behind her eyes.

"Well, I gather it didn't warrant that much alarm," said the doctor, smiling. "Now you take it easy today, Frau Hagnauer, and I'll make the appointment with Dr. Widmer tomorrow for you, if you like, and let you know."

That suited Renate. "I was warned about my retina."

"Didn't I also warn you to try to relax more? Remember when you had those fast heartbeats and you were told it was due to stress?" He turned, smiling, to Luisa. "Good-bye, dear Luisa, and take care of our patient."

"Of course," said Luisa.

Renate decided to remain in bed, and she wanted the Sunday papers, extra coffee, her cigarettes within reach. Possibly an omelette for lunch with a small salad. And could Luisa wheel the TV set in? "Come back at once after you fetch the *Sonntags Blick*. I'll need you near all day in case of an emergency, you know."

"Yes," said Luisa, not looking at Renate. There went her Sunday, her day off by right. There went any chance of seeing Rickie or Dorrie. And Teddie seemed suddenly very far away.

The kiosk where she bought the *Blick* was two streets beyond Jakob's, and on her return, she looked into the tavern. No Rickie. It was around ten-thirty.

Ursie was behind the bar at the espresso machine. "Rickie
hasn't shown up yet, Luisa. Sunday morning, y'know."

"Tell him hello."

"You coming back?" asked Ursie.

"Not sure. Probably not." Luisa went out, and looking left on
the pavement was delighted to see Rickie with Lulu on the lead,
one street away. "Hi, Rickie!"

"Good—morning, dear Luisa. And how did your evening
finish?"

Luisa laughed nervously. "Got to hurry home with this."
She indicated the newspaper under her arm. "Well—Dorrie
was in my room a few seconds last night, just taking a look at it,
and Renate barged in. You'd have thought Dorrie was a robber!
Renate made a big scene and after Dorrie left, Renate pre-
tended— Anyway, she thinks there's something the matter with
her *eye* now. A torn retina. I don't think anything's the matter
with it."

Rickie gave a laugh. "I can imagine *that* scene. Dorrie in your
room!"

"Rickie, I've got to go. I'm the nurse today, meals in bed. She's
going to the eye doctor tomorrow."

"*Schönen Sonntag!*"

Luisa walked toward home, toward the new chill that was settling into the apartment. She sensed something worse to come,
something heavy, indescribable, and more important than even
Dorrie.

24

Renate's appointment the next day was at 10 A.M. Luisa had
ordered a taxi. She was to accompany Renate, of course, and

had already spoken to the girls in the workroom, told them of the delicate condition of Renate's eye, and made sure they had their work laid out for the morning. At that time, a little after eight, Renate was resting.

The girls were rather surprised.

"Did she have a fall?" Vera asked.

"No, it just came on suddenly—Saturday night," Luisa answered.

Renate had created a patch for her eye out of folded dark cloth and an elastic cord. Luisa sat in a corner of the examining room which had charts on the wall and various lamps as well as a chair like a dentist's.

"Flashing lights," Renate said, "white and some pinkish. Naturally, this causes some blurred vision." Her tone was sharp, as if to order the doctor to see it her way.

In silence, Dr. Widmer examined the eye from all angles. Finally, he said, "I don't see any sign of retinal damage. No damaged blood vessels. Do you see anything like a veil obstructing your—"

"Yes! It's grayish. I had a shock, you see—a stranger standing in a room of my apartment. I felt that something burst behind my eye."

"Somebody broke in?" asked the doctor, attentive.

"A friend of one of my apprentice girls. But it was after midnight—when I opened the door and—"

"But a friend," said the doctor.

"Yes, but I'm talking about the shock."

Dr. Widmer advised resting the eye, thought the covering a good idea, and gave her something easier to wear. Drops now, when Renate's chair was reclined to horizontal. She was to take the little bottle with her. Two drops twice a day; he would see her in two days' time, or if there was improvement, there might be no need for her to come again.

Luisa sensed that Renate was disappointed at this. She had murmured something at home about "hospital rest."

At home, instead of resting, Renate at once went to check on the workroom, wearing her new black patch which looked like an item from a pirate's costume. Renate made light of her trouble now, and cut an imposing figure as she inspected work-in-progress, and checked an autumn coat in Vera's charge, which had to be finished by Wednesday morning: the client was coming. This was Frau Loser of Kuesnacht, for whom Renate always had to make out two bills, one the real bill, the second for Frau Loser to show her husband.

Renate even examined the kitchen floor—the girls had had their midmorning coffee and cake—and asked Luisa in a brusque way to give it another sweeping.

The worst was dinner that evening. They were to have lamb chops, two smallish ones each, baked potato, and salad. Often they cooked together, but now all was for Luisa to do, including the table-setting (the bridge table in the TV sitting room, more elegant than the kitchen), while Renate watched the TV, now back in the sitting room, or did some one-eyed reading of the newspapers.

Renate waited until they were seated, glasses of wine poured, the first silent bites consumed, then said, "Luisa, you may consider yourself no longer obliged to take your meals with me. I admit— I confess—I can't bring myself to treat as normal what I saw Saturday night—or what that will lead to." Despite the vagueness of her words, Renate spoke as if she had a hardened conviction of what she was saying, and would never be budged on it.

"I—" At a loss, Luisa shrugged. "Dorrie asked if she could see my room. What's wrong with that?"

"You know the people she associates with—homos, lesbians— because she's one herself." Renate forked a lamb morsel into her mouth. "You think I want girls in my establishment friendly with such people? I do not!"

Luisa chose her words. "It seems to me people can have all kinds of *friends*. Rickie has become a friend. And you're mistaken about Teddie, who's not a homo."

Renate twitched. "Worse—the two-faced kind. Bisexual—dangerous and dishonest." Her uncovered eye bored into Luisa's face.

Luisa gathered herself, making sure her knife and fork were secure on her plate, then rose with her plate and wine glass. "Since I am not obliged to share the same table—" Luisa carried these items to the kitchen. She drew up a chair, no longer hungry, but she was able to eat the rest and intended to.

Tonight she'd try to get out—for half an hour anyway.

Renate clumped up the hall, clump, scrape, clump, scrape, and appeared in the doorway, looking angry enough to give her other eye a rupture. "If you are thinking of going out tonight to see your sordid friends—go ahead. But you will not get back in."

Luisa did not answer, only stared back at Renate.

"Good night. And wash the dishes before you go to bed."

Luisa's mind spun. The nearest telephone was L'Eclair. Was her post going to be safe? Well, yes, Luisa could get there first (downstairs), unless Renate went down earlier and waited for the postman at eight-thirty or nine.

She tidied the kitchen, while Renate watched a program that they usually looked at together. As she was pulling the rubbish bag up to tie it for removal, a thought struck her: if she tried to quit Renate's employ, Renate could give her bad references.

But as yet the idea of leaving Renate was shocking. Nearly a year she'd been with Renate, who had befriended her, given her room and board (provided them for a modest sum, anyway), who had instructed her and encouraged her almost as if she were Renate's own daughter. It was impossible to imagine that all that could be swept away, overnight. It simply didn't make sense.

She took a second shower before she went to bed. She had found herself stinking from anxiety and fear, something she hadn't known since running away from her family, when she had ended up in the Zurich railway station, full of strangers who looked at her directly, some hostilely, men and women too, and she had been scared, sensing odd and dangerous thoughts running through their heads.

She was in bed before eleven, reading a biography of Chopin, an old hardback from Renate's bedroom shelves. Yesterday it had been interesting; tonight Chopin seemed unimportant. She got up and went to her table, and tore off a sheet of notepaper.

She wrote:

Dear Rickie,

Please tell Dorrie, also Teddie, that Renate is on the warpath and it is maybe impossible to phone and just as bad if they phone me. Maybe I said some of this, but things are worse. I'll try to get this to you in Jakob's tomorrow morning—else drop it in your postbox.

Love,
L.

RENATE HAGNAUER'S HOUSEHOLD began to stir before seven, as usual. Renate and Luisa were on their feet, Luisa in the kitchen making coffee. Both had always liked to breakfast in their dressing gowns in the kitchen.

Now Renate came in with her eye patch in place, and said, "Would you bring my breakfast on a tray this morning, Luisa? I want to rest my eye as much as possible."

Luisa prepared the usual, coffee with milk separate, sliced bread, butter, and strawberry jam this morning. After serving this, Luisa breakfasted alone in the kitchen.

It was almost a joy to ready the long worktable, definitely a joy to greet the smiling faces of Vera, dear Elsie, and Stefanie. Each asked Renate how she was faring, and had the doctor said what was the trouble?

Renate replied with an air of suffering. "I am sure I am better. No, no pain, thank you."

Then came the nine-thirty break, always initiated by Renate and made definite by her departure from the house.

"You don't have to come if you don't want to," said Renate coolly, when she and Luisa were in the apartment hall.

"Oh, but—well, I'd like to," said Luisa. Up to now she had served as escort for Renate.

A first-floor tenant exclaimed at the sight of Renate. "Oh, Madame! What happened?"

"Nothing! Maybe a torn retina. Not—"

"Ach! Retina—"

Passersby on the street of course gave Renate a glance: here came the grim, one-eyed pirate Captain Kidd, and with a limp too, as if she had a wooden leg. Luisa repressed a smile.

Jakob's, and Ursie at once spotted Renate from the bar. "Madame Renate! 'Morning! And what happened to your eye?"

"Nothing at all. A little strain," replied Renate.

Luisa got a *Tages-Anzeiger* from the rack for Renate. They had just sat down, when Rickie and Lulu appeared in the doorway between the bar and the dining area.

Seeing them, Rickie bowed slightly, bowed again at the sight of Renate's convex black patch. Renate wasn't watching. There was no need for Renate and Luisa to order. Andy soon brought their espressos with cream. And Renate lit her cigarette.

"Something in the eye?" Andy asked with concern.

"No, just a little strain," Renate replied with a tight smile.

Luisa's right hand was in her pocket, her fingers on the folded note to Rickie. Couldn't she just walk over and hand it to Rickie, maybe under pretense of a handshake? Or simply drop it on the table? Luisa nursed the last third of her cup. Renate was absorbed in the newspaper. Luisa eased herself along the bench.

"Back in a minute," she said, though Renate had not lifted her eyes. She went slowly and directly toward Rickie, who at once looked at her.

"Sit down, sweetie," he said.

"Brought you this." Now with her back to Renate, she took her hand from her pocket and dropped the note by Rickie's croissant plate.

"Ah, thank you. A love letter!" Rickie pocketed it. "Teddie phoned this morning. He would love to take you out Wednesday evening for dinner. He can pick you up at an exact time in a taxi."

Luisa almost writhed. "I explained in my note—"

"Use my house as a meeting place!" he interrupted. "Think about it. I can arrange it."

"Just tell him it's tough. I don't want to make a half-promise." Luisa glanced over her shoulder, and found Renate's eye fixed on her. Smoke curled from her mouth as if from the mouth of a dragon.

Renate was now busy counting out coins. She paid for Luisa as usual. They were silent, except for murmured good-byes to Andy and Ursie.

Slap, scrape, slap, scrape went Renate's shoes. She did better with a cane, had an elegant black one at home, but detested carrying it, Luisa knew.

"I saw you passing a message to that Rickie this morning," Renate said in a staccato monotone.

"Yes. I don't think you like me phoning him from the house, otherwise I would."

"You'll make my eye worse if you keep up this nonsense!" She slowed and touched the eye patch delicately. "I can feel it throbbing."

Luisa said with deliberate calmness, "I don't know what you're angry about."

"The degenerates you seem to prefer lately! What do you think I'm angry about?"

A woman passing them in the opposite direction glanced at Renate with a surprised expression.

Luisa clenched her teeth, made herself stop. "Degenerate? Worse than that *Dorftrottel* Willi? You seem to like him all right and

he lied about the French Foreign Legion. You must've heard it—
that evening at the Wengers'. The police have his record." Luisa
had heard it from Rickie.

Since Renate couldn't deny this, she chose to say nothing. By
now they were climbing the front steps, Renate one at a time. She
pulled from her handbag an impressive ring of keys, which she
sometimes called a *trousseau* in the French manner.

Silence again.

Renate, after seeing that the work was going all right, took to
her bed. This caused Luisa to have to rap on her door at noon, to
ask if Renate wished her to bring a tray. Renate did: sardines on
buttered toast with a piece of lemon, and a sliced tomato with oil
and salt.

"And a small pot of tea, please."

Luisa prepared this in the kitchen, where two girls were
already at the table, eating the sandwiches they had brought from
home. Stefanie's school day was today, so she had not come to
work.

"She's really down, eh?" asked Vera.

"Something eating her?" Elsie whispered.

"I don't know," Luisa said, as if she were bored with Renate's
performance, which was true.

The next morning, Luisa jumped every time the telephone
rang. The sitting room telephone had been moved into Renate's
bedroom, so she could handle business calls from her bed.

Elsie, just returning from the toilet, was close to the hall telephone when it rang around three that afternoon. "For you, Luisa.
A fella," she said with a wink.

Teddie, Luisa thought. "Hello?"

"Hi, Luisa! What about tonight? I'll pick you up at seven?"
Teddie spoke in a rush. "I'll be in a taxi and ring the bell, or you
can be—"

"Just a minute," Renate's voice interrupted on the other
phone. "Luisa is not . . ."

"Teddie, I'm sorry," said Luisa, embarrassed. "You see it's—"

"Or tomorrow night," Renate's voice continued. "She is under contract with me, and until . . ."

"Get off the line, Madame!" Teddie shouted. "Chris'sake, what an old bitch!"

"Enough!" That word came like a squawk, and Renate hung up with a clatter.

Luisa could hear the girls in the workroom whispering and tittering. "It's sort of a crisis, Teddie—Rickie knows."

"I talked with Rickie half an hour ago," said Teddie. "Can you come to his apartment?"

"Got to sign off, Teddie. I'll be here, you know."

"Yeah, I *know.*"

Luisa hung up softly, hating to face the girls.

"Is he nice? He sounded nice," Elsie whispered.

"*Luisa!*" That was from Renate.

Luisa went to Renate's room.

Renate had a nosebleed, and Luisa had the feeling she had made the most of it by getting a stain on the top sheet. She wanted more paper tissues, though a goodly supply was within her reach.

"This absurd excitement!" said Renate with contempt.

Luisa was to make a pot of tea, bring a damp cloth—no, bring a clean top sheet for the bed, please. Meanwhile Renate muttered about rudeness. Luisa changed the top sheet while Renate lay with head back, though the bleeding seemed to have stopped.

It was another evening when Renate dined by herself, served by Luisa, and had the TV set for company, while Luisa tried to eat something in the kitchen. Luisa wanted to run out, to escape, and forever.

When the phone rang, Luisa flew for it and lifted it before the first ring was finished. "Hello?"

"Hi, I'll meet you in ten minutes downstairs, OK?" said Dorrie's voice, and she hung up.

So did Luisa hang up, and smiled a little, thinking of Renate with fork in hand, not fast enough to catch any of that.

"What was that?" cried Renate.

"Wrong number."

Luisa checked her watch, stuffed keys and some money in her trouser pocket, and spent what time she had tidying the kitchen. On the dot of her ten-minute command, Luisa opened the door and escaped, floated down the stairs and out.

25

The shiny black hatchback rolled into sight and stopped near a parked car. Luisa dashed for it, opened the door, and climbed in.

"Hi, Dorrie!"

"Good evening! You know—I was taking a chance and I won, didn't I?" Dorrie laughed. "Where would you like to go? We can go anywhere."

True. The black car offered concealment, at least partial, from outsiders, and Luisa imagined that it might be bulletproof too, though it probably wasn't. "I have to think."

"Rickie called me and asked me for a drink *chez lui*. Told me Teddie was turned down and was miserable. What happened?"

The car crept along in first.

"I didn't turn him down. Renate picked up the second phone and yelled at Teddie. Then when you rang I said yes right away, I was so angry."

"You said nothing. I said I'll be here in ten minutes. Did you eat yet?"

"Not really."

"Let's try the Pavilion—if we can park and there's a table. Two big ifs."

Off they went, through the Langstrasse, under the tracks of the
city's railway station. Dorrie couldn't find a legitimate parking
place, and took a chance in a narrow street off Raemistrasse, saying she felt lucky tonight. There was no table at the Pavilion for
the moment, so they bought beers at the bar with the aid of a
waitress Dorrie knew—one Marcia who promised to do her best
for a table. Dorrie introduced them.

"Luisa—pretty name, pretty girl." Marcia went off with a
heavy tray.

The place was loud with conversation. Music from somewhere was nearly drowned out. It was just what Luisa loved, at
least tonight, lots of people and anonymity.

"A table!" said Dorrie.

Marcia had signaled.

Chili con carne caught Luisa's eye on the menu. She had
heard that it was very popular in New York pubs. Then she
exclaimed softly, "Smoked salmon!" as if it were the greatest luxury in the world.

"That's cool, have it," said Dorrie.

Dorrie gave their order. She told Luisa about Bert stealing a
naked male mannequin today from a store where they were working together.

"It'll come back, of course, when he gets tired of it. One of
the shopgirls asked him was he going to sleep with it and what
would he *do* with it. 'A hard man is good to find,' Bert said." Dorrie's face grew pink with laughter.

They went to a basement bar-café near the Weinplatz, where
Dorrie dared to park her car. "For an hour—maybe less. I like to
think my black car can hide itself from cops."

Luisa stole a glance at her watch: ten forty-three. The bar-café,
rather small, was called the Shopping Center. The waitresses wore
black overalls and white shirts. Dorrie knew a few people here, a gay
bar for girls, Luisa supposed, though only two girls looked like people Luisa might have labeled gay. She ordered an espresso at the bar.

A rather large blonde girl asked Dorrie if she could "interrupt," meaning dance with Luisa.

"No, thanks," Luisa said. "We want to talk."

"See? Easy," said Dorrie.

It was all easy, and smooth, until she and Dorrie were rolling along in Dorrie's car again, getting ever nearer the street where Luisa lived. Then everything shifted into a tight gear, as if in readiness for a war.

"I'll say it again. If she locks you out tonight, you stay at my place. No problem. So I'll wait—ten minutes? And if you don't come down I'll know you got in."

Luisa, peering, saw no light at the sitting room window. She was poised to open the car door. "She can play a game for ten minutes, knowing I'm trying my key—keeping the door bolted."

"Then I'll wait fifteen minutes," Dorrie said. "Or get a taxi to my place. Or—well, Rickie would let you sleep at his apartment, wouldn't he?"

"Oh, certainly."

"I'd hate that, but it's closer," said Dorrie. "Try it, sweetie, and I'll be here fifteen minutes."

Luisa climbed the front steps and used her front door key. It was half-past midnight, late for the people in this building. Luisa climbed the stairs softly, and inserted her key. The first bolt moved, but she couldn't open the door. She took a breath, then knocked gently.

Silence, and she listened hard. She could hear her heart beating, but what she listened for was Renate's step, which however soft she tried to make it would be audible where Luisa stood. She knocked again, more loudly. Unthinkable to ring the bell, it was loud and shrill.

Still nothing happened. Six, seven minutes had passed? She could still run down and rejoin Dorrie, go to Dorrie's place, and Dorrie would bring her back before eight. Luisa started down the stairs, softly but still audibly in her sneakers, and a step creaked. She went down more steps, then paused.

She heard a bolt slide. The door opened a crack, a very small crack, and Luisa climbed the stairs again. The crack stayed the same, as if Renate were ascertaining that it was she and not some stranger. "Thanks," Luisa whispered.

Renate took a few seconds to open the door wider. The apartment hall light was on.

Luisa slipped in.

Renate muttered, "You should be glad I let you in. Thankful!"

"I'm sorry you put the bolt on. I needn't have woken you."

"Needn't have woken me, when you ran out this evening to God knows where? How do I know what you'll come home with! I saw who you were with. You think I'm running a whorehouse—a place for call girls?"

Luisa kept a calm silence, her objective being to get to bed as soon as possible. She turned in the hall, because she intended to be polite. "Good night." Then Luisa saw and recognized a couple of blouses, beige trousers, pajamas that had been tossed out onto the hall floor. Her clothes, from the basket in the big bathroom with the bath.

"I don't want your filthy clothes with mine. Wash yours separately, I don't care where! You understand?"

Luisa picked her clothes up. "Yes," she said firmly. She took the clothes into her room.

"*And,*" yelled Renate, advancing with a slap, scrape, "you are not to use the big bathroom again, understand? Take your things and you can start using the shower bathroom only."

Luisa hoped that was Renate's last message for tonight. From the big bathroom, Luisa collected her spare toothbrush, towel, and a few items from the medicine cabinet. Now she'd have to use the washing machine separately in the basement on Tuesdays, Luisa supposed. Was Renate going to hand her her own dirty clothes in the basket and expect her to wash them as if she were a servant, Luisa wondered, and had to smile at the thought. She washed and put on pajamas. She longed for a glass of milk, but was afraid of another yell from Renate, whose door down the hall was still slightly open.

"Luisa!" The yell had come.

Renate wanted cold tea with ice, sugar, and lemon on the side. Luisa set about this, and managed to take a glass of milk to her room.

Renate claimed to feel pressure behind her eye, and a weight on her chest. In bed, she kept her good eye mostly closed, and maintained a miserable expression. Luisa did all her biddings and said not a word.

Around ten that evening, Freddie Schimmelmann had telephoned Rickie (not having found him in Jakob's), and said he was in the neighborhood and could he come by? Rickie had hesitated, then said yes. Freddie might have news.

Freddie appeared in uniform, even long-sleeved shirt and jacket. "I have just talked with our mutual friend," he announced to Rickie, removing his cap as he entered the apartment.

"Which one?"

"Willi—our *Dorftrottel*," said Freddie with his wrinkled grin. "May I?" He removed his jacket, then loosened his tie. "Surprise visit, you know. I thought it would be better if I went alone and in uniform."

"Did he *say* anything?"

Freddie chuckled. "No. Not at first and not at the end. He got such a shock at the sight of me, he nearly pissed in his pants. Had to let the poor guy go to the toilet."

"You saw him alone?" asked Rickie, surprised.

"No—because those people—Frau Wenger, she followed close behind me. She heard me knock on his door. So I had to take the gentle tack. 'Maybe you remember a little more now—about

the boy who got hit in the back? With something *hard*?'" Freddie
said "hard," shoving his fist as if to jab someone at kidney height.
"And he did maybe, but he kept saying 'No, no' and shaking his
head. Same as last time. Pity. If I'd been alone with him—"

Rickie took a breath. "So Frau Wenger said you were being
cruel tonight?"

"No. She couldn't. No possibility. It's unhealthy the way she
takes care of that fellow. Very handsome doors there now, Rickie.
Stained dark brown and varnished. Have you seen them?"

"Not in their finished state," said Rickie primly. "But that was
fun, Freddie. Worth it! The only punishment Willi's ever going to get,
it looks like, my intrusion with Ernst. The only thing that impressed
him—his doors kicked in! Let's have a beer—or something."

They drank small beers out of the bottle. Freddie was still
sweating, despite a faint breeze through Rickie's window.

"Could I have a shower, Rickie?" Freddie's tone was almost
pleading.

"But—naturally." It was natural, after a long day, to want a
shower. And Freddie had tried tonight, tried beyond his assigned
work or duties, to help. Rickie got a big towel.

Freddie had hung his jacket on the back of a chair and his
damp shirt over that. "Y'know, Rickie, we'll never get the truth
out of Willi unless we can get him in a room and bust him. His—
stupidity is going to save him."

Rickie knew. "I wonder what else he's going to do," he mused,
"if Renate programs him? Maybe a girl next time."

"A girl?"

Rickie laughed. "Oh, Dorrie's getting fond of Luisa, I think.
Remember Dorrie—the blonde girl who's a good dancer? I don't
mean it's serious—but Renate's jealousy knows no bounds."

Freddie chuckled, not very interested, and went off to the
bathroom.

When he returned, he rather shyly proposed what Rickie had
expected him to propose. "Why not?" Freddie asked.

Rickie hadn't told him that he was "clean." And Freddie wasn't clean. "Did I tell you—I was summoned by my doctor—and I'm not HIV positive." Rickie's voice was firm. "Dr. Oberdorfer said he was testing me for two months—making me practice safe sex."

Freddie looked dumbstruck. He stared at Rickie for a few seconds. "Really, Rickie? But that's *wonderful*! Neither am I HIV positive, y'know? I was only—"

"But you said you were."

Freddie shook his head, smiling. "I thought with both of us playing it safe—I said it so I could be with you. Thought I had to, from what you said."

No HIV, plural the two of them. And Freddie willing to lie about a thing like that! "You're telling me the truth now?"

"I swear. I am." Freddie raised his right hand. "I get my checkups. So why not, Rickie?"

Rickie thought also, why not? He could trust Freddie. So Rickie headed for his third shower that day, then for another pair of small beers to take to the bedside.

They both laughed: safe sex again. It was almost like being married, Rickie thought. In certain ways, better. Freddie wasn't a teenager. Freddie wasn't a thief, either. Rickie had grown used to finding his wallet empty in the morning, or earlier, if his young companion—one of the "little ones"—had wanted to depart, say, at 3 A.M. How many gold or silver cigarette lighters—?

The curious thing was that despite Freddie being thirty-eight, Rickie's sex life was becoming better. Certainly better than—if he faced it—with the pretty boys. So rambled Rickie's thoughts as he lay smoking a cigarette, sipping from the still cold bottle. Freddie seemed to be dozing. Long-distance telephone calls too, Rickie remembered, to impress a former or even current boyfriend, now holidaying in Acapulco or Florida. People like himself, dumb enough to pick up such boys, simply had to pay, pay also with being abandoned. And with Freddie he could feel safe in regard to

HIV. It was the horrid existence of the HIV virus, Rickie thought, that made one think: It floats in the air, it can be exchanged with a glance, it rubs off on sheets, though he knew that was not true. HIV had become a specter, however; that much was true.

Wakening, Freddie said, "Oh, I almost forgot something." He eased himself out of bed. He swung his big towel round himself, then reached into a pocket of his jacket. He produced a little gift-wrapped box.

Rickie felt embarrassed. "For me? Oh, you *shouldn't* have."

Under the gift-wrapping Rickie found a white box from a jewelry store whose name he knew. Inside was a silver key ring—his initials in a flat silver circle attached by braided black leather to the key ring proper.

"It's really good-looking. Thank you very much, Freddie—looks very expensive."

"Na-aa, I swear."

"I'll start using it right away."

Rickie had a happy idea—ice cream. There was a box of vanilla in his fridge. Rickie put on pajama pants and top and fetched it, plus spoons. Freddie donned his undershorts, his now dry blue shirt, and they sat on the edge of Rickie's bed, spooning delicious bites. "You know, Freddie—I think Dorrie and Luisa have a date tonight—if Luisa can escape." Rickie gave a short laugh. "Luisa's having it rough—Renate trying to coop her up."

"What's happened?"

"Nothing—apart from Renate seeing Dorrie—fully clothed—standing in Luisa's room." Rickie smiled. He'd told Freddie about that on the phone. "But Renate doesn't want Luisa to have any—well, boyfriends, I suppose. They're maybe 'bad for her work,' and girlfriends—gay ones out! Dorrie's got a crush on Luisa."

"But Luisa doesn't like girls, does she?"

"No. Maybe she could, I dunno. Renate kept Luisa from seeing Teddie tonight—the first night since that injury he could go out. And he's had another good word from the *Tages-Anzeiger*, he told me, so he may get his second article published. And there's Renate—the old closet dyke, listening in on Luisa's phone calls! Oh, and the *crise* now with Renate's eye." Rickie filled Freddie in on that, which Luisa thought an imaginary ailment.

"What Renate needs is a real shock," said Freddie. "A prank—a surprise party. Make her blow up! Drop dead! Think of something, Rickie. You're good at that."

"All right, I'll think."

26

For the second weekend, Renate managed to keep Luisa at home and away from her friends. This was fairly easy: she reminded Luisa that the ophthalmologist had said that she wasn't to lift anything, even a kettle of hot water.

On Monday, Renate and Luisa made another trip to Dr. Widmer for a ten o'clock appointment. He pronounced the eye "all right." No inflammation. Renate spoke of a sensation of pressure, still. The doctor tested the vision. It was equal to the other eye.

"If you want to see me—I am here," said Dr. Widmer, as if he didn't want to see her, but if she insisted—

That was not very nice of him, Renate thought, not a professional tone to use. In the taxi riding homeward, Renate mulled over Dr. Widmer's attitude, even his remark that the black patch seemed unnecessary.

"From now on too," Renate said to Luisa, "you can keep your food separate from mine in the fridge."

"Oh—I was already doing that," Luisa said calmly.

Renate hated her calm. There was something the matter with the girl. Well, that was plain, wasn't it? Renate, her one eye gazing out the window as the taxi sped along, looked at Luisa suddenly and said, "Taking on a girl like you—from nowhere—I should have known." She said it firmly, as if there were something in Luisa that rendered her hopeless, unredeemable, for the rest of her life.

At home, Renate saw that the girls had their work assigned for the day, and instructed Vera to double-check on a navy blue jacket whose gores were tricky. Renate was slowly making Vera her foreman, which she was already, but she was nudging Luisa out of any and all vantage grounds of the past.

Still feeling the sting of Dr. Widmer's offhand treatment, Renate announced to the workroom that she would be out for lunch, back she hoped before three. She went into her bedroom and telephoned for a taxi to arrive in forty-five minutes. That would give her time to freshen up and apply a little makeup.

Renate asked the driver to go to the Hotel zum Storchen, which had a rooftop restaurant, but en route she decided to try the Storchen's bar instead. It was of a comfortable size, with a piano, and some tables for two at which one person did not look odd. She had removed her eye patch as soon as she was out the door of her apartment house.

What a shame the old days were past, Renate thought as she savored her lobster meat, when she and Luisa might have been enjoying a similar lunch together. Once in a while she had given the girl a treat, of course. Those days were before Luisa had plunged herself into the homosexual scene. Who would've thought it! Renate took consolation in sips of delicious white wine. The meal was followed by an espresso and a cigarette.

At the hotel door, she asked the porter to summon a taxi. She had given him a two-franc piece, and he held the taxi door open for her. Renate was not sure how it happened, but suddenly her face was on the taxi floor, her nose scraping along the corrugated rubber mat.

Renate gasped.

The taxi driver opened the other door. The porter was trying to take her arm to help her. Renate had to crawl backward out of the taxi in order to get to her feet. And was her long skirt up at the back? Certainly the porter would've had a fine view of her feet, one in a slipper, the other in an ugly boot!

"Madame!" said the porter, extending a forearm.

"Are you all right?" asked the taxi driver.

"Thank you. Thank you."

Finally settled in the taxi, Renate gave the driver her address, and turned her attention to keeping the blood from dropping on to her dress front. She thought she had a slight nosebleed, and some kind of scratch along the bridge of her nose. She put the eye patch on before she opened the apartment door.

From the workroom, she heard the murmur of voices, and a shrill "Ha-a—*ha-a!*" which Renate recognized as Stefanie's.

Renate entered her bathroom, and washed the smeared blood from her nose and cheeks. She was glad no neighbor had seen her downstairs just now! A nasty scrape on her nose. That would create little dark red scabs. Renate applied alcohol.

Then she entered the workroom, where the conversation died at once, though Vera and Luisa did not stop their work.

Stefanie looked at her, and said, "Oh, Madame Renate, what happened?"

Renate noticed that Luisa glanced at her face, then continued to pin something. "Oh, nothing! It's because with this eye patch I can't judge distances, you know."

Renate sent Luisa down to the local pharmacy for calcium tablets and more aspirin.

FROM RICKIE, LUISA LEARNED THAT Teddie had had his second article, "A Night in Town," accepted by the *Tages-Anzeiger*, which proved to Luisa that a letter to her from Teddie was missing.

Luisa was convinced that there was no limit to the twists that people in authority could invent. Rickie saw things the same way, though he had never said it in so many words. This was why Luisa liked being with him and talking with him. And he took chances. He had told her a story of being in a hotel in Istanbul in which the air-conditioning didn't work, and his windows were not made to open, the hotel told him. Rickie had finally driven his right fist through a windowpane. He had shown Luisa a scar on the outer edge of his right hand.

"Have another evening with Dorrie," Rickie said. "What's the harm? Or with Teddie. He'll want to celebrate when that second article comes out."

Yes, Luisa was sure of that. "Tell him I'll try."

"Try? You'll make it! You make a date with him now—and we'll make it." Rickie meant if she rang Teddie up now.

Luisa didn't. She was then in Rickie's flat, at just before seven on a Thursday evening.

Rickie saw her hesitation and said, "Come on then, you and I are going to a cinema tonight. It's a new film made in China. All right? Do you want to ring the old witch?" He gestured gracefully toward his telephone.

It seemed so easy. Luisa dialed, stood up straight, and informed Renate that she was going to a cinema and would be home later. Before twelve, she added for politeness's sake, and hung up before Renate could reply.

"Splendid! Now we're free."

She felt free. They shared a cold beer, checked the film time in Rickie's newspaper, then rang for a taxi. In town they had time for a wiener before the film started. They'd go to a Chinese place afterward, said Rickie.

The picture was not as great as they had expected. In the talky parts, Luisa's thoughts wandered to the prison that the apartment, the workroom had become. Renate was trying to push Vera into her place. Well, so be it, Luisa didn't care. Vera, who was a *Schneiderin* anyway, higher than Luisa, didn't want a "favored" place, because she didn't like Renate. Who did like her? Vera realized that she could get excellent training from Renate, and that was all she

wanted—plus perhaps a good recommendation from Renate
when her contract was finished. What did the girls think of the
present state of affairs? They'd never guess that—or would they?—
that Renate had blown her stack over a date or two with a
boyfriend, then a girlfriend? Luisa was learning not to underesti-
mate what another person might guess or divine. But Luisa
doubted if Vera and the others could imagine Renate's intensity,
once she realized that she, Renate, might not be number one in
Luisa's—what? Affections? Luisa's eyes focused as a ball of red fire
sank into a horizon of dark blue water.

"FIN" appeared in large white letters on the screen, and the
audience began to stir.

"You see? You're going to need it," said Rickie when they
were out on the pavement. He handed her the tweed jacket that
he had insisted on taking from his closet.

"Rickie!" a voice cried.

It came from a tall young man in a beige summer suit, who
was going into the cinema for the next show. Rickie introduced
him as Markus. The young man grinned.

"*So*, Rickie," he said, glancing at Luisa.

"Yes. Isn't she a darling? She has metamorphosed my life.
Wears my clothes!"

"Hah–ho–o!" said Markus, and drifted away.

Luisa was smiling. She felt happy—for the first time in days.

They walked to the Chinese restaurant.

With a taxi, Luisa was in front of her house before midnight.
Rickie paid the taxi off, and insisted on waiting until he was sure
she could get in. If she couldn't, she was to come home with him.

Luisa entered the house and climbed the stairs. Rickie had
told her to keep his jacket "till next time."

The apartment door opened easily, and then Luisa was con-
fronted by Renate looking shocked.

"Don't bring *that* in the house! Whose is it?"

"I had to borrow it. I was cold."

"Get it out of here! Out!" Renate snatched the jacket, which Luisa was carrying over her arm, clumped into the sitting room, and without putting the light on raised the window higher and threw the jacket out.

"All right, I'm going to get it!" Luisa headed for the door.

"You do and you won't get back in tonight!"

Luisa went out the door and closed it, and sped down the stairs. Rickie was just bending over a bush by the front step, retrieving the jacket.

Rickie laughed softly. "I could *hear* her!" he whispered. With a movement of his head, he indicated that she should come with him.

27

Luisa awakened just after six on Rickie's big sofa, clad in large yellow pajamas, under a white sheet folded double. She felt happy and rested too, though she'd slept hardly six hours. Soon she'd be drinking coffee with Rickie here in a pleasant atmosphere, maybe eating bread and jam with him. Enjoy this while you can, Luisa told herself.

She walked barefoot on Rickie's wall-to-wall carpeting. Luisa put on water and accidentally clanked the kettle on the hotplate. "Damn!"

Rickie slowly awakened. He wanted tea this morning instead of coffee, because it was a special morning. He appeared in pajamas and a striped cotton dressing gown. "Ah, Markus should see us now, breakfasting together!"

"Oh-h—the fellow at the cinema! Yes! Bread, Rickie?"

"No, my dear, my diet. I try. I give up a lot of things, but not my beer or my croissant in the morning."

"Arf!" said Lulu.

"Lulu, at Jakob's—not here. It's the word 'croissant.'"

They sat at Rickie's polished dining table. Butter and jam and
sliced bread for Luisa. A cigarette and tea without sugar for Rickie.
Luisa stopped herself from saying thank you again to Rickie. She
felt so happy and secure with him, as if he could arrange anything,
protect her, hide her, if necessary. "Renate took a bowl out of my
hands and threw it in the sink—about four days ago."

"Broke it in the sink?"

"I'd nearly finished a bowl of soup—out of a can—so in she
comes humming, not saying anything. Then, 'Filthy soup!' she says,
and *bang*! I rinsed the pieces and dropped them in the bin. My
heart was beating like blazes. 'Now you can complain!' she said
and—when I didn't react at all, she hit me with her fist on the
shoulder. Can you imagine? I saw the blow coming so I just tensed
my shoulder and she fairly bounced!" Luisa laughed, remembering.

"I think you're taking it all very well."

"The bowl was one I'd brought from home—made by a
woman potter I knew when I was about eight. And like a fool I'd
told Renate this."

"It won't last forever—this monster in your life," said Rickie.
"I'm sorry you have another six months of it."

"Five months and a week. Even so." She looked at her watch:
seven twenty-two already.

Rickie went to a cabinet in his living room and pulled out a
drawer. "My apartment here." He held a key between his fingertips. "Give me your key ring, I'll put it on for you. Anytime, day
or night—just come."

Wordless, Luisa put the key ring back in her trouser pocket.

"Use the bathroom. I have plenty of time."

When she came out of the bathroom, dressed, Rickie said,
"Shall we have lunch? What time? I'll meet you at Jakob's."

Luisa twisted on her toes, nervous. "She'll say she needs me to
make her lunch. She's playing the invalid now."

At ten minutes before eight, Luisa encountered the cheerful Stefanie on the front path.

"Out already or out all night?" asked Stefanie.

Luisa whispered, grinning, "Don't you recognize my same clothes?"

"*Yes.*" She sounded impressed. "Hey—" But she was whispering, glancing up quickly as if she expected Renate to be leaning out of a front window. "What's she up to—treating you like a servant?"

Luisa shrugged. "Her nature. Got to crack the whip, you know."

"But what did you *do*—anything? Or maybe you don't want to tell me." Stefanie smiled mischievously.

"Nothing!" Luisa said firmly, believing it.

They climbed the steps to the front door.

"Got a nice boyfriend?" Stefanie asked, with hopeful air.

"Very."

In the presence of so many others, Renate took the tack of ignoring Luisa that morning. Luisa had gone at once to her room to put on a fresh shirt. Renate had removed her eye patch, and from time to time put her cupped palm carefully over her right eye, as if it hurt, though it looked no different from the other.

Luisa did not go out with Renate for the nine-thirty coffee break, but took coffee in the kitchen with the girls.

Around eleven, the doorbell rang. Renate sent Vera down to see who it was.

Vera returned in less than five minutes with a big bouquet in her arms. "For you, Luisa!" Vera said, smiling.

"*Me?*" Luisa stood up from her sewing machine. She was aware that Renate stared with disapproval, as Luisa took the cellophane-wrapped bouquet from Vera. "Thanks for bringing it, Vera."

"Oh, that's OK! Seems to be roses." Vera winked.

Luisa took the bouquet to the kitchen to make use of the big table. The flowers required snipping of thin wire, disposal of damp

tissue. And she had to find a vase, or vases. A dozen red roses!
Long-stemmed. An envelope held a card. It said:

> I am walking on air, my
> darling. I hope you are
> too. Your Moritz.

Luisa bit her underlip quickly, repressed a giggle. She found two
vases, put seven roses in one and five in the other. Then mustering
courage, she went into the workroom with the larger vase.

"Oo-ooh! Look!" cried Stefanie.

"Oh, gorgeous!" From Elsie.

"Aren't they? I hope they'll brighten up the workroom!" said
Luisa, setting the vase down in the middle of the long table, where
today there was room.

"You will take those to your own room, Luisa. This is a workplace." Renate's thin black brows came down.

"But I have another vase for myself. I thought the girls might
like to—"

"Take them out!"

Luisa did. And dear Stefanie groaned loudly in sympathy. Luisa
vowed to herself, she would manage to let the girls know they
were welcome to one or two roses to take home. How often did
something pretty come into the workshop?

At noon, Luisa asked Renate what she might like for lunch. A
tuna fish salad with lemon, onion, and buttered toast. Luisa delivered her creation on a tray in the TV-sitting room, then with keys
in pocket slipped out the door. She had passed a message to Stefanie in the kitchen: the girls could go into her room and take a
couple of roses before they departed this afternoon, if they wished.

Luisa trotted toward Jakob's, aware that, if Rickie weren't
there, she would be badly disappointed. Sometimes he had to work
over the lunch hour. Rickie was not at his usual table, but suddenly

she saw him standing in the doorway that led to the back terrace. They took a table under the grapevines, with more shade than sun.

"Rickie, the roses are beautiful! Thank you."

Rickie lightly blew her a kiss. "My love! I have had a good morning's work and I've been thinking."

Ursie arrived, beaming with good spirits, her fair hair streaked with perspiration and her white apron rather soiled for this time of day. Rickie ordered a Coke at once for Luisa and beer for himself. Cold cuts and bread for both.

"We must somehow make better use of Dorrie—in regard to Renate." Rickie's brow wrinkled. "If you moved to my atelier to sleep—to make your breakfast, to live—she'd consider you a delinquent. Fine. We have to make her *throw* you out, so you can finish your apprenticeship with another seamstress."

"Yes. With bad references," Luisa said at once.

Their plates arrived.

"Another beer, Rickie?" asked Ursie. "While I'm here."

"*Ja*—um—*ein kleines*," said Rickie. He pushed the mustard pot closer to Luisa. "Ah, these Renate types. They occur among men too, you know? Didn't happen to me, but to a young friend of mine about eight years ago. Heinz. Apprentice advertising artist and *again* the man who befriended him—Heinz was living in his big studio—was a closet queen. Most people assumed he was straight. He had *no* sex life, so as soon as Heinz met a boy and fell in love"—Rickie lowered his voice, glanced at the next table which was noisy with its own conversation—"Meyer the older man blew up. He kicked Heinz out like something filthy. That wasn't disastrous, because Meyer wasn't his teacher, just his landlord. But it's the same situation, you see, Luisa."

Luisa did see. She sought for the right word and came out with "possessiveness."

"More profound," said Rickie darkly. "The Meyers and the Renates see their protégés meeting people who will give them something they can't give—or won't. Sex. I doubt if you'd accept any advances from Renate if they came, would you?"

"No." Luisa smiled nervously, because it was weird to imagine, yet not impossible to imagine. Luisa had always been aware that it pleased Renate to think that she, Luisa, had a slight crush on her, or more than slight. Luisa didn't want to say this, and she felt Rickie knew, anyway.

A certain recollection had jolted Rickie: Heinz had died young. AIDS. And from whom? Who knew? Heinz had wasted away fast, was already in hospital when Rickie had paid his first and last visit. He'd looked like a skeleton, something to be afraid of. Rickie was ashamed of himself. Why hadn't he found the time to visit twice, three times, even though Heinz hadn't been a close friend? Philip Egli had done better as a friend, Rickie remembered. He remembered Heinz's smile from his hospital pillows. Rickie had brought some peaches and a book. Pitiful.

"To change the subject— Ah, most welcome, Ursie!" His beer had arrived. "Teddie phoned me this morning. He's having a birthday in about a week—wants to invite you and me and a few others for dinner at the Kronenhalle. And—said his mother will pay for a year at journalism school."

How nice for him, Luisa thought. "It sounds like a happy future." She pushed back her empty plate, aware that Rickie was watching for some reaction in regard to Teddie.

"Oops," Rickie said quietly. "Our Willi has reappeared. Behind you. He's standing in the doorway looking around at people. Coffee, dear Luisa?"

"No time. You know, we don't get quite an hour."

"Lunch is on me. Now you run if you must."

"Thank you, Rickie." Luisa stood up, glanced behind her long enough to see Willi Biber's figure—sporting his gray hat—slowly turn in the doorway. "You know, Rickie, I think you're looking trimmer." She slapped her own waist.

Rickie beamed.

She bent toward Rickie. "Even Frau Wenger at L'Eclair asked me what happened—because Renate's so hostile to me. She told me Renate said, 'It's something so shocking, I prefer not to tell you or anyone.' Ha-ha!" Luisa was off, trotting toward the back garden gate.

Typical, Rickie was thinking. Renate Hagnauer was a classic case indeed—with a list of symptoms as definite as those of Spanish flu or meningitis. Rickie had forgotten to pass on something else Teddie had said. He wanted to invite Luisa for a cruise on the Nile. Rickie had reminded Teddie of certain dangers from fundamentalist attacks on tourists lately. Teddie had said, "A cruise down the Mississippi then. A steamboat down to New Orleans!"

"Come on, dear Lulu. Back to the factory."

Rickie had work, and his work went well that afternoon. But he was aware of feeling lonely. He hadn't a date that night, certainly not with Teddie Stevenson, of whom he sometimes thought, or daydreamed, even when he was working. Or with Freddie Schimmelmann either. He felt like ringing Freddie up. But where was he, at work, at home, in one of his classes for detection training? Working out at a gym?

One telephone call that afternoon was from a salad-sauce company, Rainbow, whose representative wanted to tell Rickie that "the boss" liked his waterfall idea. With an effort, Rickie recalled: a façade of falling water of various delicate of colors.

"I'm glad," Rickie said. "Thanks for telling me."

The rep did sound happy about it. Rickie felt just as down, however, after he had hung up. He looked over at Mathilde who was addressing envelopes, then at the phone on his long table.

Rickie dialed Freddie's home number.

A woman answered.

"Hello," said Rickie. "Is—Officer Schimmelmann there, please?"

"Not here now. He's going to phone in before six. Who shall I say called?"

Rickie hesitated, then took the plunge. "Rickie. It's—"

"Rickie. Oh yes, he's mentioned your name," the voice said on a cheerful note. "Any message?"

"No-o. It's not important. Just say I phoned, please."

"Certainly will, Rickie."

They hung up. Was that his wife? Rickie supposed so. Amazing. How did Freddie do it?

28

A few days passed before Rickie had a glimpse of Luisa, and that was around 10 A.M. at Jakob's, when she appeared with Renate—a rare sight these days. Renate often came alone.

"Wah-wah-wah," Rickie said silently with his lips, and gestured with thumb and fingers to Luisa. *Yack!* He pointed to himself. *Call me up. Something to say.* Rickie wanted to discuss his and Dorrie's idea for giving Renate a shock.

When the telephone rang around four that afternoon, Rickie had hopes. Renate sometimes sent Luisa out for pastry around this time. To Rickie's surprise, his caller was Ursie.

"It's Ruth," said Ursie. "You know, Frau Riester? She's been drinking a lot this afternoon." The idea was, could Rickie help her get home?

"Of course," Rickie said at once, and only fifteen seconds later felt rather annoyed. Pity there wasn't another friend of Ruth's at Jakob's to do the favor.

Rickie explained the situation to Mathilde. Ruth lived in Rickie's atelier building.

At Jakob's, Rickie found Ruth gazing into space with an empty wine glass before her. At the same time he saw Luisa near the telephone booth, and she saw him.

"Rickie, I was just going to phone you!"

"Hello, my sweet! Got to see Ruth home—to my studio building. Hello, Ruth! Rickie."

Ursie hovered. "She wouldn't eat lunch, though I offered her a plate. It's the anniversary of her husband's death, she says."

"I'll walk you home, OK?" Was that hostility he saw in those milky eyes under the gray brows?

"Oh-h—Rickie—n-nice boy!"

Rickie grasped the hand she extended, and thought: Thank God! Up, up and away.

Luisa helped.

"You know—a year ago m'husband died," murmured Ruth. The front of her gray dress was wet with something she'd spilled, maybe white wine. "I mean—"

"I understand," said Rickie. He nodded at Ursie. They were going to make it. Ruth swayed, but she didn't sag.

"Thank you, Rickie," said Ursie, sighing with relief.

On the pavement, Rickie said, "Take some deep breaths, Ruth."

"I'm *fine*!" said Ruth, supported under each elbow now.

"Luisa, I'm so happy to see you!" said Rickie. "Did you hear from Teddie?"

"You mean about the newspaper article, yes. He phoned. I had luck. Rather I just hung up after half a minute. Had to!"

"My husband Eric—it was a year—no, many years. It was *today*," said Ruth.

"True. It was," said Rickie.

"'S natural to remember—"

"Listen, Dorrie and I have an idea. Can you come in my studio for—even two minutes?"

"I'm supposed to be buying sweet rolls at L'Eclair," said Luisa, ready to laugh at the incongruity of what she was actually doing.

Rickie said, "Almost there, Ruth. Got your key?"

She woke up a bit at the sight of the six steps up to the front door of the apartment house. Rickie and Luisa wafted her up. The key was in her purse, good. Then another aerial flight up some polished granite steps to Ruth's door.

They left Ruth with a glass of water by her bedside table, and Ruth lying on her own double bed in her bedroom. He made sure that the window was slightly open.

Outside, they were only a couple of steps from the stairs that went down to his studio. Luisa said she had to start back now, as she was off course for L'Eclair anyway. Rickie knew.

"Look—" He began to walk back with her, slowly as he dared. "Renate—" Here he laughed. "She finds Dorrie in bed with you one night—or even early evening. Opens your room door, for instance. A shriek of horror. Renate—she's bound to fire you. Or she may have a real heart attack!"

Luisa gave a laugh. "Dorrie's idea?"

"Ours. You can count on me for a roof over your head—money if you need it. Philip Egli's sister thinks her boss might take on another apprentice."

"But Rickie—it's so uncertain. And getting Dorrie into it—"

"I know Renate's type. What other way is there?"

"Got to say g'bye, Rickie." Luisa turned and trotted away.

Trotting, Rickie thought with some resentment, watching her figure grow ever smaller, trotting back toward Renate Hagnauer.

Rickie realized that Ruth's keys were in his trouser pocket, that he'd been squeezing them while he talked with Luisa. He walked back a few steps and went down his atelier steps. His own door was locked, and he had to ring for Mathilde. "Rickie!"

She opened. "Hi. Mr. Hallauer phoned again—you know, about the aluminum spoons."

"The aluminum spoons—"

"It's your airplane idea."

"Ah—right."

"He doesn't like the crossed spoons but he likes the spoon design you did. Wants you to phone him."

"Ok. Just now I have to go back to Frau Riester's—upstairs. I came away with her keys."

Mathilde's full red lips smiled. "I *saw* you two—with that pretty girl Luisa. What a sight! Ha-*hah*!" She slapped a thigh.

"Back in a couple of minutes."

Rickie rang Ruth's bell, knocked, and loudly announced himself before he used her apartment door key. Nothing had changed, Ruth seemed asleep. He went to the fridge, which to his surprise looked rather clean and tidy. He cut several cubes of cheese that looked like Tilsiter. These he put on a small plate.

"Ruth?"

She was sound asleep with mouth slightly open. So many wrinkles in her face! Horrible to grow old, he thought. And not a damn thing to do about it—except painful facelifts, of course, which soon became visible, and one got chided for that. Or an early death or suicide. Easy to see, looking at Ruth Riester's now meaningless body, her gray hair, puckered face, why some people preferred suicide.

Rickie forced himself to remove Ruth's shoes, dreading her waking up.

"Aw-wr—"

"Rickie, Ruth," he whispered.

"Aw-wr—" She relapsed with closed eyes again.

Rickie found a light blanket, and covered her with it. One never knew with elderly people. Philip Egli had sounded optimistic about Luisa's finding a slot. A couple of words about Renate had been enough to apprise Philip of the situation. "One of *those*," Philip had said drearily. "Yes, I remember her from Jakob's, sure."

He left a note under Ruth's keys:

> Couldn't double-lock. Keep
> well, dear Ruth. Rickie.

29

They chose the following Saturday night—late. Luisa was to stay at home all evening, and open the door for Dorrie at a quarter past 1 A.M., by which time Luisa was ninety percent sure Renate would be in bed and asleep, and if not, then absorbed in a TV program. The TV set was in Renate's room, whose door was always closed or almost closed. Renate had announced that she wasn't going to Jakob's this Saturday. Luisa reasoned that even if Renate spotted them in the hall as Dorrie came in, she'd be furious enough on finding her entering the house at that hour. But better yet would be to find the two of them in bed. Luisa had after a couple of days become so used to the idea of both of them piling into her single bed, that it seemed they had rehearsed. When Luisa thought of the scene, a laugh started, but at once another thought sobered her: it was going to be a turning point. Luisa saw her life kicked upside down. She was braced for being out on the street.

Rickie as ever was an angel—so calm, so sure all would go well, that she would soon be a "free human being," as he had said a few times.

The Saturday arrived, a sunny day—promising success, smiles, freedom, laughter, and goodwill tomorrow from her friends. Would that be? Luisa had done the shopping, using Renate's little two-wheel trolley to roll it all back. It had taken several trips up the stairs. Renate, still resting her eye, hadn't wanted to drive. Renate was having a leisurely morning at L'Eclair, over tea and light lemon cake that Frau Wenger claimed to have created.

That evening, Luisa studied her English, and went over at least five pages in her big book of textiles with illustrations in color, and its names of fabrics in four languages.

Nearly eleven. Renate seldom knocked or barged into her room after this hour. Luisa relaxed a little, and imagined the scene at Jakob's now. She imagined Dorrie, behaving as usual with Rickie and others, having a beer, maybe dancing. Rickie intended to walk with Dorrie part of the way, he had told Luisa, to see if Luisa were free to open the front door for Dorrie. So at five, then ten past one, Luisa checked that Renate's bedroom door was closed, and at thirteen minutes past, she went softly down the stairs in her slippers, slacks, and a blouse.

There was Dorrie, half visible in the dark, advancing as Luisa opened the front door. No need to signal nor to speak; Luisa led the way upstairs.

What was she to expect on the other side of the apartment door? Luisa steadily pushed it open: nothing. She took Dorrie's hand to guide her in, released her to relock the door.

They tiptoed into Luisa's room and shut the door. Both bent with silent laughter for a moment. A single lamp partly lit the room, and Dorrie looked round as if the room were new to her. She started removing her blue cotton jacket, still silent, glancing at Luisa.

Luisa had turned her bed down—the sheet and the light counterpane. A blue blanket lay folded across the foot of the bed. Luisa slipped out of her shoes. She felt suddenly shy, and it was like a pain, paralyzing her. Next her slacks. Dorrie was moving faster.

"Gonna keep my socks on," Dorrie whispered. "I'm the one who's got to leave in a hurry!"

Dorrie also kept her underpants on, but stripped on top. Luisa felt obliged to do the same.

"Got to look good on top," said Dorrie. "That's fine. OK?" She gestured to the bed.

Luisa got under the sheet, then Dorrie slipped in beside her.

"Good to leave the light on—don't you think?" said Dorrie. "We're that type, y'know, like to do it with the light on?" She struggled, but a laugh came out.

They listened for a few seconds. Nothing.

"We've got to make some noise," Dorrie whispered.

"I know. I could turn my radio on."

"Can you reach it?"

Luisa turned on her abdomen, extended an arm beyond the pillows. The radio sat on a bookcase. Classical music, and Luisa left it, rather low. She did want to hear Renate in the hall, when she came.

"Luisa—" said Dorrie, squeezing Luisa round the waist with one arm. "You don't know how I've waited for this moment!"

Now Luisa laughed loudly, really shrieked.

"Shall I do it again?" Dorrie giggled. "*Ahem!*"

Silence still.

"When I think, I could've visited you many a night!" said Dorrie. "She *is* a sound sleeper! *Wow!*"

Silence. Then Luisa heard something in the hall.

"Luisa?" That was it, Renate.

A pause.

Dorrie, her arm round Luisa's waist, said, "Put your arm around me. This has to look right."

"Luisa?" The door was opening. "*Wha-at*—" It was like a scream. "*What're* you doing here? Luisa! Get up, you—get out!"

Dorrie was out and up, dressing. "We'll be out, don't you worry!"

Renate's arms flailed. "Out! *Out!*" She addressed Dorrie who was zipping her slacks.

Luisa, on her feet, grabbed her blouse.

Dorrie dodged Renate's fists, though one blow did land on her neck.

"*What* kind of place do you think this *is?*" Renate cried. "Get out, get *out!*"

"'Bye, Luisa!" said Dorrie at the room door, and Luisa had a glimpse of Dorrie's shining eyes and wide, amused grin before she vanished in the direction of the apartment door.

Renate was limping after her. "Human filth! *Filth!*"

When Luisa entered the hall, Renate was at the apartment

door, still yelling, following Dorrie down the stairs now. The *minu-terie* was on.

"*Out!—ah-h!*" That was a cry of terror.

Luisa got to the open door in time to see Renate tumbling down the stairs, bare feet visible for an instant amid the fabric of the Chinese dressing gown, and to see Dorrie's figure in the hall below, heading for the next stairs. A loud crack and bumping sound followed: Renate's head had struck the wall at the foot of the stairs.

"What in heaven—" cried a female voice from a door below.

Renate, a crumpled heap, lay against the wall she had hit.

Dorrie reappeared in the hall. Another neighbor opened a door.

"It's Frau Hagnauer!"

"Knocked senseless! I'll get a wet towel!"

A woman pulled at Renate's arm, while a man tried to move her lower legs so she could sit up on the landing.

Luisa had descended half the steps. Someone was asking her what had happened. Renate was dead, Luisa thought; her eyes stayed half open like her mouth, her head lolled on one shoulder.

"Call a doctor!"

"An ambulance!"

"Luisa, what happened?"

Luisa glanced at Dorrie. "She followed my friend out—and she fell."

Two men insisted over a woman's protest in carrying Renate into an apartment, where she was carefully placed on a sofa. Some-one mentioned tea.

"I'm staying with you, Luisa," Dorrie said.

Dorrie looked white as chalk, Luisa thought, as if she were dead. Suddenly Luisa's ears were ringing, her knees seemed to sag. A woman seized her elbow, and Luisa sat down awkwardly in an armchair. Then Dorrie poked a damp towel into her hands.

"Head down in-in-into this," Dorrie said. "Face down, go ahead!"

There was a long doorbell ring, plus knocking. The police arrived, accompanied by a doctor.

"This has sugar. Good for you," a woman said, handing Luisa a mug of hot tea with a spoon in it.

Dorrie held the mug for Luisa.

The other people in pajamas and dressing gowns were answering the questions of the police who had clustered at the sofa.

"Her card of identity?"

Luisa told them where it would be, in Renate's purse in her bedroom, in her wallet there, and Luisa would have gone up herself, if Dorrie and a couple of the women hadn't restrained her.

"I'll get your keys, dear," Dorrie said. "Where are they? You can't stay here tonight."

Sympathetic words from a couple of the women. A shocking accident! So sudden! Luisa was welcome to stay with either of them, to sleep on a spare bed. Renate had vanished from the sofa. The police took Luisa's name, looked at her card of identity, which she had got from the wallet Dorrie had brought. One policeman asked what had happened, and both Luisa and Dorrie said that Dorrie had left the apartment, and Renate Hagnauer had started down the stairs. A neighbor could confirm this: Luisa standing outside the apartment door, and the other girl Dorrie down in the next hall, when the neighbor had opened her door and seen Renate on the landing where she had just fallen.

"She'd been shouting at someone," the woman said. "I heard her—that's why I opened the door."

"Shouting?" said the officer.

"As if she were angry. Sometimes she gets angry, I know. I can hear her voice."

Luisa swallowed tea. Then Dorrie was beside her.

"I've phoned. Let's go," Dorrie said.

"Phoned?"

"I spoke with Rickie. He told me to phone—later tonight, you know? And I locked the apartment door."

The one policeman who remained was leaving too, and Dorrie was saying to one of the women that Luisa shouldn't sleep in the apartment upstairs tonight, and the woman agreed.

Luisa and Dorrie were down in the street, walking, Dorrie holding Luisa's arm. Dorrie had brought a tweed jacket of Luisa's. Luisa's keys were in her pocket.

"Rickie's waiting for us at the Small g," Dorrie said, walking faster. "Come on, do you good!"

Luisa took deep breaths of the cool night air, and saw again the shocking image of Renate's bare feet, one small and normal, the other rather like a thick S—Renate's feet seen from three meters away, motionless after the fall. "You told Rickie?"

Dorrie gripped Luisa's hand. "No—I just said we'd be there in a couple of minutes."

Luisa relaxed her arm. Dorrie had been partly supporting her.

"You're OK now. Good," Dorrie said. "Look, you sleep at my place tonight or at Rickie's. But it's your decision. No arguments about it with Rickie."

"OK."

There was Rickie with Lulu under the grapevine trestle at Jakob's main entrance. "*Both* of you!" he said, laughing.

Dorrie glanced at Luisa. "I was thrown out, but—" Dorrie lowered her voice. "Renate fell down the stairs." She fairly whispered the last word. "She's dead, Rickie."

Rickie frowned. "You're—"

"It's true," Luisa said. "She fell. She was wearing a long dressing gown—tripped."

"The police came just now," Dorrie went on softly, though there was no one around, except a single man who came out of Jakob's and passed them, paying them no mind.

The Small g seemed unusually quiet just then, even its lights weaker. Ursie's voice from somewhere inside shouted, "*Ja—OK—we are closing*! Finish your drinks, please!"

"Dead," Rickie said, stunned.

"Rickie, Luisa can sleep at my place tonight or yours, but now we—"

"At mine. Come on, we'll go to mine."

They began to walk, Lulu leading, heading for home.

"I didn't bring my car," Dorrie said to Rickie. "I could phone for a taxi from your place."

"Or you stay at my place!" Rickie felt expansive, hospitable. Tonight had presented a crisis, *une vraie crise*. Renate dead, her apprentices without a master, Luisa—free of Renate! Rickie was aware that he had had a few on this special evening when Dorrie was expected to liberate Luisa, and that the reality of Renate's demise had not sunk into his brain.

Rickie put his key into his lock. Then he switched on lights in his flat.

"Come, now we make the bed," Rickie said, pulling back the dark blue counterpane that covered his double bed.

With three changing the sheets, the work seemed done in a trice.

"Stay with me tonight, Dorrie. It's a very strange night."

Dorrie nodded. "Sure, Luisa."

Rickie was to take the sofa. "If you ladies don't mind," he added, "I shall be here in the morning to prepare your tea or coffee."

Rickie poured himself a small Scotch, straight, and easily persuaded Dorrie to have the same. "You'll sleep better," said Rickie.

By now Dorrie had told him about Renate plunging down the stairs, just as she rounded the banister into the hall, and of hearing the terrible *crack*. Dorrie said the doctor had pronounced Renate's neck broken. Now Rickie believed. Luisa was free, and also jobless. But tomorrow they would talk about all that.

Luisa had washed at the basin, and now she lay face down, head turned toward Dorrie in the big bed. St. Jakob's church clock tolled one note for the half hour. Which? Rickie was out of sight

SMALL g   269

in the living room. "Thank you," Luisa said softly, not sure if Dorrie was awake or not.

"Nothing to thank me for. Go to sleep."

30

A telephone call just before ten that morning woke Rickie up,
and he took the phone which was at one end of the sofa.

It was his sister Dorothea. "How are you, Rickie? I thought it
was time we had lunch together. Are you free today? Maybe at the
Kronenhalle?"

"Ah, Dorothea—" He could still lunch with his sister, he
supposed, but he wanted to be on hand to help Luisa if he
were needed. "I'm not sure, thank you. There's some news here.
Luisa's boss—you remember I told you about Luisa, the apprentice
seamstress?"

"Of course. Luisa. With the boyfriend."

Rickie continued. His bedroom door was shut. "Her boss died
last night—fell down her apartment stairs and broke her neck."

"Goodness, Rickie!"

"It happened around one in the morning. So Luisa slept here.
She's still here."

Dorothea understood. They would talk later.

Rickie heard the girls stirring, called a "Good morning!" and
invited them to make use of the bathroom first. He donned a
dressing gown and started the coffee, then set the table. He had
some sliced ham, and plenty of bread, luckily.

"I was thinking—we should walk over to the apartment,
Luisa, the workplace," Rickie said tentatively. He knew it would
be easier if Luisa went with someone, and he hoped Dorrie was

free. "You'll have to tell the girls, too. They've all got phone numbers, I suppose." Rickie was thinking of Monday morning, and the
girls arriving just before eight, as Luisa had told him.

"I know. I'll do it," said Luisa.

"Renate must have a lawyer. Do you know of any relatives?"

"She has a lawyer. I'll know his name when I see it. She said
something about a sister in Romania."

The girls made the bed (Rickie said to leave the sheets on),
and the apartment was neat again when Rickie emerged from the
bathroom, shaved and dressed.

"Shall we go?" said Rickie. "And can Lulu come?"

Luisa managed a smile. "Sure. Of course."

Luisa dreaded this, a neighbor on the street saying, "Oh, Luisa,
I heard the sad news!" but they encountered no one Luisa knew,
even in the house. Luisa unlocked, and there was the long hall, the
sitting room door and Renate's bedroom door a little open as she
had left them. Beside Renate's bed lay the embroidered slippers
that Renate had not taken time to put on last night, and which
would not have saved her if she had. Everything looked familiar,
yet this morning everything was different, eerie and frozen.

Rickie calmly took charge, with support from Dorrie.

Luisa knew where the brown leather business address book lay
in the workroom, and she telephoned Vera first.

"I can't believe it!" said Vera.

Luisa explained. "She was angry with a friend of mine—
scolding, you know—not watching where she was going." If she
didn't say it, the neighbors would.

Elsie reacted in the same manner, shocked nearly speechless.

"We'll have to finish all the work that's been ordered," Luisa
said. "So come in tomorrow, of course. Please."

Stefanie was not in, and Luisa did not want to leave the message with her parents.

"Luisa," Rickie said, "Renate's lawyer. Do you want to look
for his name?"

It began with an R, and Luisa finally recognized it in the business address book. She copied his name and number on a piece of paper, as Rickie suggested, and did the same for Renate's bank and the man she dealt with there.

"If Renate had a will, the lawyer probably has a copy, and maybe the bank too," Rickie said. "We may find the sister's address there."

Lulu was going from room to room with lively curiosity. In contrast, Luisa felt unsure of what to do next. She made her own bed, started to make Renate's, then began taking the sheets off. Dorrie helped her. All went into the laundry basket. Luisa checked the fridge, thinking of the girls tomorrow and their coffee breaks, threw out a couple of items and put a pot in the sink to soak. Would she ever have a real meal here again?

"Can I do something?" Rickie asked. "Is the workroom ready for tomorrow morning?"

"I'm sure it's OK, I checked it."

Luisa looked into Renate's room with its clutter of nail-polish bottles, mascara boxes, eau-de-cologne, hairbrushes, combs, a silver tray of hairpins. Behind two closed cupboard doors hung racks of long dresses, skirts, blouses, Luisa knew.

"Don't think about all this today, Luisa," said Dorrie. "Do it with one of the girls. Or they might want some of the things."

"That's true." The idea made Luisa feel less depressed.

"Pack a small suitcase—for tonight," Rickie said. "You'll be in my studio, you know." He had already reminded Luisa that neither he nor Mathilde ever got to the studio before nine-thirty.

Luisa did. Her pajamas, slippers, something different to wear tomorrow, a book, then another book, toothbrush.

Out into the sunlight again, Rickie carrying her case, and Luisa in charge of Lulu. They met a neighbor whose face Luisa remembered from last night.

"Oh, I'll be back tomorrow," Luisa replied to her question. "Eight o'clock or before."

"You know we're here, if we can help," the woman said.

"Thank you!"

A few moments later, Dorrie said to Luisa, "Just think, we can *reach* you now! *I* can, Teddie can—Rickie. We can telephone you!" Dorrie burst out in a happy laugh.

The telephone was ringing when they entered Rickie's studio.

"Who could that be on a Sunday?" Rickie murmured, thinking it might be his sister with an idea for a drink or dinner.

"Hello, Rickie!" said Teddie Stevenson. "I was just about to give up. Listen, it's all fixed for tomorrow night. My birthday bash, you know? Seven-thirty at the Kronenhalle, reservation in my name. For at least twelve people, I said, in case I think of a couple of others at the last minute. Can you make it, Rickie? Please."

"Yes—I'm pretty sure I can. Thank you, Teddie."

"And Luisa's got to be there. You can bring her, can't you? I could, of course, but if the atmosphere's so ugly there, even down on the street—"

"I'm sure Luisa can be there," Rickie said, watching Luisa set her small case now in the room off the kitchenette. Dorrie was absorbed in his cartoons tacked to the wall. "There's been a change here, Teddie. The old witch is no more—she is dead."

"Dead? You're kidding."

"I am *not*."

"What do you mean, Rickie?"

"Luisa will sleep in my studio tonight. She's here—if you don't believe me. Luisa!"

She came and took the phone. "Hello, Teddie. Yes, it is true." Now Luisa squirmed and frowned. "Fell down the stairs, just outside the apartment. No, in the house. Her neck was broken." Luisa said she supposed she could come tomorrow evening, but couldn't be sure, and thanked Teddie for inviting her.

"You're going to keep on *living* there? At Renate's?"

"It's all just happened, Teddie. I can't answer a question like that. The girls and I too—we have to work there tomorrow as usual."

"Gosh," said Teddie. "C-can you put Rickie back on?"

Teddie asked Rickie to invite the fellow called Philip, if he wished. Rickie asked if he could bring Freddie instead.

"The police officer, you know? I'm not sure he'll be free tomorrow evening."

"Sure, Rickie, invite both. It's a shame my article won't be out by tomorrow, but they're postponing it *again*."

ON MONDAY MORNING, though it was raining lightly (she had taken a raincoat from Rickie's cupboard), Luisa stood at seven-thirty down on the pavement in front of Renate's apartment house. Here came Stefanie, holding a newspaper over her head, and an oversized white plastic handbag in her other hand, smiling mischievously at Luisa.

"You're up early. Been out all night?"

Stefanie had noticed the raincoat. "You didn't talk with Vera?"

"No. Why?"

"Renate had a fall—Saturday night. On the staircase. She's dead."

"Oh, my God!" Frowning, Stefanie took the newspaper from her head. "Just suddenly dead, you mean?"

"Yes. It broke her neck."

"What're we going to do?"

"Not sure yet. We've got to finish our assignments—the orders, you know. Vera will know what to do. I'll be there in a minute." Luisa saw tears gather in Elsie's eyes.

"It's just so hard to believe," said Elsie.

As Luisa had supposed, Vera took charge. It was like the army; Vera was next in rank to Renate, after all, and had Elsie in charge, whereas Luisa and Stefanie had been Renate's two apprentices. First they would take care of the orders.

"Then there's the *Frauenfachschule* to help us out, you know,"

Vera went on, her dark eyes earnest, "with maybe the name of a good *Damenschneiderin* for us."

A new mistress, boss. The idea left the girls solemn and wide-eyed.

"Now let's get to work on what we must do," said Vera.

Luisa plunged in with the rest. Seams, bastings and plannings, and full use of the long table. Only Stefanie was able to talk, to make a joke about the rain. For the coffee break at ten, the girls would have only the unfinished cake from Friday, Luisa thought, as she hadn't gone to L'Eclair yesterday.

The telephone rang now; Vera answered it. One call was from a private client asking about a finishing date for a suit. Vera gave an approximate date, and Luisa thought she would have said the same. This morning Rickie was to phone Renate's bank, then ring Luisa, and shortly before ten, Vera summoned Luisa to the phone.

Rickie told her he had spoken to a man at UBS called Gamper, who seemed well acquainted with Renate Hagnauer. "I explained that I was a friend of yours, and that you were one of Frau Hagnauer's apprentices. He seemed shocked at the news—also seemed to know your name. Now, Luisa—"

"Yes."

"Mr. Gamper said the bank has a copy of Renate's will, but her lawyer handles that. We must take a certificate of death to the—to Renate's lawyer. Did anybody give you a certificate Saturday night?"

"No. I'm sure of that."

"Then we'll have to get it from the hospital where they took her. Or the morgue." Rickie sighed. "What's your house number there, my sweet?"

"One forty-five."

"Thanks. Luisa—I can't do much without you, you know. You have the same address as Renate, so they'd give the certificate to you—"

Luisa explained that she couldn't leave at eleven, as Rickie proposed, because she had to be here, and the girls took just forty-five minutes for lunch, because they brought their own, and, and . . .

"But this is an emergency! If we don't do it today, we'll have to do it tomorrow. Who's the girl you said could take charge?"

"Vera."

So Luisa met Rickie at eleven at the corner of Jakob's. He had ordered a taxi. Then to the hospital, which Rickie had traced that morning, the hospital whose ambulance had come to Renate's dwelling. Luisa showed her identification, and with this obtained a certificate of death, signed by the doctor who had come to the house.

"Step number one," said Rickie when this was over. "I'll drop you back home—and myself at Jakob's for lunch. Can I persuade you?"

Luisa shook her head. "I'd best go back. And you—lost the whole morning, I realize, Rickie."

"I'll survive. I'll be in my studio all afternoon."

By now they were in a taxi, which had been easy to get at the hospital doors.

"Would you give me that certificate, my sweet, and I'll make a photocopy or two in my studio. Might be useful. And I'll give the original back to you tonight. You'll be there, won't you?"

The Kronenhalle. It was hard to imagine, a few hours from now, being in that elegant restaurant where she and Renate had gone on rare occasions to celebrate something. She was supposed to look cheerful tonight. Teddie's birthday. "I haven't even a present for him."

Rickie laughed. "Teddie can telephone you now! Come to see you—I suppose. That's a nice present for him."

They had arrived at Luisa's destination.

"Pick you up at a quarter past seven?" Rickie asked. "And try to reach the lawyer this afternoon, Luisa. Make a date and I'll try to join you—whenever it is—if you want me to come with you."

"Of course, I do, Rickie."

Upstairs, the girls were half finished with their lunch. They knew Luisa had been out on an essential errand, and were curious. Luisa washed her hands at the sink.

"I had to find the doctor who was here," Luisa said, relieved to talk about it. "I had to get the death certificate."

"Oooh—of course, that's normal!"

"Do you know when's the funeral yet?"

Luisa, buttering a piece of bread, felt flustered. "It's got to be tomorrow, I suppose. I've got to ring the hospital again." But Renate's body wasn't at the hospital, it would very likely be at an undertaker's parlor. Luisa wanted to ring Rickie again. But wouldn't he get fed up with doing services for her?

"Do you know, Luisa—"

"Oh Luisa, you're supposed to telephone—a certain number. It's by the hall phone."

Elsie and Vera had spoken at once, and Luisa chose to listen to Vera. An office of some kind had left a number.

After two o'clock, Luisa rang this number. It was the morgue, and what funeral arrangements had she made?

"I'll have to phone you back," Luisa stammered, feeling at a total loss, inadequate, stupid.

But there was Vera, twenty-two years old, much more in command. Vera and Luisa consulted in Luisa's room. Perhaps Renate had expressed a preference in her will? That was certainly possible, and the thought shocked Luisa into action.

Vera stood by Luisa at the telephone. The lawyer Rensch was busy for another half hour, Luisa was told. She washed her best foulard scarf, which had a rather masculine pattern, she thought, and took it damp to the cheerful Stefanie who was wielding the iron today. Luisa tried again for Rensch.

"Oh yes, Frau Hagnauer! A colleague told me. He had seen it in the newspaper. What a shocking thing!"

Luisa recalled that Stefanie had been about to say, at lunch, that there had been a small item about Renate in the *Tages-*

Anzeiger that morning, which she had with her. Stefanie had looked for such an item and found it. Luisa didn't want to see it, but she didn't say so. She felt embarrassed, constricted, but she forced the question out.

"Do you know if Frau Hagnauer had a preference as to where she would like to be buried?"

"No, I do not. It may be in the will. Have you the certificate of death?"

It was arranged in seconds: Luisa was to come to Dr. Rensch's office at three-thirty. Luisa so informed Vera (to whom Luisa had given Renate's set of keys), and Luisa set off for Rickie's studio without phoning him. Rickie gave her the original certificate, and called a taxi for her. He also offered to come with her.

"I've got to learn," Luisa said. She took off alone.

Luisa felt weakened by the heavy leather-upholstered chairs in the waiting room of Rensch and Kuenzler in the Bahnhofstrasse. Renate would have been dressed for this formal setting. Luisa wore white cotton slacks and her best rubber-soled shoes. A door opened and she was beckoned in.

Dr. Rensch, a plump man with gray hair, laid an envelope with a visible red seal on his desk. He looked carefully at the death certificate. "A fall down the stairs, you say—horrid." Then he opened the envelope with a penknife. "You will permit me—the burial matter first, I think."

Luisa kept silent. The will seemed to be about six pages long and on heavy paper.

Frowning, the lawyer read on, turned a page. "Ah yes, I remember now. Frau Hagnauer preferred cremation."

An ugly thought flew across Luisa's mind: Renate preferred cremation because it would burn her crippled foot to ashes, never to be seen again.

Dr. Rensch was saying, "We can give you some counsel about that, if you like. These are heavy responsibilities for one as young as you."

"Yes," Luisa agreed politely.

Dr. Rensch read on. "She still owns the apartment, I presume?"

"Yes." Months ago Renate had mentioned that she owned the apartment.

"And her sister? Is she in touch?"

"I don't know."

"The sister in Zagreb?" Dr. Rensch looked at Luisa. "We've got to notify her. This will was updated this year, so I'll assume the address here is still valid for the sister. Edwiga Elisabeta Dvaldivi," the lawyer said carefully. "You and she are the co-inheritors, you know. I suppose you know."

Co-inheritors. Fifty-fifty. It was as unreal as the sister, whose name Luisa had never heard Renate utter. "No, I didn't know."

"Oh, Frau Hagnauer thought most highly of you—and of your talent." He gave a restrained smile, lifted his glasses and looked at Luisa.

Was that true, Luisa thought. Thought highly, yes, in the sense that she was so special, she had to be imprisoned. Luisa felt her heart beating heavily. "I'm sorry but I have to ask you what I'm supposed to do about the cremation."

Dr. Rensch nodded. "We'll take care of that for you—with your consent, I trust." He pushed a button.

A woman opened a door on the lawyer's right.

"Can you make a copy of Frau Hagnauer's will, please, Christina?"

Less than twenty minutes later, Luisa was on a tram, riding toward Aussersihl and home. The will in its envelope made her handbag bulge. Co-inheritor. Half the apartment, what did that mean? Half Renate's bank account? Luisa felt quite neutral, uninterested. It somehow wasn't true. It was like Renate's death, which had happened "early yesterday, Sunday," today being Monday, but her death didn't seem true, or real.

Duties next: check with Vera on the progress of the day's work, and be sure they had not neglected any client they were supposed

to speak to today. Luisa was to ring Rickie, if she had time, and
report on the lawyer.

"Look, Luisa, perfect," said Stefanie with a proud gesture. The
foulard square hung over a line by the ironing board. "I'd get full
marks for that."

"It does look prettier than when I bought it!" In a beam of
sunlight, the gold, blue, and tan of the pattern came up like a
stained-glass window. "Now I need a gift wrap."

"You're giving that *away*?" cried Stefanie.

"Aw-wr," said Elsie, glad to have something to smile at.

"I'm going—I have to go to a birthday party tonight," Luisa
explained, "and I didn't do any shopping."

Vera told Luisa that everything was in control. She beckoned
Luisa into a corner of the workroom. "And the funeral?" she whispered. "What's happening?"

"I just found out—it's supposed to be a cremation. The
lawyer's going to see about that. It's bound to be tomorrow—don't
you think?"

Vera nodded. "Sure. Very likely. The lawyer's going to phone
you?"

Luisa nodded.

The girls were winding things up for the day, as usual trying
to leave the worktable reasonably tidy. Luisa did not ring Rickie,
because there was hardly time, if she swept the workroom and got
dressed. She realized she didn't want to say anything to Rickie
about being co-inheritor, or about cremation. Not now, not
tonight.

"I almost forgot," Vera said, "your friend Dorrie rang twice,
and she'd like you to ring back. Left a number. It's there."

Then Luisa was suddenly alone in the flat. She looked at the
message Vera had written: Dorrie and a number. She wanted Dorrie with her this evening, wanted Dorrie's smile and her easy manner. In her room, Luisa reached for her German dictionary (the
safest place she'd been able to think of) on the top shelf of her

bookcase, and got from it the card Teddie had given her, one of his mother's personal cards, with home address and number. Teddie had drawn a line through "Frau Katarina Stevenson" and written "Teddie" above.

Teddie's mother answered. "Oh, hello, Luisa!" she said, more friendly than Luisa had expected. "Yes, Teddie's here—in the bath—but I'll ask."

Teddie came on, using a bathroom phone, he said. "What's the matter? You're coming tonight, aren't you?"

"Oh yes, I was wondering, could I invite a friend—who's been very helpful—"

"Sure!" said Teddie.

"Dorrie. Thanks, Teddie . . . of course. I look forward."

Then Luisa dialed the number for Dorrie. It was still only five to five, and she knew Dorrie didn't usually stop work at five. A man's voice answered (not Bert), then Dorrie came on.

"Yes, a busy day!" Luisa said. "I just spoke with Teddie. Can you join us tonight? Kronenhalle at seven-thirty?"

"I could. I heard about it from Rickie. You're sure it's OK?"

It was OK. Teddie had said it was a buffet.

31

Rickie had walked over to Luisa's, and had ordered a taxi to come there. Luisa was down on the pavement, in a longish blue-and-gray cotton skirt with pleats and her finest white blouse, with a generous black shawl to guard against the evening cool.

The taxi arrived at almost the same time as Rickie.

"Kronenhalle, *bitte*," said Rickie, looking at the flat square box Luisa carried, with its thin blue ribbon. "I didn't bring anything,

I'm afraid, so Teddie will have to forgive me. I was busy today. So
you won't tell me what the lawyer said?"

"Not now. Not that he said much."

"Gave you a copy of the will?"

"Oh, yes. Dorrie's coming tonight."

Rickie smiled. "So is Philip Egli. Lots of work for you to do—
in regard to the will?"

Luisa shook her head. "No."

Rickie wanted to ask when the funeral would be, but now
didn't seem the time. However, when would be the right time?
Luisa looked rather paralyzed by events.

When they were inside the Kronenhalle's doors, Rickie said,
"The funeral—it's tomorrow?"

"It's a cremation. The lawyer's going to let me know the time.
I suppose tomorrow."

Rickie was sure Luisa would go to the service, and there was
always a service. "Let's go up. It's on the floor above this."

Teddie's party was in a big room which held two long tables,
set at a wide angle. Teddie came at once to greet them, very dapper in a blue summer suit and a red bow tie.

He kissed Luisa's cheek. "You look beautiful! Hi, Rickie!
These are for you, Luisa." Teddie extended a pair of gardenias,
which he had been carrying delicately on one palm. "Ribbon has
a little safety pin to—" he explained anxiously, ready to help, but
Luisa said she could manage.

"Thank you, Teddie. Such a fresh smell! This little item is for
you. Happy birthday!"

"You didn't have to bring me *anything*!" Grinning, he turned
the flat box over. "I'm going to leave this at the front desk or I'll
lose it. Please—welcome to the party. Have a drink. I'll be back."
He dashed out of sight down some stairs.

Waiters fussed around the two linen-covered tables, bringing
stacks of plates in addition to the glasses and cutlery. Wine bottles
stood in ice buckets.

"Good evening," said Freddie Schimmelmann, bowing to Luisa. "And Rickie." To Luisa he added, "I heard the—about the accident. I don't think any of us expected a mishap like that."

"No, we didn't," said Luisa, at once conscious of the "we." Meaning who?

Teddie was back with a tall, blond young man. "Eric—my military training pal. Luisa—Rickie—"

Eric, staring at Luisa, said, "'Evening."

Then came Philip Egli and a dark-haired young man. "Hello. This is Walter Boehler. You know, Rickie, from the travel bureau." Philip looked radiantly happy.

Rickie did remember, somebody new. "Walter of the travel bureau!" Rickie echoed, as if greeting a great poet. "And Andreas! Can't believe my eyes!"

Andy, in a proper suit and tie, drifted forward, smiling. "'Evening, Teddie. *Ein* Appenzeller, Rickie? Ha-ha!"

"What a surprise!" Rickie said.

"For me too, but I can't stay long. Half an hour, Ursie said."

"I invited Ursie," Teddie said to Rickie, "but she absolutely couldn't come even for twenty minutes. Andy—please make these people take some drinks. You know how to do it!"

"Teddie—for you." Andy pulled a white envelope from a jacket pocket. "A card from us all. We all say happy birthday."

"Thank you, Andy."

They moved toward the drinks table. There was lots of Coca-Cola and tomato juice.

"Fraulein Luisa," said Andy, ducking his head an instant. "Ursie and I and Hugo—all of us are very sorry to hear about Madame."

"Thank you, Andy—for your sympathy. I think we are all shocked."

Long-stemmed dahlias stood in vases on both tables, and shorter tulips and white roses. Suddenly it wasn't like "a funeral," as Luisa had thought moments ago, but like a burst of pretty things, and special food and drink. A waiter was lighting the candelabra.

"Mademoiselle?" A waiter offered a tray of stemmed glasses, all half full of bubbling champagne.

Everyone took a glass, even two or three young-looking girls whose names Luisa didn't know, and who looked so shy, Luisa felt herself a picture of poise by comparison.

"Happy birthday, Teddie!"

"And many more!"

"To Teddie!"

"Speech, Teddie!"

"Ye-es-s! Some words from the great journalist!"

Rickie exchanged a smile with Luisa. He had a Scotch on the rocks, thanks to Andy.

"Thank you all—very much—for being here," said Teddie.

"More!"

"Yes—OK. Finally I'm twenty-one." Teddie looked at the floor, lifted a foot as if he were about to stomp on the carpet. "Can't believe I've reached the age that Americans tell you to wait for. Wait till you're twenty-one before you do this and that." He cleared his throat. "At least tonight I have the right to gather my favorite people around me: a few school friends, military training pal—Eric—who may have saved my life and did save my self-respect, when he told me to lie flat. Otherwise I'd have got a live bullet—in the backside. Wrong side for a soldier."

"Hah-ho." A murmur of laughter.

"Tonight Franzi is here, my school friend with whom I shared almost everything, boxes from home, books, secondhand cars—a room, yes—girls, no. And tonight Luisa is here, the girl who says 'I'm not sure, I have to think about it.' Even about a date."

Whispers: "Who's Luisa?"

"Last but not least—my friend Rickie, who took me in one night, when I wasn't the equal of a street attacker. My all-round pal, Rickie Markwalder. Now let's eat, drink, and have a good time!"

"Ye-eay, Rickie!" a male voice shouted. Whose voice?

Luisa just then saw Dorrie's black-clad figure in the doorway, raising a hand to acknowledge Luisa's wave.

A patter of applause. A little laughter.

People became interested in the buffet tables.

Teddie drifted toward Rickie. "I hadn't counted on making a speech." Teddie passed a hand across his forehead.

"You did quite well!"

"I thought later—you know—some of us might go to Jakob's. Nightcap. OK, Rickie?"

"Of course it's OK," Rickie replied, dubious about Luisa's and his own energy level later. "Freddie's on duty tonight at ten, I know."

Not far away from Rickie, Dorrie was saying to Luisa, "I brought this for Teddie. Is he collecting presents now?" She held a small rectangular box.

"I suppose so. What did you get him?"

"Joke pens. Well, they work. I happened to have them because I'd just bought them! Hah!"

Now Luisa smiled. "I brought something I had too. No time today for shopping."

"Did you have to see—well—her lawyer?"

"Yes."

"What happened?"

Luisa felt like ducking the question, and held herself straight. "I don't want to talk about it just now. Sorry."

"Let's get something to eat. Somebody said there was beef Stroganoff."

A couple of smaller tables had now been covered with white linen and chairs set round, for those who wished to sit. Luisa and Dorrie chose to sit, and were soon joined by Rickie. Beef Stroganoff and rice was the hot dish, and the cold offerings pâté, sliced ham, sausages, and salads.

"Everything all right?" Teddie was on his feet, wine glass in hand, and with no intention of sitting, it seemed.

Luisa was looking at Teddie, when her vision went gray, and sounds became blurred. She laid down the fork she had just picked up. "I can't—" Then she was dropping to her right, the side where Dorrie wasn't.

Cold water on a napkin across Luisa's forehead. She saw an unfocused cream-colored ceiling with panels.

". . . heavy day . . . tomato juice . . ."

Luisa realized that she lay on her back on a couple of benches; that she must have been quite unconscious for a minute or two.

"Feeling steadier now?" Dorrie was asking, pressing her hand.

"Oh, sure."

"Don't eat anything if you don't want to," someone said.

"A little is good," Rickie's voice said.

Luisa ate a bite, slowly.

Rickie's deep voice said, "A little beef, a sip of wine—"

The morsel of beef brought the scene back. Tonight she would sleep in Rickie's studio, as she had last night. She sipped some water. "I'm OK," she said to Dorrie and Teddie, because he was seated opposite her now, looking at her. He stood up and bowed a little.

"I'll be back."

"A cake!" a girl shouted.

A cake was arriving, inspiring applause. It was carried by two waiters and sat on a rather large tray, but the cake with twenty-one candles ablaze was not huge. This was deposited in the center of the buffet table, which had been partly cleared.

"No more speeches!" yelled Teddie. "And I'm not going to blow all these out. It's unsanitary! Come up and I'll cut!"

Luisa stayed where she was, so did Dorrie. Rickie came back with three plates of cake, held somewhat dangerously.

"What kind? Looks homemade," Dorrie said.

"Coconut meringue."

Rickie wanted to see Luisa home early, he explained to Teddie, as she was tired. Teddie of course had to stay with his guests.

Dorrie said her thanks and good night to Teddie, and she and Luisa
and Rickie departed.

In the taxi, Rickie kept silent. If Luisa wanted Dorrie to stay
the night, he thought, she could as far as he was concerned, but he
was not going to say anything about it. As it turned out, Dorrie
asked to be dropped at a corner which she said wasn't far from
where she lived.

Then Rickie and Luisa went on to the studio. Rickie
unlocked with his own key.

"It's weird," Luisa said when she was down in the big white
room. She tossed her handbag onto the single bed that she had
made neatly that morning. "I really feel weird now."

Rickie glanced at the floor. "It is weird—yes, that's the word.
A very strange two days. Sit down on Mathilde's chair." Rickie
pulled out the swivel chair. "Mind if I look for a small beer?" He
opened the fridge. There were two.

"I must tell you something. I mean—I feel like telling you."

He thought of Mathilde's confession of pregnancy, which
hadn't been true. "Yes. What, my dear?"

"Renate made me co-inheritor in her will. The other is her
sister in Zagreb."

"In a way, I am not surprised, you know?" But Rickie felt very
surprised, and was sure he even looked surprised. "Everything?"

"I suppose. The lawyer Rensch said half and half—with the
sister. Of course they have to find the sister. Then I've heard people always have to wait for months—proving things."

"Yes. Six months usually. Then you'll have death duties, maybe
eight percent." Rickie sipped his Heineken from the cold bottle.
"Didn't Renate own that apartment too?"

"Yes." It hit Luisa again as a frightening responsibility: a big
property tax (maybe) to pay before she could touch any of
Renate's money to cover the bills. Electricity and telephone bills.
She'd have to talk to Gamper at UBS, certainly. Then a happier
thought came. "You know, Rickie, Vera—one of the girls—she's a

'coworker,' higher than apprentice. She's got an idea. We're going to visit the women's technical school at Kreuzplatz, and look for a dressmaker who could take Renate's place. There may be a person who'd be glad of an apartment to live in, Vera thinks."

The thought cheered Rickie too. "Of course! You could keep the same girls—the same clientele! But you ought to get the place repainted. I don't mean it's shabby now, but to pick yourself up. Pick the girls up too. Luisa, I'll leave you. You're OK? Will you get to bed? Soon?"

Luisa nodded. "*Yes.*"

"I've got to put in an appearance at Jakob's, you know." He tipped the little bottle and finished it. "'Bye, my dear. I'll lock from the outside. Got your keys?"

"Yes."

ON THE WAY TO JAKOB'S, Rickie undid his bow tie, stuck it in his pocket, and opened the top button of his shirt. He was thinking that Luisa had looked unusually pretty tonight with her brown hair shining as usual, her small gold circles of earrings, her wonderful mixture of shyness and good humor. Co-inheritor! What would Renate have left in stocks and bonds? More than a million francs, he'd guess, Renate being thrifty by nature and having had a long working life. Would that make any difference at all in regard to Teddie? No, why should it? Who did Luisa like better, Teddie or Dorrie?

Lulu, he thought, as he neared his apartment house. Rickie unlocked his front door, then his apartment door, and heard Lulu scampering toward him. He felt for her lead in the dark: it hung from a row of coat hooks on the left in the hall. Out again, and Lulu went tidily into the gutter for a pee. He didn't put her lead on till they were almost at the door of Jakob's.

Ursie was the first familiar figure he saw, Ursie behind the bar, drawing two beers. "Rickie! A good evening?"

"Yes, and so elegant! Ursie, we missed you!"

"I know, I know, thank you," pouring wine now, eyes on the glass.

"Teddie's due here tonight."

"Ah, good!"

The second figure to catch his eye was that of Willi Biber, hunched over white wine, his big hand concealing the stem of the glass and part of the bowl. He wore his old gray broad-brimmed hat, and was slow to look up at Rickie. Then Willi tensed, and his feet shifted as if he might leave.

Rickie looked away. That had been a "hostile" glance from Willi. Rickie knew he was one of the "others," the enemy, the wrong kind of people, the people that Renate Hagnauer had not cared for, and about whom she had been scathing. Rickie realized that he would be, therefore, among the curious few who might be glad of Renate's death, whereas Willi Biber in losing Renate had lost a *protectrice*, a comforter, a friend. Small wonder that Willi looked dejected and melancholic tonight! He sat at the end of the table, where Rickie had often seen him when Renate had been at the table, seated at right angles to Willi. Willi might have been conjuring up memories of Renate, Rickie thought, seated close to him, drawing on her cigarette holder, eyeing the goings on with disapproval—though often making a sketch. Rickie stood at the bar.

"What will you have, Rickie?" asked Ursie. "A small beer?"

"No. I'll wait a minute." He reached for his cigarettes.

"Andreas said the party was just *grand*! The *Kronenhalle*!"

"It was—pretty. Teddie's birthday, you know."

"I know! And Luisa was there?"

"Ye-es."

After wiping the stems of two glasses, Ursie set two beers proudly on a tray on the counter. "Ah, poor girl! A shock, you know? What's going to become of the apartment?"

"I don't know," said Rickie.

"Will all the girls look for other jobs?"

Rickie took his time. "I dunno. There's a helper there—Vera. Older, you know. She may take over. We'll see."

"Ah Rickie, welcome back!" Andy laughed. He wore his familiar dark trousers, white shirt, and black vest unbuttoned. "Two reds and three beers, Ursie. Teddie coming tonight?"

"Supposed to."

"And poor Willi," Ursie went on, setting two glasses under the taps. "He's a lost soul. He's hardly eaten since he heard the news— so Frau Wenger told somebody. He did worship Frau Renate!" Ursie rolled her eyes, reached for another maroon-colored tray and slapped it down on the counter.

Too damn bad if Willi lost his appetite, Rickie thought. Had Ursie forgotten the night Teddie got hit in the back; all the suspicions, the interviews later with Willi Biber? Rickie wasn't going to jog her memory.

"One small beer, Rickie," said Ursie. "On the house. A big beer, if you want it."

"Small. Thank you."

"Teddie hasn't been here in quite a while, has he? And here he is! Look!"

Teddie, with a big smile for Rickie, entered with two young men from the party, Eric and another whose name Rickie didn't know.

"Hello again, Rick," said Teddie. "By yourself?" He nodded to Ursie. "'Evening, Ursie!"

"Except for Lulu. A beer, Teddie?" The boys seemed content to stay at the bar, where only two or three other customers stood.

"This round is on the house!" Ursie said. "In honor of Teddie's birthday."

Diplomacy rampant again, Rickie thought, watching the young fellows say their thanks. Beer all round. He also saw Teddie's gaze move to Willi Biber at the table inside.

"Yep, still around," said Rickie, "and in his usual place."

Teddie shook his head. "Poor old son of a bitch," he murmured.

Rickie gave a laugh. "Teddie, you're growing up!"

Teddie frowned. "Wasn't I always growing up?"

Eric cleared his throat and said to Rickie, "Teddie says you make wonderful layouts—for advertisements. He showed me one in a magazine. I have a friend . . ."

Rickie, a bit drunk, answered Eric's questions politely. Eric had a friend finishing his apprenticeship as *Grafiker*, commercial artist. What kind of job should he aim for? "He should aim for the kind of stuff he likes to draw," Rickie said, determined to go no further. Instantly, the Custom account invaded his brain, took over. Rickie much wanted to get that account. He liked the name, the people at Custom. He had to invent a trademark, a logo, and series of ads for men's luxury goods. Was this a noble aspiration for a grown man? No.

Then Teddie asked how Luisa was doing. How was she really doing? And when the other two fellows weren't listening, was Dorrie in love with Luisa? What was Luisa's attitude toward Dorrie?

"Dorrie's been very helpful. That's all I know. Luisa needs a little help now, you know. Moral support."

"I'm here too. Tell her. Well, I did tell her."

The fellows wanted to walk Rickie home, because Teddie had said Rickie's flat was in the neighborhood. Rickie had explained in Jakob's that he couldn't ask them in, because it was late and tomorrow was a working day. So Eric in Jakob's had rung for a taxi to come to Rickie's address.

"Big deal," Rickie said to Teddie. "You're allowed to come to Jakob's neighborhood again."

Teddie laughed. "I said to my mother, since I'm twenty-one—just this once—in a taxi. It won't be just this once." His smile was confident.

"What did you do with your presents?"

"I went to my house—and left them."

32

Tuesday morning. Luisa's first thought was: the cremation. The lawyer Rensch was supposed to telephone about that. Or was it the bank? No, the lawyer. Luisa leapt out of bed. Five past seven now. Coffee, a slice from a sweet bun in the fridge. Get dressed, make the bed. The studio should look neat when Mathilde came in at nine-thirty or so.

Luisa was unlocking the apartment door by seven-thirty, unpleasantly aware of the closed door of Renate's bedroom as she walked past it. For today, try not to see it, she told herself. She would go to the cremation, of course—there was some kind of ceremony, she thought.

Vera was the first arrival, well before eight, when Luisa was making coffee in the kitchen. Again Vera mentioned the cremation, and said she would be glad to accompany Luisa if Luisa didn't mind.

"Mind? Of course *not*," said Luisa. "Thank you, Vera."

Dr. Rensch rang before nine. He informed Luisa that the "ceremony" for Frau Hagnauer would take place at two-thirty that afternoon, and would last less than an hour.

"The cremation itself will take about two hours, and it is not necessary to stay for that unless you wish to." He then gave the address of the crematorium. "Do you want the ashes preserved?"

"No," said Luisa, not very firmly but firmly enough.

"The bill will be taken care of out of the assets here. All right?"

End of conversation.

Luisa returned to her coffee cup, trying to draw courage from it. Vera's dark eyes met hers, and Luisa beckoned to her. They spoke in the long hall. Luisa told Vera the time of the ceremony.

"I know where that place is," Vera said. "We can get a tram and then a taxi."

"OK. And I think we should let the girls off at lunch, don't you? After lunch?"

"Certainly, yes. We can manage." Vera's long dark hair moved emphatically with her nod. "I'll tell them. And also—"

"Yes?"

"I'll come back and help you with Renate's things." She nodded toward the closed door. "I can imagine you don't want to do it alone."

Luisa reminded herself that she had to stand on her own. To open that door and enter seemed as depressing as entering a tomb, but who else but herself should do it? "My job," said Luisa.

"All right. If you'd rather."

"No." Luisa smiled nervously. "I hadn't *rather*. It's—I'd be *glad* if you helped me."

So the girls at lunch were informed that they were free for the rest of the day. Vera made the announcement, "Frau Hagnauer's ceremony is at two-thirty this afternoon—followed by a cremation—"

Someone gasped.

"You are of course welcome to come, but it is not obligatory. I shall be going with Luisa."

Murmurs. No one accepted the invitation.

Stefanie and Elsie drifted off after one o'clock, both making an effort to say the right thing to Luisa. The only words that came clearly were, "See you tomorrow."

Luisa changed her white slacks for a dark skirt from her room. Then before she and Vera departed, Luisa opened the door of Renate's room. Again Luisa was aware of holding herself straight, shoulders back, lest she shrink from this.

"I think the two cupboards are pretty full," she said to Vera. "There are some of those white bags in the kitchen, I know."

The white bags were for clothing to be given away to the poor, and there were several collections a year on the streets in Zurich.

Vera gave the cupboards a serious glance and said, "We'll manage. We'll make a good start today, anyway."

Then Luisa closed Renate's door once more. "Let's take a taxi. Let's do it right." She went to the telephone.

The crematorium was in a stone edifice that might have been an office building or a bank, except for a smallish sign in brass beside the wide doors. Renate Hagnauer's name was the open sesame, bringing first a male attendant, who showed them into a room he called "the chapel." This softly lit and dark-curtained room was lined with chairs, had chairs also in its center, enough to seat at least forty, Luisa thought. Now only Therese Wenger of L'Eclair was present. Luisa had telephoned Ursie just before noon, but Ursie had begged off: she couldn't leave her duties, really. Francesca, who had inquired the time of the event this morning, came in just after Luisa and Vera. They all gave silent nods to one another. The stocky coffin sat already on a dais more than a meter high, its end aimed at dark brown curtains which covered a wide area and overlapped at the center.

A man in a dark robe, of no particular religious order (Luisa thought), came out, greeted them softly, and read from a book which he held in one hand. Death calls us all. Renate was a part of all of us (really?), a woman acquainted with work, skilled in her profession, respected by friends and neighbors, *instructrice* to generations of young women who had followed in her footsteps . . . Then Luisa noticed a small-looking man seated in the corner, dark mustache, solemn. A friend of Renate's?

Amen. It was over, and the speaker turned away, a mechanism began grinding audibly. The casket glided away from them, through the brown curtains, and the curtains swung and closed again. The lights grew brighter.

Therese Wenger said softly, as they were walking out of the room, "Willi didn't want to come. I asked him, of course. I think he's too sad. A strange one is our Willi."

The small man slipped out and on to the pavement.

"Do you know who he is?" Luisa whispered.

Vera pondered, recognition coming. "Yes—Edouard something. French. Renate used to play chess with him, I think. Haven't
seen him in a year or more!"

Frau Wenger said her good-bye. She was going to take a tram
home.

Vera had a thought: they could go now to the *Frauenfachschule*
at Kreuzplatz to speak with someone about finding a dressmaker.
"The sooner the better. We'll find out what we have to do."

They also sought a tram. Luisa found herself feeling optimistic
for no reason at all, happy, or happier. It was the wrong kind of
feeling for today, but she couldn't stop it. The world looked different as she gazed out of the tram window. The dark-haired and
pale-skinned Vera Riedli looked different, though she had known
Vera exactly as long as she had known Renate. Vera glanced at her
and smiled shyly.

"I was thinking," Vera said, "I don't think I'd like to be cre-
mated. I know it saves space and all that. But I think I'd rather be
just buried."

"After you're dead, of course."

Then they both laughed, giggled, and had to force themselves
back to sobriety.

At the Women's Technical School, they spoke to a woman
who took down the address of the apartment of the late Frau Hagnauer. A new dressmaker could live there, if she wished, and Vera
(with Luisa's accord) said that such an arrangement would be
preferable, the dressmaker after all being the manager.

"That may be possible—to find someone and soon. But one
never knows," the woman at the desk added with professional cau-
tion. "I shall consult my records and let you know."

That had been a little misleading, Luisa thought, as they made
their way back to the tram stop. They had explained that Luisa and
Frau Hagnauer's sister inherited the flat, which would make
Renate's room occupied, if the sister chose to live there. But still,

a new dressmaker could keep her present dwelling and inherit a fine clientele, which might be a step up for her.

Then they were opening the apartment, and the ringing telephone stopped before they could reach it.

"A rubbish bag first, don't you think, Luisa?" Frowning, with an air of taking charge, Vera stood sideways on the threshold of Renate's room.

Luisa fetched a couple from the kitchen.

"I thought—these little things that no one will ever use—" Vera meant the nail-polish bottles, the lipsticks, on Renate's dressing table. "I'll let you do it while I phone my mother and tell her I'll be late."

Luisa got to work, slowly at first, then more rapidly, making decisions. Nearly all had to go, drawers full of stockings, underwear. Handkerchieves were another matter, some quite pretty. Would Francesca, for example, like a few?

Vera was now tossing skirts and dresses onto the floor. "I can't see—well, anyone wanting these. Long skirts—should we have any cleaned for the white bags?"

Luisa agreed: a few could be cleaned, if they looked as if they needed it, of course. Renate had always had her clothes cleaned frequently.

The telephone again. Luisa went to it.

"How was it? How are you?" asked Dorrie's voice.

"Vera's here now. She's helping with—with Renate's room. The clothes, you know."

"I'll come over. I'm free now. I'll give you a hand."

"It's *boring*."

Dorrie had hung up.

Luisa went back to her work. They were filling the third thirty-five-liter gray bag for the rubbish. The shoes. Luisa forced herself to handle them. Out, all of them.

Dorrie arrived in no time, it seemed.

"This is Dorrie Wyss," Luisa said. "Vera Riedli."

"Oh Dorrie—yes,"Vera said. "You're the one who was leaving that night."Vera's fingers tightened on the three belts she was holding. "You saw her fall."

"Well, no—"

"I saw her fall," said Luisa. "Dorrie was walking in the hall below—and she looked back." Luisa continued. "Renate went down two or three steps before she tripped." She intended to say no more to Vera.

They put the last shoes into yet another rubbish bag.

The desk. Luisa looked at the open *secrétaire* with its six busy pigeonholes, at the letters in opened envelopes in a surprisingly disorderly heap to the left, a flat transparent box of paper clips, drawing pins, and pencils on the right.

"I can't face that today," Luisa said, feeling suddenly not tired but bored with the task.

"OK, dear Luisa," Vera said. "We've done quite a lot today. Look!" She indicated the nearly empty cupboards.

"The bathroom. Let's make a start, at least," Luisa said. "We'll need another sack. But *you* don't have to stay, Vera."

Vera wanted to stay a few minutes more.

Toothbrushes, old pill boxes and bottles from the medicine cabinet shelves, aspirin—Luisa didn't want even Renate's aspirin, nor the round mirror which on one side enlarged, but Vera said she could use that, with Luisa's permission. Toothpaste out.

"Laundry bag?" asked Dorrie, holding a couple of towels. "The other's full."

Another was found.

"The cleaning women can wash that," Luisa said, meaning the medicine cabinet.

Then Vera said good-bye to Luisa and Dorrie. "Don't work anymore, Luisa. There's tomorrow." Smiling, Vera waved and departed, carrying one of the gray rubbish bags for tomorrow Tuesday's collection.

"I'm going to wash my hands in my own, small bathroom," Luisa said, heading down the hall.

"I too, may I?"

They both washed with soap and warm water, and watched the gray dirt swirl away down the drain.

"I want to get out of this skirt." Luisa went to her room, and took a pair of white cotton slacks from a hanger. In a few seconds, the slacks were on.

"Knock-knock," said Dorrie.

Suddenly they both laughed. Luisa's room seemed big and friendly, familiar. Dorrie took her hands, and suddenly they were kissing. Dorrie put her arms round Luisa and held her tight. And they kissed again. Dorrie, like Vera, was among the trusted.

The telephone rang in the hall.

"Hell and damnation," said Dorrie.

"Can you answer?"

"Me?" said Dorrie, but she turned and went into the hall.

"Rickie," Dorrie said, coming back. "Wants to talk with you. He sounds very happy."

"Hello, *Liebes*," said Rickie. "How are you doing? I'm glad it's over . . . My dear Luisa, I have news. I got the Custom account. I can't say it in a few words but—it's big and *important* for me. That's it."

"The men's gloves."

Rickie laughed. "That was my first ad you saw. I've got the rest of the account. It's an advertising campaign, you know? With logo . . . So meet me later, please, you and Dorrie. We'll have a bite at Jakob's, all right?"

It was hard to say no to Rickie, and Luisa didn't want to say no. Luisa informed Dorrie. Jakob's at eight. It was after seven now.

Where was Luisa sleeping tonight, Dorrie asked. In Rickie's studio. They tidied, drifted, talked about nothing. Dorrie closed Renate's room door once more, and set a rubbish bag at the apartment door, so they wouldn't forget it. Luisa swept the workroom hastily, amassing as ever bits of thread, snippets of material, pins.

They were early at Jakob's, and Dorrie ordered two Kirs, after making sure Andreas knew how a Kir was made.

"We don't start with beer on a day like today," said Dorrie.

Standing at the bar, they raised the pink drinks and sipped.

"Something to show you." Luisa reached into a back pocket and pulled out a bent and creased snapshot. She handed it to Dorrie.

It was of Luisa aged fifteen or sixteen, taken in the neighborhood of her mother and stepfather's home. Luisa's dark brows scowled at the photographer, the wind made her short, tousled hair look wild. She wore a dark green shirt with rumpled collar, and the picture stopped at the waist. There was a pole of some kind and a hedge in the background. "It's me."

"That's *you*?" said Dorrie, unbelieving.

"Just before I met Renate. I was pulling out a drawer in her room today, and it fell out on the floor. I had no idea she had it. Isn't it incredible?"

"Can't believe it—but I've got to. Were you trying to be a gangster?"

"Yes. Exactly. This was in Brig. I was going to apprentice school but—hanging around boys all the time. Motorcycles, you know. I never owned one, but the boys let me drive theirs—without a license."

"Wow," said Dorrie, impressed.

"I wanted to look as ugly as possible. Really!"

"Why?"

Luisa thought of her stepfather, and bit her underlip. She took the picture back and calmly tore it in half, then tore it once more.

Dorrie's blue eyes stared, as if she had destroyed something important.

"It's not worth keeping. I don't want to think about those days."

"*Les girls!*" said Rickie, entering with Lulu on the lead.

They took a corner table, far across from the bar. A beer for Rickie, and with consent all around potato salad and cold cuts, and two small beers.

"Now first—" Rickie began with an effort at seriousness. "How was the cremation?" He addressed both.

"I wasn't there," Dorrie said.

"Yes—first," Luisa began, "you don't see anything except the coffin—closed. It's on a sort of stage. In a round room like a chapel. Vera Riedli went with me. She was a wonderful help today!" Today already seemed like yesterday.

Luisa went on. The words by the minister, and then—the coffin moving away, through the curtains and out of sight. She felt as if she were narrating a miracle, and Rickie listened, fascinated. "Francesca was there—but so few others." Luisa saw Rickie press his lips together, and knew he was thinking: Because so few people liked Renate.

"Well, I won't ask any more questions about *that* tonight," Rickie said, putting his hand over his eyes for a moment.

The beers arrived.

Rickie asked about Vera's "taking over." She couldn't assume total authority, Luisa explained, because she was not yet a "master cutter." They had to find a *Damenschneiderin*, and they had made a start today at the Women's Technical School.

"And then, dear Luisa, we must get that big apartment repainted. That slightly dirty cream—is just not cheerful."

"I talked with Bert about that," Dorrie said. "Bert has a friend who's a professional housepainter."

"When am I going to meet Bert?" asked Rickie.

Dorrie and Luisa laughed.

They walked from Jakob's to Rickie's studio. He wanted them to see his Custom efforts.

Rickie had made twenty or more sketches, most in soft pencil, some with color added: an Edwardian top hat with lining

showing, a vertical design suggesting a tiepin, a belt buckle that
was a *C*. They lay in disorder on the longest table in his studio.

"Now the finale," he said, pulling a tissue covering back from
a more finished creation "Simply a peacock feather. But they like
this best. In fact, so do I."

The feather was vertical, broad at the top, blue and green, with
a circle of red not quite in the center.

"We can have lots of color variations. This'll be on everything
they make, ties, shirts—just one feather somewhere, not too obvi-
ous." Rickie deliberately ended his speech. "So good night, girls,
sleep well. I shall return—to this factory—*all too soon!*" He made
an unsteady bow, and departed.

Dorrie looked at the nook of a room where the single bed
stood against the wall. "Really very snug here. Can I stay with
you?"

"Tonight?" Luisa without thinking had started to unbutton
her shirt. She was suddenly tired enough to drop.

"Yes. Just five minutes—maybe." She pulled her cotton blouse
over her head.

Luisa hardly glanced at Dorrie's bare breasts. She continued
undressing.

Dorrie pulled the counterpane back, and the sheet, and beckoned. Five minutes, Luisa thought, like an echo. She and Dorrie
were in bed, embracing, unwashed, Luisa realized, and heavy with
fatigue. Then Dorrie was almost on top of her, kissing her lips. The
light here was dim, coming from the studio. Both of them sighed,
like one person. They were still, until Dorrie squeezed her closer,
and Luisa did the same. Luisa moved her hand from Dorrie's waist
up her smooth side with its hint of ribs. Let her hand move down
Dorrie's spine, tense and muscular. Luisa was thinking, she had not
been in bed, horizontal, with anyone since she had been with her
stepfather, at least a year ago—the one awful time when he had
persisted, threatened her with a wallop, unless she "tried it in bed"
with him. In bed instead of on the bed, dressed. Luisa's room door

did not lock. Penetration, they called it in the books, but nothing else had happened—which sounded like a joke. What else was supposed to happen? A climax, of course. That hadn't happened.

"Agh-h!" Luisa said, like a very loud gasp.

"What's up?"

Luisa took a breath. "I was thinking of something—not important. Maybe I was half asleep."

"It *must* be important!" Dorrie was propped on an elbow.

Luisa couldn't say it now, in bed with Dorrie. She squirmed and jumped out of bed, hardly aware of the fact she was naked. "It's my stepfather—I was thinking of. I didn't want to say it now—really."

"Oh. The child-molester," Dorrie said flatly.

"I just couldn't say it—in bed with you."

Dorrie looked at her. "And how long—did you say this went on? It began—"

"Oh—little things. But awful. Maybe I was ten—eleven. Went on really till I ran away. He'd say he'd swat me if I said anything to my mother. And once or twice he swatted me for nothing. But essentially nobody made a move. You understand?"

Dorrie was silent.

"All my friends were boys and he'd say he'd tell my mother I was screwing them if I said anything about him. It was a fine mess, believe me!" Luisa tried to laugh and could not.

"Didn't your mother know?"

Luisa shrugged. "Must have. Sure. She didn't like me because I didn't like her." She let out a sigh, and reached for her robe behind the bathroom door, struggled into it. "I feel finished with that—from today on. Somehow. All that just doesn't matter anymore."

Dorrie stirred as if to get up, and didn't. "You told Renate all this?"

"No. She probably guessed. She knew a lot just by guessing—she was so often right."

Dorrie was still propped on her elbow. "You were how old when your mother married your stepfather? Maybe you told me but I forgot."

Luisa forgot too, unless she thought hard about it, which she did not want to do. "Maybe nine when he moved in. But they couldn't marry before the divorce was legal. Takes five years, you know. My father had left my mother. Had another girlfriend. Can't blame him."

"You liked him?"

"Better than I did my mother, sure. That's not saying much." Her father had written at least once to her, had telephoned once, but Luisa's mother had screamed at him over the phone, Luisa recalled. Luisa told Dorrie this, then said she did not want to talk anymore about it.

"It's grim—all that," Dorrie said, "but it happens often, you know? Lots of people—I know there's no consolation in thinking of other people who—"

"Oh, but there is! I used to read magazine articles—all of them that I came across! It *does* help. If I saw a magazine on a newsstand, you know—child abuse—I'd buy it."

Dorrie slowly got out of bed, then it seemed in seconds she had her dark trousers on and was pulling her blouse down.

"It's so different—since today," Luisa said. "The whole world is different, I swear it."

"It's going to be easier now. Everything. You'll see. What's there to worry about?" Dorrie opened her arms quickly and smiled. "I'll take off."

"You don't have to take off so soon."

"I was intending to. Honestly."

"You've got your car?"

"Other side of Jakob's. 'Bye, my dear."

Luisa had walked part of the way across the studio when Dorrie turned at the door. "I'm locked in. Got your key?"

Rickie had locked automatically, Luisa knew. She got her set of keys and opened the door.

"Talk to you tomorrow," Dorrie said. "Or if I don't, don't worry. I'm all over town tomorrow." A blown kiss, and Dorrie was out the door like a wraith.

Luisa put out the ceiling light, and walked to her bed. Tonight she wouldn't take a shower, just to be different. A sharp pain made her lift her foot. She'd almost stepped hard on a drawing pin! Smiling, Luisa pulled it from the ball of her foot. Off with her robe then, and into bed. Dorrie had just lain here. Wasn't it still a little warm from her? Luisa spread her left hand, palm down, pretending that the warmth was still there.

33

Teddie Stevenson's article came out two days later in the *Tages-Anzeiger* under the name Georg Stefan. Here were the events of the National Holiday, August the first, the gaiety of Jakob's on that night, a walk to his mother's car, a hard swat from behind, and he had been flat on the ground with a tree trunk against his face. The helpful strangers, the walk to Jakob's, and the attention that couldn't have been warmer from his own family.

To Luisa and to Rickie, Teddie had quietly delivered two copies of the paper, in case either missed it. In a telephone call to each, Teddie said that he had another article due out about his efforts to gain entry to journalism school, and that he was hopeful about another piece on young people's holidays. Teddie was starting journalism school in early October.

Emboldened by his success, and cheered by Luisa's availability, Teddie vowed to her by letter and over the telephone that he would sit on her doorstep "maybe not all the time but now and then, just because I haven't been able to." He and Luisa had an evening at a Greek restaurant, and another in a disco.

But Luisa's mind was on managing the atelier. The first candidate for "dressmaker" had not worked out: a woman in her forties, rather nervous and unsmiling, Luisa and the girls had thought, married and not enthusiastic about living in the apartment even Monday to Friday.

Dorrie's friend Bert brought his friend Gerhard (the professional housepainter), plus a friend of Gerhard's. The work would require an electrician too, to be expected, considering the age of the wires and fixtures. A two-week job was agreed upon, with two painters at work. Luisa had seen Mr. Gamper at the bank again, and had been assured of enough money from Renate's account to cover present expenses.

It was simple, after all. The bank gave Luisa a current account out of which she paid the girls' wages, while the telephone and electricity were deducted automatically, as ever, from Renate's account now in Luisa's name. This account Luisa could add to when necessary from a deposit account, which Mr. Gamper called "comfortably high" now. Luisa had inquired about Renate's sister, and Mr. Gamper had said there had been no reply as yet from Zagreb.

At least two dozen letters of condolence trickled in from Renate's clients, including one from the woman who had always wanted a second, lower bill to show her husband. "We must answer these," Luisa said. Vera agreed, and volunteered to share the duty with Luisa.

The girls were given three weeks off with pay during the painting of the apartment. Luisa had been sleeping at the workshop, as she called the apartment now. With all the preparation for the painters, the expectation of their early arrival, Luisa had found it not at all difficult to spend the nights alone there.

It was Vera's idea that Luisa go for a week in the country during the worst of the painting. "Paint fumes can give you a headache, you know." Of course, Luisa had heard that. Dorrie knew of a nice country inn. So did Rickie. Inquiries. Dorrie's was closer, the price about the same. So Dorrie drove Luisa there one morning with a suitcase and a bag of books and sketching material. Besides a greensward where a few cows grazed, there was a brook. Best of all was the room itself with an irregular corner, and old-fashioned wallpaper of a tiny pink floral design. Dorrie drove out twice and spent two afternoons with Luisa. They made excursions and had dinner once at a different hostelry. Luisa felt changed completely, as if she had spent these days in another country. Teddie telephoned and arrived in the brown Audi, and Luisa was able to invite him for lunch. Rickie did not visit, but phoned to acquaint her with the painters' progress.

In Aussersihl, Luisa's room was now painted white, the bed in a different place, her pin-up board on another wall. Teddie's latest article was pinned up, and the paper showed signs of yellowing after only a month.

Dorrie Wyss came to the Small g every Saturday night. Bert turned up on a Saturday night with one of the two painters who had worked in the apartment. By now Rickie had met both. Bert was a skinhead unless he wore a wig. He put on lipstick and eyeliner at weekends, and wore untidy blue work clothes nearly all the time. A medium-sized, real (Bert said) gold earring set the picture off. "If anybody grabs this earring, my ear comes with it," Bert said, "and I don't think anybody wants that."

Now when Luisa entered the big, newly painted workroom, she felt herself the manager of the house, payer of the rent, the salaries, the utilities—answerable for everything. When she remembered being sent to the kitchen to eat her meals, with telephone calls and evenings out forbidden, she wondered what had been the matter with *herself* to have put up with it for weeks? And what a very odd person Renate Hagnauer had been to treat her so, and then to reward her with half her estate!

Teddie was going to journalism school, which meant not only more writing for him but study of "early and contemporary journalists and reporters." He was proud of his work, Luisa felt, and she knew he had to apply himself to make a favorable impression on his mother who, Teddie told her, sometimes said he was "drifting, like so many young people." Teddie could usually come to the Small g on Saturday nights, but often he worked on weekday evenings. Therefore, Luisa made the same excuse, if Teddie wanted to see her several times in the week: she would say that her "final" was coming up before too long, which was true. She had to pass and pass it well. She was conscious that she had more to prove than Teddie. He would be able to keep up a rather high standard of living, whether he succeeded in journalism or not.

It was more than two months after Renate's death that the third applicant for "dressmaker" came to the workshop, sent by the *Frauenfachschule*. This was a lively, rather short woman with reddish blonde hair and a Schaffhausen accent, which Luisa had always found a little comical. Her name was Helen Suhner, she was unmarried, forty-five years old, and willing to live in. Indeed, she seemed happy with the idea of living in the high-ceilinged, newly decorated apartment. Renate's room stood ready with the double bed, the dressing table, the *secrétaire*, all placed differently now from the Renate days. Luisa on her own had discarded the curtains almost at once after Renate's death, and made new ones of yellow silk lined with white material.

Dorrie, because of her acquaintance with set designers, got free theater tickets sometimes for herself and Luisa. Luisa was glad that Dorrie seemed to take their relationship lightly. Luisa would have been frightened of anything else, and perhaps Dorrie understood this. They didn't telephone every day, or write intimate notes to each other. If they wanted to spend a night together, Luisa went to Dorrie's flat, and Helen Suhner asked no questions. For her an eighteen-year-old had the right to privacy, Luisa supposed. Dorrie showed no jealousy of Teddie, even when Teddie and Luisa danced on Saturday evenings. And Teddie was quiet in regard to Dorrie.

With Helen Suhner, Luisa went to the Kunsthaus now and then on Sundays, more to see the exhibitions than to sketch what the women were wearing. Like the rest of the world for Luisa, the Kunsthaus with its great stairways, its coffee shop, had become what it was, transformed by the absence of Renate, and a little by the presence of another person, the more youthful Helen.

One morning came a letter from Mr. Gamper of UBS. Their investigations into Renate Hagnauer's sister's whereabouts had led them to Goerlitz in the former GDR, and the authorities had been slow in replying. They had found out that the sister had died nearly a year ago. Therefore Luisa was the sole beneficiary. It was a working day before 10 A.M. when Luisa read this news. She said nothing to Vera or to Helen, and told herself that it made no change, that she had half expected it, anyway. Luisa found that she didn't think about it—it being the fact of having, pretty soon, maybe after three months more, a seven-figure sum in the charge of UBS and Mr. Gamper in her name, a comfortable current account all her own with which she could buy a coat or a pair of shoes whenever she wished. It wasn't quite imaginable to Luisa.

Some two weeks after she had learned this, Rickie asked Luisa what she had heard from "Renate's bank."

"Oh yes. Mr. Gamper said they've found out that the sister is dead. So I'm the only—inheritor."

"Really," said Rickie, suddenly earnest. "That's—well—congratulations."

One evening when she had been alone, Luisa had plucked up her courage and read through the copy of Renate's will, not understanding every phrase. But she understood that there were two or three other banks with stocks and bonds, and also two bonds held by UBS.

The same evening she had told Rickie, she had said, "Don't

mention this to anyone, will you, Rickie? I'm not telling even Dorrie—or Vera at the workshop. I don't want anyone to think that I'm conceited—or changed." She patted Lulu's white head. The dog had been staring, listening intently.

"I am honored that you told me," said Rickie. "I shall keep it quiet."

"Even from Freddie."

"Agreed."

In March, Luisa was to receive her inheritance, a mystery or problem that no longer troubled her, because she had talked with Mr. Gamper at UBS and also with Rickie. One kept the investments on, and spent what one needed to from the interest—as a rule, said Rickie. Also in March would come her final exam after which, if she passed it, she could take on one apprentice of her own.

Often Helen and Luisa took mid-morning coffee at Jakob's. Almost never was Willi Biber to be seen. Luisa had steered Helen toward the long table at which Luisa and Renate had usually sat. The atmosphere was now so different that Luisa hardly ever thought of Renate at Jakob's. Rickie was generally opposite, for a time hidden behind the *Tages-Anzeiger*, then greeting them with a "Good morning!" and sometimes he came over to sit for a few minutes, and they would exchange news, if there was any.

"Well, which do you really prefer, Dorrie or me?" Teddie asked a couple of times, and each time Luisa had answered, "Must I be so precise—definite? It's casual—light—"

Yes, she had gone to bed with Teddie too, two or three times when Helen had been out for the evening, once when Teddie's mother had been away for a weekend. How could she or anyone make a decision based on something like that?

The scar on Teddie's back was now a shrinking spot, and he was proud of it, Luisa thought. Teddie was in no position to demand decisions from her, hard and fast, unless he was proposing marriage, which he wasn't. After his journalism school, he would have to find well-paid work, if he expected to acquire his own apartment. It seemed to Luisa that an ocean of time lay between now and that future, plenty of time for Teddie to meet another girl or two. Rickie said that to Luisa and maybe to Teddie. Meanwhile, Luisa thought, what was the matter with her being his favorite girlfriend? Maybe even second favorite? Teddie's mother liked her better, Luisa could feel, maybe because she, Luisa, had acquired some independence, and because Teddie no longer had his head in the clouds.

"Are you going to be one of those AC-DCs?" asked Teddie. "You'll have to decide sometime."

Would she? If Teddie felt unhappy with the situation, he could part company with her, Luisa thought, though that would be harsh to say, and in fact she didn't want that. What was wrong with taking it easy? Luisa loved Dorrie for not making things heavy.

And Rickie—Luisa liked him for being always there, reachable, if she wanted to talk to him about something. Even when he and Freddie went to Paris for a long weekend, Rickie left his hotel name and number.

Rickie met Freddie's wife Gertrud after prodding Freddie, and inquiring Gertrud's preference as to restaurant.

"Gypsy," Freddie had said, puzzling Rickie.

Hungarian? All right. Rickie played host, first in his apartment, for pre-dinner drinks—he had been told Gertrud preferred Cinzano and soda—then a taxi to a fine Hungarian restaurant. Gertrud was blondish, not very tall, and worked as bookkeeper for at least three orchestral groups in the Zurich area, as Rickie understood it. The important thing to Rickie was that she seemed friendly. He had been every bit as nervous as when he had met Teddie's mother, and Gertrud's smile, the way she had extended her hand, had suddenly put him at ease. She looked a healthy and well-kept forty, with a nice haircut and good but conservative clothes. She talked easily about Freddie's progress in detection school, and said with a glance at her spouse that soon his hours would be even odder.

"I never know when to cook a good meal, so this is a treat," she said to Rickie.

She had chosen roast duck with hot apple sauce, red cabbage, potato dumpling, which had sounded so attractive, the men had followed suit.

Gertrud and Freddie had been married ten years, Rickie knew, and Freddie had told him that Gertrud had been married once before. It was a mutually satisfactory marriage, Rickie thought, and he judged from little things—the way Freddie held her chair for her at the restaurant, and his air of pride, even satisfaction, when he looked at her. Strange, Rickie thought, but then a lot of life was strange.

A successful evening and a milestone, Rickie felt. Would his relationship with Freddie grow into something as strong and steady as Freddie's and Gertrud's? No use in asking himself, he knew. No use in asking Freddie. The funny thing was, Rickie in a quiet way felt happy.

About the Author

Born in Forth Worth, Texas, in 1921, Patricia Highsmith spent much of her adult life in Switzerland and France. She was educated at Barnard College, where she studied English, Latin, and Greek. Her first novel, *Strangers on a Train*, published initially in 1950, proved to be a major commercial success, and was filmed by Alfred Hitchcock. Despite this early recognition, Highsmith was unappreciated in the United States for the entire length of her career.

Writing under the pseudonym of Claire Morgan, she then published *The Price of Salt* in 1953, which had been turned down by her previous American publisher because of its frank exploration of homosexual themes. Her most popular literary creation was Tom Ripley, the dapper sociopath who first debuted in her 1955 novel, *The Talented Mr. Ripley*. She followed with four other Ripley novels. Posthumously made into a major motion picture, *The Talented Mr. Ripley* has helped bring about a renewed appreciation of Highsmith's work in the United States, as has the posthumous publication of *The Selected Stories* and *Nothing That Meets the Eye: The Uncollected Stories*, both of which received widespread acclaim when they were published by W. W. Norton & Company.

The author of more than twenty books, Highsmith has won the O. Henry Memorial Award, the Edgar Allan Poe Award, Le Grand Prix de Littérature Policière, and the Award of the Crime Writers' Association of Great Britian. She died in Switzerland on February 4, 1995, and her literary archives are maintained in Berne.